P9-CKT-155

Sicilian Stories

Novelle siciliane

A Dual-Language Book

Giovanni Verga

Edited and Translated by
STANLEY APPELBAUM

DISCARD

DOVER PUBLICATIONS, INC.
Mineola, New York

Pacific Grove Public Library

853.8
VER

Copyright

Translations, Introduction, and footnotes copyright © 2002 by Dover Publications, Inc.

All rights reserved under Pan American and International Copyright Conventions.

Published in Canada by General Publishing Company, Ltd., 895 Don Mills Road, 400-2 Park Centre, Toronto, Ontario M3C 1W3.

Published in the United Kingdom by David & Charles, Brunel House, Forde Close, Newton Abbot, Devon TQ12 4PU.

Bibliographical Note

This Dover edition, first published in 2002, contains the full Italian text of twelve stories by Giovanni Verga (see Introduction for bibliographic details), reprinted from a standard edition, plus new translations of each by Stanley Appelbaum, who also made the selection, wrote the Introduction, and supplied the footnotes.

Library of Congress Cataloging-in-Publication Data

Verga, Giovanni, 1840–1922.
  Sicilian stories/Novelle siciliane : a dual-language book / Giovanni Verga ; edited and translated by Stanley Appelbaum.
      p. cm.
  Stories taken from his Vita dei campi and Novelle rusticane.
  Contains the full Italian text with English translation.
  ISBN 0-486-41945-2 (pbk.)
      1. Verga, Giovanni, 1840–1922—Translations into English. I. Title: Novelle siciliane. II. Appelbaum, Stanley. III. Title.

PQ4734.V5 A22 2001
853'.8—dc21

2001042396

Manufactured in the United States of America
Dover Publications, Inc., 31 East 2nd Street, Mineola, N.Y. 11501

Contents

INTRODUCTION

Giovanni Verga: Life and Work

The family background of the man who has been called the greatest Italian short-story writer between Boccaccio and the 20th century was one of well-to-do comfort, with homes both in Catania (on the east coast of Sicily, just south of Mount Etna, it is the island's second largest city, after Palermo) and in the countryside, where the Vergas possessed estates. Far from being grasping conservatives, however, the Vergas were liberal in politics and aspired toward the unification of Italy long before the actual event, which occurred during Giovanni's lifetime. (Until he was twenty, Sicily was part of the Bourbon Kingdom of Naples, or "Two Sicilies.")

Giovanni Verga was born in 1840, either in Catania (the "big city" of his Sicilian stories) or in Vizzini, a small town in the Iblei hills about thirty miles southwest of Catania, where he vacationed frequently as a child and teenager; Vizzini is the setting, whether named or not, of some of his most famous stories. Verga's talent for writing was in evidence from his youth; by 1856 he had begun a novel (unpublished) about the American Revolution. His vocation as a writer quickly cut short his law-school days (1858). The year 1860 was of great significance to Sicily (conquest by Garibaldi and annexation to the Kingdom of Piedmont, which championed the unification of Italy) and to Verga personally, who became involved in the publication of periodicals and who published his novel *I Carbonari della montagna* (The Carbonari[1] of the Mountain). From 1860 to 1864 Verga served in the National Guard.

In 1865 Verga first ventured north, to the more cosmopolitan and progressive areas of Italy, spending two months in Florence, which had just become the capital of the country (after Turin, in Piedmont). Besides working on novels, his favorite literary medium, he began trying his hand at plays in that year, though it would be nearly two

---

1. The Carbonari of the early 19th century were a Mason-inspired secret society that combated the repressive governments of the Italy of their day. One of Verga's grandfathers had been a Carbonaro.

decades before he really made a name for himself in the theater. From 1869 to 1871 he lived mainly in Florence, where he became part of the foremost literary circles, and continued to write novels and plays. In 1870, the year in which Rome was won for the Italian nation (it became the capital in 1871), Verga published in magazine installments the novel that first won him fame and income, *Storia di una capinera* (The History of a Blackcap [a species of bird]), about a girl who goes mad after her sweetheart marries her wealthier stepsister.

In 1872 Verga made his important move to Milan, which was to be his main base of operations until 1885 (or even until 1893, according to some chroniclers). At the time, Milan was at the cutting edge of Italian intellectual life, the home of the Second Romantic Movement and of Scapigliatura ("dissolute ways," a movement in arts and letters that championed realism and naturalism as already practiced in France and elsewhere). In Milan, where he associated with writers of the stature of Arrigo Boito and composers of the stature of Giuseppe Verdi, his output of novels continued. His novels up to 1875 tend to be passionate love stories, often involving artists and writers moving in high society in northern Italy.

The 1874 short story "Nedda," in which Verga nostalgically returned to Sicilian themes, with an amazing ability to recall the slightest, most telling details of the rural life he had observed as a well-to-do youngster, is universally considered to be the great breakthrough work that set his career in a new, and ultimately its most significant, direction. (Like the other stories included in this Dover volume, it is discussed in greater detail later in this Introduction.) However, he was slow to follow up that lead. His next novel, *Eros,* published in 1875, was in his earlier Milanese vein (translated into German the following year, it first made him known outside Italy). Before 1875 was over, though, he had begun sketches for a Sicilian novel.

Meanwhile, "Nedda" had made Verga more amenable to short-story writing (he hadn't favored that form), which was, among other things, a quicker way to earn money than novel writing. Over the next two decades, he wrote dozens of stories for newspapers and magazines, most of which he would periodically gather into volumes, usually retouching or rewriting them. His first such volume, with no Sicilian story, was the 1876 *Primavera e altri racconti* (Spring, and Other Stories; "Nedda," though out of place there, was added to the second edition of *Primavera* in 1877).

Between 1878 and 1880 Verga published in newspapers and magazines the eight Sicilian stories that were collected in the 1880 volume

Vita dei campi (Rural Life), six of which are included in this Dover edition (the last two in the 1880 volume were "Guerra di Santi" [War of Saints] and "Pentolaccia"; a story of a different type was arbitrarily included by the publisher in the second edition of 1881, and in later editions the stories were further revised—to their detriment, it is generally thought—and placed in a new, less cogent sequence).

Also in 1880, Verga met again, after a ten-year separation, the writer Giselda Fojanesi, who was by then the wife of the writer Mario Rapisardi, an old school friend of Verga's who had helped introduce him to Florentine society. This didn't prevent Verga from beginning a three-year relationship with her (a confirmed bachelor, he was no celibate), which may be reflected in the story "Di là del mare" (Beyond the Sea) that concludes the volume *Novelle rusticane* (see below).

In 1881 Verga finally published the Sicilian novel he had been working on for at least six years: *I Malavoglia* (a family name; the book is generally known in English as The House by the Medlar Tree), which many critics consider his masterpiece (see the discussion of the story "Fantasticheria," below). Luchino Visconti's Neorealist film of 1948, *La terra trema* (The Earth Trembles), is based on *I Malavoglia*.

In 1882, the publication year of another non-Sicilian, "modern," psychological novel, Verga visited his spiritual mentor Emile Zola at his retreat in Médan (near Versailles), and made a trip to London.

In 1883, Verga published two volumes of short stories, the poor-people-of-Milan collection, *Per le vie* (On the Streets), and the second Sicilian collection, *Novelle rusticane* (Rustic Stories). *Novelle rusticane,* consisting of twelve stories, all or most of which had been published in periodicals between 1880 and 1882, is considered to contain his best short-story work, along with *Vita dei campi;* five pieces from *Novelle rusticane* are included in this Dover volume. (The others are: "Il Reverendo" [The Reverend], "Cos'è il Re" [What Is the King], "Don Licciu Papa," "Il mistero" [The Mystery], "Gli orfani" [The Orphans], "I galantuomini" [The Gentry], and the above-mentioned "Di là del mare.")

Also in 1883, Verga wrote his best and most successful play, *Cavalleria rusticana,* based on his story of the same name in *Vita dei campi.* It was first performed in 1884; in the later course of that year Verga visited London and Paris.

After 1885, Verga lived chiefly in Sicily, making many trips to Rome and continuing to write extensively, although his later works, with one enormous exception, are not as highly regarded as *Vita dei campi, I Malavoglia,* and *Novelle rusticane.* That exception is his second

Sicilian novel, which some critics call his very best effort, *Mastro-don Gesualdo* (prefigured in the 1880 story "La roba" [see below]), published in installments in 1888 and in book form in 1889.

In the 1887 short-story volume *Vagabondaggio* (Roaming), only the title story is Sicilian. Verga's last two short-story collections were *I ricordi del Capitano d'Arce* (The Reminiscences of Captain d'Arce), 1891, and *Don Candeloro e C.i* (Don Candeloro and His Company; about provincial strolling players), 1894.

In 1889 Verga entered into a relationship, which would last the rest of his life, with the pianist Dina Castellazzi di Sordevolo. In 1895 he wrote a play version of the story "La Lupa" from *Vita dei campi;* it was performed in 1896. His writing continued at a slower rate; he spent a lot of his time revising his earlier works for new editions, which discerning critics don't prize as highly as the original versions. Between 1912 and 1919 he was involved in screenwriting and film production, especially cinematic versions of his own stories and novels.

In 1920 he received great honors on the occasion of his eightieth birthday, and he was made an Italian senator. He died of thrombosis in 1922 at his ancestral home in Catania. Both in his lifetime and afterward, his reputation had its ups and downs. His greatest achievements as a writer—both his concern for the lowly and downtrodden, and the colloquial, unrhetorical style of his best Sicilian stories—were not always appreciated in his lifetime, but the critical tide turned in his favor in the 1920s, and at the present time it seems safe to say that he is an imperishable classic in Italy, if still not universally recognized elsewhere.

The Sicilian Stories: General Remarks

Generally considered Verga's best work, along with his two Sicilian novels, are "Nedda" (1874, Brigola, Milan) and the stories in the two volumes *Vita dei campi* (Rural Life; published in 1880 by Emilio Treves, Milan) and *Novelle rusticane* (Rustic Stories; published at the end of 1882, dated 1883, by Felice Casanova, Turin). These stories typify Verga's *verismo* (true-to-life) style, based on French realists such as Flaubert and naturalists such as Zola, and championed in Italy by Verga's Sicilian friend, the writer Luigi Capuana.

During the decades after the first book publications (themselves revisions of the very-first periodical publications), Verga undertook further rewriting, and changed the contents of the volumes by adding or

removing stories and by altering their sequence within the volumes. This Dover edition preserves the text of the first book publications, and presents twelve stories ("Nedda," six from *Vita dei Campi,* and five from *Novelle rusticane*) in their original sequence (details below). Each of at least four of the stories included here has been singled out by various critics as Verga's best single story.

Generally speaking, the *Vita dei campi* stories present their characters unpolemically as part of an almost mythically unchanging natural and social environment, whereas the *Novelle rusticane* stories contain more unveiled social protest, and reflect their specific era, during which the bourgeoisie was being enriched at the expense of the nobility and the clergy, while the peasantry remained exploited. Additional major themes, as throughout Verga's entire oeuvre, are love and solitude.

These stories present an entire sociology and ethnography of the time and place concerned. Verga's Sicily is not the whole island, but an area within a 30-mile radius north, west, and particularly south-southwest of Catania. The time is more or less the time of writing, or shortly before. Unobtrusively, but skillfully, the stories reveal the social classes, a wide variety of occupations, home life, popular amusements, religion and superstitions—the entire life of the people down to their characteristic sayings and gestures. A strong feeling of fatalism emerges, which the author appears to share (his two Sicilian novels were intended to be parts of a large cycle to be called *I Vinti* (Those Defeated by Life).

Unlike many sentimentalizing 19th-century depictors of village life, Verga doesn't paint an idyllic picture. The landscape has its own beauties, but it is a hard one to live in. Ignorance and envy are almost institutionalized. Of course, Verga does indicate that poverty is to blame for many individual or societal character defects; and he is fair enough to point out occasionally that even the gentry can suffer and become impoverished. (The "gentry," *galantuomini,* of his stories are usually small or middle-range landowners, not the immensely wealthy and powerful owners of huge "latifundia.")

Verga's style in the Sicilian stories, in many ways a contrast to his earlier "Milanese" approach, is plain and straightforward, largely avoiding active participation by the author as an all-knowing figure who feels free to address the reader directly. He makes much use of the technique of reporting his characters' thoughts and plans in their own personal phraseology and diction even when he isn't using dialogue (direct discourse). He employs very little actual Sicilian dialect,

but his standard Italian frequently contains thoughts, proverbs, and turns of phrase that are translated or adapted from Sicilian. There are numerous rare and unusual words, and uncommon spellings of common words. All of these demands on the reader are worth the trouble, though, because the material is so rich and rewarding.

The Sicilian stories constantly use certain terminology (sometimes in a standard Italian form, sometimes in Sicilian) that calls for clarification:

Forms of Address. To retain the flavor of the original, the English translation herein uses equivalents or near-equivalents in English of certain courtesy titles that precede people's baptismal names. *Compare*, literally "godfather," commonly prefixed to names of rural men, is rendered as "neighbor" in this volume; the feminine equivalent is *comare*. *Zio* ("uncle"), a term of respect for older rural men, is rendered as "'Uncle.'" (Feminine: *zia*.) *Gnà*, which some scholars have seen as derived from *signora* and others from *donna*, is used when addressing rural women; its English equivalent here is "Mis'," the American rural form of "Mrs." or "Miss." *Massaro*, literally "tenant farmer" or "smallholder," is rendered (when a title) as "farmer." *Curatolo* is rendered literally as "sheep farmer," or just "farmer." *Mastro*, a term applied to artisans and skilled workmen, is rendered as "Master." *Don*, a courtesy title for men of the gentry, or at least well-to-do men, is now familiar to Americans and is left unchanged; its feminine form is *donna*. The title character of Verga's second great Sicilian novel, Mastro-don Gesualdo, is so termed because he has ascended from the artisan class to the gentry (among whom he is extremely unhappy: an example of the people who have unwisely broken with "their own kind," as mentioned at the end of the story "Fantasticheria"). On the subject of forms of address, the reader of the Italian texts should pay very close attention to the social and psychological underpinnings of the use of the familiar *tu* and the polite *voi* for "you"; this couldn't be rendered in the English, but is an important feature of the stories.

Money. For the sake of historical precision, all terms designating specific sums of money, and weights and measures, have been left in their Italian forms in the translation. The basic unit of currency is the *lira*, which was worth about 20 cents (U.S.) at the time. The *lira* is divided into a hundred *centesimi*. A *tarì* was worth 42½ *centesimi*; a *carlino*, 25 *centesimi*; a *soldo*, 5 *centesimi*; a *grano*, 2½ *centesimi*. An *onza* (or *oncia*) was worth 12¾ *lire*. The terms *baiocco* and *quattrino* refer to very small denominations, and aren't used specifically (thus they are translated into equivalent English expressions).

Weights and Measures. A *cafiso* was about 6 pounds, but it varied according to place and time. A *quintale* equals 100 kilograms (about 220 pounds). A *rotolo* was about 800 grams (about 1¾ pounds). The cereal measure *tumolo* varied in nature, but was about 15 pounds.

The Individual Stories in This Volume

"Nedda." This breakthrough work in Verga's career, which led him to concentrate on the short-story form and on Sicilian subject matter, is said to have been written in Florence in three days' time during a period of discouragement when Verga was thinking of returning home for good. It was first published in Milan in the June 15, 1874 issue of the *Rivista italiana di Scienze, Lettere e Arti*. Later that year it was published in book form, as an offprint from the magazine, by Brigola in Milan, with the subtitle "Bozzetto siciliano" (Sicilian Sketch).

The prologue (first paragraph) reflects the author's actual situation as a Sicilian far from home who is recalling his native soil after some time away. It also provides a sample of Verga's "fancy" style when he isn't treating rural subject matter in colloquial terms.

The names of the two main characters are typical Sicilian nicknames derived from the stressed syllables of their full baptismal names. Nedda is short for Bastianedda, which would be (Se)bastianella in standard Italian (Sicilian *dd* equals Italian *ll*). Janu would be Sebastiano in its full Italian form (with Sicilian *u* for Italian *o*).

Besides a mention of the Plain of Catania (Piana di Catania), which lies south of the city, and Mascali as a source of wine (that town is two-thirds of the way from Catania to Taormina), the towns and villages locatable on a good commercial map of Sicily[2] (Viagrande, Pedara, Nicolosi, Trecastagni, Aci Catena, Valverde, and Mascalucia) are all on the southern slope of Mount Etna, very close to Catania.

"Fantasticheria." First published in Rome in the August 24, 1879 issue of *Il Fanfulla della Domenica*,[3] this became the first story in the 1880 volume *Vita dei Campi*.

2. For this Introduction, the translator used the Michelin folding map No. 432 (scale of 1/400,000; 1 cm : 4 km). Place names in Verga's stories not on that map may be considered to be names of specific farms, local nicknames of geographical features, localities that would appear only on Ordnance Survey–type maps, street names, neighborhood names, and the like.   3. The Sunday literary supplement of *Il Fanfulla*. This highly regarded daily was originally published in Florence, but moved to Rome when that city became the new capital of Italy in 1871. Fanfulla was a devil-may-care 16th-century soldier who had already been made a character in 19th-century fiction.

It serves as a manifesto for Verga's new *verismo*. Basically a plotless meditation that refers to the decline of a fisherman's family, it reflects Verga's own tensions between his Sicilian roots and his deep involvement with the haughty, disdainful, and exploitative high society of northern Italy as embodied in a glamorous sweetheart. He treats the woman here with open sarcasm, his sympathies clearly going to the Sicilian characters.

This dissatisfaction in love and contrast between North and South are picked up in the final story, "Di là del mare" (Beyond the Sea) of his next collection of Sicilian stories, *Novelle rusticane* (1883), in which he may be referring specifically to Giselda Fojanesi. Thus, the two stories provide a framework for his two greatest story collections, considered as a unit.

"Fantasticheria" is also significant as an unmistakable projection of a great work in progress: the novel *I Malavoglia*. The fortunes of the fisher family are substantially the same in both works, even down to the lost medlar tree in their yard.

With regard to geography, Aci Trezza is on the coast, slightly northeast of Catania. The small prison island of Pantelleria lies about sixty miles southwest of the westernmost tip of Sicily, and is actually closer to Tunisia than to Sicily.

"Jeli il pastore." Written in November 1879, this was partially published in Florence in the February 29, 1880 issue of *La Fronda*, then placed as the second story in the 1880 *Vita dei campi*.

In his amicable simplicity, coupled with a difficulty in expressing himself that unavoidably breaks out into violent action, Jeli is much like Melville's Billy Budd. The final story in the original 1880 edition of *Vita dei campi*, "Pentolaccia," also concerns a placid cuckold who suddenly erupts.

"Jeli il pastore" is remarkably well observed, and very well written in detail, but a little choppy as a whole, because (1) it covers many years, and with unequal passage of time, (2) its incidents are more strung-along than cogently connected, and (3) at times its point-of-view shifts uneasily between Jeli and Don Alfonso, especially in the amazing long final sentence of the opening paragraph, in the course of which the reader realizes that the shared experiences of the boys are now being perceived solely in the thoughts, and by the standards, of Don Alfonso. (Verga himself was aware of the problem, because he began his next paragraph with: "Jeli himself didn't suffer from that melancholy.")

The problem arose from Verga's close identification of Don Alfonso

with himself. The story takes place in Verga's childhood-and-adolescence vacation area; the Vergas owned the estate near Vizzini called Tebidi ("warm, sunny [houses]") in the story, and numerous place names too local to appear on commercial maps are identifiable features in the nearby countryside. Besides Vizzini itself, the place names that *are* on the map include Licodia (Licodia Eubea), Caltagirone, Buccheri, and Marineo, none of them very far from Vizzini.

Jeli is short for some name ending in -*ele* (in standard Italian; -*eli* in Sicilian), most likely Raffaele, but possibly Gabriele. Mara is short for Maria; Menu, for Carmelo.

"Rosso Malpelo." This story was first published (as "Scene popolari") in Rome in the August 2 and 4, 1878 issues of *Il Fanfulla*. It appeared as a separate small book in 1880, published by Forzani, Rome, under the imprint Patto di Fratellanza. Then it became the third story in the 1880 *Vita dei campi*.

The literal translation of the hero's name is Red Evil-hair. The story is a perfect exemplification of the English saying, "Give a dog a bad name, and then hang him." As far as plot cohesion and continuity are concerned, this may be Verga's most successful story; the sandpit locale, which even has a mythology of its own, creates a microcosm symbolic of human existence, while the author employs detached irony perfectly to cloak his enormous sympathy with his main character. As elsewhere, but with especial artistry here, Verga associates the fate of animals with that of people, not only manifestly, as with the donkey Gray, but even in such details as the nickname of Rosso's father, "Bestia" (only an insensitive translator would totally disguise that connection with the animal world).

The name Misciu is a nickname for Domenico; Mommu might stand for Domenico, Girolamo, or Romolo. The locality Monserrato is now within the city limits of Catania. Plaja, the seashore slaughterhouse, is either at the mouth of the river Simeto, somewhat south of the city, or else corresponds to the present-day Lido di Plaia, to the immediate south of the city. Cifali, now called Cibali, is very close to Catania.

"Cavalleria rusticana." This story, the one most closely associated with Verga's name (but largely because of its later adaptations), was originally an offshoot of his work on the novel *I Malavoglia*; the basic plot appears in an early sketch for the novel, circa 1875. The story as we have it was first published in Rome in the March 14, 1880 issue of *Il Fanfulla della Domenica*, and then became the fourth story in the 1880 *Vita dei campi*.

This brief story about the blustering but vulnerable knave and fool Turiddu (= [Salva]torello) bears a surprising amount of weight and intensity when "primitive" passions of jealousy and revenge are unleashed.

Licodia (Alfio's birthplace, not far from Vizzini) and Sortino (the birthplace of his mules; about fifteen miles east of Vizzini) are the only place-names mentioned that can be found on a commercial map, but it is almost axiomatic that the story takes place in Vizzini itself (where "Cavalleria" tours are currently available). The Canziria where the duel is fought among the prickly pears is said to be the Cunzirìa ("tanners' district") just outside of town.

This story inspired numerous adaptations. Verga himself wrote a play version (his best stage work) in 1883. Its first performance, on January 14, 1884, at the Teatro Carignano in Turin, with the superb actress Eleonora Duse in the leading feminine role (now called Santuzza), was a spectacular success. When the pioneering French producer-director André Antoine mounted a French translation at his Théâtre Libre in 1888, the Parisians didn't take to it; but in Italy the play was already inspiring musical works. A tone poem by Giuseppe Perrotta was performed in Catania in 1886. The opera *Mala Pasqua* (Evil Easter), based on Verga's play, with music by Stanislao Gastaldon, was performed at the Teatro Costanzi in Rome on April 8, 1890. May 17 of the same year, at the same house, was the date of the premiere of Pietro Mascagni's *Cavalleria rusticana*, a tremendous success and the breakthrough work of operatic *verismo*. (It wasn't until 1893 that Verga obtained a payment of 143,000 *lire* from Mascagni and the music publisher Sonzogno.) In 1902 another opera based on the play, this one by Domenico Monleone, was performed in Amsterdam. (In 1907 it was Sonzogno who won a lawsuit after Monleone's opera was illegally performed in Italy.) In 1910 the important French film director Emile Chautard did a screen version of the play, and two different Italian film versions appeared in 1916 (just to mention the versions of Verga's play in his own lifetime).

"La Lupa." First published in the February 1880 issue of the *Rivista nuova di Scienze, Lettere e Arti*, probably in Milan,[4] this subsequently became the fifth story in the 1880 *Vita dei campi*.

---

4. The translator has been unable to locate a city of publication for this magazine, but its title differs by only one word, *nuova* ("new"), from that of the magazine in which "Nedda" was first published (see above). The inference is strong that this was substantially the same magazine, which had now become a monthly. (No reference known to the translator gives the cities of publication of the periodicals mentioned, and he was compelled to do tedious independent research.)

Like "Cavalleria rusticana," this story is brief and passionate, a study in monomania. Pina, the real name of La Lupa, is short for Giuseppina; Nanni is short for Giovanni; Maricchia is a form of Maria.

The only firm geographical indication in the story is that Mount Etna can be seen in the distance. St. Agrippina, prominently mentioned, was the patron saint of Mineo, which is slightly closer to Catania than Vizzini is. But there is a strong tradition that the characters live in Vizzini itself.

Verga wrote a play version of "La Lupa" in 1895, and tried to interest Puccini in composing an opera based on it. The play was first performed at the Teatro Gerbino in Turin on January 26, 1896. An opera based on the play was eventually published in 1919 (music by Pierantonio Tasca), but wasn't performed until 1933 (in Noto, Sicily).

"L'amante di Gramigna." When this story was first published in the February 1880 issue of the *Rivista minima* in Milan, it was called "L'amante di Raja"; in this case, the bandit's name means "(the fish) skate, or ray." When it appeared as the sixth story in the 1880 *Vita dei campi*, the prefatory letter to the editor of the magazine, Salvatore Farina, was abridged, while the incidents were expanded.

The letter to Farina is a major theoretical statement of the methods and aims of Verga's *verismo*, and deserves close attention. The story is a fascinating psychological study of love inspired by hearsay alone; unlike analogous situations in folktales, the unseen hero is not a handsome knight or a gilded youth, but a grimy, hunted outlaw, loved for the suffering that he endures. The story, which basically consists of merely a beginning and an end, as Verga in his letter says it will, is extremely well told; the opening paragraph of the actual story, after the letter, is an absolutely brilliant piece of exposition.

The name Peppa would seem to be a short form of Giuseppa. All three geographical references are on commercial maps. We have already encountered Licodia and the river Simeto. Palagonia is about 20 miles southwest of Catania.

"Malaria." First published in Florence in the August 14, 1881 issue of *La Rassegna settimanale di Politica, Scienze, Lettere ed Arti*, this became the fifth story in the 1883 volume *Novelle rusticane*.

The title is translated here as "Pestilential Air," not only because that is the literal meaning (the compound noun is formulated exactly like *malocchio*, "evil eye," and numerous other words beginning with *mal-*), but also because the true origin of the chills-and-fever disease was not yet known when the story was written, and it was attributed

to the unwholesome air of certain low-lying regions. The first two paragraphs of the story make this abundantly clear.[5]

This is not so much of a plotted story as it is the general portrait of an entire district, with just a few victims singled out for special mention. Lentini, with its then stagnant lake, is roughly 10 miles south of Catania. Agnone is nearby, on the coast. Francofonte is roughly 5 miles southwest of Lentini. Paternò, on the other hand, is about 10 miles from Catania in a northwesterly direction. The name Turi is short for Salvaturi (Salvatore).

"La roba." There is conflicting information about the first publication of this story. According to one trustworthy source, it was one of three recently written stories (the others being "Storia dell'asino di San Giuseppe" and "Cos'è il Re") that Verga suggested for inclusion in the forthcoming second edition of *Vita dei campi* instead of another story, thematically unrelated to the rest, that the publisher, Emilio Treves, wished to insert to expand the volume. Treves is said to have considered the three new stories too good to be introduced so inconspicuously; they deserved to be saved for a brand-new volume of stories. When *Vita dei campi* was reprinted in 1881, that unrelated story *was* added to it. The source in question allows the reader to infer *ex silentio* that the new volume, *Novelle rusticane* (which eventually was published by someone else in 1883) marked the first appearance anywhere of the three stories Verga had suggested, "La roba" being the seventh story in the book. On the other hand, another source states categorically that "La roba" was first published in Florence in the December 26, 1880 issue of *La Rassegna settimanale* (the other two stories aren't mentioned apart from *Novelle rusticane*).

Again, this is not a story with a plot (unless Mazzarò's career is considered to have a story line). Instead, it is an elaborate character sketch, and, as such, an important "rehearsal" for Verga's second great Sicilian novel, *Mastro-don Gesualdo*. In both cases, a poor lower-class man pulls himself up by his own bootstraps and becomes rich through his overpowering acquisitiveness.

Geographically, we are once more south of Catania, in the neighborhood of Lentini and Francoforte, and in the fertile Piana di Catania. A few of the little, off-the-map places mentioned in "Jeli il pastore" recur here.

"Storia dell'asino di S. Giuseppe." Apparently this story was

---

5. In a couple of the other stories, the translator has used "malaria" in English for the sake of concision, but only when the cause of the disease is not under discussion.

first published in the 1883 collection *Novelle rusticane* (see the comments on "La roba," above) as the eighth item in the book.

In numerous ways, this is an animal counterpart to "Rosso Malpelo," which itself featured a donkey prominently. Just as Rosso's red hair, which he was born with, was superstitiously viewed, ruining his life, so the pied coat of "St. Joseph's" donkey condemns him from birth. Rosso was emotionally and economically a prisoner of his sand quarry, but "St. Joseph's" donkey wanders from master to master, deteriorating physically and valued at a lower price each time, in what Verga called elsewhere a *via dolorosa* or a *via crucis,* the Stations of the Cross. The religious aura becomes crystal clear when "St. Joseph's" donkey falls to his knees like the donkey that adored the Christ Child. Naturally, the donkey's fate is meant to be read as an all-too-common Sicilian human destiny as well; Rosso Malpelo constantly compares himself to animals, and in another story from *Novelle rusticane,* "Gli orfani" (The Orphans), worn-out peasant women are specifically equated with domestic animals that have served their turn and are expendable. With regard to geography, we already have encountered Buccheri, Licodia, and the Piana di Catania.

"Pane nero." This story was first published in Turin between the issues of February 25 and March 18, 1882 of *La Gazzetta letteraria,* a weekly supplement of the daily *Gazzetta piemontese.* In May of 1882, in an expanded form, it was published separately by Giannotta in Catania. Finally it was placed as the ninth story in the 1883 *Novelle rusticane.*

The content is absorbing, but the narrative technique is unusual, and perhaps not entirely successful. Verga here attempts to follow the fortunes of an entire household, and, as it becomes progressively dispersed, the reader never knows which individual will be in the limelight next, or for how long. The effect is somewhat like that of the summary of a novel, a little bewildering though undoubtedly overpowering.

The name Nena is short for a name ending in *-ena,* such as Nazarena or Filomena. Cheli is short for the Sicilian version of Michele; while Brasi stands for (standard-Italian) Biagio, and Decu for Diego.

Geographically, we encounter Francofonte once more. The other place-names refer to individual farms or to other very small localities.

"Libertà." This story was published in Rome in the March 12, 1882 issue of *La Domenica letteraria,* a weekly that existed for only

three years. It then became the eleventh story in the 1883 *Novelle rusticane.*

This is the only Verga story that deals with a specific historical event (though he mentions neither the time nor the place). In July 1860, while Garibaldi's armies of liberation were making their successful way eastward through Sicily, the lower-class villagers of Bronte, on the western slope of Mount Etna, roughly 15 miles northwest of Catania, were deluded into a "liberty" craze and massacred the rich and noble. Garibaldi's general Nino (actually, Gerolamo) Bixio (1821–1873), who was no friend to anarchy and who wished no disturbance left in the rear as his army advanced, administered swift, hard justice.

In some ways this story summarizes many themes of the entire collection *Novelle rusticane.* A venal, corrupt police constable occurs in the story "Don Licciu Papa." A greedy, exploitative parish priest occurs in "Il Reverendo." Members of the gentry who are themselves impoverished (like Don Paolo in "Libertà") occur in "I galantuomini."

In his description of the uprising, Verga employs a nervous, telegraphic style (with many verbless sentences) that reflects the excitement of the events. With regard to names of characters: Neddu is short for Bastianeddu (Sebastianello), and Pippo for Giuseppe.

Sicilian Stories

Novelle siciliane

NEDDA

Il focolare domestico era per me una figura rettorica, buona per incorniciarvi gli affetti più miti e sereni, come il raggio di luna per baciare le chiome bionde; ma sorridevo allorquando sentivo dirmi che il fuoco del camino è quasi un amico. Sembravami in verità un amico troppo necessario, a volte uggioso e dispotico, che a poco a poco avrebbe voluto prendervi per le mani, o per i piedi, e tirarvi dentro il suo antro affumicato per baciarvi alla maniera di Giuda. Non conoscevo il passatempo di stuzzicare la legna, né la voluttà di sentirsi inondare dal riverbero della fiamma; non comprendevo il linguaggio del cepperello che scoppietta dispettoso, o brontola fiammeggiando; non avevo l'occhio assuefatto ai bizzarri disegni delle scintille correnti come lucciole sui tizzoni anneriti, alle fantastiche figure che assume la legna carbonizzandosi, alle mille gradazioni di chiaroscuro della fiamma azzurra e rossa che lambisce quasi timida, accarezza graziosamente, per divampare con sfacciata petulanza. Quando mi fui iniziato ai misteri delle molle e del soffietto, mi innamorai con trasporto della voluttuosa pigrizia del caminetto. Io lascio il mio corpo su quella poltroncina, accanto al fuoco, come vi lascerei un abito, abbandonando alla fiamma la cura di far circolare più caldo il mio sangue e di far battere più rapido il mio cuore; e incaricando le faville fuggenti, che folleggiano come farfalle innamorate, di farmi tenere gli occhi aperti, e di far errare capricciosamente del pari i miei pensieri. Cotesto spettacolo del proprio pensiero che svolazza vagabondo senza di voi, che vi lascia per correre lontano, e per gettarvi a vostra insaputa come dei soffi, di dolce e d'amaro in cuore, ha attrattive indefinibili. Col sigaro semispento, cogli occhi socchiusi, le molle fuggendovi dalle dita allentate, vedete l'altra parte di voi andar lontano, percorrere vertiginose distanze: vi par di sentirvi passar per i nervi correnti di atmosfere sconosciute, provate, sorridendo, l'effetto di mille sensazioni che farebbero incanutire i vostri capelli e solcherebbero di rughe la vostra fronte, senza muovere un dito, o fare un passo.

NEDDA

For me the household hearth was a figure of speech, a suitable frame-work for the gentlest, calmest emotions, just as a moonbeam is a proper light for enhancing blonde tresses; but I used to smile when-ever I was told that firelight is virtually a friend. To tell the truth, it seemed to me like a friend who is too compulsory, at times tiresome and despotic, one who'd gradually want to take you by the hands or feet and pull you into his smoky cave to give you a Judas kiss. I was unfamiliar with the pastime of poking the logs and the pleasure of feeling myself washed over by the reverberation of the flames; I didn't understand the language of the log that crackles teasingly, or grumbles as it blazes; my eyes weren't accustomed to the odd patterns of the sparks running like fireflies over the blackened brands, the fan-tastic figures taken on by the wood as it carbonizes, the thousand chiaroscuro gradations of the blue-and-red flame that licks as if timidly, caresses gracefully, and then flares up with impudent petu-lance. When I became initiated into the mysteries of the tongs and the bellows, I fell madly in love with the voluptuous laziness of the fire-side. I drop my body onto that armchair next to the fire the way I would drop a garment onto it, abandoning to the flames the task of making my blood circulate more hotly and my heart beat faster, and charging the flying sparks, which flit about giddily like lovesick but-terflies, with the duty of keeping my eyes open and making my thoughts roam just as capriciously. This spectacle of your own thoughts fluttering at random out of your control, leaving you behind while they dash off into the distance and, without your knowledge, waft sweet or bitter gusts into your heart, possesses attractions that can't be defined. Your cigar half-extinguished, your eyes partly shut, the tongs slipping out of your relaxed fingers, you see the other part of yourself traveling far away, covering dizzying distances; you seem to feel currents of unknown atmospheres passing through your sinews as you smile; you feel the effect of a thousand sensations that would turn your hair gray and dig wrinkles into your brow, though you don't stir a finger or take a step.

3

E in una di coteste peregrinazioni vagabonde dello spirito la fiamma che scoppiettava, troppo vicina forse, mi fece rivedere un'altra fiamma gigantesca che avevo visto ardere nell'immenso focolare della fattoria del Pino, alle falde dell'Etna. Pioveva, e il vento urlava incollerito; le venti o trenta donne che raccoglievano le ulive del podere facevano fumare le loro vesti bagnate dalla pioggia dinanzi al fuoco; le allegre, quelle che avevano dei soldi in tasca, o quelle che erano innamorate, cantavano; le altre ciarlavano della raccolta delle ulive, che era stata cattiva, dei matrimoni della parrocchia, o della pioggia che rubava loro il pane di bocca: la vecchia castalda filava, tanto perché la lucerna appesa alla cappa del focolare non ardesse per nulla, il grosso cane color di lupo allungava il muso sulle zampe verso il fuoco, rizzando le orecchie ad ogni diverso ululato del vento. Poi, nel tempo che cuocevasi la minestra, il pecorajo si mise a suonare certa arietta montanina che pizzicava le gambe, e le ragazze si misero a ballare sull'ammattonato sconnesso della vasta cucina affumicata, mentre il cane brontolava per timore che gli pestassero la coda. I cenci svolazzavano allegramente, mentre le fave ballavano anch'esse nella pentola, borbottando in mezzo alla schiuma che faceva sbuffare la fiamma. Quando tutte furono stanche, venne la volta alle canzonette, *Nedda! – Nedda la varannisa!* esclamarono parecchie. Dove s'è cacciata la *varannisa*?

Son qua; rispose una voce breve dall'angolo più buio, dove s'era accoccolata una ragazza su di un fascio di legna.

– O che fai tu costà?

– Nulla.

– Perché non hai ballato?

– Perché son stanca.

– Cantaci una delle tue belle canzonette.

– No, non voglio cantare.

– Che hai?

– Nulla.

– Ha la mamma che sta per morire, rispose una delle sue compagne, come se avesse detto che aveva male ai denti.

La ragazza che stava col mento sui ginocchi alzò su quella che aveva parlato certi occhioni neri, scintillanti, ma asciutti, quasi impassibili, e tornò a chinarli, senza aprir bocca, sui suoi piedi nudi.

Allora due o tre si volsero verso di lei, mentre le altre si sbandavano ciarlando tutte in una volta come gazze che festeggiano il lauto pascolo, e le dissero:

And in one of those vagabond pilgrimages of the spirit, the crackling flames, perhaps too close to me, made me see again another, gigantic flame that I had once seen burning in the huge hearth of the Pine farmhouse on the slopes of Etna. It was raining, and the wind was howling angrily; the twenty or thirty women who were harvesting the olives on the farm were letting their rain-soaked clothes dry off in front of the fire; the cheerful ones, those with money in their pockets, or those who were in love, were singing; the others were chatting about the olive harvest, which had been poor, about the marriages in the parish, or about the rain, which was taking the food out of their mouths. The elderly wife of the farm manager was spinning, mainly to keep the oil lamp hanging from the hood of the fireplace from burning for nothing. The big wolf-colored dog had his muzzle extended over his paws facing the fire, and he'd prick up his ears at every different howl of the wind. Then, while the food was cooking, the shepherd began playing some mountain tune that tickled your feet, and the girls started dancing on the disjointed tile floor of the vast smoky kitchen, while the dog growled in fear of having his tail stepped on. The ragged clothes were fluttering cheerfully, while the beans were dancing, too, in the pot, muttering amid the froth puffed up by the fire. When all the women were tired, it was time for songs, and several of them called: "Nedda! Nedda from Viagrande! Where's the girl from Viagrande hiding herself?"

"Here I am," answered a small voice from the darkest corner, where a girl was squatting on her heels on top of a bundle of firewood.

"What are you doing over there?"

"Nothing."

"Why didn't you dance?"

"Because I'm tired."

"Sing us one of your pretty songs."

"No, I don't feel like singing."

"What's wrong with you?"

"Nothing."

"It's because her mother is going to die," one of her companions answered, in the same tone as if she had said that Nedda had a toothache.

The girl, who had been resting her chin on her knees, looked up at the woman who had spoken, her eyes wide, dark and sparkling, but dry and almost expressionless; then once again, without opening her mouth, she lowered them to look at her own bare feet.

Then two or three of the women turned toward her and, while the others scattered, all chattering at once like magpies rejoicing over a rich pasture, they said to her:

– O allora perché hai lasciato tua madre?

– Per trovar del lavoro.

– Di dove sei?

– Di Viagrande, ma sto a Ravanusa.

Una delle spiritose, la figlioccia del castaldo, che dovea sposare il terzo figlio di Massaro Jacopo a Pasqua, e aveva una bella crocetta d'oro al collo, le disse volgendole le spalle: – Eh! non è lontano! la cattiva nuova dovrebbe recartela proprio l'uccello!

Nedda le lanciò dietro un'occhiata simile a quella che il cane accovacciato dinanzi al fuoco lanciava agli zoccoli che minacciavano la sua coda.

– No! lo zio Giovanni sarebbe venuto a chiamarmi! esclamò come rispondendo a se stessa.

– Chi è lo zio Giovanni?

– È lo zio Giovanni di Ravanusa; lo chiamano tutti così.

– Bisognava farsi imprestare qualche cosa dallo zio Giovanni, e non lasciare tua madre, disse un'altra.

– Lo zio Giovanni non è ricco, e gli dobbiamo diggià dieci lire! E il medico? e le medicine? e il pane di ogni giorno? Ah! si fa presto a dire: aggiunse Nedda scrollando la testa, e lasciando trapelare per la prima volta un'intonazione più dolente nella voce rude e quasi selvaggia, ma a veder tramontare il sole dall'uscio, pensando che non c'è pane nell'armadio, né olio nella lucerna, né lavoro per l'indomani, la è una cosa assai amara, quando si ha una povera vecchia inferma, là su quel lettuccio!

E scuoteva sempre il capo dopo aver taciuto, senza guardar nessuno, con occhi asciutti, che tradivano tale inconscio dolore quale gli occhi più abituati alle lagrime non saprebbero esprimere.

– Le vostre scodelle, ragazze! gridò la castalda scoperchiando la pentola in aria trionfale.

Tutte si affollarono attorno al focolare, ove la castalda distribuiva con sapiente parsimonia le mestolate di fave. Nedda aspettava ultima, colla sua scodelletta sotto il braccio. Finalmente ci fu posto anche per lei, e la fiamma l'illuminò tutta.

Era una ragazza bruna, vestita miseramente, dall'attitudine timida e ruvida che danno la miseria e l'isolamento. Forse sarebbe stata bella, se gli stenti e le fatiche non avessero alterato profondamente non solo le sembianze gentili della donna, ma direi anche la forma umana. I suoi capelli erano neri, folti, arruffati, appena annodati con dello spago, aveva denti bianchi come avorio, e una certa grossolana avvenenza di lineamenti che rendeva attraente il suo sorriso. Gli

"Then why did you leave your mother?"

"To find work."

"Where are you from?"

"From Viagrande, but I'm staying at Ravanusa."

One of the witty girls, the farm manager's goddaughter, who was to marry farmer Jacopo's third son at Easter, and who was wearing a lovely gold cross around her neck, said to her, while turning her back to her: "Oh, that's not far! A little bird could bring the bad news to you!"

Nedda darted at her back a look like the one that the dog curled up in front of the fire was darting at the wooden clogs that were threatening his tail.

"No! 'Uncle' Giovanni would have come to call me!" she exclaimed as if in answer to herself.

"Who's 'Uncle' Giovanni?"

"He's 'Uncle' Giovanni from Ravanusa; everyone calls him that."

"You should have borrowed some money from 'Uncle' Giovanni instead of leaving your mother," another woman said.

"'Uncle' Giovanni isn't rich, and we already owe him ten *lire!* And the doctor? And the medicine? And our daily bread? Oh, it's easy enough to say," Nedda added, shaking her head, and for the first time allowing a more sorrowful tone to tinge her rough, almost savage voice, "but to stand in your doorway watching the sun go down, knowing that there's no bread in the cupboard, no oil in the lamp, and no work for the next day—that's a very bitter thing when you've got a poor old woman lying ill on her cot!"

And after falling silent, she kept shaking her head, looking at nobody; her eyes were dry but revealed an unwitting sorrow of a kind that eyes more used to weeping couldn't express.

"Your bowls, girls!" shouted the farm manager's wife, raising the lid of the pot with a look of triumph.

They all crowded around the hearth, where the farm manager's wife was ladling out the beans with prudent frugality. Nedda waited till she was the last, her little bowl under her arm. Finally there was room for her, too, and she was totally illuminated by the flames.

She was a swarthy girl, shabbily dressed, with that shy, coarse bearing produced by poverty and isolation. She might have been pretty, had not privations and labors thoroughly ruined not only her sweet womanly features, but even her human shape, as it were. Her hair was black, thick, tousled, contained only by a bit of string; she had teeth white as ivory, and a certain rough charm in her face that made her smile attractive. Her eyes were big and dark, swimming in a bluish

occhi avea neri, grandi, nuotanti in un fluido azzurrino, quali li
avrebbe invidiati una regina a quella povera figliuola raggomitolata
sull'ultimo gradino della scala umana, se non fossero stati offuscati
dall'ombrosa timidezza della miseria, o non fossero sembrati stupidi
per una triste e continua rassegnazione. Le sue membra schiacciate
da pesi enormi, o sviluppate violentemente da sforzi penosi erano di-
ventate grossolane, senza esser robuste. Ella faceva da manovale,
quando non avea da trasportare sassi nei terreni che si andavano dis-
sodando, o trasportava dei carichi in città per conto altrui, o faceva
altri di quei lavori più duri che da quelle parti stimansi inferiori al
compito dell'uomo. I lavori più comuni della donna, anche nei paesi
agricoli, la vendemmia, la messe, la ricolta delle ulive, erano delle
feste, dei giorni di baldoria, proprio un passatempo anziché una fatica. È vero bensì che fruttavano appena la metà di una buona giornata estiva da manovale, la quale dava 13 bravi soldi! I cenci sovrap-
posti in forma di vesti rendevano grottesca quella che avrebbe dovuto
essere la delicata bellezza muliebre. L'immaginazione più vivace non
avrebbe potuto figurarsi che quelle mani costrette ad un'aspra fatica
di tutti i giorni, a raspar fra il gelo, o la terra bruciante, o i rovi e i
crepacci, che quei piedi abituati ad andar nudi nella neve e sulle roccie infuocate dal sole, a lacerarsi sulle spine, o ad indurirsi sui sassi,
avrebbero potuto esser belli. Nessuno avrebbe saputo dire quanti
anni avesse cotesta creatura umana; la miseria l'avea schiacciata da
bambina con tutti gli stenti che deformano e induriscono il corpo,
l'anima e l'intelligenza – così era stato di sua madre, così di sua
nonna, così sarebbe stato di sua figlia – e dell'impronta dei suoi
fratelli in Eva bastava che le rimanesse quel tanto che occorreva per
comprenderne gli ordini e per prestar loro i più umili, i più duri
servigi.

Nedda sporse la sua scodella, e la castalda ci versò quello che rimaneva di fave nella pentola, e non era molto!

– Perché vieni sempre l'ultima? Non sai che gli ultimi hanno quel
che avanza? le disse a mo' di compenso la castalda.

La povera ragazza chinò gli occhi sulla broda nera che fumava nella
sua scodella, come se meritasse il rimprovero, e andò pian pianino
perché il contenuto non si versasse.

– Io te ne darei volentieri della mia, disse a Nedda una delle sue
compagne che aveva miglior cuore; ma se domini continuasse a piovere . . . davvero! . . . oltre a perdere la mia giornata non vorrei anche
mangiare tutto il mio pane.

– Io non ho questo timore! rispose Nedda con un tristo sorriso.

fluid, and a queen might have envied them, though she was just a poor girl huddled on the lowest rung of the social ladder, if they hadn't been dulled by the melancholy timidity of poverty, or if they didn't look stupid because of her constant sad resignation. Her limbs, crushed by enormous weights, or violently strengthened by painful efforts, had become coarse without being robust. She worked as a construction laborer when she wasn't carrying rocks on land that was being tilled, bringing loads into town for other people, or performing other, harder labors of the kind that are considered in those areas to be beneath a man's dignity. The tasks more common to women, even in farm regions—grape and grain harvesting and olive gathering— were like holidays to her, days of merrymaking, a pastime rather than a chore. Although, to tell the truth, they brought in barely half the income from a good summer's day as a construction worker, which would produce a whopping 13 *soldi!* The layers of rags in lieu of a dress made a grotesquerie of what should have been her delicate female beauty. The most vivid imagination couldn't conceive that those hands compelled to do rough work every day, scraping in the ice, the burning soil, the brambles, or rock clefts, that those feet accustomed to go bare on the snow and on boulders scalded by the sun, to be cut with thorns or callused on the rocks, might have been beautiful. No one could have told the age of that human creature; from her childhood on, poverty had crushed her with every privation that stunts and toughens the body, soul, and mind—it had been that way with her mother and grandmother, it would be that way with her daughter— and it was sufficient for her to have retained that little bit of the imprint of her brothers-in-Eve which would allow her to understand their orders and to perform the lowest and hardest services for them.

Nedda held out her bowl, and the farm manager's wife poured into it the beans remaining in the pot, and it wasn't a lot!

"Why do you always show up last? Don't you know that those who are last get only what's left over?" the farm manager's wife said, as if to make things up to her.

The poor girl looked down at the black broth that was steaming in her bowl, as if she deserved the reproach, and she walked away very slowly, so that it wouldn't spill out.

"I'd gladly give you some of mine," Nedda was told by one of her companions who had a kinder heart, "but if it should keep on raining tomorrow—honestly!—on top of losing my day's pay, I wouldn't want to eat up all my bread, too."

"I don't have that worry," Nedda replied with a mean smile.

– Perché?

– Perché non ho pane di mio. Quel po' che ci avevo, insieme a quei pochi quattrini li ho lasciati alla mamma.

– E vivi della sola minestra?

– Sì, ci sono avvezza; rispose Nedda semplicemente.

– Maledetto tempaccio, che ci ruba la nostra giornata! imprecò un'altra.

– To' prendi dalla mia scodella.

– Non ho più fame; riprese la *varannisa* ruvidamente a mo' di ringraziamento.

– Tu che bestemmi la pioggia del buon Dio, non mangi forse del pane anche tu! disse la castalda a colei che avea imprecato contro il cattivo tempo. E non sai che pioggia d'autunno vuol dire buon anno!

Un mormorìo generale approvò quelle parole.

– Sì, ma intanto son tre buone mezze giornate che vostro marito toglierà dal conto della settimana!

Altro mormorìo d'approvazione.

– Hai forse lavorato in queste tre mezze giornate perché ti s'abbiano a pagare? rispose trionfalmente la vecchia.

– È vero! è vero! risposero le altre con quel sentimento istintivo di giustizia che c'è nelle masse, anche quando questa giustizia danneggia gli individui.

La castalda intuonò il rosario, le avemarie si seguirono col loro monotono brontolìo accompagnate da qualche sbadiglio. Dopo le litanie si pregò per i vivi e per i morti; allora gli occhi della povera Nedda si riempirono di lagrime, e dimenticò di rispondere *amen*.

– Che modo è cotesto di non rispondere *amen*! le disse la vecchia in tuono severo.

– Pensava alla mia povera mamma che è tanto lontana: rispose Nedda facendosi seria.

Poi la castalda diede la *santa notte,* prese la lucerna e andò via. Qua e là, per la cucina o attorno al fuoco, s'improvvisarono i giacigli in forme pittoresche; le ultime fiamme gettarono vacillanti chiaroscuri sui gruppi e su gli atteggiamenti diversi. Era una buona fattoria quella, e il padrone non risparmiava, come tant'altri, fave per la minestra, né legna pel focolare, né strame pei giacigli. Le donne dormivano in cucina, e gli uomini nel fienile. Dove poi il padrone è avaro, o la fattoria è piccola, uomini e donne dormono alla rinfusa, come meglio possono, nella stalla, o altrove, sulla paglia o su pochi cenci, i figliuoli accanto ai genitori, e quando il

"Why not?"

"Because I have no bread. The little I had, I left with my mother, along with our few coins."

"And you live on just the food they dish out?"

"Yes, I'm used to that," Nedda replied simply.

"Damn this bad weather that's robbing us of our day's pay!" another woman cursed.

"Here, take some from my bowl."

"I'm not hungry anymore," the girl from Viagrande replied roughly as a way of saying thank you.

"You, the one cursing the good Lord's rain, don't you eat bread like everyone else?" said the farm manager's wife to the woman who had damned the bad weather. "Don't you know that rain in autumn means a good crop?"

A general murmuring gave approval to her speech.

"Yes, but in the meantime your husband will deduct three good half-days from our weekly pay!"

Another murmur of approval.

"And did you work during those three half-days to earn any pay?" the old woman replied triumphantly.

"It's true! It's true!" the others replied with that instinctive feeling for justice that people possess in the aggregate, even when that same justice harms them individually.

The farm manager's wife recited the rosary, and the Hail Marys succeeded one another with their monotonous rumble, accompanied by a few yawns. After the litanies they prayed for the dead and for the living; then Nedda's eyes filled with tears, and she forgot to say amen.

"What manners are these, not to say amen?!" the old lady said to her in severe tones.

"I was thinking about my poor mother who's so far away," replied Nedda, becoming serious.

Then the farm manager's wife wished them a "blessed night," took the oil lamp, and left. Here and there, in the kitchen or around the fire, they improvised sleeping places in picturesque forms; the last flames cast wavering chiaroscuros on the groups and their various postures. That tenant farmhouse was a good one, and the owner wasn't stingy, like so many others, with beans for the soup, wood for the hearth, or straw for the pallets. The women slept in the kitchen, the men in the hayloft. Where the boss is cheap, or the farmhouse is small, men and women sleep all together, as best they can, in the stable or elsewhere, on the straw or on a little heap of rags, the children

genitore è ricco, e ha una coperta di suo, la distende sulla sua famigliuola; chi ha freddo si addossa al vicino, o mette i piedi nella cenere calda, o si copre di paglia, s'ingegna come può; dopo un giorno di fatica, e per ricominciare un altro giorno di fatica, il sonno è profondo, come un despota benefico, e la moralità del padrone non è permalosa che per negare il lavoro alla ragazza che, essendo prossima a divenir madre, non potesse compiere le sue dieci ore di fatica.

Prima di giorno le più mattiniere erano uscite per vedere che tempo facesse, e l'uscio che sbatteva ad ogni momento sugli stipiti spingeva turbini di pioggia e di vento freddissimo su quelli che intirizziti dormivano ancora. Ai primi albori il castaldo era venuto a spalancare l'uscio, per svegliare anche i più pigri, giacché non è giusto defraudare il padrone di un minuto della giornata lunga dieci ore che egli paga il suo bravo tarì, e qualche volta anche tre carlini (sessantacinque centesimi!) oltre la minestra!

– Piove! era la parola uggiosa che correva su tutte le bocche con accento di malumore. La Nedda, appoggiata all'uscio, guardava tristamente i grossi nuvoloni color di piombo che gettavano su di lei le livide tinte del crepuscolo. La giornata era fredda e nebbiosa; le foglie avvizzite si staccavano dal ramoscello, strisciavano lungo i rami, e svolazzavano alquanto prima di andare a cadere sulla terra fangosa, e il rigagnolo s'impantanava in una pozzanghera dove s'avvoltolavano voluttuosamente dei maiali: le vacche mostravano il muso nero attraverso il cancello che chiudeva la stalla, e guardavano la pioggia, che cadeva, con occhio malinconico; i passeri, rannicchiati sotto le tegole della gronda, pigolavano in tuono piagnoloso.

– Ecco un'altra giornata andata a male! mormorò una delle ragazze addentando un grosso pan nero.

– Le nuvole si distaccano dal mare laggiù, disse Nedda stendendo il braccio; sul mezzogiorno forse il tempo cambierà.

– Però quel birbo del fattore non ci pagherà che un terzo della giornata!

– Sarà tanto di guadagnato.

– Sì, ma il nostro pane che mangiamo a tradimento?

– E il danno che avrà il padrone delle ulive che andranno a male, e di quelle che si perderanno fra la mota?

– È vero! disse un'altra.

– Ma provati ad andare a raccogliere una sola di quelle ulive che andranno perdute fra una mezz'ora, per accompagnarla al tuo pane asciutto, e vedrai quel che ti darà di giunta il fattore.

alongside the parents; when the father is wealthy enough to have a blanket of his own, he spreads it out over his family; anyone who's cold presses up against his neighbor, or puts his feet in the warm ashes, or covers himself with straw—whatever he can devise. After a hard day's work, and when the next day will be just as hard, sleep is deep, like a well-meaning despot, and the owner's morals are fastidious only when it comes to denying work to a girl who's close to giving birth and thus couldn't put in ten strenuous hours.

Before daybreak the earliest risers had gone out to see what the weather was like, and the door, slamming between its jambs every minute, drove in whirlwinds of rain and freezing air onto those who were still asleep, all numb. At the first gleam of dawn the farm manager had come to throw the door wide open and to arouse even the laziest, since it's unfair to cheat the proprietor out of even a minute of the ten-hour day that he pays for with a good *tarì*, and sometimes even with three *carlini* (seventy-five *centesimi!*) besides the food!

"It's raining," was the gloomy phrase on everyone's lips, in a discontented tone. Nedda, leaning against the door jamb, was looking gloomily at the huge, lead-colored clouds that were casting the livid tints of dawn upon her. The day was cold and foggy; the withered leaves were becoming detached from their twigs, were slithering down the boughs, and fluttering a little before they finally fell onto the muddy ground; and the streamlet was swelling into a big puddle in which pigs were wallowing voluptuously. The cows were showing their black muzzles through the gate that barred the stable, and were looking at the falling rain with melancholy eyes. The sparrows, huddled beneath the tiles of the eaves, were peeping in querulous tones.

"Here's another day gone to waste!" murmured one of the girls, biting into a large loaf of dark bread.

"The clouds are pulling away from the sea over yonder," said Nedda, stretching out her arm. "By noon, maybe, the weather will change."

"But that scoundrelly farm manager will pay us only a third of our day's wages!"

"It will still be that much earned."

"Yes, but what about our bread that we're eating at our own expense?"

"And what about the loss that the owner will take for the olives that rot on the trees and the ones that get lost in the mud?"

"That's true!" another woman said.

"But just try to go and pick up just one of those olives, which will get spoiled in a half-hour, so you can eat it along with your dry bread, and you'll see what a bonus the farm manager will give you!"

– È giusto, perché le ulive non sono nostre!

– Ma non son nemmeno della terra che se le mangia!

– La terra è del padrone to'! replicò Nedda trionfante di logica, con certi occhi espressivi.

– È vero anche questo; rispose un'altra che non sapeva che rispondere.

– Quanto a me preferirei che continuasse a piovere tutto il giorno piuttosto che stare una mezza giornata carponi in mezzo al fango, con questo tempaccio, per tre o quattro soldi.

– A te non ti fanno nulla tre o quattro soldi, non ti fanno! esclamò Nedda tristamente.

La sera del sabato, quando fu l'ora di fare il conto della settimana, dinanzi alla tavola del fattore, tutta carica di cartaccie e di bei gruzzoletti di soldi, gli uomini più turbolenti furono pagati i primi, poscia le più rissose delle donne, in ultimo, e peggio, le timide e le deboli. Quando il fattore le ebbe fatto il suo conto Nedda venne a sapere che, detratte le due giornate e mezzo di riposo forzato, restava ad avere quaranta soldi.

La povera ragazza non osò aprir bocca. Solo le si riempirono gli occhi di lagrime.

– E lamentati per giunta, piagnucolona! gridò il fattore, il quale gridava sempre da fattore coscienzioso che difende i soldi del padrone. Dopo che ti pago come le altre, e sì che sei più povera e più piccola delle altre! e ti pago la tua giornata come nessun proprietario ne paga una simile in tutto il territorio di Pedara, Nicolosi e Trecastagne! Tre carlini, oltre la minestra!

– Io non mi lamento! disse timidamente Nedda intascando quei pochi soldi che il fattore, come ad aumentarne il valore, avea conteggiato per grani. La colpa è del tempo che è stato cattivo e mi ha tolto quasi la metà di quel che avrei potuto buscarmi.

– Pigliatela col Signore! disse il fattore ruvidamente.

– Oh, non col Signore! ma con me che son tanto povera!

– Pagagli intiera la sua settimana a quella povera ragazza; disse al fattore il figliuolo del padrone che assisteva alla ricolta delle ulive. Non sono che pochi soldi di differenza.

– Non devo darle che quel ch'è giusto!

– Ma se te lo dico io!

"That's only fair, because the olives don't belong to us!"

"No more do they belong to the ground that swallows them up!"

"Look, the ground belongs to the proprietor!" Nedda retorted, proud of her logic, her eyes very expressive.

"That's true, too," replied another woman, who didn't know how to reply.

"As for me, I'd prefer it to keep raining all day long rather than remaining on all fours for half a day in the middle of the mud, in this rotten weather, for three or four *soldi*."

"Three or four *soldi* make no difference to you, none at all!" exclaimed Nedda gloomily.

On Saturday evening, when it was time to be paid for the week, in front of the farm manager's table, which was loaded down with stacks of papers and beautiful piles of coins, the more turbulent men were the first to be paid; then the more quarrelsome of the women; then, last and most poorly, the shy and weak women. When the farm manager had paid her, Nedda learned that, after deducting the two-and-a-half days of enforced leisure, she was left with only forty *soldi*.

The poor girl didn't dare open her mouth. Her eyes merely filled with tears.

"Go around moaning, on top of everything else, crybaby!" yelled the farm manager, who always yelled like a conscientious manager defending his employer's pocketbook. "After I give you the same pay as the rest, even though you're poorer and smaller than the rest! And I pay you a wage that no other proprietor pays in the whole territory of Pedara, Nicolosi, and Trecastagni! Three *carlini* besides the chow!"

"I'm not complaining," Nedda said timidly, pocketing the small sum of money that the farm manager had dealt out coin by coin, as if to make it look like more. "The weather's to blame, which has been bad and has deprived me of almost half of what I could have made."

"Take it up with God!" said the farm manager rudely.

"Oh, not with God, but with myself, for being so poor!"

"Pay that poor girl for a full week," the proprietor's son,[1] who was attending the olive harvest, said to the manager. "There's only a slight difference in the amount."

"I mustn't give her more than is fair!"

"But I'm authorizing you to!"

---

1. The author may be referring to himself in younger years, because the Vergas had property in the area.

– Tutti i proprietari del vicinato farebbero la guerra a voi e a me se *facessimo delle novità.*

– Hai ragione! rispose il figliuolo del padrone, che era un ricco proprietario e avea molti vicini.

Nedda raccolse quei pochi cenci che erano suoi, e disse addio alle compagne.

– Vai a Ravanusa a quest'ora! dissero alcune.

– La mamma sta male!

– Non hai paura?

– Sì, ho paura per questi soldi che ho in tasca; ma la mamma sta male, e adesso che non son costretta a star più qui a lavorare mi sembra che non potrei dormire se mi fermassi ancora stanotte.

– Vuoi che t'accompagni? le disse in tuono di scherzo il giovane pecorajo.

– Vado con Dio e con Maria; disse semplicemente la povera ragazza prendendo la via dei campi a capo chino.

Il sole era tramontato da qualche tempo e le ombre salivano rapidamente verso la cima della montagna. Nedda camminava sollecita, e quando le tenebre si fecero profonde cominciò a cantare come un uccelletto spaventato. Ogni dieci passi voltavasi indietro, paurosa, e allorché un sasso, smosso dalla pioggia che era caduta, sdrucciolava dal muricciolo, e il vento le spruzzava bruscamente addosso a guisa di gragnuola la pioggia raccolta nelle foglie degli alberi, ella si fermava tutta tremante, come una capretta sbrancata. Un assiolo la seguiva d'albero in albero col suo canto lamentoso, ed ella tutta lieta di quella compagnia lo imitava col fischio di tempo in tempo, perché l'uccello non si stancasse di seguirla. Quando passava dinanzi ad una cappelletta, accanto alla porta di qualche fattoria, si fermava un istante nella viottola per dire in fretta un'avemaria, stando all'erta che non le saltasse addosso dal muro di cinta il cane di guardia che abbaiava furiosamente; poi partiva di passo più lesto rivolgendosi due o tre volte a guardare il lumicino che ardeva in omaggio alla Santa e rischiarava la via al fattore quando egli tornava tardi alla sera. – Quel lumicino le dava coraggio, e la faceva pregare per la sua povera mamma. Di tempo in tempo un pensiero doloroso le stringeva il cuore come una fitta improvvisa, e allora si metteva a correre, e contava ad alta voce per stordirsi, o pensava ai giorni più allegri della vendemmia, o alle sere d'estate, quando, con la più bella luna del mondo, si tornava a stormi dalla Piana, dietro la cornamusa che suonava allegramente; ma il suo pensiero ritornava sempre là, dinanzi al misero giaciglio della sua inferma. Inciampò in una scheggia di lava tagliente come un

"Every landowner in these parts would declare war on you and me both if we followed new ways."

"You're right," replied the son of the proprietor, who was a wealthy landowner and had many neighbors.

Nedda gathered up her few rags and said good-bye to her companions.

"You're going to Ravanusa at this hour!" some of them said.

"My mother is ill!"

"Aren't you afraid?"

"Yes, I'm afraid for this money I've got in my pocket; but my mother is ill, and now that I'm not forced to remain here and work anymore, I don't think I could sleep if I stayed here tonight."

"Do you want me to escort you?" the young shepherd said jokingly.

"I'm going with God and His Mother," the poor girl said simply, as she set out toward the fields with bowed head.

The sun had set some time earlier, and the shadows were rapidly climbing toward the summit of the mountain. Nedda was worried as she walked, and when the darkness became deep she began singing like a frightened songbird. Every ten paces she turned around fearfully, and whenever a stone, loosened by the rain that had fallen, rolled down from the low wall and the wind suddenly sprayed her with a shower of the rain that had collected in the leaves of the trees, she would halt all a-tremble, like a young goat that had strayed from the flock. A scops owl was following her from tree to tree with its mournful call, and she, overjoyed at having that company, whistled in imitation of it every once in a while so that the bird wouldn't grow tired of following her. Whenever she passed by a small shrine near the gate to some farm, she'd stop on the path for a moment to utter a rapid Hail Mary, keeping alert lest the furiously barking watchdog leap onto her from the enclosing wall; then she'd resume her journey at a brisker pace, turning back two or three times to look at the little lamp that was burning in honor of the Blessed Virgin and lighting the way for the farm manager when he came home in the late evening.—That little lamp gave her courage, and made her pray for her poor mother. From time to time a sorrowful thought gripped her heart with a sudden twinge, and then she'd start to run, singing aloud to numb her mind, or she'd think about the happier days of the grape harvest or about the summer evenings when, in the loveliest imaginable moonlight, crowds of folk would come back from the Plain of Catania, following the merrily playing bagpipe. But her thoughts always reverted to her sick mother's wretched bedside. She stumbled over a sliver of lava as sharp

rasojo, e si lacerò un piede, l'oscurità era sì fitta che alle svolte della viottola la povera ragazza spesso urtava contro il muro o la siepe, e cominciava a perder coraggio e a non sapere dove si trovasse. Tutt'a un tratto udì l'orologio della Punta che suonava le nove così vicino che sembrolle i rintocchi le cadessero sul capo, e sorrise come se un amico l'avesse chiamata per nome in mezzo ad una folla di stranieri.

Infilò allegramente la via del villaggio cantando a sguarciagola la sua bella canzone, e tenendo stretti nella mano, dentro la tasca del grembiule, i suoi quaranta soldi.

Passando dinanzi alla farmacia vide lo speziale ed il notaro tutti inferraiuolati che giocavano a carte. Alquanto più in là incontrò il povero matto di Punta che andava su e giù, da un capo all'altro della via, colle mani nelle tasche del vestito, canticchiando la solita canzone che l'accompagna da venti anni, nelle notti d'inverno e nei meriggi della canicola. Quando fu ai primi alberi del diritto viale che fa capo a Ravanusa incontrò un pajo di buoi che venivano a passo lento ruminando tranquillamente.

– Ohé! Nedda! gridò una voce nota.

– Sei tu! Janu?

– Sì, son io, coi buoi del padrone.

– Da dove vieni? domandò Nedda senza fermarsi.

– Vengo dalla Piana. Son passato da casa tua; tua madre t'aspetta.

– Come sta la mamma?

– Al solito.

– Che Dio ti benedica! esclamò la ragazza come se avesse temuto di peggio, e ricominciò a correre.

– Addio! Nedda! le gridò dietro Janu.

– Addio, balbettò da lontano Nedda.

E le parve che le stelle splendessero come soli, che tutti gli alberi, che conosceva ad uno ad uno, stendessero i rami sulla sua testa per proteggerla, e che i sassi della via le accarezzassero i piedi indolenziti.

L'indomani, poiché era domenica, venne la visita del medico, che concedeva ai suoi malati poveri il giorno che non poteva consacrare ai suoi poderi. Una triste visita davvero! perché il buon dottore che non era abituato a far complimenti coi suoi clienti, e nel casolare di Nedda non c'era anticamera, né amici di casa ai quali potere annunziare il vero stato dell'inferma.

Nella giornata seguì anche una mesta funzione; venne il curato in rocchetto, il sagrestano coll'olio santo, e due o tre comari che

as a razor and cut her foot; the darkness was so dense that at the bends in the path the poor girl often bumped into a wall or a hedge. She was starting to lose courage, not recognizing where she was. All at once she heard the tower clock at Punta ringing nine so close by that she thought the strokes were falling on her head, and she smiled as if a friend had called her by name in the midst of a throng of strangers.

Cheerfully she entered the village street, singing her lovely song at the top of her lungs and holding her forty *soldi* tightly in her hand inside the pocket of her overalls.

As she passed in front of the pharmacy she saw the druggist and the notary, all wrapped up in their cloaks, playing cards. A little farther along she met the poor madman of Punta; he was walking up and down, from one end of the street to the other, with his hands in his jacket pockets, humming his usual song, which had kept him company for twenty years, in the winter nights and the dog-day noons. When she reached the first trees on the straight road leading to Ravanusa, she met a team of oxen coming slowly toward her as they calmly chewed their cud.

"Hey, Nedda!" shouted a familiar voice.

"Is that you, Janu?"

"Yes, it's me, with the boss's oxen."

"Where are you coming from?" Nedda asked without stopping.

"I'm coming from the Plain. I looked in at your place; your mother's expecting you."

"How is Mother?"

"Same as usual."

"God bless you!" the girl explained, as if she had feared something worse, and she started to run again.

"Good-bye, Nedda!" Janu called after her.

"Good-bye!" Nedda stammered from a distance.

And it seemed to her that the stars were shining like suns, that all the trees, which she knew one by one, were extending their boughs over her head to protect her, and that the stones on her path were caressing her aching feet.

The next day, because it was Sunday, they were visited by the doctor, who granted his unmonied patients the day he couldn't devote to his profitable cases. A sad visit, in truth, because the good doctor wasn't accustomed to stand on ceremony with his patients, and because in Nedda's cottage there was no waiting room, nor friends of the family to whom he could report the sick woman's real condition.

During the day another sad function followed; the parish priest came in his surplice, the sacristan with the consecrated oil, and two or three

borbottavano non so che preci. La campanella del sagrestano squillava acutamente in mezzo ai campi, e i carrettieri che l'udivano fermavano i loro muli in mezzo alla strada, e si cavavano il berrreto. Quando Nedda l'udì per la sassosa viottola che metteva dallo stradale al casolare tirò su la coperta tutta lacera dell'inferma, perché non si vedesse che mancavano le lenzuola, e piegò il suo più bel grembiule bianco sul deschetto zoppo che avea reso fermo con dei mattoni. Poi, mentre il prete compiva il suo ufficio, andò ad inginocchiarsi fuori dell'uscio, balbettando macchinalmente delle preci, guardando come trasognata quel sasso dinanzi alla soglia su cui la sua vecchierella soleva scaldarsi al sole di marzo, e ascoltando con orecchio disattento i consueti rumori delle vicinanze, ed il via vai di tutta quella gente che andava per i proprii affari senza avere angustie pel capo. Il curato partì, ed il sagrestano indugiò invano sull'uscio perché gli facessero la solita limosina pei poveri.

Lo zio Giovanni vide a tarda ora della sera la Nedda che correva sulla strada di Punta.

– Ohé! dove vai a quest'ora?

– Vado per una medicina che ha ordinato il medico.

Lo zio Giovanni era economo e brontolone.

– Ancora medicine! borbottò, dopo che ha ordinato la medicina dell'olio santo! già loro fanno a metà collo speziale, per dissanguare la povera gente! Fai a mio modo, Nedda, risparmia quei quattrini e vatti a star colla tua vecchia.

– Chissà che non avesse a giovare! rispose tristamente la ragazza chinando gli occhi, e affrettò il passo.

Lo zio Giovanni rispose con un brontolìo. Poi le gridò dietro: – Ohé la *varannisa!*

– Che volete?

– Anderò io dallo speziale. Farò più presto di te, non dubitare. Intanto non lascerai sola la povera malata.

Alla ragazza vennero le lagrime agli occhi.

– Che Dio vi benedica! gli disse, e volle anche mettergli in mano i denari.

– I denari me li darai poi; le disse ruvidamente lo zio Giovanni, e si diede a camminare colle gambe dei suoi vent'anni.

La ragazza tornò indietro e disse alla mamma: – C'è andato lo zio Giovanni, – e lo disse con voce dolce insolitamente.

La moribonda udì il suono dei soldi che Nedda posava sul deschetto, e la interrogò cogli occhi. – Mi ha detto che glieli darò poi; rispose la figlia.

neighbor women who muttered some prayers or other. The sacristan's high-pitched handbell rang across the fields, and the carters who heard it stopped their mules in the middle of the road and doffed their caps. When Nedda heard it on the stony path leading from the highroad to her cottage, she pulled up the sick woman's tattered blanket so no one could see there were no sheets, and she folded her prettiest white apron over the wobbly little table she had shored up with bricks. Then, while the priest was performing his rite, she went and knelt down outside the door, mechanically stammering out prayers and, as if in a daze, staring at the stone in front of the threshold on which her old mother used to warm herself in the March sun, and listening with an inattentive ear to the familiar sounds of her surroundings and the comings and goings of all those people occupied with their own business without worries in their heads. The priest left, while the sacristan lingered in vain at the door to receive the customary alms for the poor.

"Uncle" Giovanni saw Nedda running down the road to Punta late in the evening.

"Hey! Where are you going at this hour?"

"I'm going for a medicine that the doctor prescribed."

"Uncle" Giovanni was thrifty and grumpy.

"More medicine," he muttered, "after prescribing the medicine of the consecrated oil! They're in cahoots with the druggists to bleed poor folk dry! Take my advice, Nedda, save that money and go stay at your mother's side."

"But it might possibly do her some good!" the girl replied roughly, lowering her eyes, and she ran faster.

"Uncle" Giovanni replied with a grumble. Then he called after her: "Hey, girl from Viagrande!"

"What do you want?"

"*I'll* go to the druggist's. I'll get there before you would, take my word for it. Meanwhile you won't be leaving the poor sick woman alone."

Tears came to the girl's eyes.

"God bless you!" she said, and she tried to put the money in his hand.

"You'll give me the money later," said "Uncle" Giovanni harshly, and he started to walk as if he were still twenty.

The girl returned home and told her mother: "'Uncle' Giovanni has gone." She said this with a sweet voice unusual for her.

The dying woman heard the clink of the coins that Nedda was placing on the table, and questioned her with her eyes. "He said I should give it to him later," her daughter replied.

– Che Dio gli paghi la carità! mormorò l'inferma, così non resterai senza un quattrino.

– Oh, mamma!

– Quanto gli dobbiamo allo zio Giovanni?

– Dieci lire. Ma non abbiate paura, mamma! Io lavorerò!

La vecchia la guardò a lungo coll'occhio semispento, e poscia l'abbracciò senza aprir bocca. Il giorno dopo vennero i becchini, il sagrestano e le comari. Quando Nedda ebbe acconciato la morta nella bara, coi suoi migliori abiti, le mise fra le mani un garofano che avea fiorito dentro una pentola fessa, e la più bella treccia dei suoi capelli; diede ai becchini quei pochi soldi che le rimanevano perché facessero a modo, e non scuotessero tanto la morta per la viottola sassosa del cimitero; poi rassettò il lettuccio e la casa, mise in alto, sullo scaffale, l'ultimo bicchiere di medicina, e andò a sedersi sulla soglia dell'uscio guardando il cielo.

Un pettirosso, il freddoloso uccelletto del novembre, si mise a cantare fra le frasche e i rovi che coronavano il muricciolo di faccia all'uscio, e alcune volte, saltellando fra le spine e gli sterpi, la guardava con certi occhietti maliziosi come se volesse dirle qualche cosa: Nedda pensò che la sua mamma, il giorno innanzi, l'avea udito cantare. Nell'orto accanto c'erano delle ulive per terra, e le gazze venivano a beccarle, ella le avea scacciate a sassate, perché la moribonda non ne udisse il funebre gracidare, adesso le guardò impassibile, e non si mosse, e quando sulla strada vicina passarono il venditore di lupini, o il vinaio, o i carrettieri, che discorrevano ad alta voce per vincere il rumore dei loro carri e delle sonagliere dei loro muli, ella diceva: costui è il tale, quegli è il tal altro. Allorché suonò l'avemaria, e s'accese la prima stella della sera, si rammentò che non doveva andar più per le medicine alla Punta, ed a misura che i rumori andarono perdendosi nella via, e le tenebre a calare nell'orto, pensò che non avea più bisogno di accendere il lume.

Lo zio Giovanni la trovò ritta sull'uscio.

Ella si era alzata udendo dei passi nella viottola, perché non aspettava più nessuno.

– Che fai costà? le domandò lo zio Giovanni. Ella si strinse nelle spalle, e non rispose.

Il vecchio si assise accanto a lei, sulla soglia, e non aggiunse altro.

– Zio Giovanni, disse la ragazza dopo un lungo silenzio, adesso che non ho più nessuno, e che posso andar lontano a cercar lavoro, partirò

"May God repay his kindness!" the sick woman murmured. "This way you won't be left penniless."

"Oh, Mother!"

"How much do we owe 'Uncle' Giovanni?"

"Ten *lire*. But don't be afraid, Mother! I'll work for it!"

The old woman gave her a long look with her dying eyes, and then hugged her without saying a word. The next day the undertakers arrived, as did the sacristan and the neighbor women. When Nedda had laid out the dead woman in the coffin with her best clothes, she placed in her hands a carnation that had bloomed in a cracked cooking pot, and the most beautiful tress of her own hair; she gave the undertakers the little money she had left so they would do a proper job and not shake the dead woman too much on the stony path to the cemetery; then she made up the cot again, straightened up the house, placed the last glass of medicine up on a high shelf, and sat down on the threshold, looking at the sky.

A robin, that songbird of November so sensitive to the cold, began singing in the bushes and brambles that crowned the low wall opposite the door and, at times, as it hopped among the thorns and the dry branches, it would look at her with mischievous eyes, as if it wanted to tell her something: it occurred to Nedda that, just one day before, her mother had heard it sing. In the adjoining vegetable garden there were olives on the ground, and the magpies were coming to peck at them; she had been chasing them away with stones so the dying woman wouldn't hear their gloomy croaking, but now she looked at them impassively, and didn't budge. And when there passed down the nearby road the lupin vendor, or the wineseller, or the carters, who were talking loud to drown out the noise of their carts and the harness bells of their mules, she'd say: this is so-and-so, that's so-and-so. When the Angelus sounded, and the first star of evening appeared, she recalled that it was no longer necessary to go to Punta for medicine, and, as the sounds of the road gradually diminished and darkness fell on the garden, it occurred to her that she had no further need to light the lamp.

"Uncle" Giovanni found her standing in the doorway.

She had stood up when she heard footsteps on the path, because she was no longer expecting anyone.

"What are you doing there?" "Uncle" Giovanni asked her. She shrugged her shoulders and made no answer.

The old man sat down next to her, on the threshold, and added nothing further.

"'Uncle' Giovanni," the girl said after a long silence, "now that I have no one left in the world, and I can travel far looking for work, I'll

per la Roccella ove dura ancora la ricolta delle ulive, e al ritorno vi restituirò i denari che ci avete imprestati.

– Io non son venuto a domandarteli, i tuoi denari! le rispose burbero lo zio Giovanni.

Ella non disse altro, ed entrambi rimasero zitti ad ascoltare l'assiolo che cantava.

Nedda pensò ch'era forse quello stesso che l'avea accompagnata dal *Pino*, a sentì gonfiarlesi il cuore.

– E del lavoro ne hai? domandò finalmente lo zio Giovanni.

– No, ma qualche anima caritatevole troverò che me ne darà.

– Ho sentito dire che ad Aci Catena pagano le donne abili per incartare le arancie in ragione di una lira al giorno, senza minestra, e ho subito pensato a te; tu hai già fatto quel mestiere lo scorso marzo, e devi esser pratica. Vuoi andare?

– Magari!

– Bisognerebbe trovarsi domani all'alba al giardino del Merlo, sull'angolo della scorciatoia che conduce a S. Anna.

– Posso anche partire stanotte. La mia povera mamma non ha voluto costarmi molti giorni di riposo!

– Sai dove andare?

– Sì. Poi mi informerò.

– Domanderai all'oste che sta sulla strada maestra di Valverde, al di là del castagneto ch'è sulla sinistra della via. Cercherai di Massaro Vinirannu, e dirai che ti mando io.

– Ci andrò, disse la povera ragazza tutta giuliva.

– Ho pensato che non avresti avuto del pane per la settimana, disse lo zio Giovanni, cavando un grosso pan nero dalla profonda tasca del suo vestito, e posandolo sul deschetto.

La Nedda si fece rossa, come se facesse lei quella buona azione. Poi dopo qualche istante gli disse:

– Se il signor curato dicesse domani la messa per la mamma io gli farei due giornate di lavoro alla ricolta delle fave.

– La messa l'ho fatta dire; rispose lo zio Giovanni.

– Oh! la povera morta pregherà anche per voi! mormorò la ragazza coi grossi lagrimoni agli occhi.

Infine, quando lo zio Giovanni se ne andò, e udì perdersi in lontananza il rumore dei suoi passi pesanti, chiuse l'uscio, e accese la candela. Allora le parve di trovarsi sola al mondo, ed ebbe paura di dormire in quel povero lettuccio ove soleva coricarsi accanto alla sua mamma.

go to Roccella, where they're still harvesting the olives, and when I'm back I'll return the money you've lent us."

"I didn't come to ask for your money!" "Uncle" Giovanni replied gruffly.

She said no more, and the two of them sat there in silence listening to the call of the scops owl.

Nedda thought it might be the same one that had accompanied her from the Pine farm, and she felt her heart swelling.

"And do you have work?" "Uncle" Giovanni finally asked.

"No, but I'll find some charitable soul who'll give me some."

"I've heard tell that at Aci Catena they're paying women who know how to wrap oranges a *lira* a day, without food, and I immediately thought about you; you already did that kind of work last March, and you must be experienced at it. Do you want to go?"

"If I only could!"

"You'd have to show up at dawn tomorrow at Blackbird orchard, at the corner of the shortcut that leads to Sant' Anna."

"I can even set out tonight. My poor mother didn't want to cost me many days of idleness!"

"You know where to go?"

"Yes. Besides, I'll ask the way."

"Ask the proprietor of the inn on the main road to Valverde, beyond the chestnut grove to the left of the road. Look for farmer Vinirannu, and tell him *I* sent you."

"I'll go," said the poor girl, quite jolly.

"It occurred to me that you might not have enough bread for the week," said "Uncle" Giovanni, producing a large dark loaf from the deep pocket of his jacket and placing it on the table.

Nedda blushed as if she were the one doing that good deed. Then, a few moments later, she said:

"If the priest were to say a Mass for Mother tomorrow, I'd work for him for two days at bean harvest."

"I've already paid for the Mass," replied "Uncle" Giovanni.

"Oh, my poor dead mother will pray for you too!" the girl murmured with big tears in her eyes.

Finally, when "Uncle" Giovanni departed and she heard the sound of his heavy steps dying away in the distance, she shut the door and lit the candle. Then she really felt all alone in the world, and she was afraid to sleep in that poor cot on which she used to lie down beside her mother.

❖   ❖   ❖

E le ragazze del villaggio sparlarono di lei perché andò a lavorare subito il giorno dopo la morte della sua vecchia, e perché non aveva messo il bruno; e il signor curato la sgridò forte quando la domenica successiva la vide sull'uscio del casolare che si cuciva il grembiule che avea fatto tingere in nero, unico e povero segno di lutto, e prese argomento da ciò per predicare in chiesa contro il mal uso di non osservare le feste e le domeniche. La povera fanciulla, per farsi perdonare il suo grosso peccato, andò a lavorare due giorni nel campo del curato, perché dicesse la messa per la sua morta il primo lunedì del mese e la domenica. Quando le fanciulle, vestite dei loro begli abiti da festa, si tiravano in là sul banco, o ridevano di lei, e i giovanotti, all'uscire di chiesa le dicevano facezie grossolane, ella si stringeva nella sua mantellina tutta lacera, e affrettava il passo, chinando gli occhi, senza che un pensiero amaro venisse a turbare la serenità della sua preghiera, e alle volte diceva a se stessa, a mo' di rimprovero che avesse meritato: Son così povera! – oppure, guardando le sue due buone braccia: – Benedetto il Signore che me le ha date! e tirava via sorridendo.

Una sera – aveva spento da poco il lume – udì nella viottola una nota voce che cantava a squarciagola, e con la melanconica cadenza orientale delle canzoni contadinesche: «*Picca cci voli ca la vaju' a viju. – A la mi' amanti di l'arma mia*».

– È Janu! disse sottovoce, mentre il cuore le balzava nel petto come un uccello spaventato, e cacciò la testa fra le coltri.

E l'indomani, quando aprì la finestra, vide Janu col suo bel vestito nuovo di fustagno, nelle cui tasche cercava di far entrare le sue grosse mani nere e incallite al lavoro, con un bel fazzoletto di seta nuova fiammante che faceva capolino con civetteria dalla scarsella del farsetto, e che si godeva il bel sole d'aprile appoggiato al muricciolo dell'orto.

– Oh, Janu! diss'ella, come se non ne sapesse proprio nulla.

– *Salutamu!* esclamò il giovane col suo più grosso sorriso.

– O che fai qui?

– Torno dalla Piana.

La fanciulla sorrise, e guardò le lodole che saltellavano ancora sul verde per l'ora mattutina. – Sei tornato colle lodole.

*   *   *

And the village girls maligned her because she went off to work the very day after her mother died, and because she hadn't put on mourning; and the priest gave her a good dressing-down when, on the following Sunday, he saw her at her cottage doorway sewing her overalls, which she had had dyed black, the single, poor symbol of her mourning; and he used this as the subject of a sermon inveighing against the evil practice of desecrating Sundays and holy days. To have her great sin pardoned, the poor girl went to work in the priest's field for two days, so he would say a Mass for her dead mother on the first Monday of every month and on Sundays. When the girls, dressed in their holiday best, moved away from her on the pew, or laughed at her, and the young men greeted her with coarse jokes on leaving church, she would draw her tattered shoulder cape tightly around her and walk faster, her eyes cast down, but no bitter thought disturbed the serenity of her prayers; and at times she said to herself, as if it were a reproach she had deserved: "I'm so poor!" Or else, looking at her two strong arms, she'd say: "Bless the Lord, who gave me them," and she'd walk away with a smile.

One evening, not long after she had extinguished the lamp, she heard on the path a familiar voice singing very loud, with that melancholy Arabic intonation of Sicilian rural songs: "Before very long I'll pay a visit to the sweetheart of my soul."[2]

"It's Janu!" she said quietly, while her heart bounded in her breast like a frightened bird, and she buried her head in the bedclothes.

The next day, when she opened her window she saw Janu with his beautiful new fustian jacket, into the pockets of which he was trying to thrust his large hands, blackened and callused with toil. A beautiful handkerchief of brand-new silk was peeping coquettishly out of his vest pocket. Leaning against the low wall of the vegetable garden, he was enjoying the fine April sunshine.

"Oh, Janu!" she said, as if she had no idea what was going on.

"Greetings!" the young man exclaimed with his widest smile.

"What are you doing here?"

"I've just come back from the Plain."

The girl smiled and looked at the larks that still hopped through the grass at that morning hour. "You've come back with the larks."

---

2. A standard-Italian equivalent to the Sicilian-dialect text would be: "Poco ci vuole che la vado a vedere / Alla mia amante dell'anima mia."

– Le lodole vanno dove trovano il miglio, ed io dove c'è del pane.

– O come?

– Il padrone m'ha licenziato.

– O perché?

– Perché avevo preso le febbri laggiù, e non potevo più lavorare che tre giorni per settimana.

– Si vede, povero Janu!

– Maledetta Piana! imprecò Janu stendendo il braccio verso la pianura.

– Sai, la mamma! . . . disse Nedda.

– Me l'ha detto lo zio Giovanni.

Ella non disse altro e guardò l'orticello al di là del muricciolo. I sassi umidicci fumavano; le goccie di rugiada luccicavano su di ogni filo d'erba; i mandorli fioriti sussurravano lieve lieve e lasciavano cadere sul tettuccio del casolare i loro fiori bianchi e rosei che imbalsamavano l'aria; una passera petulante e sospettosa nel tempo istesso schiamazzava sulla gronda, e minacciava a suo modo Janu, che avea tutta l'aria, col suo viso sospetto, di insidiare al suo nido, di cui spuntavano fra le tegole alcuni fili di paglia indiscreti. La campana della chiesuola chiamava a messa.

– Come fa piacere a sentire la *nostra* campana! esclamò Janu.

– Io ho riconosciuto la tua voce stanotte, disse Nedda facendosi rossa e zappando con un coccio la terra della pentola che conteneva i suoi fiori.

Egli si volse in là, ed accese la pipa, come deve fare un uomo.

– Addio, vado a messa! disse bruscamente la Nedda, tirandosi indietro dopo un lungo silenzio.

– Prendi, ti ho portato codesto dalla città; le disse il giovane sciorinando il suo bel fazzoletto di seta.

– Oh! com'è bello! ma questo non fa per me!

– O perché? se non ti costa nulla! rispose il giovanotto con logica contadinesca.

Ella si fece rossa, come se la grossa spesa le avesse dato idea dei caldi sentimenti del giovane, gli lanciò, sorridente, un'occhiata fra carezzevole e selvaggia, e scappò in casa, e allorché udì i grossi scarponi di lui sui sassi della viottola, fece capolino per vederlo che se ne andava.

Alla messa le ragazze del villaggio poterono vedere il bel fazzoletto di Nedda, dove c'erano stampate delle rose *che si sarebbero mangiate,* e su cui il sole, che scintillava dalle invetriate della

"The larks go wherever they find millet, and I go wherever there's bread."

"How's that?"

"My boss let me go."

"Why?"

"Because I'd caught a fever down there, and I could work only three days a week."

"I can see it, poor Janu!"

"Damn the Plain!" Janu cursed, stretching out an arm toward the lowlands.

"You know, my mother . . . ," Nedda began.

"'Uncle' Giovanni told me."

She said no more, but merely gazed at the garden beyond the wall. The damp rocks were steaming; the dewdrops were glistening on every blade of grass; the blossoming almond trees were whispering softly, dropping onto the cottage roof their white and pink flowers that scented the air; a hen sparrow, petulant and mistrustful at the same time, was squawking on the eaves and, in her own fashion, was threatening Janu, who, with his suspect face, looked exactly as if he had evil designs on her nest, of which some telltale wisps of straw protruded from the tiles. The bell of the little church was calling to Mass.

"What a pleasure it is to hear *our* bell!" exclaimed Janu.

"I recognized your voice last night," said Nedda, blushing and digging with a potsherd in the soil of the cooking pot that contained her flowers.

He turned away and lit his pipe, as a man should do.

"Good-bye, I'm going to Mass!" Nedda announced brusquely, moving away after a long silence.

"Here, I brought you this from town," said the young man, spreading out his beautiful silk handkerchief.

"Oh, how beautiful! But it's much too good for me!"

"Why, if it doesn't cost you anything?" the young man replied with rural logic.

She blushed, as if that great expense had informed her of the young man's tender feelings. Smiling, she darted a glance at him that was half-loving and half-savage, and she ran into the house. When she heard his heavy shoes on the stones of the path, she peeked out to watch him depart.

At Mass the village girls were able to see Nedda's beautiful handkerchief, on which were printed roses "pretty enough to eat," and onto which the sun, reflected from the stained-glass church windows,

chiesuola, mandava i suoi raggi più allegri. E quand'ella passò dinanzi a Janu, che stava presso il primo cipresso del sacrato, colle spalle al muro e fumando nella sua pipa tutta intagliata, ella sentì gran caldo al viso, e il cuore che le faceva un gran battere in petto, e sgusciò via alla lesta. Il giovane le tenne dietro zufolando, e la guardava a camminare svelta e senza voltarsi indietro, colla sua veste nuova di fustagno che faceva delle belle pieghe pesanti, le sue brave scarpette, e la sua mantellina fiammante – ché la povera formica, or che la mamma stando in paradiso non l'era più a carico, era riuscita a farsi un po' di corredo col suo lavoro. – Fra tutte le miserie del povero c'è anche quella del sollievo che arrecano quelle perdite più dolorose pel cuore!

Nedda sentiva dietro di sé, con gran piacere o gran sgomento (non sapeva davvero che cosa fosse delle due) il passo pesante del giovanotto, e guardava sulla polvere biancastra dello stradale tutto diritto e inondato di sole un'altra ombra che qualche volta si distaccava dalla sua. Tutt'a un tratto, quando fu in vista della sua casuccia, senza alcun motivo, si diede a correre come una cerbiatta innamorata. Janu la raggiunse, ella si appoggiò all'uscio, tutta rossa e sorridente, e gli allungò un pugno sul dorso. – To'!

Egli ripicchiò con galanteria un po' manesca.

– O quanto l'hai pagato il tuo fazzoletto? domandò Nedda togliendoselo dal capo per sciorinarlo al sole e contemplarlo tutta festosa.

– Cinque lire; rispose Janu un po' pettoruto.

Ella sorrise senza guardarlo; ripiegò accuratamente il fazzoletto, cercando di farlo nelle medesime pieghe, e si mise a canticchiare una canzonetta che non soleva tornarle in bocca da lungo tempo.

La pentola rotta, posta sul davanzale, era ricca di garofani in boccio.

– Che peccato, disse Nedda, che non ce ne siano di fioriti, e spiccò il più grosso bocciolo e glielo diede.

– Che vuoi che ne faccia se non è sbocciato? diss'egli senza comprenderla, e lo buttò via. Ella si volse in là.

– E adesso dove andrai a lavorare? gli domandò dopo qualche secondo. Egli alzò le spalle.

– Dove andrai tu domani!

– A Bongiardo.

– Del lavoro ne troverò; ma bisognerebbe che non tornassero le febbri.

– Bisognerebbe non star fuori la notte a cantare dietro gli usci! gli diss'ella tutta rossa, dondolandosi sullo stipite dell'uscio con certa aria civettuola.

projected its most cheerful rays. And when she walked by Janu, who was standing near the first cypress in the churchyard, his back to the wall, smoking his richly carved pipe, she felt her face flushing hotly and her heart beating wildly in her breast, and she slipped away quickly. The young man kept after her, whistling, and watched her walking briskly, never looking back, with her new fustian dress that threw fine, heavy folds, her charming slippers, and her brand-new shoulder cape—because the poor hardworking ant, now that her mother was in Heaven and no longer a burden to her, had managed to amass a little wardrobe from her wages. Among all the wretched aspects of the life of the poor, one must also include that feeling of relief which comes even after suffering the losses that are the most painful to the heart!

With great pleasure or great alarm (she really didn't know which) Nedda heard the young man's heavy steps behind her; on the whitish dust of the perfectly straight, sun-drenched highroad she watched another shadow that sometimes detached itself from hers. All at once, when she was within sight of her cottage, for no reason she began to run like a love-struck doe. Janu caught up with her; she leaned against her door, all red and smiling, and gave him a punch on the back: "Take that!"

He hit her back with somewhat rough gallantry.

"How much did you pay for your handkerchief?" asked Nedda, taking it off her head, spreading it out in the sun, and gazing at it with great glee.

"Five *lire*," replied Janu, somewhat conceitedly.

She smiled, not looking at him; she carefully refolded the handkerchief, trying to retain the same folds, and began to hum a song that she hadn't sung for a long time.

The broken cooking pot on the windowsill was full of budding carnations.

"What a shame," Nedda said, "that there aren't any fully opened," and she picked the largest bud and gave it to him.

"What am I supposed to do with a flower that hasn't opened?" he said, failing to understand her, and he threw it away. She turned to one side.

"And where will you go to work now?" she asked him a few seconds later. He shrugged his shoulders.

"Where will *you* go tomorrow?" he asked.

"To Bongiardo."

"I'll find work, as long as the fever doesn't come back."

"You shouldn't stay out at night serenading at people's doors," she said, red in the face, swinging on the door jamb coquettishly.

– Non lo farò più se tu non vuoi.

Ella gli diede un buffetto e scappò dentro.

– Ohé! Janu! chiamò dalla strada la voce dello zio Giovanni.

– Vengo! gridò Janu; e alla Nedda: Verrò anch'io a Bongiardo, se mi vogliono.

– Ragazzo mio, gli disse lo zio Giovanni quando fu sulla strada, la Nedda non ha più nessuno, e tu sei un bravo giovinotto; ma insieme non ci state proprio bene. Hai inteso?

– Ho inteso, zio Giovanni: ma se Dio vuole, dopo la messe, quando avrò da banda quel po' di quattrini che ci vogliono, insieme ci staremo bene.

Nedda, che avea udito da dietro il muricciolo, si fece rossa, sebbene nessuno la vedesse.

L'indomani, prima di giorno, quand'ella si affacciò all'uscio per partire, trovò Janu, col suo fagotto infilato al bastone. – O dove vai? gli domandò. – Vengo anch'io a Bongiardo a cercar del lavoro.

I passerotti, che si erano svegliati alle voci mattiniere, cominciarono a pigolare dentro il nido. Janu infilò al suo bastone anche il fagotto di Nedda, e s'avviarono alacremente, mentre il cielo si tingeva sull'orizzonte, delle prime fiamme del giorno, e il venticello era frizzante.

A Bongiardo c'era proprio del lavoro per chi ne voleva. Il prezzo del vino era salito, e un ricco proprietario faceva dissodare un gran tratto di chiuse da mettere a vigneti. Le chiuse rendevano 1200 lire all'anno in lupini ed ulivi, messe a vigneto avrebbero dato, fra cinque anni, 12 o 13 mila lire, impiegandovene soli 10 o 12 mila; il taglio degli ulivi avrebbe coperto metà della spesa. Era un'eccellente speculazione, come si vede, e il proprietario pagava, di buon grado, una gran giornata ai contadini che lavoravano al dissodamento, 30 soldi agli uomini, 20 alle donne, senza minestra; è vero che il lavoro era un po' faticoso, e che ci si rimettevano anche quei pochi cenci che formavano il vestito dei giorni di lavoro; ma Nedda non era abituata a guadagnar 20 soldi tutti i giorni.

Il soprastante si accorse che Janu, riempiendo i corbelli di sassi, lasciava sempre il più leggiero per Nedda, e minacciò di cacciarlo via. Il povero diavolo, tanto per non perdere il pane, dovette accontentarsi di discendere dai 30 ai 20 soldi.

Il male era che quei poderi quasi incolti mancavano di fattoria, e la notte uomini e donne dovevano dormire alla rinfusa nell'unico

"I won't do it anymore if you don't want me to."

She gave him a cuff and dashed inside.

"Hey, Janu!" "Uncle" Giovanni's voice called from the road.

"Coming!" Janu shouted, adding, to Nedda: "I'll come to Bongiardo, too, if they want me."

"My boy," said "Uncle" Giovanni when he reached the road, "Nedda has nobody anymore, and you're a good lad; but you're not really suited to each other. Get me?"

"I get you, 'Uncle' Giovanni; but, God willing, after the grain harvest, when I've laid aside the little bit of money that's necessary, we'll get along together very well."

Nedda, who had heard this from behind the wall, blushed, though no one could see her.

The next day, before daybreak, when she came to the door on her way out, she found Janu with his bundle tied to his staff. "Where are you going?" she asked him. "I'm coming along to Bongiardo to look for work."

The baby sparrows, which had awakened on hearing those early-morning voices, began to peep inside the nest. Janu tied Nedda's bundle to his staff as well, and they set out eagerly while the sky was taking on color at the horizon from the first rays of the sun, and the breeze was bitingly cold.

At Bongiardo there really was work for anyone who wanted it. The price of wine had risen, and a wealthy landowner was having a large area of enclosed parcels of land tilled to be planted with vines. The parcels produced 1,200 *lire*'s worth of lupins and olives annually, but if planted with vines, they'd yield 12 or 13 thousand *lire* in five years, with an investment of only 10 or 12 thousand; the timber from the felled olive trees would cover half of that expense. It was an excellent speculation, as can be seen, and the landowner was gladly paying a handsome daily wage to the farmhands working at the tilling, 30 *soldi* to the men and 20 to the women, without food. It's true that the work was a little heavy, and that the workers had to wear out even those few ragged garments that they wore on workdays, but Nedda wasn't used to earning 20 *soldi* every day.

The overseer noticed that when Janu filled the baskets with stones he always left the lighter one for Nedda, and he threatened to discharge him. The poor devil, so as not to lose all income, had to agree to a pay cut from 30 to 20 *soldi* a day.

The trouble was that those all but uncultivated properties had no big farmhouse, and at night the men and women had to sleep here

casolare senza porta, e sì che le notti erano piuttosto fredde. Janu avea sempre caldo e dava a Nedda la sua casacca di fustagno perché si coprisse bene. La domenica poi tutta la brigata si metteva in cammino per vie diverse.

Janu e Nedda avevano preso le scorciatoie, e andavano attraverso il castagneto chiacchierando, ridendo, cantando a riprese, e facendo risuonare nelle tasche i grossi soldoni. Il sole era caldo come in giugno; i prati lontani cominciavano ad ingiallire; le ombre degli alberi avevano qualche cosa di festevole, e l'erba che vi cresceva era ancora verde e rugiadosa.

Verso il mezzogiorno sedettero al rezzo per mangiare il loro pan nero e le loro cipolle bianche. Janu avea anche del vino, del buon vino di Mascali che regalava a Nedda senza risparmio, e la povera ragazza, che non c'era avvezza, si sentiva la lingua grossa, e la testa assai pesante. Di tratto in tratto si guardavano e ridevano senza saper perché.

– Se fossimo marito e moglie si potrebbe tutti i giorni mangiare il pane e bere il vino insieme; disse Janu con la bocca piena, e Nedda chinò gli occhi perché egli la guardava in un certo modo. Regnava il profondo silenzio del meriggio, le più piccole foglie erano immobili; le ombre erano rade; c'era per l'aria una calma, un tepore, un ronzìo di insetti che pesava voluttuosamente sulle palpebre. Ad un tratto una corrente d'aria fresca, che veniva dal mare, fece sussurrare le cime più alte de' castagni.

– L'annata sarà buona pel povero e pel ricco, disse Janu, e se Dio vuole alla messe un po' di quattrini metterò da banda . . . e se tu mi volessi bene! . . . – e le porse il fiasco.

– No, non voglio più bere; disse ella colle guance tutte rosse.

– O perché ti fai rossa? diss'egli ridendo.

– Non te lo voglio dire.

– Perché hai bevuto?

– No!

– Perché mi vuoi bene?

Ella gli diede un pugno sull'omero e si mise a ridere.

Da lontano si udì il raglio di un asino che sentiva l'erba fresca. – Sai perché ragliano gli asini? domandò Janu.

– Dillo tu che lo sai.

– Sì che lo so; ragliano perché sono innamorati, disse egli con un riso grossolano, e la guardò fisso. Ella chinò gli occhi come se ci vedesse delle fiamme, e le sembrò che tutto il vino che aveva bevuto le montasse alla testa, e tutto l'ardore di quel cielo di metallo le penetrasse nelle vene.

and there in the one and only hut, which had no door, while the nights were rather cold. Janu always felt warm and he gave Nedda his fustian cloak so she'd be well covered. Then on Sunday the whole company set out on different paths.

Janu and Nedda had taken shortcuts, and were walking through the chestnut grove, chattering, laughing, singing songs with refrains, and making the big coins clink in their pockets. The sun was as hot as in June; the distant meadows were beginning to grow yellow; the shade of the trees had a festive air, and the grass that grew there was still green and laden with dew.

Around noon they sat down in the shade to eat their dark bread and white onions. Janu had wine, too, good wine from Mascali which he offered to Nedda unsparingly; and the poor girl, who wasn't used to it, felt her tongue get thick and her head get very heavy. From time to time they looked at each other and laughed without knowing why.

"If we were husband and wife, we could eat bread and drink wine together every day," Janu said with his mouth full, and Nedda lowered her eyes because of the way he was looking at her. The deep silence of noon prevailed, and even the smallest leaves were still; the patches of shade were few and far between; in the air there was a calm, a warmth, a buzzing of insects that weighed voluptuously on one's eyelids. Suddenly a fresh breeze from the sea made the highest tops of the chestnut trees rustle.

"This will be a good growing year for rich and poor alike," said Janu, "and, God willing, at the grain harvest I'll lay aside a little money . . . and if you loved me! . . ." And he handed her the wine flask.

"No, I don't want to drink anymore," she said, her cheeks all red.

"Why are you turning red?" he asked with a laugh.

"I don't want to tell you."

"Because you've been drinking?"

"No!"

"Because you love me?"

She gave him a punch on the shoulder and started to laugh.

In the distance was heard the braying of a donkey that smelled the fresh grass. "Do you know why donkeys bray?" asked Janu.

"Since you know, tell me."

"Sure, I know: they bray because they're in love," he said with a coarse laugh, and he stared hard at her. She lowered her eyes as if she had looked into a fire, and she felt as if all the wine she had drunk were going to her head, and all the heat of that metallic sky were piercing into her veins.

– Andiamo via! esclamò corrucciata, scuotendo la testa pesante.

– Che hai?

– Non lo so, ma andiamo via!

– Mi vuoi bene?

Nedda chinò il capo.

– Vuoi essere mia moglie?

Ella lo guardò serenamente, e gli strinse forte la mano callosa nelle sue mani brune, ma si alzò sui ginocchi che le tremavano per andarsene. Egli la trattenne per le vesti, tutto stravolto, e balbettando parole sconnesse, come non sapendo quel che si facesse.

Allorché si udì nella fattoria vicina il gallo che cantava, Nedda balzò in piedi di soprassalto, e si guardò attorno spaurita.

– Andiamo via! andiamo via! disse tutta rossa e frettolosa.

Quando fu per svoltare l'angolo della sua casuccia si fermò un momento trepidante, quasi temesse di trovare la sua vecchierella sull'uscio deserto da sei mesi.

Venne la Pasqua, la gaia festa dei campi, coi suoi falò giganteschi, colle sue allegre processioni fra i prati verdeggianti e sotto gli alberi carichi di fiori, colla chiesuola parata a festa, gli usci delle casipole incoronati di festoni, e le ragazze colle belle vesti nuove d'estate. Nedda fu vista allontanarsi piangendo dal confessionale, e non comparve fra le fanciulle inginocchiate dinanzi al coro che aspettavano la comunione. Da quel giorno nessuna ragazza onesta le rivolse più la parola, e quando andava a messa non trovava posto al solito banco, e bisognava che stesse tutto il tempo ginocchioni – se la vedevano piangere pensavano a chissà che peccatacci, e le volgevano le spalle inorridite.

– E quelli che le davano da lavorare ne approfittavano per scemarle il prezzo della sua giornata.

Ella aspettava il suo fidanzato che era andato a mietere alla Piana per raggruzzolare i quattrini che ci volevano a metter su un po' di casa, e a pagare il signor curato.

Una sera, mentre filava, udì fermarsi all'imboccatura della viottola un carro da buoi, e si vide comparir dinanzi Janu pallido e contraffatto.

– Che hai? gli disse.

– Sono stato ammalato. Le febbri mi ripresero laggiù, in quella

"Let's get out of here!" she exclaimed angrily, shaking her heavy head.
"What's wrong with you?"

"I don't know, but let's leave!"

"Do you love me?"

Nedda nodded her head.

"Do you want to be my wife?"

She looked at him serenely, and squeezed his callused hand tightly
with her own swarthy hands, but she raised herself to her knees,
which were trembling, in order to leave. He held her back by her
clothes; he was violently agitated, and was stammering out discon-
nected words, as if he didn't know what he was doing.

When they heard the rooster crowing in the nearby farmhouse,
Nedda leaped to her feet with a start, and looked around in fright.

"Let's get out of here! Let's get out of here!" she said, red in the face
and in a hurry to go.

When she was about to turn the corner of her own cottage, she
halted anxiously for a moment, as if afraid of finding her old mother
in the doorway that had been deserted for six months.

Easter came, that cheerful holiday for rural folk, with its giant bonfires, its merry processions across the newly green meadows and beneath
the blossom-laden trees, with the little church decked out for the holiday, the cottage doors hung with festoons, and the girls in their beautiful
new summer dresses. Nedda was seen leaving the confessional in tears,
and she didn't take her place among the girls kneeling in front of the
altar awaiting Communion. From that day on, no decent girl spoke to
her anymore, and when she attended Mass she couldn't find a place on
her regular pew, but had to remain on her knees the whole time; if the
girls saw her cry, they imagined she had committed unspeakable sins,
and they turned their backs on her in horror. And the people who gave
her jobs took advantage of this to reduce her daily wage.

She was waiting for her fiancé, who had gone off to the grain harvest in the Plain in order to accumulate the money they'd need to set
up housekeeping and to pay the priest.

One evening, while she was spinning, she heard an oxcart stop at
the entrance to the path, and she saw Janu appear before her, pale and
looking terrible.

"What's wrong with you?" she asked.

"I've been sick. The fevers attacked me again down there in that

maledetta Piana; ho perso più di una settimana di lavoro, ed ho mangiato quei pochi soldi che avevo fatto.

Ella rientrò in fretta, scucì il pagliericcio, e volle dargli quel piccolo gruzzolo che aveva legato in fondo ad una calza.

– No, diss'egli. Domani andrò a Mascalucia per la rimondatura degli ulivi, e non avrò bisogno di nulla. Dopo la rimondatura ci sposeremo.

Egli aveva l'aria triste facendole questa promessa, e stava appoggiato allo stipite, col fazzoletto avvolto attorno al capo, e guardandola con certi occhi luccicanti.

– Ma tu hai la febbre! gli disse Nedda.

– Sì, ma spero che mi lascerà ora che son qui; ad ogni modo non mi coglie che ogni tre giorni.

Ella lo guardava senza parlare, e sentiva stringersi il cuore vedendolo così pallido e dimagrato.

– E potrai reggerti sui rami alti? gli domandò.

– Dio ci penserà! rispose Janu. Addio, non posso fare aspettare il carrettiere che mi ha dato un posto sul suo carro dalla Piana sin qui. A rivederci presto! e non si muoveva. Quando finalmente se ne andò, ella lo accompagnò sino alla strada maestra, e lo vide allontanarsi senza una lagrima, sebbene le sembrasse che stesse a vederlo partire per sempre; il cuore ebbe un'altra strizzatina, come una spugna non spremuta abbastanza, nulla più, ed egli la salutò per nome alla svolta della via.

Tre giorni dopo udì un gran cicaleccio per la strada. Si affacciò al muricciolo, e vide in mezzo ad un crocchio di contadini e di comari Janu disteso su di una scala a piuoli, pallido come un cencio lavato, e colla testa fasciata da un fazzoletto tutto sporco di sangue. Lungo la via dolorosa che dovette farsi prima di giungere al casolare di lui, egli, tenendola per mano, le narrò come, trovandosi così debole per le febbri, era caduto da un'alta cima, e s'era concio a quel modo. – Il cuore te lo diceva! mormorò egli con un triste sorriso. Ella l'ascoltava coi suoi grand'occhi spalancati, pallida come lui, e tenendolo per mano. L'indomani egli morì.

Allora Nedda, sentendo muoversi dentro di sé qualcosa che quel morto le lasciava come un triste ricordo, volle correre in chiesa a pregare per lui la Vergine Santa. Sul sacrato incontrò il prete che sapeva la sua vergogna, si nascose il viso nella sua mantellina e tornò indietro derelitta.

damned Plain. I lost more than a week's work, and I used up the little money that I had earned."

She went back into the house hastily, ripped up the straw mattress, and offered him the tiny pile of coins that she kept tied up in the foot of a stocking.

"No," he said. "Tomorrow I'll go to Mascalucia for the olive-tree pruning, and I won't need a thing. After the pruning we'll get married."

He looked sad as he made her that promise; he remained leaning against the door jamb, his bandanna wrapped around his head, looking at her with strangely gleaming eyes.

"But you've got a fever!" Nedda said.

"Yes, but I hope it will leave me, now that I'm here; in any case, it only attacks me every three days."

She was looking at him in silence, feeling her heart tighten to see him so pale and emaciated.

"But will you be able to keep your balance on the high boughs?" she asked.

"God will see to it!" Janu replied. "Good-bye, I can't keep the carter waiting. He gave me a seat on his cart from the Plain all the way here. I'll see you again soon!" But he didn't budge. When he finally left, she accompanied him as far as the highroad, and tearlessly watched him depart, though she felt as if she were seeing him go for the last time; her heart felt one more brief pressure, like a sponge not sufficiently wrung dry—no more than that—and he called out her name at the bend in the road.

Three days later she heard loud chattering on the road. She came out to the wall and saw Janu stretched out on a ladder in the midst of a group of farmhands and neighbor women. He was as pale as a washed-out rag, and his head was bound with a handkerchief that was soaked in blood. Along the way of sorrows they had to pass before reaching his cottage, he held her by the hand and told her how, weakened by his fever, he had fallen from a tall treetop and had been injured so badly. "Your heart predicted it!" he murmured with a sad smile. She listened to him with her big eyes wide open, while, just as pale as he was, she held him by the hand. The next day he died.

Then Nedda, feeling something stirring inside her that the dead man had left her as a sad souvenir, decided to run to the church to pray to the Blessed Virgin for him. In the churchyard she met the priest, who knew of her shame; she hid her face in her shoulder cape and went back home, abandoned.

Adesso, quando cercava del lavoro, le ridevano in faccia, non per schernire la ragazza colpevole, ma perché la povera madre non poteva più lavorare come prima. Dopo i primi rifiuti e le prime risate ella non osò cercare più oltre, e si chiuse nella sua casipola, come un uccelletto ferito che va a rannicchiarsi nel suo nido. Quei pochi soldi raccolti in fondo alla calza se ne andarono l'un dopo l'altro, e dietro ai soldi la bella veste nuova, e il bel fazzoletto di seta. Lo zio Giovanni la soccorreva per quel poco che poteva, con quella carità indulgente e riparatrice senza la quale la morale del curato è ingiusta e sterile, e le impedì così di morire di fame. Ella diede alla luce una bambina rachitica e stenta: quando le dissero che non era un maschio pianse come avea pianto la sera in cui avea chiuso l'uscio del casolare e s'era trovata senza la mamma, ma non volle che la buttassero alla Ruota.

– Povera bambina! che incominci a soffrire almeno il più tardi che sarà possibile! disse. Le comari la chiamavano sfacciata, perché non era stata ipocrita, e perché non era snaturata. Alla povera bimba mancava il latte, giacché alla madre scarseggiava il pane. Ella deperì rapidamente, e invano Nedda tentò spremere fra i labbruzzi affamati il sangue del suo seno. Una sera d'inverno, sul tramonto, mentre la neve fioccava sul tetto, e il vento scuoteva l'uscio mal chiuso, la povera bambina, tutta fredda, livida, colle manine contratte, fissò gli occhi vitrei su quelli ardenti della madre, diede un guizzo, e non si mosse più.

Nedda la scosse, se la strinse al seno con impeto selvaggio, tentò di scaldarla coll'alito e coi baci, e quando s'accorse ch'era proprio morta, la depose sul letto dove avea dormito sua madre, e le s'inginocchiò davanti, cogli occhi asciutti e spalancati fuor di misura.

– Oh! benedette voi che siete morte! esclamò. – Oh benedetta voi, Vergine Santa! che mi avete tolto la mia creatura per non farla soffrire come me!

Now when she sought work, people laughed in her face, not in mockery of the sinning girl, but because the poor mother could no longer work as hard as she used to. After the first rejections and the first bursts of laughter she no longer dared to keep looking, and she shut herself up in her cottage like a wounded bird huddling in its nest. Those few coins saved in the stocking foot departed one after the other, and, after the coins, her beautiful new dress and the lovely silk handkerchief. "Uncle" Giovanni aided her to the small extent that he could, with that indulgent, life-restoring charity in the absence of which a priest's morality is unjust and barren; and in that way he kept her from starving to death. She gave birth to a stunted and undernourished girl. When she was told it wasn't a boy, she cried the way she had cried on the evening when she had shut her cottage door and found herself motherless. But she wouldn't allow the girl to be left as a foundling in the convent.[3]

"Poor girl! At least let her not begin suffering until the last possible moment!" she said. Her neighbors called her shameless because she wasn't a hypocrite and because she wasn't an unnatural mother. The poor baby lacked milk, since its mother was short of bread. It wasted away rapidly, and it was in vain that Nedda tried to squeeze blood from her breasts into those starving little lips. One winter evening, at sunset, while the snow was falling on the roof and the wind was shaking the disjointed door, the poor baby, chilled, livid, her little hands clenched, stared with her glazed eyes into the burning eyes of her mother, gave one wriggle, and moved no more.

Nedda shook her, hugged her to her breast with savage violence, tried to warm her with her breath and with kisses. When she realized she was really dead, she placed her on the bed where her mother had slept, and knelt down in front of her, her eyes dry but open unnaturally wide.

"Oh, the two of you who are dead, how blessed you are!" she exclaimed. "Oh, how blessed you are, Holy Virgin, for taking away my baby so she wouldn't suffer the way I have!"

---

3. Literally, "to be thrown onto the wheel." This particular "wheel" is the turntable device at convent entrances on which objects can be brought in or taken out with no personal contact occurring.

FANTASTICHERIA

Una volta, mentre il treno passava vicino ad Aci-Trezza, voi, affacciandovi allo sportello del vagone, esclamaste: «Vorrei starci un mese laggiù!».

Noi vi ritornammo e vi passammo non un mese, ma quarantott'ore; i terrazzani che spalancavano gli occhi vedendo i vostri grossi bauli avranno creduto che ci sareste rimasta un par d'anni. La mattina del terzo giorno, stanca di vedere eternamente del verde e dell'azzurro, e di contare i carri che passavano per via, eravate alla stazione, e gingillandovi impaziente colla catenella della vostra boccettina da odore, allungavate il collo per scorgere un convoglio che non spuntava mai. In quelle quarantott'ore facemmo tutto ciò che si può fare ad Aci-Trezza: passeggiammo nella polvere della strada, e ci arrampicammo sugli scogli; col pretesto d'imparare a remare vi faceste sotto il guanto delle bollicine che rubavano i baci; passammo sul mare una notte romanticissima, gettando le reti tanto per far qualche cosa che a' barcaiuoli potesse parer meritevole di buscare dei reumatismi; e l'alba ci sorprese nell'alto del *fariglione,* un'alba modesta e pallida, che ho ancora dinanzi agli occhi, striata di larghi riflessi violetti, sul mare di un verde cupo; raccolta come una carezza su quel gruppetto di casuccie che dormivano quasi raggomitolate sulla riva, e in cima allo scoglio, sul cielo trasparente e profondo, si stampava netta la vostra figurina, colle linee sapienti che ci metteva la vostra sarta, e il profilo fine ed elegante che ci mettevate voi. – Avevate un vestitino grigio che sembrava fatto apposta per intonare coi colori dell'alba. – Un bel quadretto davvero! e si indovinava che lo sapevate anche voi dal modo col quale vi modellavate nel vostro scialletto, e sorridevate coi grandi occhioni sbarrati e stanchi a quello strano spettacolo, e a quell'altra stranezza di trovarvici anche voi presente. Che cosa avveniva nella vostra testolina mentre contemplavate il sole nascente? Gli domandavate forse in qual altro emisfero vi avrebbe ritrovata fra un mese?

REVERIE

Once, while our train was passing close to Aci Trezza, you looked out the window of the coach and exclaimed: "I'd like to spend a month down there!"

We returned there and spent not a month, but forty-eight hours; the villagers, whose eyes opened wide at the sight of your heavy trunks, probably thought you were going to stay for a couple of years. On the morning of the third day, weary of the eternal green and blue you were seeing, and of counting the carts going by in the street, you were at the station; impatiently toying with the little chain of your perfume bottle, you stretched out your neck to catch sight of a train that seemed never to appear. During those forty-eight hours we did all that can be done in Aci Trezza: we strolled through the dust in the road, and we climbed the sea cliffs; under the pretext of learning how to row, you made little blisters under your glove that demanded kisses to heal them. We spent a most romantic night on the sea, throwing out fish nets, if only to do something that would make the boatmen find some merit in catching rheumatism; and dawn overtook us atop the lone rock in the sea, a modest, pale dawn that I can still see before me, striped with broad violet reflections, over a dark-green sea. It gathered like a caress over that little cluster of cottages that slept as if curled up on the shore; and at the summit of the rock, against the deep, transparent sky, your delicate figure was clearly stamped, with the expert outlines that your dressmaker had created for it, and the subtle, elegant profile that you provided personally.—You were wearing a little gray dress that seemed made on purpose to harmonize with the colors of the dawn.—Really a lovely picture! And it was easy to guess that you knew it, too, from the way in which you draped yourself in your shawl and smiled with big, wide-open, weary eyes at that strange spectacle and at the additional oddity of finding yourself present there. What was going on in that sweet little head while you were contemplating the rising sun? Were you perhaps asking it in what

Diceste soltanto ingenuamente: «Non capisco come si possa viver qui tutta la vita».

Eppure, vedete, la cosa è più facile che non sembri: basta non possedere centomila lire di entrata, prima di tutto; e in compenso patire un po' di tutti gli stenti fra quegli scogli giganteschi, incastonati nell'azzurro, che vi facevano batter le mani per ammirazione. Così poco basta perché quei poveri diavoli che ci aspettavano sonnecchiando nella barca, trovino fra quelle loro casipole sgangherate e pittoresche, che viste da lontano vi sembravano avessero il mal di mare anch'esse, tutto ciò che vi affannate a cercare a Parigi, a Nizza ed a Napoli.

È una cosa singolare; ma forse non è male che sia così – per voi, e per tutti gli altri come voi. Quel mucchio di casipole è abitato da pescatori; «gente di mare», dicon essi, come altri direbbe «gente di toga», i quali hanno la pelle più dura del pane che mangiano, quando ne mangiano, giacché il mare non è sempre gentile, come allora che baciava i vostri guanti . . . Nelle sue giornate nere, in cui brontola e sbuffa, bisogna contentarsi di stare a guardarlo dalla riva, colle mani in mano, o sdraiati bocconi, il che è meglio per chi non ha desinato; in quei giorni c'è folla sull'uscio dell'osteria, ma suonano pochi soldoni sulla latta del banco, e i monelli che pullulano nel paese, come se la miseria fosse un buon ingrasso, strillano e si graffiano quasi abbiano il diavolo in corpo.

Di tanto in tanto il tifo, il colèra, la malannata, la burrasca, vengono a dare una buona spazzata in quel brulicame, il quale si crederebbe che non dovesse desiderar di meglio che esser spazzato, e scomparire; eppure ripullula sempre nello stesso luogo; non so dirvi come, né perché.

Vi siete mai trovata, dopo una pioggia di autunno, a sbaragliare un esercito di formiche tracciando sbadatamente il nome del vostro ultimo ballerino sulla sabbia del viale? Qualcuna di quelle povere bestioline sarà rimasta attaccata alla ghiera del vostro ombrellino, torcendosi di spasimo; ma tutte le altre, dopo cinque minuti di pànico e di viavai, saranno tornate ad aggrapparsi disperatamente al loro monticello bruno. Voi non ci tornereste davvero, e nemmen io; ma per poter comprendere siffatta caparbietà, che è per certi aspetti eroica, bisogna farci piccini anche noi, chiudere tutto l'orizzonte fra due zolle, e guardare col microscopio le

other hemisphere you would be located a month from then? But all you said, ingenuously, was: "I don't understand how people can live their whole lives here."

And yet, you see, it's easier than it looks: all that's necessary is not to possess a yearly income of a hundred thousand *lire,* first of all; and, to make up for that, to undergo a little of all the hardships encountered amid those gigantic cliffs, set like gems in the blue, that made you clap your hands in admiration. It takes just as little as that for those poor devils who were dozing in the boat, while waiting for you, to be able to find amid their ramshackle, picturesque huts (which, when you saw them from a distance, seemed to you to be seasick, too) everything that you ardently search for in Paris, Nice, and Naples.

It's odd, but maybe it's not a bad thing that life is like that—for you, and for everyone else like you. That heap of cottages is inhabited by fishermen; "sea folk," they call themselves, just as someone else might say "long-robed people."[1] Their hide is tougher than the bread they eat, when they have any to eat, because the sea isn't always as kind as when it was kissing your gloves. . . . On its black days, when it rumbles and sprays, they have to be content to stand on the shore looking at it, hand in hand, or stretched out on their stomachs, which is better for someone who hasn't dined. On such days there's a crowd at the inn door, but not many coins jingle on the tin of the bar, and the urchins who teem in the village, as if poverty were a good fattening-feed, yell and scratch one another as if they had the devil in them.

Every so often, typhus, cholera, crop failure, or a storm sweeps away a large number of that swarm, which you'd think would want nothing better than to be swept away and disappear; and yet, the population is always replenished in the same spot, I couldn't tell you how or why.

Have you ever, after an autumn rainfall, scattered an army of ants when you were inattentively writing the name of your most recent dancing partner on the sand of the garden path? Some of those poor tiny creatures were probably impaled on the ferrule of your umbrella, writhing in agony; but all the rest, after five minutes of panicky scurrying to and fro, were probably clinging desperately to their little brown hill again. I'm sure *you* wouldn't go back to it, and neither would I. But to be able to understand that kind of obstinacy, which is heroic in some ways, we must imagine ourselves just as diminutive as they, our entire horizon enclosed between two sods of turf; we must

---

1. Judges, lawyers, university professors, and the like. The ancient Romans called themselves *togati,* "people who wear the toga," that is, "Roman citizens."

piccole cause che fanno battere i piccoli cuori. Volete metterci un occhio anche voi, a cotesta lente, voi che guardate la vita dall'altro lato del cannocchiale? Lo spettacolo vi parrà strano, e perciò forse vi divertirà.

Noi siamo stati amicissimi, ve ne rammentate? e mi avete chiesto di dedicarvi qualche pagina. Perché? *à quoi bon?* come dite voi. Che cosa potrà valere quel che scrivo per chi vi conosce? e per chi non vi conosce che cosa siete voi? Tant'è, mi son rammentato del vostro capriccio un giorno che ho rivisto quella povera donna cui solevate far l'elemosina col pretesto di comperar le sue arancie messe in fila sul panchettino dinanzi all'uscio. Ora il panchettino non c'è più; hanno tagliato il nespolo del cortile, e la casa ha una finestra nuova. La donna sola non aveva mutato, stava un po' più in là a stender la mano ai carrettieri, accocolata sul mucchietto di sassi che barricano il vecchio *posto* della guardia nazionale; ed io girellando, col sigaro in bocca, ho pensato che anche lei, così povera com'è, vi avea vista passare, bianca e superba.

Non andate in collera se mi son rammentato di voi in tal modo a questo proposito. Oltre i lieti ricordi che mi avete lasciati, ne ho cento altri, vaghi, confusi, disparati, raccolti qua e là, non so più dove; forse alcuni son ricordi di sogni fatti ad occhi aperti; e nel guazzabuglio che facevano nella mia mente, mentre io passava per quella viuzza dove son passate tante cose liete e dolorose, la mantellina di quella donnicciola freddolosa, accocolata, poneva un non so che di triste e mi faceva pensare a voi, sazia di tutto, perfino dell'adulazione che getta ai vostri piedi il giornale di moda, citandovi spesso in capo alla cronaca elegante – sazia così da inventare il capriccio di vedere il vostro nome sulle pagine di un libro.

Quando scriverò il libro, forse non ci penserete più; intanto i ricordi che vi mando, così lontani da voi in ogni senso, da voi inebbriata di feste e di fiori, vi faranno l'effetto di una brezza deliziosa, in mezzo alle veglie ardenti del vostro eterno carnevale. Il giorno in cui ritornerete laggiù, se pur ci ritornerete, e siederemo accanto un'altra volta, a spinger sassi col piede, e fantasie col pensiero, parleremo forse di quelle altre ebbrezze che ha la vita altrove. Potete anche immaginare che il mio pensiero siasi raccolto in quel cantuccio ignorato del mondo, perché il vostro piede vi si è posato, – o per distogliere i miei occhi dal luccichìo che vi segue dappertutto, sia di gemme o di febbri – oppure perché vi ho cercata inutilmente per tutti i luoghi che la

use a microscope to observe the small causes that make small hearts beat. Do you, too, want to put your eyes to this lens, you who look at life from the other end of the telescope? You'll find the spectacle strange, and thus you may be amused by it.

We were very close friends, remember? And you asked me to dedicate one of my pieces to you. Why? *"A quoi bon?"* as you would say. What would anything I write mean to anyone who knows you? And for anyone who doesn't know you, what are you? At any rate, I recalled that whim of yours one day when I saw again that poor woman to whom you used to give alms under the pretext of buying her oranges, which were set out in a row on the little bench outside her door. Now the bench is no longer there; the medlar tree in the yard has been cut down, and the house has a new window. Only the woman hadn't changed; she stood a little more off to the side as she held out her hand to the carters, while crouching on the little heap of stones that blocks the entrance to the former post of the National Guard. I, gadding about with my cigar in my mouth, remembered that she, too, poor as she is, had seen you passing by, fair-complexioned and magnificent.

Don't get angry if I recalled you in that way and in that connection. In addition to the happy memories you left me with, I have a hundred others, vague, confused, ill-assorted, gathered here and there, I no longer recall where. Maybe some of them are recollections of daydreams I saw with my eyes open; amid the hodgepodge they created in my mind as I walked down that alley where so many happy and sad things have occurred, the shoulder cape of that little woman, suffering from the cold as she crouched there, added some element of sorrow and made me think of you: you, sated with everything, even with the flattery that the fashion magazine heaps upon you, often naming you first in its society pages—so sated that you came up with the whim of seeing your name in the pages of a book.

When I write that book, perhaps you will no longer recall that request; meanwhile, the recollections I now send you, which are so remote from you in every sense of the word, as you revel in parties and flowers, will appear to you like a delightful breeze amid the lamplit waking nights of your eternal Carnival. The day you go back down there, if you ever do, and we sit beside each other once again, shoving stones with our feet and daydreaming, perhaps we'll talk about those other intoxicating delights that life offers elsewhere. You can also imagine that my thoughts are clustering around that unknown corner of the world because you once set your feet there—or in order to tear my eyes away from the dazzle that follows you everywhere, whether

moda fa lieti. Vedete quindi che siete sempre al primo posto, qui come al teatro.

Vi ricordate anche di quel vecchietto che stava al timone della nostra barca? Voi gli dovete questo tributo di riconoscenza perché egli vi ha impedito dieci volte di bagnarvi le vostre belle calze azzurre. Ora è morto laggiù all'ospedale della città, il povero diavolo, in una gran corsìa tutta bianca, fra dei lenzuoli bianchi, masticando del pane bianco, servito dalle bianche mani delle suore di carità, le quali non avevano altro difetto che di non saper capire i meschini guai che il poveretto biascicava nel suo dialetto semibarbaro.

Ma se avesse potuto desiderare qualche cosa egli avrebbe voluto morire in quel cantuccio nero vicino al focolare, dove tanti anni era stata la sua cuccia «sotto le sue tegole», tanto che quando lo portarono via piangeva guaiolando, come fanno i vecchi. Egli era vissuto sempre fra quei quattro sassi, e di faccia a quel mare bello e traditore col quale dové lottare ogni giorno per trarre da esso tanto da campare la vita e non lasciargli le ossa; eppure in quei momenti in cui si godeva cheto cheto la sua «occhiata di sole» accoccolato sulla pedagna della barca, coi ginocchi fra le braccia, non avrebbe voltato la testa per vedervi, ed avreste cercato invano in quegli occhi attoniti il riflesso più superbo della vostra bellezza; come quando tante fronti altere s'inchinano a farvi ala nei saloni splendenti, e vi specchiate negli occhi invidiosi delle vostre migliori amiche.

La vita è ricca, come vedete, nella sua inesauribile varietà; e voi potete godervi senza scrupoli quella parte di ricchezza che à toccata a voi, a modo vostro. Quella ragazza, per esempio, che faceva capolino dietro i vasi di basilico, quando il fruscìo della vostra veste metteva in rivoluzione la viuzza, se vedeva un altro viso notissimo alla finestra di faccia, sorrideva come se fosse stata vestita di seta anch'essa. Chi sa quali povere gioie sognava su quel davanzale, dietro quel basilico odoroso, cogli occhi intenti in quell'altra casa coronata di tralci di vite? E il riso dei suoi occhi non sarebbe andato a finire in lagrime amare, là, nella città grande, lontana dai sassi che l'avevano vista nascere e la conoscevano, se il suo nonno non fosse morto all'ospedale, e suo padre non si fosse annegato, e tutta la sua famiglia non fosse stata dispersa da un colpo di vento che vi avea soffiato

caused by gems or by fever—or else because I've sought you in vain in every place that fashion makes joyous. So, you see: you're always in the best seat, in my mind and at the theater.

Do you also remember that little old man who sat at the tiller of our boat? You owe him that tribute of gratitude because ten times he kept you from getting your beautiful blue stockings wet. Now he's died down there in the big-city hospital, poor devil, in a large, all-white ward, between white sheets, where he chewed on white bread served by the white hands of the sisters of mercy, whose only shortcoming was their inability to understand the petty complaints that the poor fellow was mumbling in his half-barbarous dialect.

But if he had been able to request one thing, he would have wanted to die in the dark corner near his hearth, where his tumbledown bed had stood for so many years "beneath his own rooftiles"; so much so that, when they took him away, he wept and whimpered, the way old men do. He had always lived between those four stone walls, facing that beautiful, treacherous sea with which he had had to contend daily, to draw from it enough to live on, without losing his life in it. And yet, in those moments when he was quietly enjoying his "look-around in the sunshine," squatting on the rower's bench of his boat, his knees clasped in his arms, he wouldn't have turned his head to look at you, and you would have sought in vain in those astonished eyes for the most proud reflection of your beauty—the thing that occurs when all those haughty heads are bowed, making an aisle for you to pass through in the glittering salons, and you see your image in the envious eyes of your best women friends.

Life is rich, as you see, in its inexhaustible variety, and you need have no scruples in enjoying that part of its riches that have fallen to your lot, in your own way. For example, if that girl who peeped out from behind the pots of basil,[2] when the rustling of your dress created a revolution in her narrow lane, saw another very well-known face at the window opposite hers, she smiled as if she, too, had been dressed in silks. Who knows what humble joys were in her thoughts at that windowsill, behind that fragrant basil, while her eyes were fixed on that other house wreathed in vines? And the laughter in her eyes wouldn't have ended as bitter tears there in the big city, far from the stone house walls that had seen her born, and that knew her, had not her grandfather died in the hospital, and her father been drowned, and all her family scattered by a gust of wind that had blown upon

2. This, to a lover of literature, is reminiscent of the Boccaccio story (*Decameron*, IV, 5) that Keats used as the basis of his narrative poem "Isabella; or, The Pot of Basil." Boccaccio's story, in turn, was based on a Sicilian folk ballad.

sopra – un colpo di vento funesto, che avea trasportato uno dei suoi
fratelli fin nelle carceri di Pantelleria: «nei guai!» come dicono
laggiù.

Miglior sorte toccò a quelli che morirono; a Lissa l'uno, il più
grande, quello che vi sembrava un David di rame, ritto colla sua
fiocina in pugno, e illuminato bruscamente dalla fiamma dell'ellera.
Grande e grosso com'era, si faceva di brace anch'esso se gli fissavate
in volto i vostri occhi arditi; nondimeno è morto da buon marinaio,
sulla verga di trinchetto, fermo al sartiame, levando in alto il berretto,
e salutando un'ultima volta la bandiera col suo maschio e selvaggio
grido d'isolano. L'altro, quell'uomo che sull'isolotto non osava toccarvi
il piede per liberarlo dal lacciuolo teso ai conigli nel quale v'eravate
impigliata da stordita che siete, si perdé in una fosca notte d'inverno,
solo, fra i cavalloni scatenati, quando fra la barca e il lido, dove stavano
ad aspettarlo i suoi, andando di qua e di là come pazzi, c'erano ses-
santa miglia di tenebre e di tempesta. Voi non avreste potuto immaginare di qual disperato e tetro coraggio fosse capace per lottare
contro tal morte quell'uomo che lasciavasi intimidire dal capolavoro
del vostro calzolaio.

Meglio per loro che son morti, e non «mangiano il pane de re,»
come quel poveretto che è rimasto a Pantelleria, e quell'altro pane
che mangia la sorella, e non vanno attorno come la donna delle arancie, a viver della grazia di Dio; una grazia assai magra ad Aci-Trezza.
Quelli almeno non hanno più bisogno di nulla! Lo disse anche il
ragazzo dell'ostessa, l'ultima volta che andò all'ospedale per chieder
del vecchio e portargli di nascosto di quelle chiocciole stufate che son
così buone a succiare per chi non ha più denti, e trovò il letto vuoto,
colle coperte belle e distese, e sgattaiolando nella corte andò a pian-
tarsi dinanzi a una porta tutta brandelli di cartaccie, sbirciando dal
buco della chiave una gran sala vuota, sonora e fredda anche di estate,
e l'estremità di una lunga tavola di marmo, su cui era buttato un
lenzuolo, greve e rigido. E dicendo che quelli là almeno non avevano
più bisogno di nulla, si mise a succiare ad una ad una le chiocciole che
non servivano più, per passare il tempo. Voi, stringendovi al petto il
manicotto di volpe azzurra, vi rammenterete con piacere che gli avete
dato cento lire al povero vecchio.

them—a direful gust of wind that had even brought one of her brothers to the prison on Pantelleria: "into trouble," as people down there say.

Those of her brothers who died had a better fate; one at Lissa,[3] the eldest, the one who resembled a bronze David, standing tall with his harpoon in his fist and brusquely illuminated by the ivy-wood fire.[4] Big and tall as he was, he, too, turned as red as embers whenever you stared at his face with your bold eyes. All the same, he died like a good sailor, on the foremast, clinging to the rigging, raising his cap aloft and once more saluting the flag with his wild, masculine islander's cry. The other one, the man who, on the little island, didn't dare touch your foot to free it from the rabbit snare in which you had become entangled, careless woman that you are, was lost on a gloomy winter's night, alone, amid the unleashed fury of the breakers, when sixty miles of storm and darkness separated his boat from the shore, where his family was awaiting him, scurrying to and fro like lunatics. You couldn't have imagined with what desperate, cheerless courage that man was capable of struggling against such a death, even though he had let himself be intimidated by your shoemaker's masterpiece.

Better off, the brothers who are dead and aren't "eating the king's bread" like that poor fellow on Pantelleria, or that other bread which their sister is eating, and who aren't roaming about like that orange vendor, living off charity; charity is very hard to come by in Aci Trezza. At least the dead have no more need of anything! The young son of the inn proprietress said the same thing the last time he went to the hospital to ask about the old man, and to sneak in for him some of those stewed snails that are so good to suck on for someone who's lost all his teeth, and he found the bed empty, the blankets all spread out neatly on it. Slinking away into the courtyard, he took up his stand in front of a door covered with torn shreds of paper; squinting through the keyhole, he saw a big empty room, echoing and cold even in summer, and one end of a long marble table on which had been thrown something stiff and heavy wrapped in a sheet. After saying that the dead, at least, have no more need of anything, in order to pass the time he started sucking out the snails one by one, since they had lost their original purpose. You, clutching your blue-fox muff to your bosom, will recall with pleasure that you gave the poor old man a hundred *lire*.

---

3. An island off the coast of Croatia, now called Vis. It was the scene of a naval battle in 1866, in which the Italians were defeated by the Austrians, during the Austro-Prussian War. 4. The unusual word *ellera* was rendered as "lanterns" in a previous translation.

Ora rimangono quei monellucci che vi scortavano come sciacalli e assediavano le arancie; rimangono a ronzare attorno alla mendica, a brancicarle le vesti come se ci avesse sotto del pane, a raccattar torsi di cavolo, buccie d'arancie e mozziconi di sigari, tutte quelle cose che si lasciano cadere per via ma che pure devono avere ancora qualche valore, perché c'è della povera gente che ci campa su; ci campa anzi così bene che quei pezzentelli paffuti e affamati cresceranno in mezzo al fango e alla polvere della strada, e si faranno grandi e grossi come il loro babbo e come il loro nonno, e popoleranno Aci-Trezza di altri pezzentelli, i quali tireranno allegramente la vita coi denti più a lungo che potranno, come il vecchio nonno, senza desiderare altro; e se vorranno fare qualche cosa diversamente da lui, sarà di chiudere gli occhi là dove li hanno aperti, in mano del medico del paese che viene tutti i giorni sull'asinello, come Gesù, ad aiutare la buona gente che se ne va.

– Insomma l'ideale dell'ostrica! direte voi. – Proprio l'ideale dell'ostrica, e noi non abbiamo altro motivo di trovarlo ridicolo che quello di non esser nati ostriche anche noi. Per altro il tenace attaccamento di quella povera gente allo scoglio sul quale la fortuna li ha lasciati cadere mentre seminava principi di qua e duchesse di là, questa rassegnazione coraggiosa ad una vita di stenti, questa religione della famiglia, che si riverbera sul mestiere, sulla casa, e sui sassi che la circondano, mi sembrano forse pel quarto d'ora – cose serissime e rispettabilissime anch'esse. Parmi che le irrequietudini del pensiero vagabondo s'addormenterebbero dolcemente nella pace serena di quei sentimenti miti, semplici, che si succedono calmi e inalterati di generazione in generazione. – Parmi che potrei vedervi passare, al gran trotto dei vostri cavalli, col tintinnìo allegro dei loro finimenti e salutarvi tranquillamente.

Forse perché ho troppo cercato di scorgere entro al turbine che vi circonda e vi segue, mi è parso ora di leggere una fatale necessità nelle tenaci affezioni dei deboli, nell'istinto che hanno i piccoli di stringersi fra loro per resistere alle tempeste della vita, e ho cercato di decifrare il dramma modesto e ignoto che deve aver sgominati gli attori plebei che conoscemmo insieme. Un dramma che qualche volta forse vi racconterò e di cui parmi tutto il nodo debba consistere in ciò: – che allorquando uno di quei piccoli, o più debole, o più incauto, o più egoista degli altri, volle staccarsi dal gruppo per vaghezza dell'ignoto, o per brama di meglio, o per curiosità di conoscere il mondo, il mondo

Now there still remain those urchins who escorted you like jackals and laid siege to the oranges; they're still there buzzing around the beggar woman, pawing her clothes as if she had bread under them, picking up cabbage stalks, orange peels, and cigar butts, all those things that are dropped in the street but must surely still have some value, because there are poor folk who live off them; in fact, they live off them so well that those hungry little paupers with puffy stomachs will grow up amid the mud and dust of the street. They'll get as big and tall as their fathers and grandfathers, and they'll populate Aci Trezza with other little paupers, who will cheerfully eke out their own difficult living just as long as they're able to, like that old grandfather, without wishing for anything different. If they do want to do something he couldn't do, it's to be able to close their eyes for the last time in the same place where they first opened them, treated by the village doctor who rides over every day on his little donkey, like Jesus, to help out good people who are leaving this world.

"In short, an oyster's aim in life!" you'll say. Yes, exactly an oyster's aim in life, and the only reason we have to find it ridiculous is that we weren't born as oysters ourselves. In other respects, those poor people's tenacious attachment to the rock onto which Fortune let them fall while she was planting princes here and duchesses there; that courageous resignation to a life of hardships; that religious love of family, which is reflected in their attitude to their work, their home, and the stones around it—all these things seem to me (perhaps only momentarily) very significant and honorable in their own right. I think that the restlessness of our vagabond thoughts would be softly lulled asleep in the serene peace of those gentle, simple feelings, which continue in unchanging calm from generation to generation.—I think that I could watch you riding by in your carriage, your horses trotting smartly and their harness bells tinkling merrily, and wave to you in peace of mind.

Perhaps because I've tried too hard to look into the whirlwind that surrounds you and follows you around, I now seem to have discerned a necessity ordained by fate in the tenacious affections of the weak, in little people's instinct for sticking together to combat the storms of life; and I've tried to decipher the modest, unseen drama that must have dispersed the humble actors whom we met together. A drama that I may recount to you some day, of which the entire plot seems to me to consist of this: whenever any one of those little people, because he was either weaker, more incautious, or more selfish than the others, decided to detach himself from the group out of infatuation with

da pesce vorace com'è, se lo ingoiò, e i suoi più prossimi con lui. – E sotto questo aspetto vedete che il dramma non manca d'interesse. Per le ostriche l'argomento più interessante deve essere quello che tratta delle insidie del gambero, o del coltello del palombaro che le stacca dallo scoglio.

the unknown, or a yearning for better things, or curiosity about what the big world was like, that world, like the voracious fish that it is, swallowed him whole, and his nearest and dearest with him.—And, looked at in this way, you see that the drama is not without interest. For oysters, the most interesting story line must be one that concerns the danger of prawns or the knife of the diver who detaches them from their rock.

JELI IL PASTORE

Jeli, il guardiano di cavalli, aveva tredici anni quando conobbe don Alfonso, il signorino; ma era così piccolo che non arrivava alla pancia della *bianca,* la vecchia giumenta che portava il campanaccio della mandra. Lo si vedeva sempre di qua e di là, pei monti e nella pianura, dove pascolavano le sue bestie, ritto ed immobile su qualche greppo, o accoccolato su di un gran sasso. Il suo amico don Alfonso, mentre era in villeggiatura, andava a trovarlo tutti i giorni che Dio mandava a Tebidi, e divideva con lui il suo pezzetto di cioccolata, e il pane d'orzo del pastorello, e le frutta rubate al vicino. Dapprincipio, Jeli dava dell'*eccellenza* al signorino, come si usa in Sicilia, ma dopo che si furono accapigliati per bene, la loro amicizia fu stabilita solidamente. Jeli insegnava al suo amico come si fa ad arrampicarsi sino ai nidi delle gazze, sulle cime dei noci più alti del campanile di Licodia, a cogliere un passero a volo con una sassata, e montare con un salto sul dorso nudo delle sue bestie mezze selvaggie, acciuffando per la criniera la prima che passava a tiro, senza lasciarsi sbigottire dai nitriti di collera dei puledri indomiti, e dai loro salti disperati. Ah! le belle scappate pei campi mietuti, colle criniere al vento! i bei giorni d'aprile, quando il vento accavallava ad onde l'erba verde, e le cavalle nitrivano nei pascoli; i bei meriggi d'estate, in cui la campagna, bianchiccia, taceva, sotto il cielo fosco, e i grilli scoppiettavano fra le zolle, come se le stoppie si incendiassero! il bel cielo d'inverno attraverso i rami nudi del mandorlo, che rabbrividivano al rovajo, e il viottolo che suonava gelato sotto lo zoccolo dei cavalli, e le allodole che trillavano in alto, al caldo, nell'azzurro! le belle sere di estate che salivano adagio adagio come la nebbia; il buon odore del fieno in cui si affondavano i gomiti, e il ronzìo malinconico degli insetti della sera, e quelle due note dello zufolo di Jeli, sempre le stesse – iuh! iuh! iuh! che facevano pensare alle cose lontane, alla festa di San Giovanni, alla notte di Natale, all'alba della scampagnata, a tutti quei grandi avvenimenti trascorsi, che sembrano mesti, così lontani, e facevano guardare in alto, cogli occhi

JELI THE HERDSMAN

Jeli, the horseherd, was thirteen when he met Don Alfonso, the child of the gentry; but he was so small that he didn't even come up to the belly of Whitie, the old mare who wore the bell of the herd. He was always to be seen here and there, in the mountains and on the plain, where his animals were grazing; he'd be standing motionless on some embankment or squatting on some big stone. All the time that his friend Don Alfonso was on vacation in the country at Tebidi, he'd go out to meet him without fail every day. They'd share Alfonso's bar of chocolate, the little herd boy's loaf of barley bread, and the fruit filched from the neighbor's orchard. At first Jeli addressed the young gentleman as "your excellence," as the custom is in Sicily, but after they had a real knockdown fight, their friendship was firmly established. Jeli taught his friend how to climb up to magpies' nests or to the tops of walnut trees taller than the bell tower in Licodia, how to hit a sparrow on the wing with a stone, and how to leap onto the bare back of his half-wild horses, seizing the first one that came within reach by the mane and not allowing yourself to be alarmed by the angry neighing of the unbroken colts, or by their desperate bucking. Oh, the lovely rides across the harvested fields, with manes flying in the wind; the beautiful April days when the wind raised waves in the green grass and the horses neighed in the pastures; the lovely summer noontides when the bleached countryside lay silent beneath the overcast sky, and the crickets chirped in the turf as if the stubble were on fire; the beautiful winter sky seen through the naked boughs of the almond tree, shuddering in the north wind, and the frozen path echoing beneath the horses' hooves, and the larks trilling up there, in the warm blue sky; the lovely summer evenings rising very slowly, like the mist; the good smell of the hay in which your elbows sank, and the melancholy buzz of the insects at evening, and that two-note piping of Jeli's, always the same—ee-oo, ee-oo—which made you think about faraway things, about St. John's Day,[1] Christmas Eve, the dawn of a picnic day, all those great events of

---

1. June 24.

umidi, quasi tutte le stelle che andavano accendendosi in cielo vi
piovessero in cuore, e l'allagassero!

Jeli, lui, non pativa di quella malinconia; se ne stava accoccolato sul
ciglione, colle gote enfiate, intentissimo a suonare iuh! iuh! iuh! Poi
radunava il branco a furia di gridi e di sassate, e lo spingeva nella
stalla, di là del *poggio alla Croce.*

Ansando, saliva la costa, di là dal vallone, e gridava qualche volta
al suo amico Alfonso: – Chiamati il cane! ohé, chiamati il cane; oppure: – Tirami una buona sassata allo *zaino,* che mi fa il signorino,
e se ne viene adagio adagio, gingillandosi colle macchie del vallone; oppure: – Domattina portami un ago grosso, di quelli della
gnà Lia.

Ei sapeva fare ogni sorta di lavori coll'ago; e ci aveva un batuffoletto di cenci nella sacca di tela, per rattoppare al bisogno le
brache e le maniche del giubbone; sapeva anche tessere dei trec-
ciuoli di crini di cavallo, e si lavava anche da sé colla creta del vallone il fazzoletto che si metteva al collo, quando aveva freddo.
Insomma, purché ci avesse la sua sacca ad armacollo, non aveva
bisogno di nessuno al mondo, fosse stato nei boschi di Resecone, o
perduto in fondo alla piana di Caltagirone. La gnà Lia soleva dire:
– Vedete Jeli il pastore? è stato sempre solo pei campi come se
l'avessero figliato le sue cavalle, ed è perciò che sa farsi la croce
con le due mani!

Del rimanente è vero che Jeli non aveva bisogno di nessuno, ma
tutti quelli della fattoria avrebbero fatto volentieri qualche cosa per
lui, poiché era un ragazzo servizievole, e ci era sempre il caso di bus-
carci qualche cosa da lui. La gnà Lia gli cuoceva il pane per amor del
prossimo, ed ei la ricambiava con bei panieri di vimini per le ova, ar-
colai di canna, ed altre coserelle. – Facciamo come fanno le sue
bestie, diceva la gnà Lia, che si grattano il collo a vicenda.

A Tebidi tutti lo conoscevano da piccolo, che non si vedeva fra le
code dei cavalli, quando pascolavano nel *piano del lettighiere,* ed era
cresciuto, si può dire, sotto i loro occhi, sebbene nessuno lo vedesse
mai, e ramingasse sempre di qua e di là col suo armento! «Era piovuto dal cielo, e la terra l'aveva raccolto» come dice il proverbio; era
proprio di quelli che non hanno né casa né parenti. La sua mamma
stava a servire a Vizzini, e non lo vedeva altro che una volta all'anno
quando egli andava coi puledri alla fiera di San Giovanni; e il giorno

the past that seem sad at such a distance, and which made you look upward with moist eyes, as if all the stars lighting up in the sky were raining into your heart and flooding it!

Jeli himself didn't suffer from that melancholy; he would remain crouched on the embankment, his cheeks puffed out, all his attention fixed on that piping, ee-oo, ee-oo, ee-oo! Then he'd assemble the herd with wild shouts and stone tossing, and drive it into the stable, on the other side of Cross Hill.

Panting, he'd climb up the slope, past the ravine, at times shouting to his friend Alfonso: "Call over the dog, hey, call over the dog!," or else: "Throw a stone at Brownie!² He's acting like a young lord, walking too slow, and loitering over the bushes in the ravine," or else: "Tomorrow morning bring me a thick needle, one of Mis' Lia's."

He knew how to do all sorts of needlework, and he had a wad of rags in his canvas bag for mending his pants and his jacket sleeves whenever necessary. He also knew how to weave braids out of horsehair, and he himself even washed, with chalk from the ravine, the cloth he wore around his neck when he felt cold. In short, as long as he had his bag slung over his shoulder, he didn't need a person in the world, whether he was in the Resecone woods or lost in the middle of the Caltagirone plain. Mis' Lia used to say: "See Jeli the herdboy? He's always been alone in the countryside as if his own mares had given birth to him, and that's why he knows how to do a little of everything!"

For the rest, it's true that Jeli had no need of anyone, but everyone on the farm would gladly have given him a hand, because he was a helpful boy, and you could always ask him for something. Mis' Lia baked his bread out of neighborly love, and in return he made beautiful osier egg baskets for her, reed wool-winders, and other small objects. "Let's behave the way his horses do," Mis' Lia used to say. "They scratch each other's necks when they itch."

At Tebidi everyone had known him since he was a tot who couldn't be seen amid the horses' tails when they pastured on the Litter-driver's Plain, and you might say he had grown up in their sight, even though no one ever saw him, because he was constantly roaming all over with his herd. "He had rained down from the sky, and the earth had taken him up," as the proverb goes; he was really one of those who have no home and no relatives. His mother had been a servant at Vizzini, and had seen him only once a year, when he went to the fair of St. John with

---

2. *Zaino* literally is an animal of a uniform color, but usually a dark one with no white hairs; a previous translator says "chestnut."

in cui era morta, erano venuti a chiamarlo, un sabato sera, ed il lunedì
Jeli tornò alla mandra, sicché il contadino che l'aveva surrogato nella
guardia dei cavalli, non perse nemmeno la giornata; ma il povero
ragazzo era ritornato così sconvolto che alle volte lasciava scappare i
puledri nel seminato. – Ohé! Jeli! gli gridava allora Massaro
Agrippino dall'aja; o che vuoi assaggiare le nerbate delle feste, figlio
di cagna? – Jeli si metteva a correre dietro i puledri sbrancati, e li
spingeva mogio mogio verso la collina; però davanti agli occhi ci
aveva sempre la sua mamma, col capo avvolto nel fazzoletto bianco,
che non gli parlava più.

Suo padre faceva il vaccaro a Ragoleti, di là di Licodia, «dove la
malaria si poteva mietere» dicevano i contadini dei dintorni; ma nei
terreni di malaria i pascoli sono grassi, e le vacche non prendono le
febbri. Jeli quindi se ne stava nei campi tutto l'anno, o a Don
Ferrante, o nelle chiuse della Commenda, o nella valle del Jacitano, e
i cacciatori, o i viandanti che prendevano le scorciatoie lo vedevano
sempre qua e là, come un cane senza padrone. Ei non ci pativa, perché era avvezzo a stare coi cavalli che gli camminavano dinanzi, passo
passo, brucando il trifoglio, e cogli uccelli che girovagavano a stormi,
attorno a lui, tutto il tempo che il sole faceva il suo viaggio lento lento,
sino a che le ombre si allungavano e poi si dileguavano; egli avea il
tempo di veder le nuvole accavallarsi a poco a poco e figurar monti e
vallate; conosceva come spira il vento quando porta il temporale, e di
che colore sia il nuvolo quando sta per nevicare. Ogni cosa aveva il suo
aspetto e il suo significato, e c'era sempre che vedere e che ascoltare
in tutte le ore del giorno. Così, verso il tramonto quando il pastore si
metteva a suonare collo zufolo di sambuco, la cavalla mora si accostava
masticando il trifoglio svogliatamente, e stava anch'essa a guardarlo,
con grandi occhi pensierosi.

Dove soffriva soltanto un po' di malinconia era nelle lande deserte
di Passanitello, in cui non sorge macchia né arbusto, e ne' mesi caldi
non ci vola un uccello. I cavalli si radunavano in cerchio colla testa
ciondoloni, per farsi ombra scambievolmente, e nui lunghi giorni della
trebbiatura quella gran luce silenziosa pioveva sempre uguale ed afosa
per sedici ore.

Però dove il mangime era abbondante, e i cavalli indugiavano volentieri, il ragazzo si occupava con qualche altra cosa: faceva delle gab-
bie di canna per i grilli, delle pipe intagliate, e dei panierini di giunco;
con quattro ramoscelli, sapeva rizzare un po' di tettoia, quando la tramontana spingeva per la valle le lunghe file dei corvi, o quando le
cicale battevano le ali nel sole che abbruciava le stoppie; arrostiva le

his colts. On the day she died, a Saturday evening, they had come to call him, and on Monday Jeli was back with the herd, so that the farmhand who had taken his place as horseherd didn't even lose his regular day's pay; but the poor boy was so upset on his return that he sometimes let his colts wander onto sown fields. "Hey, Jeli!" farmer Agrippino would then yell to him from the threshing floor, "do you want a healthy taste of my whip, you son of a bitch?" Jeli would start running after the stray colts, driving them dejectedly toward the hill; but before his eyes he always saw his mother, her white kerchief wrapped around her head, not speaking to him anymore.

His father worked as a cowherd at Ragoleti, on the other side of Licodia, "where the malaria was thick enough to harvest," as the local farmhands said; but in malarial areas the pastures are rich, and cows don't catch the fever. So Jeli remained out in the fields all year long, either at Don Ferrante, or in the enclosures of Commenda, or in the valley of Jacitano, and the hunters, or the wayfarers who took the shortcuts, would always see him here and there, like a dog without a master. He didn't suffer from this, because he was accustomed to be with the horses, which walked in front of him at a slow pace, nibbling the clover, and with the birds, which circled around him in flocks, all the time that the sun performed its very slow journey, until the shadows lengthened and then disappeared. He had the time to watch the clouds pile up gradually, forming hills and valleys; he knew how the wind blows when it carries a storm, and the color that the clouds take on before a snowfall. Everything had its own special appearance and meaning, and there was always something to see and hear at each hour in the day. And so, toward sunset, when the herdboy started playing on his elder-wood pipe, the dark mare would approach him, chewing the clover listlessly, and she, too, would stand there looking at him with her large, thoughtful eyes.

The place where he felt just a bit of melancholy was on the deserted heaths of Passanitello, where no shrub or brush grows, and where no bird flies in the hot months. The horses would gather in a circle, their heads hanging, to cast some shade on one another, and during the long days of threshing that broad, silent light would fall with uniform sultriness for sixteen hours.

But where there was abundant grazing and the horses enjoyed lingering, the boy would spend his time with other things: he'd make cricket cages out of reed, carve tobacco pipes, and weave little rush baskets; with four branches he knew how to erect a small shed when the north wind drove long files of crows through the valley, or when the cicadas rubbed their wings in the sunshine that scorched the

ghiande del quarceto nella brace de' sarmenti di sommacco, che
pareva di mangiare delle bruciate, o vi abbrustoliva le larghe fette di
pane allorché cominciava ad avere la barba dalla muffa, perché
quando si trovava a Passanitello nell'inverno, le strade erano così cattive che alle volte passavano quindici giorni senza che si vedesse passare anima viva.

Don Alfonso che era tenuto nel cotone dai suoi genitori, invidiava
al suo amico Jeli la tasca di tela dove ci aveva tutta la sua roba, il pane,
le cipolle, il fiaschetto del vino, il fazzoletto pel freddo, il batuffoletto
dei cenci col refe e gli aghi grossi, la scatoletta di latta coll'esca e la
pietra focaja; gli invidiava pure la superba cavalla *vajata,* quella bestia
dal ciuffetto di peli irti sulla fronte, che aveva gli occhi cattivi, e gon-
fiava le froge al pari di un mastino ringhioso quando qualcuno voleva
montarla. Da Jeli invece si lasciava montare e grattar le orecchie, di
cui era gelosa, e l'andava fiutando per ascoltare quello che ei voleva
dirle. – Lascia stare la *vajata,* gli raccomandava Jeli, non è cattiva, ma
non ti conosce.

Dopo che Scordu il Bucchierese si menò via la giumenta calabrese
che aveva comprato a San Giovanni, col patto che gliela tenessero nel-
l'armento sino alla vendemmia, il puledro zaino rimasto orfano non
voleva darsi pace, e scorazzava su pei greppi del monte con lunghi nitriti lamentevoli, e colle froge al vento. Jeli gli correva dietro, chia-
mandolo con forti grida, e il puledro si fermava ad ascoltare, col collo
teso e le orecchie irrequiete, sferzandosi i fianchi colla coda. – È perché gli hanno portato via la madre, e non sa più cosa si faccia – osservava il pastore. – Adesso bisogna tenerlo d'occhio perché sarebbe
capace di lasciarsi andar giù nel precipizio. Anch'io, quando mi è
morta la mia mamma, non ci vedevo più dagli occhi.

Poi, dopo che il puledro ricominciò a fiutare il trifoglio, e a darvi
qualche boccata di malavoglia – Vedi! a poco a poco comincia a
dimenticarsene.

– Ma anch'esso sarà venduto. I cavalli sono fatti per esser venduti;
come gli agnelli nascono per andare al macello, e le nuvole portano la
pioggia. Solo gli uccelli non hanno a far altro che cantare e volare tutto
il giorno.

Le idee non gli venivano nette e filate l'una dietro l'altra, ché di
rado aveva avuto con chi parlare e perciò non aveva fretta di scovarle
e distrigarle in fondo alla testa, dove era abituato a lasciare che sbuc-
ciassero e spuntassero fuori a poco a poco, come fanno le gemme dei

stubble; he'd roast acorns from the oak grove over the embers of sumac runners, and it felt as if he were eating roast chestnuts; or else he'd toast broad slices of bread when it began to be bearded with mold, because when he was at Passanitello in the wintertime, the roads were so bad that sometimes two weeks would go by in which he wouldn't see a living soul passing.

Don Alfonso, whom his parents mollycoddled, envied his friend Jeli that canvas bag in which he kept all his possessions, his bread, his onions, his little wine flask, his neckerchief for cold weather, his wad of rags with thread and thick needles, the little tin box with tinder and flint. He also envied him the magnificent mare Dapple.[3] She had a protruding tuft of hair on her forehead, and malevolent eyes, and she distended her nostrils like a bad-tempered mastiff when someone wanted to ride her. But she let Jeli ride her and scratch her ears, about which she was very apprehensive, and she would sniff him to hear what he wanted to tell her. "Leave Dapple alone," Jeli recommended to him. "She's not vicious, but she doesn't know you."

After Scordo from Buccheri took away with him the Calabrian mare he had bought at St. John's fair, with the understanding that she would be kept in the herd until the grape harvest, the all-black colt, now orphaned, could find no rest; he would race up to the mountain ridges with long, mournful neighs, his nostrils in the air. Jeli would run after him, shouting at him loudly, and the colt would stop to listen, his neck extended and his ears twitching, lashing his sides with his tail. "It's because they took away his mother, and he doesn't know what to do anymore," the herdboy observed. "Now we've got to keep an eye on him because he's liable to fall over the cliff. It was the same with me when my mother died; I couldn't see a thing in front of me."

Then, after the colt began to sniff at the clover again, and to chew a mouthful of it listlessly: "See! Little by little he's beginning to forget her.

"But he'll be sold, too. Horses are made to be sold, just as lambs are born to go to the slaughterhouse and the clouds bring rain. Only birds have nothing to do but sing and fly around all day."

Ideas didn't come to him in a neat row one behind the other, because he had seldom had anyone to talk with, and so he was in no hurry to dredge them up and disentangle them in his mind, but was accustomed to let them shed their covering there and peep out little by little, like buds on branches in the sunshine. "Even birds," he

---

3. Or: "variegated, vair-colored."

ramoscelli sotto il sole. – Anche gli uccelli, soggiunse, devono buscarsi il cibo, e quando la neve copre la terra se ne muoiono.

Poi ci pensò su un pezzetto. – Tu sei come gli uccelli; ma quando arriva l'inverno te ne puoi stare al fuoco senza far nulla.

Don Alfonso però rispondeva che anche lui andava a scuola, a imparare. Jeli allora sgranava gli occhi, e stava tutto orecchi se il signorino si metteva a leggere, e guardava il libro e lui in aria sospettosa, stando ad ascoltare con quel lieve ammiccar di palpebre che indica l'intensità dell'attenzione nelle bestie che più si accostano all'uomo. Gli piacevano i versi che gli accarezzavano l'udito con l'armonia di una canzone incomprensibile, e alle volte aggrottava le ciglia, appuntava il mento, e sembrava che un gran lavorìo si stesse facendo nel suo interno; allora accennava di sì e di sì col capo, con un sorriso furbo, e si grattava la testa. Quando poi il signorino mettevasi a scrivere per far vedere quante cose sapeva fare, Jeli sarebbe rimasto delle giornate intiere a guardarlo, e tutto a un tratto lasciava scappare un'occhiata sospettosa. Non poteva persuadersi che si potesse poi ripetere sulla carta quelle parole che egli aveva dette, o che aveva dette don Alfonso, ed anche quelle cose che non gli erano uscite di bocca, e finiva col fare quel sorriso furbo.

Ogni idea nuova che gli picchiasse nella testa per entrare, lo metteva in sospetto, e pareva la fiutasse colla diffidenza selvaggia della sua *vajata*. Però non mostrava meraviglia di nulla al mondo; gli avessero detto che in città i cavalli andavano in carrozza, egli sarebbe rimasto impassibile con quella maschera d'indifferenza orientale che è la dignità del contadino siciliano. Pareva che istintivamente si trincerasse nella sua ignoranza, come fosse la forza della povertà. Tutte le volte che rimaneva a corto di argomenti ripeteva: – Io non ne so nulla. Io sono povero – con quel sorriso ostinato che voleva essere furbo.

Aveva chiesto al suo amico Alfonso di scrivergli il nome di Mara su di un pezzetto di carta che aveva trovato chi sa dove, perché egli raccattava tutto quello che vedeva per terra, e se l'era messo nel batuffoletto dei cenci. Un giorno, dopo di esser stato un po' zitto, a guardare di qua e di là soprappensiero, gli disse serio serio:

– Io ci ho l'innamorata.

Alfonso, malgrado che sapesse leggere, sgranava gli occhi. – Sì, ripeté Jeli, Mara, la figlia di Massaro Agrippino che era qui; ed ora sta a Marineo, in quel gran casamento della pianura che si vede dal *piano del lettighiere,* lassù.

– O ti mariti dunque!

added, "have to look for their food, and when the snow covers the ground, they die of that."

Then he reflected on this for a while. "You're like the birds; but when winter comes, you can stay by the fire and not do a thing."

But Don Alfonso replied that he *was* occupied: he went to school to learn. Then Jeli opened his eyes wide and was all ears when the young gentleman started to read; he'd look at both him and his book suspiciously, listening with that slight blinking of the eyes which is the sign of intense attention in those animals which are closest to man. He liked poetry, which caressed his sense of hearing with the harmony of an incomprehensible song; at times he wrinkled his brow and thrust out his chin, and a great stirring seemed to be taking place within him. At those times he'd nod approvingly with a sly smile, and he'd scratch his head. After that, when the young gentleman started to write to show how many things he knew how to do, Jeli could have kept on watching him for days at a time, then he'd suddenly dart a suspicious glance. He couldn't be convinced that it was possible to repeat on paper the words that he had spoken, or that Don Alfonso had spoken, and even the things that hadn't escaped his lips, and he'd end up by giving that sly smile.

Every new idea that knocked at his head seeking entry made him suspicious, and he seemed to be sniffing at it with the savage distrust of his mare Dapple. But he didn't show surprise at anything whatsoever; if people had told him that in town horses rode in carriages, he would have remained impassive, with that mask of Oriental indifference which constitutes the dignity of the Sicilian peasant. He seemed to be making a protective wall out of his ignorance, as if that were the true strength of poor folk. Every time he ran out of arguments, he'd repeat: "I know nothing about that; I'm poor," with that stubborn smile that was meant to be sly.

He had asked his friend Alfonso to write Mara's name on a little piece of paper which he had found somewhere (he picked up everything he saw on the ground) and had stored away in his wad of rags. One day, after a short period of remaining silent and looking all around, lost in thought, he said with the greatest seriousness:

"I *have* a sweetheart."

Despite his ability to read, Alfonso opened wide eyes. "Yes," Jeli repeated, "the daughter of farmer Agrippino who was here; now she's staying at Marineo, in that big housing compound in the lowlands that you can see from the Plain of the Litter-driver up there."

"So you're getting married, then?"

– Sì, quando sarò grande, e avrò sei onze all'anno di salario. Mara non ne sa nulla ancora.

– Perché non gliel'hai detto?

Jeli tentennò il capo, e si mise a riflettere. Poi svolse il batuffoletto e spiegò la carta che s'era fatta scrivere.

– È proprio vero che dice Mara; l'ha letto pure don Gesualdo, il campiere, e fra Cola, quando venne giù per la cerca delle fave.

– Uno che sappia scrivere, osservò poi, è come uno che serbasse le parole nella scatola dell'acciarino, e potesse portarsele in tasca, ed anche mandarle di qua e di là.

– Ora che ne farai di quel pezzetto di carta tu che non sai leggere? gli domandò Alfonso.

Jeli si strinse nelle spalle, ma continuò ad avvolgere accuratamente il suo fogliolino scritto nel batuffoletto dei cenci.

La Mara l'aveva conosciuta da bambina, che avevano cominciato dal picchiarsi ben bene, una volta che s'erano incontrati lungo il vallone, a cogliere le more nelle siepi di rovo. La ragazzina, la quale sapeva di essere «nel fatto suo», aveva agguantato pel collo Jeli, come un ladro. Per un po' s'erano scambiati dei pugni nella schiena, uno tu ed uno io, come fa il bottaio sui cerchi delle botti, ma quando furono stanchi andarono calmandosi a poco a poco, tenendosi sempre acciuffati.

– Tu chi sei? gli domandò Mara.

E come Jeli, più salvatico, non diceva chi fosse. – Io sono Mara, la figlia di Massaro Agrippino, che è il campaio di tutti questi campi qui.

Jeli allora lasciò la presa dell'intutto, e la ragazzina si mise a raccattare le more che le erano cadute nella lotta, sbirciando di tanto in tanto il suo avversario con curiosità.

– Di là del ponticello, nella siepe dell'orto, ci son tante more grosse; aggiunse la piccina, e se le mangiano le galline.

Jeli intanto si allontanava quatto quatto, e Mara, dopo che stette ad accompagnarlo cogli occhi finché poté vederlo nel querceto, volse le spalle anche lei, e se la diede a gambe verso casa.

Ma da quel giorno in poi cominciarono ad addomesticarsi. Mara andava a filare la stoppa sul parapetto del ponticello, e Jeli adagio adagio spingeva l'armento verso le falde del *poggio del Bandito.* Da prima se ne stava in disparte ronzandole attorno, guardandola da lontano in aria sospettosa, e a poco a poco andava accostandosi coll'andatura guardinga del cane avvezzo alle sassate. Quando finalmente si trovavano accanto, ci stavano delle lunghe ore senza aprir bocca. Jeli

"Yes, when I grow up and earn six *onze* a year. Mara doesn't know anything about it yet."

"Why haven't you told her?"

Jeli shook his head and began to think. Then he opened the wad of rags and unfolded the paper he had had written for him.

"It's really true that it says 'Mara;' Don Gesualdo, the field watchman, read it, too, and so did Friar Cola when he came down collecting beans as alms.

"A person who can write," he then observed, "is like a person who keeps words in his tinder box and can carry them in his pocket, and can also send them here or there."

"Now, since you can't read, what will you do with that scrap of paper?" Alfonso asked him.

Jeli shrugged his shoulders, but continued wrapping up his little written sheet carefully in the wad of rags.

He had known Mara since she was little; they had begun their acquaintance by beating each other hard, upon meeting in the ravine, while gathering blackberries from the bramble hedges. The little girl, who was very conscious of being "on her own property," had seized Jeli by the neck like a thief. For a while they had exchanged punches on the back, in alternation, the way a cooper hammers on barrel hoops, but once they were tired they calmed down little by little, though they still had a grip on each other.

"Who are you?" Mara asked him.

And when Jeli, who was more of a savage, refused to reveal his identity, she said: "I'm Mara, the daughter of farmer Agrippino, who controls all the farm land around here."

Then Jeli completely released his prisoner, and the little girl began picking up the blackberries that she had dropped during the fight, occasionally squinting at her adversary with curiosity.

"Across the little bridge, in the vegetable-garden hedge, there are loads of big blackberries," the girl added, "and the chickens eat them."

Meanwhile Jeli was walking away very quietly. After Mara watched him go as far as she could see him in the oak grove, she turned away, too, and ran home.

But from that day on, their acquaintance deepened. Mara would go to the railing of the little bridge to spin her tow, and Jeli would slowly drive his herd toward the slopes of Bandit's Hill. At first he kept his distance, lingering around her and watching her suspiciously from afar, but he gradually came closer, with that watchful gait of a dog accustomed to having stones thrown at it. When they were finally next to each other, they didn't say a word for hours and hours. Jeli would

osservando attentamente l'intricato lavorìo delle calze che la mamma aveva messo al collo alla Mara, oppure costei gli vedeva intagliare i bei zig zag sui bastoni di mandorlo. Poi se ne andavano l'uno di qua e l'altro di là, senza dirsi una parola, e la bambina, com'era in vista della casa, si metteva a correre, facendo levar alta la sottanella sulle gambe rosse.

Al tempo dei fichidindia poi si fissarono nel folto delle macchie, sbucciando dei fichi tutto il santo giorno. Vagabondavano insieme sotto i noci secolari, e Jeli ne bacchiava tante delle noci, che piovevano fitte come la gragnuola; e la ragazzina si affaticava a raccattarle con grida di giubilo più che ne poteva; e poi scappava via, lesta lesta, tenendo tese le due cocche del grembiale, dondolandosi come una vecchietta.

Durante l'inverno Mara non osò mettere fuori il naso, in quel gran freddo. Alle volte, verso sera, si vedeva il fumo dei fuocherelli di sommacchi che Jeli andava facendo sul *piano del lettighiere,* o sul *poggio di Macca,* per non rimanere intirizzito al pari di quelle cinciallegre che la mattina trovava dietro un sasso, o al riparo di una zolla. Anche i cavalli ci trovavano piacere a ciondolare un po' la coda attorno al fuoco, e si stringevano gli uni agli altri per star più caldi.

Col marzo tornarono le allodole nel piano, i passeri sul tetto, le foglie e i nidi nelle siepi, Mara riprese ad andare a spasso in compagnia di Jeli nell'erba soffice, fra le macchie in fiore, sotto gli alberi ancora nudi che cominciavano a punteggiarsi di verde. Jeli si ficcava negli spineti come un segugio per andare a scovare delle nidiate di merli che guardavano sbalorditi coi loro occhietti di pepe; i due fanciulli portavano spesso nel petto della camicia dei piccoli conigli allora stanati, quasi nudi, ma dalle lunghe orecchie diggià inquiete. Scorazzavano pei campi al seguito del branco dei cavalli, entrando nelle stoppie dietro i mietitori, passo passo coll'armento, fermandosi ogni volta che una giumenta si fermava a strappare una boccata d'erba. La sera, giunti al ponticello, se ne andavano l'uno di qua e l'altra di là, senza dirsi addio.

Così passarono tutta l'estate. Intanto il sole cominciava a tramontare dietro il *poggio alla Croce,* e i pettirossi gli andavano dietro verso la montagna, come imbruniva, seguendolo fra le macchie dei fichidindia. I grilli e le cicale non si udivano più, e in quell'ora per l'aria si spandeva una grande malinconia.

In quel tempo arrivò al casolare di Jeli suo padre, il vaccaro, che aveva preso la malaria a Ragoleti, e non poteva nemmen reggersi sull'asino che l'aveva portato. Jeli accese il fuoco, lesto lesto, e corse «alle

study attentively the intricate work in the knitting that Mara's mother had saddled her with, or else she would watch him carving beautiful zigzag patterns onto almond-wood staffs. Then they'd go off in different directions without addressing a word to each other, and the girl, who could see her house from there, would start running, making her little petticoat rise high against her pink legs.

Then, in prickly-pear season, they took their post in the densest part of the thicket, peeling pears all day long. They'd roam together below the centuries-old walnut trees, and Jeli would beat down great numbers of nuts, which rained down as thick as hail; and the little girl would tire herself out picking up as many as she could with jubilant shouts. Then she'd dart away, very briskly, stretching out the two corners of her apron and swaying like an old woman.

During the winter Mara didn't dare to stick her nose out, it was so very cold. At times, toward evening, she could see the smoke from the little sumac-runner campfires that Jeli built on the Plain of the Litter-driver or on Macca's Hill so he wouldn't become stiff like those titmice he'd find in the morning behind a stone, or in the lee of a clod. The horses, too, took pleasure in dangling their tails a bit around the fire, snuggling up to one another to be warmer.

With March the larks returned to the plain, the sparrows to the roof, the leaves and nests to the hedges, and Mara resumed her strolls together with Jeli on the soft grass, amid the flowering bushes, beneath the still bare trees that were beginning to be dotted with green. Jeli would plunge into thorn patches like a hound to discover nests of blackbirds, which would look at him in bewilderment with their little peppercorn eyes. The two children would often carry in their shirt front little rabbits just out of the burrow, nearly hairless, though their long ears already twitched nervously. They'd scurry through the fields following the herd of horses, running into the stubble behind the reapers, keeping pace with the herd and stopping every time a mare stopped to pull up a mouthful of grass. In the evening, when they had reached the little bridge, they'd go off in different directions without saying good-bye.

They spent the whole summer that way. Meanwhile the sun was beginning to set behind Cross Hill, and the robins were going after it toward the mountain, as twilight fell, following it amid the prickly-pear plants. The crickets and cicadas were no longer heard, and at that hour a deep melancholy spread through the atmosphere.

At that season Jeli's cottage was visited by his father, the cowherd, who had caught malaria at Ragoleti and couldn't even sit up straight on the donkey that had brought him. Jeli briskly lit the fire and ran "to the big houses"

case» per cercargli qualche uovo di gallina. – Piuttosto stendi un po'
di strame vicino al fuoco, gli disse suo padre; ché mi sento tornare la
febbre.

Il ribrezzo della febbre era così forte che compare Menu, seppellito sotto il suo gran tabarro, la bisaccia dell'asino, e la sacca di Jeli,
tremava come fanno le foglie in novembre, davanti alla gran vampa di
sarmenti che gli faceva il viso bianco bianco come un morto. I contadini della fattoria venivano a domandargli: – Come vi sentite, compare
Menu? Il poveretto non rispondeva altro che con un guaito come fa
un cagnuolo di latte. – È malaria di quella che ammazza meglio di una
schioppettata, dicevano gli amici, scaldandosi le mani al fuoco.

Fu chiamato anche il medico, ma erano denari buttati via, perché
la malattia era di quelle chiare e conosciute che anche un ragazzo
saprebbe curarla, e se la febbre non era di quelle che ammazzano ad
ogni modo, col solfato si sarebbe guarita subito. Compare Menu ci
spese gli occhi della testa in tanto solfato, ma era come buttarlo nel
pozzo. – Prendete un buon decotto di *ecalibbiso* che non costa nulla,
suggeriva Massaro Agrippino, e se non serve a nulla come il solfato,
almeno non vi rovinate a spendere. – Si prendeva anche il decotto di
eucaliptus, eppure la febbre tornava sempre, e anche più forte. Jeli
assisteva il genitore come meglio sapeva. Ogni mattina, prima
d'andarsene coi puledri, gli lasciava il decotto preparato nella ciotola,
il fascio dei sarmenti sotto la mano, le uova nella cenere calda, e
tornava presto alla sera colle altre legne per la notte e il fiaschetto del
vino e qualche pezzetto di carne di montone che era corso a comperare sino a Licodia. Il povero ragazzo faceva ogni cosa con garbo,
come una brava massaia, e suo padre, accompagnandolo cogli occhi
stanchi nelle sue faccenduole qua e là pel casolare, di tanto in tanto
sorrideva pensando che il ragazzo avrebbe saputo aiutarsi, quando
fosse rimasto solo.

I giorni in cui la febbre cessava per qualche ora, compare Menu si
alzava tutto stravolto e col capo stretto nel fazzoletto, e si metteva sul-
l'uscio ad aspettare Jeli, mentre il sole era ancora caldo. Come Jeli lasciava cadere accanto all'uscio il fascio della legna e posava sulla tavola
il fiasco e le uova, ei gli diceva: – Metti a bollire l'*ecalibbiso* per
stanotte, – oppure – guarda che l'oro di tua madre l'ha in consegna la
zia Agata, quando non ci sarò più. – Jeli diceva di sì col capo.

– È inutile; ripeteva Massaro Agrippino ogni volta che tornava a
vedere compare Menu colla febbre. Il sangue oramai è tutto una
peste. – Compare Menu ascoltava senza batter palpebra, col viso più
bianco della sua berretta.

to ask for some hen's eggs for him. "Rather than that, lay a little straw next to the fire," his father said, "because I feel the fever coming back."

The chills from the fever were so strong that neighbor Menu, even when buried beneath his great cloak, the donkey's saddlebag, and Jeli's knapsack, still trembled like leaves in November, in front of the large blaze from the vine runners that made his face look as pale as a dead man's. The farmhands from the main house came to ask him: "How do you feel, neighbor Menu?" The poor man answered only with a whine like that of a suckling puppy. "It's the kind of malaria that kills you more surely than a gunshot," his friends said, warming their hands at the fire.

The doctor was called, too, but that was money thrown out, because (as he said) the illness was of that familiar, clearly recognizable kind which even a boy could attend to, and, if the fever wasn't of the sort that infallibly kills the patient, it would be cured at once with sulphur. Neighbor Menu spent an arm and a leg on loads of sulphur, but it was like throwing his money down a well. "Drink a good infusion of *ecalibbiso,* which doesn't cost anything," farmer Agrippino suggested, "and if it doesn't help you any more than the sulphur, at least you won't be ruined by the cost." He drank this infusion of eucalyptus, too, but the fever kept coming back, and was even stronger. Jeli tended to his father as best he could. Every morning, before leaving with the colts, he'd leave him the prepared infusion in a bowl, the bundle of vine runners under his hand, and the eggs in the warm ashes; and in the evening he'd come home quickly with more firewood for the night, a flask of wine, and some little bit of mutton that he had run all the way to Licodia to buy. The poor boy did everything neatly, like a good housewife, and his father, watching with weary eyes as he did his chores up and down the cottage, would occasionally smile at the thought that the boy would be able to fend for himself when he was left on his own.

On the days when the fever was in remittance for a few hours, neighbor Menu would get up, quite distraught, a bandanna wrapped around his head, and would post himself in the doorway to wait for Jeli while the sunshine was still warm. When Jeli dropped the bundle of firewood next to the door and placed the flask and the eggs on the table, his father would say: "Start the *ecalibbiso* boiling for tonight," or, "Listen, after I'm gone, your aunt Agata has your mother's gold jewelry in safekeeping." Jeli would nod affirmatively.

"It's no use," farmer Agrippino would repeat every time he revisited the feverish neighbor Menu. "By this time his blood is all plague-ridden." Neighbor Menu would listen without batting an eyelid, his face whiter than his cap.

Diggià non si alzava più. Jeli si metteva a piangere quando non gli bastavano le forze per aiutarlo a voltarsi da un lato all'altro; poco per volta compare Menu finì per non parlare nemmen più. Le ultime parole che disse al suo ragazzo furono:

– Quando sarò morto andrai dal padrone delle vacche a Ragoleti, e ti farai dare le tre onze e i dodici tumoli di frumento che avanzo da maggio a questa parte.

– No, rispose Jeli, sono soltanto 2 onze e quindici, perché avete lasciato le vacche che è più di un mese, e bisogna fare il conto giusto col padrone.

– È vero! affermò compare Menu socchiudendo gli occhi.

– Ora son proprio solo al mondo come un puledro smarrito, che se lo possono mangiare i lupi! pensò Jeli quando gli ebbero portato il babbo al cimitero di Licodia.

Mara era venuta a vedere anche lei la casa del morto colla curiosità acuta che destano le cose spaventose. – Vedi come son rimasto? le disse Jeli, la ragazzetta si tirò indietro sbigottita per paura che la facesse entrare nella casa dove era stato il morto.

Jeli andò a riscuotere il denaro del babbo, e poscia partì coll'armento per Passanitello, dove l'erba era già alta sul terreno lasciato pel maggese e il mangime era abbondante; perciò i puledri vi restarono a pascolarvi per molto tempo. Frattanto Jeli s'era fatto grande, ed anche Mara doveva esser cresciuta, pensava egli sovente mentre suonava il suo zufolo; e quando tornò a Tebidi dopo tanto tempo, spingendosi innanzi adagio adagio le giumente per i viottoli sdrucciolevoli della *fontana dello zio Cosimo*, andava cercando cogli occhi il ponticello del vallone, e il casolare nella *valle del Iacitano*, e il tetto delle «case grandi» dove svolazzavano sempre i colombi. Ma in quel tempo il padrone aveva licenziato Massaro Agrippino e tutta la famiglia di Mara stava sloggiando. Jeli trovò la ragazza la quale s'era fatta grandicella e belloccia alla porta del cortile, che teneva d'occhio la sua roba mentre la caricavano sulla carretta. Ora la stanza vuota sembrava più scura e affumicata del solito. La tavola, e il letto, e il cassettone, e le immagini della Vergine e di San Giovanni, e fino i chiodi per appendervi le zucche delle sementi ci avevano lasciato il segno sulle pareti dove erano state per tanti anni. – Andiamo via, gli disse Mara come lo vide osservare. Ce ne andiamo laggiù a Marineo dove c'è quel gran casamento nella pianura.

Jeli si diede ad aiutare Massaro Agrippino e la gnà Lia nel caricare la carretta, e allorché non ci fu altro da portare via dalla stanza andò a sedere con Mara sul parapetto dell'abbeveratojo. – Anche le case, le

By now he was no longer getting out of bed. Jeli would start to cry when he didn't have the strength to help him turn over to a different side; gradually neighbor Menu even stopped speaking altogether. The last words he addressed to his boy were:

"When I'm dead, go to the owner of the cows at Ragoleti and ask for the three *onze* and the twelve *tumoli* of wheat that are coming to me from May until now."

"No," Jeli answered, "it's only two *onze* fifteen, because it's over a month since you left the cows, and we've got to deal fairly with the owner."

"It's true!" neighbor Menu agreed, partly shutting his eyes.

"Now I'm really alone in the world like a lost colt that the wolves can eat!" Jeli thought, after his father had been carried to the cemetery in Licodia.

Mara, too, had come to see the dead man's house with that keen curiosity aroused by frightening things. "Do you see what's become of me?" Jeli said to her, and the young girl drew back in alarm, afraid he would make her enter the house in which the dead man had been.

Jeli went to claim his father's money, then he departed with his herd for Passanitello, where the grass was already tall on the terrain left fallow, and the pasture was abundant, so that the colts remained grazing there for a long stretch. Meanwhile Jeli had grown up; Mara must have grown, also, he frequently reflected as he played his pipe. When he returned to Tebidi after all that time, slowly driving the mares ahead of him over the slippery paths of "Uncle" Cosimo's Fountain, his eyes sought out the little bridge in the ravine, the cottage in the Valley of Jacitano, and the roof of the "big houses," where the doves were always fluttering. But at that period the proprietor had discharged farmer Agrippino, and Mara's whole family was moving. Jeli found the girl, who had become tall and pretty, at the gate to her yard, where she was keeping an eye on her belongings while they were loaded onto the wagon. Now the empty room seemed darker and more smoke-blackened than usual. The table, the bed, the chest of drawers, the images of the Virgin and St. John, and even the nails for hanging up the gourd seed-containers, had left their traces on the walls where they had remained all those years. "We're going away," Mara said when she saw him scrutinizing the place. "We're going down to Marineo, where there's that big housing compound in the lowlands."

Jeli began helping farmer Agrippino and Mis' Lia load the wagon; when there was nothing left to carry out of the room, he sat down with Mara on the rim of the watering trough. After watching the last basket

disse quand'ebbe visto accatastare l'ultima cesta sulla carretta, anche le case, come se ne toglie via qualche oggetto non sembrano più quelle.

– A Marineo, rispose Mara, ci avremo una camera più bella, ha detto la mamma, e grande come il magazzino dei formaggi.

– Ora che tu sarai via, non voglio venirci più qui; ché mi parrà di esser tornato l'inverno a veder quell'uscio chiuso.

– A Marineo invece troveremo dell'altra gente, Pudda la rossa, e la figlia del campiere; si starà allegri, per la messe verranno più di ottanta mietitori, colla cornamusa, e si ballerà sull'aja.

Massaro Agrippino e sua moglie si erano avviati colla carretta, Mara correva loro dietro tutta allegra, portando il paniere coi piccioni. Jeli volle accompagnarla sino al ponticello, e quando Mara stava per scomparire nella vallata la chiamò: – Mara! oh! Mara!

– Che vuoi? disse Mara.

Egli non lo sapeva che voleva. – O tu, cosa farai qui tutto solo? gli domandò allora la ragazza.

– Io resto coi puledri.

Mara se ne andò saltellando, e lui rimase lì fermo, finché poté udire il rumore della carretta che rimbalzava sui sassi. Il sole toccava le roccie alte del *poggio alla Croce,* le chiome grigie degli ulivi sfumavano nel crepuscolo, e per la campagna vasta, lontan lontano, non si udiva altro che il campanaccio della *bianca* nel silenzio che si allargava.

Mara, come se ne fu andata a Marineo in mezzo alla gente nuova, e alle faccende della vendemmia, si scordò di lui; ma Jeli ci pensava sempre a lei, perché non aveva altro da fare, nelle lunghe giornate che passava a guardare la coda delle sue bestie. Adesso non aveva poi motivo alcuno per calar nella valle, di là del ponticello, e nessuno lo vedeva più alla fattoria. In tal modo ignorò per un pezzo che Mara si era fatta sposa, giacché dell'acqua intanto ne era passata e passata sotto il ponticello. Egli rivide soltanto la ragazza il dì della festa di San Giovanni, come andò alla fiera coi puledri da vendere: una festa che gli si mutò tutta in veleno, e gli fece cascare il pan di bocca per un accidente toccato ad uno dei puledri del padrone, Dio ne scampi.

Il giorno della fiera il fattore aspettava i puledri sin dall'alba, andando su e giù cogli stivali inverniciati dietro le groppe dei cavalli e dei muli, messi in fila di qua e di là dello stradone. La fiera era già sul finire, né Jeli spuntava ancora colle bestie, di là del gomito che faceva lo stradone. Sulle pendici riarse del *Calvario* e del *Mulino a vento,* rimaneva tuttora qualche branco di pecore, strette in cerchio col muso

being stacked on the wagon, he said to her: "Even houses, even houses no longer seem the same when something is taken out of them."

"At Marineo," Mara replied, "we'll have a lovelier room, Mother said, one as big as the cheese storehouse."

"Now that you're going away, I don't want to come here anymore; I'll think winter has come back if I see that closed door."

"On the other hand, at Marineo we'll find other people, redheaded Pudda and the daughter of the field watchman; we'll be jolly; at the grain harvest more than eighty reapers will come, with the bagpipes, and we'll dance on the threshing floor."

Farmer Agrippino and his wife had set out with the wagon; Mara ran after them very cheerfully, carrying the basket with the pigeons. Jeli escorted her as far as the little bridge, and when Mara was all but out of sight in the valley he called to her: "Mara! Oh, Mara!"

"What is it?" Mara asked.

He didn't know what he wanted to say. "What will *you* do here all alone?" the girl asked him then.

"I'm staying with the colts."

Mara skipped away and he stood there motionless as long as he could hear the sound of the wagon bouncing over the stones. The sun was touching the high crags of Cross Hill, the gray foliage of the olive trees was losing its color in the twilight, and far and wide in the vast countryside nothing could be heard in the spreading silence but the mare Whitie's bell.

After Mara moved to Marineo, in the midst of new people and the busy time of the grape harvest, she forgot about him; but Jeli thought constantly about her, because he had nothing else to do in the long days he spent with his eyes on his horses' tails. Now he no longer had any reason to descend to the valley, beyond the little bridge, and he was no longer seen at the main farmhouse. And so, for a while, he didn't hear that Mara had become engaged, since so much water had passed under the bridge in the interim. It was only on St. John's Day that he saw the girl again, when he went to the fair with colts to sell: a feast day that turned into pure poison for him, causing him to lose his means of support through a disaster that befell one of his master's colts, God forbid.

On the day of the fair the farm steward had been awaiting the colts since dawn, walking to and fro with his polished high boots behind the rumps of the horses and mules, which were lined up on either side of the highroad. The fair was already about to end, but Jeli had not yet showed up with the animals, beyond the bend in the road. On the scorched slopes of Calvary and the Windmill, there were still a few

a terra e l'occhio spento, e qualche pariglia di buoi, dal pelo lungo, di quelli che si vendono per pagare il fitto delle terre, che aspettavano immobili, sotto il sole cocente. Laggiù, verso la valle, la campana di San Giovanni suonava la messa grande, accompagnata dal lungo crepitìo dei mortaletti. Allora il campo della fiera sembrava trasalire, e correva un gridìo che si prolungava fra le tende dei trecconi schierate nella salita dei Galli, scendeva per le vie del paese, e sembrava ritornare dalla valle dov'era la chiesa. Viva San Giovanni!

– Santo diavolone! strillava il fattore, quell'assassino di Jeli mi farà perdere la fiera!

Le pecore levavano il muso attonito, e si mettevano a belare tutte in una volta, e anche i buoi facevano qualche passo lentamente, guardando in giro, con grandi occhi intenti.

Il fattore era così in collera perché quel giorno dovevasi pagare il fitto delle chiuse grandi, «come San Giovanni fosse arrivato sotto l'olmo,» diceva il contratto, e a completare la somma si era fatto assegnamento sulla vendita dei puledri. Intanto di puledri, e cavalli, e muli ce n'erano quanti il Signore ne aveva fatti, tutti strigliati e lucenti, e ornati di fiocchi, e nappine, e sonagli, che scodinzolavano per scacciare la noia, e voltavano la testa verso ognuno che passava, e pareva che aspettassero un'anima caritatevole che volesse comprarli.

– Si sarà messo a dormire, quell'assassino! seguitava a gridare il fattore; e mi lascia i puledri sulla pancia!

Invece Jeli aveva camminato tutta la notte acciocché i puledri arrivassero freschi alla fiera, e prendessero un buon posto nell'arrivare, ed era giunto al piano del Corvo che ancora i *tre re* non erano tramontati, e luccicavano sul *monte Arturo,* colle braccia in croce. Per la strada passavano continuamente carri, e gente a cavallo che andavano alla festa; per questo il giovanetto teneva ben aperti gli occhi, acciò i puledri, spaventati dall'insolito via vai, non si sbandassero, ma andassero uniti lungo il ciglione della strada, dietro la *bianca* che camminava diritta e tranquilla, col campanaccio al collo. Di tanto in tanto, allorché la strada correva sulla sommità delle colline, si udiva sin là la campana di San Giovanni, che anche nel bujo e nel silenzio della campagna si sentiva la festa, e

flocks of sheep, in a tight circle with their muzzles to the ground and tired eyes, and a few teams of long-haired oxen, of the type that are sold to pay the land rent, were waiting motionlessly beneath the boiling sun. Yonder, toward the valley, the St. John's Day bell[4] was calling to High Mass, accompanied by the long-drawn-out snapping of the firecrackers. Then the fairgrounds seemed to give a start, and a shouting made the rounds, becoming prolonged among the hawkers' tents aligned on Roosters' Ascent, then descending through the village streets and seeming to re-echo from the valley where the church was located: "Long live St. John!"

"The devil take it!" the steward yelled, "that scoundrel Jeli will make me miss out on the fair!"

The sheep raised their muzzles in astonishment, and all started to bleat at once, and even the oxen took a few slow steps, looking all around with big, intent eyes.

The steward was as angry as he was because on that day the rent for the big parcels of land had to be paid, "when St. John arrives under the elm tree,"[5] as the agreement stated, and to complete the sum he had been counting on the sale of the colts. Meanwhile all the colts, horses, and mules that God had created were there; currycombed and gleaming, adorned with bows, tassels, and bells, they were waving their tails to fight their boredom and turning their heads toward every passerby, seemingly awaiting a charitable soul willing to buy them.

"He's probably fallen asleep, that scoundrel!" the steward continued yelling. "And he's left me with the colts on my hands!"

But, instead, Jeli had walked all night so that the colts would be fresh when they came to the fair and would find a good spot when they got there; he had arrived at the Plain of the Crow before Orion had set, and the three stars of the Belt were twinkling over Monte Arturo.[6] Along the road there was a steady traffic of carts and people riding to the fair; therefore the young man kept his eyes wide open, so that the colts wouldn't scatter in their fright at the unaccustomed bustle, but would walk together along the road embankment behind Whitie, who was proceeding calmly in a straight line with the bell on her neck. From time to time, when the road ran along the hilltops, you could hear even the St. John's bell at that distance; even in the darkness and silence of the countryside, you could sense the festivities, and all along

---

4. Or, just possibly, "the bell at San Giovanni," if a place name is meant.   5. The village elm being a traditional place for making such agreements.   6. Literally, "before the Three Kings had set, and they were twinkling over Monte Arturo with their arms crossed."

per tutto lo stradone, lontan lontano, sin dove c'era gente a piedi o a cavallo che andava a Vizzini si udiva gridare: – Viva San Giovanni! – e i razzi salivano diritti e lucenti dietro i monti della Canziria, come le stelle che piovono in agosto.

– È come la notte di Natale! andava dicendo Jeli al ragazzo che l'aiutava a condurre il branco, – che in ogni fattoria si fa festa e luminaria, e per tutta la campagna si vedono qua e là dei fuochi.

Il ragazzo sonnecchiava, spingendo adagio adagio una gamba dietro l'altra, e non rispondeva nulla; ma Jeli che si sentiva rimescolare tutto il sangue da quella campana, non poteva star zitto, come se ognuno di quei razzi che strisciavano sul bujo taciti e lucenti dietro il monte gli sbocciassero dall'anima.

– Mara sarà andata anche lei alla festa di San Giovanni, diceva, perché ci va tutti gli anni.

E senza curarsi che Alfio il ragazzo, non rispondeva nulla:

– Tu non sai? ora Mara è alta così, che è più grande di sua madre che l'ha fatta, e quando l'ho rivista non mi pareva vero che fosse proprio quella stessa con cui si andava a cogliere i fichidindia, e a bacchiare le noci.

E si mise a cantare ad alta voce tutte le canzoni che sapeva.

– O Alfio, che dormi? gli gridò quand'ebbe finito. Bada che la *bianca* ti vien sempre dietro, bada!

– No, non dormo! rispose Alfio con voce rauca.

– La vedi la *puddara*, che sta ad ammiccarci lassù, verso Granvilla, come sparassero dei razzi anche a Santa Domenica? Poco può passare a romper l'alba; pure alla fiera arriveremo in tempo per trovare un buon posto. Ehi! morellino bello! che ci avrai la cavezza nuova, colle nappine rosse, per la fiera! e anche tu, *stellato*!

Così andava parlando all'uno e all'altro dei puledri perché si rinfrancassero sentendo la sua voce nel buio. Ma gli doleva che lo *stellato* e il *morellino* andassero alla fiera per esser venduti.

– Quando saran venduti, se ne andranno col padrone nuovo, e non si vedranno più nella mandria, com'è stato di Mara, dopo che se ne fu andata a Marineo.

– Suo padre sta benone laggiù a Marineo; ché quando andai a trovarli mi misero dinanzi pane, vino, formaggio, e ogni ben di Dio, che egli è quasi il fattore, ed ha le chiavi di ogni cosa, e avrei potuto mangiarmi tutta la fattoria se avessi voluto. Mara non mi conosceva quasi più da tanto che non ci vedevamo! e si mise a gridare: – Oh!

the highroad, way in the distance, as far as there were people walking or riding to Vizzini, you could hear the shout: "Long live St. John!" And the gleaming rockets were soaring straight up into the sky behind the mountains of Canziria, like shooting stars in August.

"It's like Christmas Eve," Jeli was saying to the boy who was helping him guide the herd, "because there are holiday illuminations in every farmhouse, and you can see bonfires all over the countryside."

The boy was dozing, slowly moving one leg after another, and he made no reply; but Jeli, who felt all his blood rushing at the sound of that bell, couldn't remain silent, as if each one of those rockets, streaking through the darkness with their silent glow, were blossoming in his soul.

"Mara has probably gone to the feast of St. John, too," he was saying, "because she goes there every year."

And, paying no heed to the continued silence of the boy, Alfio, he went on:

"Don't you know? Now Mara is as tall as this; she's taller than her mother, who gave birth to her, and when I saw her again, I couldn't believe she was really the same girl with whom I used to go and gather prickly pears and beat down walnuts."

And he started to sing aloud all the songs that he knew.

"Alfio, are you sleeping?" he shouted to him after he had finished his singing. "Watch out to make sure Whitie is always right in back of you!"

"No, I'm not sleeping," Alfio replied in a hoarse voice.

"Do you see the Pleiades[7] twinkling up there, toward Granvilla, as if rockets were being shot off at Santa Domenica, too? It can't be long before dawn breaks, and we'll get to the fair in time to find a good spot. Hey, you beautiful black colt, you'll have a new halter with red tassels for the fair. So will you, Blaze!"

He went along speaking to each of the colts that way, so that they would gain confidence hearing his voice in the darkness. But he felt bad that Blaze and Little Blackie were going to the fair to be sold.

"Once they're sold, they'll go off with their new owner, and I won't see them in the herd anymore. It was that way with Mara after she left for Marineo.

"Her father is doing very well down there in Marineo; when I went to see them they served me bread, wine, cheese, and all the good things God gives, because he's practically the steward there and he keeps the keys to everything; I could have eaten the whole farmhouse if I'd felt like it. Mara scarcely recognized me, it had been so long since

---

7. Literally, "the cluster of chickens," or something similar (Sicilian *puddu* = *pollo*).

guarda! è Jeli, il guardiano dei cavalli, quello di Tebidi! Gli è come
quando uno torna da lontano, che al vedere soltanto il cocuzzolo di
un monte gli basta a riconoscere subito il paese dove è cresciuto. La
gnà Lia non voleva che le dessi più del tu, alla Mara, ora che sua
figlia si è fatta grande, perché la gente che non sa nulla, chiacchiera
facilmente. Mara invece rideva, e sembrava che avesse infornato il
pane allora allora, tanto era rossa; apparecchiava la tavola, e spiegava la tovaglia che non pareva più quella. – O che non ti rammenti
più di Tebidi? le chiesi appena la gnà Lia fu sortita per spillare del
vino fresco dalla botte. – Sì, sì, me ne rammento, mi disse ella, a
Tebidi c'era la campana col campanile che pareva un manico di
saliera, e si suonava dal ballatoio, e c'erano pure due gatti di sasso,
che facevano le fusa sul cancello del giardino. – Io me le sentivo qui
dentro tutte quelle cose, come ella andava dicendole. Mara mi
guardava da capo a piedi con tanto d'occhi, e tornava a dire: – Come
ti sei fatto grande! e si mise pure a ridere, e mi diede uno scapac-
cione qui, sulla testa.

In tal modo Jeli, il guardiano dei cavalli, perdette il pane, perché
giusto in quel punto sopravveniva all'improvviso una carrozza che non
si era udita prima, mentre saliva l'erta passo passo, e s'era messa al
trotto com'era giunta al piano, con gran strepito di frusta e di sonagli,
quasi la portasse il diavolo. I puledri, spaventati, si sbandarono in un
lampo, che pareva un terremoto, e ce ne vollero delle chiamate, e
delle grida e degli ohi! ohi! ohi! di Jeli e del ragazzo prima di rac-
coglierli attorno alla *bianca,* la quale anch'essa trotterellava svogliatamente, col campanaccio al collo. Appena Jeli ebbe contato le sue
bestie, si accorse che mancava lo *stellato*, e si cacciò le mani nei
capelli, perché in quel posto la strada correva lungo il burrone, e fu
nel burrone che lo *stellato* si fracassò le reni, un puledro che valeva
dodici onze come dodici angeli del paradiso! Piangendo e gridando
egli andava chiamando il puledro – ahu! ahu! ahu! che non ci si
vedeva ancora. Lo *stellato* rispose finalmente dal fondo del burrone,
con un nitrito doloroso, come avesse avuto la parola, povera bestia!

– Oh! mamma mia! andavano gridando Jeli e il ragazzo. Oh! che disgrazia, mamma mia!

I viandanti che andavano alla festa, e sentivano piangere a quel
modo in mezzo al buio, domandavano cosa avessero perso; e poi,
come sapevano di che si trattava, andavano per la loro strada.

Lo *stellato* rimaneva immobile dove era caduto colle zampe in aria,
e mentre Jeli l'andava tastando per ogni dove, piangendo e parlandogli
quasi avesse potuto farsi intendere, la povera bestia rizzava il collo

we'd met, and she started shouting: 'Oh, look, it's Jeli the horseherd, the one from Tebidi!' It's like when you come home from far away, and all you need to do is see the summit of one mountain to recognize immediately the place where you grew up. Mis' Lia didn't want me to say *tu* to Mara anymore, now that her daughter is full-grown, because people who don't know the circumstances are likely to gossip. But Mara was laughing, and she was so bright and ruddy, you'd think she had just put the bread in the oven that moment; as she set the table and unfolded the tablecloth, she didn't look like the same girl. 'Don't you remember Tebidi anymore?' I asked her as soon as Mis' Lia had gone out to tap some fresh wine from the cask. 'Yes, yes, I remember,' she said, 'at Tebidi there was a bell in a tower that resembled the handle of a saltcellar, and there was music from the veranda, and there were also two stone cats that purred on the garden gate.' I felt all those things inside of me as she was mentioning them. Mara looked me up and down with wide eyes, and kept saying: 'How big you've grown!' And she also started to laugh and gave me a clout here, on the head."

That was how Jeli the horseherd, lost his means of support, because at that very moment a carriage suddenly appeared that no one had heard earlier, while it was slowly ascending the incline; but when it reached level ground, the horses had begun to trot, making a great racket of whip and bells, as if the devil were driving them. The frightened colts scattered in the twinkling of an eye—it looked like an earthquake—and it took calling, shouting, and repeated hey's by Jeli and the boy before they were reassembled around Whitie, who was also moving at a listless jogtrot, the bell on her neck. As soon as Jeli had counted his horses, he was aware that Blaze was missing. He thrust his hands into his hair, because at that spot the road ran past the gorge; and it was in the gorge that Blaze broke his back, a colt worth twelve *onze* like twelve heavenly angels! Weeping and shouting, Jeli kept calling the colt—ah-oo, ah-oo, ah-oo!—which was not yet visible. Finally Blaze answered from the bottom of the gorge with a sorrowful neigh as if he could speak, poor animal!

"Oh, God!" Jeli and the boy kept shouting. "Oh, God, what a disaster!"

The passersby on their way to the feast, hearing that kind of weeping in the dark, asked them what they had lost. Then, when they found out what it was all about, they proceeded on their way.

Blaze remained motionless where he had fallen, his legs in the air, and while Jeli felt him all over, weeping and talking to him as if he could make himself understood, the poor animal was lifting his neck

penosamente, e voltava la testa verso di lui e allora si udiva l'anelito rotto dallo spasimo.

– Qualche cosa si sarà rotto! piagnuccolava Jeli, disperato di non poter vedere nulla pel buio; e il puledro inerte come un sasso lasciava ricadere il capo di peso. Alfio rimasto sulla strada a custodia del branco, s'era rasserenato per il primo e aveva tirato fuori il pane dalla sacca. Ora il cielo s'era fatto bianchiccio e i monti tutto intorno parevano che spuntassero ad uno ad uno, neri ed alti. Dalla svolta dello stradone si cominciava a scorgere il paese, col *monte del Calvario* e *del Mulino a vento* stampato sull'albore, ancora foschi, seminati dalle chiazze bianche delle pecore, e come i buoi che pascolavano sul cocuzzolo del monte, nell'azzurro, andavano di qua e di là, sembrava che il profilo del monte stesso si animasse e formicolasse di vita. La campana dal fondo del burrone non si udiva più, i viandanti si erano fatti più rari, e quei pochi che passavano avevano fretta di arrivare alla fiera. Il povero Jeli non sapeva a qual santo votarsi in quella solitudine; lo stesso Alfio da solo non poteva giovargli per niente; perciò costui andava sbocconcellando pian piano il suo pezzo di pane.

Finalmente si vide venire a cavallo il fattore, il quale da lontano strepitava e bestemmiava accorrendo, al vedere gli animali fermi sulla strada, sicché lo stesso Alfio se la diede a gambe per la collina. Ma Jeli non si mosse d'accanto allo *stellato*. Il fattore lasciò la mula sulla strada, e scese nel burrone anche lui, cercando di aiutare il puledro ad alzarsi e tirandolo per la coda. – Lasciatelo stare! diceva Jeli bianco in viso come se si fosse fracassate le reni lui. Lasciatelo stare! Non vedete che non si può muovere, povera bestia!

Lo *stellato* infatti ad ogni movimento, e ad ogni sforzo che gli facevano fare metteva un rantolo che pareva un cristiano. Il fattore si sfogava a calci e scapaccioni su di Jeli, e tirava pei piedi gli angeli e i santi del paradiso. Allora Alfio più rassicurato era tornato sulla strada, per non lasciare le bestie senza custodia, e badava a scolparsi dicendo: – Io non ci ho colpa. Io andavo innanzi colla *bianca*.

– Qui non c'è più nulla da fare, disse alfine il fattore, dopo che si persuase che era tutto tempo perso. Qui non se ne può prendere altro che la pelle, sinché è buona.

Jeli si mise a tremare come una foglia quando vide il fattore andare a staccare lo schioppo dal basto della mula. – Levati di lì, paneperso! gli urlò il fattore, ché non so chi mi tenga dallo stenderti per terra accanto a quel puledro che valeva assai più di te, con tutto il battesimo porco che ti diede quel prete ladro!

painfully and turning his head toward him; then you could hear his uneven breathing in his pangs of agony.

"He must have broken something!" Jeli was whining, in despair because he couldn't see anything in the dark; and the colt, inert as a stone, let his head fall back heavily. Alfio, who had remained on the road in charge of the herd, had been the first to calm down, and had taken the bread out of the knapsack. Now the sky had turned whitish and the mountains all around seemed to be emerging one by one, tall and black. From the bend in the road, you could start to make out the locality, with Calvary Hill and Windmill Hill stamped against the dawn light, still dark, but dotted with the white forms of sheep; and, since the oxen grazing on the mountain summit, against the blue, were walking to and fro, the very outline of the mountain seemed to become animated and teem with life. The bell from the bottom of the gorge was no longer to be heard, the number of passersby had decreased, and those few who did go by were in a hurry to get to the fair. Poor Jeli didn't know what to do first in that lonely spot; Alfio on his own couldn't be of any help to him, and so the boy went on nibbling his piece of bread slowly.

Finally they saw, arriving on muleback, the steward, who was shouting from the distance and cursing as he approached, at the sight of the horses stationary on the road, so that Alfio ran away down the hill. But Jeli didn't leave Blaze's side. The steward left his mule on the road, and he himself climbed down into the gorge, where he tried to help the colt stand up, pulling him by the tail. "Let him be!" Jeli was saying, his face as white as if *he* were the one with a broken back. "Let him be! Don't you see he can't move, poor animal!"

Indeed, at every movement, at every effort they made him attempt, Blaze emitted a death rattle like a human being's. The steward vented his anger on Jeli with kicks and cuffs, and was cursing all the angels and saints in Paradise. By then Alfio, more reassured, had returned to the road, so that the horses wouldn't be left without supervision; he was carefully excusing himself, saying: "It's not my fault. I was walking up front with Whitie."

"There's nothing more to be done here," the steward finally said, after he was convinced it was all a waste of time. "All we can salvage from this is his hide, while it's still any good."

Jeli began trembling like a leaf when he saw the steward go and detach his rifle from the mule's packsaddle. "Get away from there, you good-for-nothing!" the steward howled at him, "because I don't know how I'm keeping myself from stretching you out on the ground next to that colt, which was worth so much more than you, for all that damned baptism the thieving priest gave you!"

Lo *stellato,* non potendosi muovere, volgeva il capo con grandi occhi sbarrati quasi avesse inteso ogni cosa, e il pelo gli si arricciava ad onde, lungo le costole, sembrava ci corresse sotto un brivido. In tal modo il fattore uccise sul luogo lo *stellato* per cavarne almeno la pelle, e il rumore fiacco che fece dentro le carni vive il colpo tirato a bruciapelo parve a Jeli di sentirselo dentro di sé.

– Ora se vuoi sapere il mio consiglio, gli lasciò detto il fattore, cerca di non farti veder più dal padrone per quel salario che avanzi, perché te lo pagherebbe salato assai!

Il fattore se ne andò insieme ad Alfio, cogli altri puledri che non si voltavano nemmeno a vedere dove rimanesse lo *stellato,* e andavano strappando l'erba dal ciglione. Lo *stellato* se ne stava solo nel burrone, aspettando che venissero a scuoiarlo, cogli occhi ancora spalancati, e le quattro zampe distese, che allora solo aveva potuto distenderle. Jeli, ora che aveva visto come il fattore aveva potuto prender di mira il puledro che penosamente voltava la testa sbigottito, e gli fosse bastato il cuore per tirare il colpo, non piangeva più, e stava a guardare lo *stellato* duro duro, seduto sul sasso, fin quando arrivarono gli uomini che dovevano prendersi la pelle.

Adesso poteva andarsene a spasso, a godersi la festa, o starsene in piazza tutto il giorno, a vedere i galantuomini nel caffè, come meglio gli piaceva, ché non aveva più né pane, né tetto, e bisognava cercarsi un padrone, se pure qualcuno lo voleva, dopo la disgrazia dello *stellato.*

Le cose del mondo vanno così: mentre Jeli andava cercando un padrone colla sacca ad armacollo e il bastone in mano, la banda suonava in piazza allegramente, coi pennacchi nel cappello, in mezzo a una folla di berrette bianche fitte come le mosche, e i galantuomini stavano a godersela seduti nel caffè. Tutta la gente era vestita da festa, come gli animali della fiera, e in un canto della piazza c'era una donna colla gonnella corta e le calze color di carne che pareva colle gambe nude, e picchiava sulla gran cassa, davanti a un gran lenzuolo dipinto, dove si vedeva una carneficina di cristiani, col sangue che colava a torrenti, e nella folla che stava a guardare a bocca aperta c'era pure massaro Cola, il quale lo conosceva da quando stava a Passanitello, e gli disse che il padrone glielo avrebbe trovato lui, poiché compare Isidoro Macca cercava un guardiano per i porci. – Però non dir nulla dello *stellato,* gli raccomandò massaro Cola. Una disgrazia come questa può accadere a tutti, nel mondo. Ma è meglio non dir nulla.

Andarono perciò a cercare compare Macca, il quale era al ballo, e nel tempo che Massaro Cola andò a fare l'imbasciata Jeli aspettò sulla

Blaze, unable to move, was turning his head with big goggling eyes, as if he had understood everything, and his skin was rippling in waves along his ribs as if a shudder were running through him. And so, on the spot, the steward killed Blaze so he could get at least his hide out of him; it seemed to Jeli that he felt in his own body the dull thud that the point-blank shot made in the living flesh.

"Now, if you want my advice," the steward declared, "don't try to see the proprietor anymore to ask for the wages he still owes you, because you wouldn't like the way he'd give them to you!"

The steward left along with Alfio and the remaining colts, which didn't even turn around to see what had become of Blaze, but were pulling up grass from the embankment. Blaze was left alone in the gorge, waiting for the skinners to come, his eyes still wide open and his four legs stretched out, because only in death had he been able to extend them. Now that Jeli had seen how the steward had been able to take aim at the colt, which was painfully turning its head in a panic, and how he had had the heart to shoot, he was no longer weeping, but stood there staring fixedly at Blaze. He remained seated on a rock until the men came to procure the hide.

Now he could stroll at leisure to enjoy the feast, or stay in the village square all day long watching the gentry in the café—whatever he liked—because he no longer had food coming in or a roof over his head. He had to look for an employer, if anyone would still take him on after the Blaze catastrophe.

That's how things go in this world: while Jeli was seeking employment, his knapsack slung over his shoulder and his staff in his hand, the band members were playing cheerfully in the square with plumes on their hats amid a crowd of white peasant caps as thick as flies, and the gentry were sitting in the café enjoying themselves. Everyone was wearing their holiday best, just like the animals at the fair, and in one corner of the square there was a woman with a short skirt and flesh-colored stockings that made her look barelegged; she was beating on a bass drum in front of a large painted cloth depicting a massacre of Christian martyrs, their blood flowing in torrents. In the crowd that was looking on open-mouthed was also farmer Cola, who had known Jeli ever since he had been at Passanitello. He told him he himself would find employment for him, because neighbor Isidoro Macca was looking for a swineherd. "But don't say anything about Blaze," farmer Cola advised him. "An accident like that can happen to anyone in the world. But it's better not to mention it."

And so they went looking for neighbor Macca, who was at the dance; while farmer Cola went to negotiate, Jeli waited on the road

strada, in mezzo alla folla che stava a guardare dalla porta della bottega. Nella stanzaccia c'era un mondo di gente che saltava e si di-
vertiva, tutti rossi e scalmanati, e facevano un gran pestare di scarponi
sull'ammattonato, che non si udiva nemmeno il ron ron del contrabasso, e appena finiva una suonata, che costava un grano, levavano il
dito per far segno che ne volevano un'altra; e quello del contrabasso
faceva una croce col carbone sulla parete, per fare il conto all'ultimo,
e ricominciava da capo. – Costoro li spendono senza pensarci, s'andava dicendo Jeli, e vuol dire che hanno la tasca piena, e non sono in
angustia come me, per difetto di un padrone, se sudano e s'affannano
a saltare per loro piacere come se li pagassero a giornata! – Massaro
Cola tornò dicendo che compare Macca non aveva bisogno di nulla.
Allora Jeli volse le spalle e se ne andò mogio mogio.

Mara stava di casa verso Sant'Antonio, dove le case s'arrampicano
sul monte, di fronte al vallone della Canziria, tutto verde di fichidindia, e colle ruote dei mulini che spumeggiavano in fondo, sul torrente;
ma Jeli non ebbe il coraggio di andare da quelle parti ora che non
l'avevano voluto nemmeno per guardare i porci, e girandolando in
mezzo alla folla che lo urtava e lo spingeva senza curarsi di lui, gli
pareva di essere più solo di quando era coi puledri nelle lande di
Passanitello, e si sentiva voglia di piangere. Finalmente massaro
Agrippino lo incontrò nella piazza, che andava di qua e di là colle braccia ciondoloni, godendosi la festa, e cominciò a gridargli dietro – Oh!
Jeli! oh! – e se lo menò a casa. Mara era in gran gala, con tanto d'orecchini che le sbattevano sulle guancie, e stava sull'uscio, colle mani
sulla pancia, cariche d'anelli, ad aspettare che imbrunisse per andare
a vedere i fuochi.

– Oh! gli disse Mara, sei venuto anche tu per la festa di San Giovanni!

Jeli non avrebbe voluto entrare perché era vestito male, però massaro Agrippino lo spinse per le spalle dicendogli che non si vedevano
allora per la prima volta, e che si sapeva che era venuto per la fiera coi
puledri del padrone. La gnà Lia gli versò un bel bicchiere di vino e
vollero condurlo con loro a veder la luminaria, insieme alle comari ed
ai vicini.

Arrivando in piazza, Jeli rimase a bocca aperta dalla meraviglia;
tutta la piazza pareva un mare di fuoco, come quando si incendiavano
le stoppie, per il gran numero di razzi che i devoti accendevano sotto
gli occhi del santo, il quale stava a godderseli dall'imboccatura del
Rosario, tutto nero sotto il baldacchino d'argento. I devoti andavano e
venivano fra le fiamme come tanti diavoli, e c'era persino una donna
discinta, spettinata, cogli occhi fuori della testa, che accendeva i razzi

amid the crowd of onlookers at the inn door. In the public room there was a throng of people dancing and having fun, all red and sweaty, stamping their heavy shoes on the tiled floor so that not even the rumble of the bass fiddle could be heard. As soon as one number was over (they cost a *grano* each), they lifted a finger to show they wanted yet another; the bass player would make a cross on the wall with charcoal, to tot up the final reckoning, and he'd start over again. "These folks spend their money without counting," Jeli kept saying, "which means they have full pockets, and aren't hard up like me, for want of employment. They're sweating and out of breath from dancing for pleasure as if they were getting paid by the day for it!" Farmer Cola came back to say that neighbor Macca didn't need anyone. Then Jeli turned around and went off dejectedly.

Mara's home was near Sant'Antonio, where the houses climb up the hill, facing the valley of Canziria, all green with prickly-pear cactus, and with the watermill wheels that froth down below in the millstream; but Jeli didn't have the heart to go there, now that he had been rejected even as a swineherd; roaming among the crowd, which jostled and shoved him, taking no heed of him, he felt more lonely than when he had been with the colts on the Passanitello heaths, and he felt like crying. Finally farmer Agrippino met him in the square; he had been walking to and fro with dangling arms, enjoying the merrymaking, and now he began to shout after him: "Hey, Jeli, hey!" And he took him home with him. Mara was all dressed up, with big earrings that swung against her cheeks; she was standing in the doorway, her ring-laden hands on her stomach, waiting for dusk so she could go see the fireworks.

"Oh," Mara said to him, "you've come for St. John's Day, too!"

Jeli wouldn't have gone in because he wasn't properly dressed, but farmer Agrippino pushed him in from behind, saying they hadn't just met and everyone knew he had come for the fair with his master's colts. Mis' Lia poured him a nice glass of wine, and they wanted to take him along to see the illuminations, together with their male and female neighbors.

When they got to the square, Jeli's mouth dropped open at the wonder of it all; the whole square resembled a sea of flames, just as when the stubble is burned, because of the great number of rockets that pious people were lighting in front of the saint, who was standing and enjoying it at the entrance to the Rosary Chapel, all in black beneath his silver canopy. The pious were walking back and forth amid the flames like so many devils, and there was even an untidy, disheveled woman, her

anch'essa, e un prete colla sottana nera, senza cappello, che pareva un ossesso dalla devozione.

– Quello lì è il figliuolo di massaro Neri, il fattore della Salonia, e spende più di dieci lire di razzi! diceva la gnà Lia accennando a un giovinotto che andava in giro per la piazza tenendo due razzi alla volta nelle mani, al pari di due candele, sicché tutte le donne se lo mangiavano cogli occhi, e gli gridavano – Viva San Giovanni.

– Suo padre è ricco e possiede più di venti capi di bestiame, aggiungeva massaro Agrippino.

Mara sapeva anche che aveva portato lo stendardo grande, nella processione e lo reggeva diritto come un fuso, tanto era forte e bel giovane.

Il figlio di massaro Neri pareva che li sentisse, e accendesse i suoi razzi per la Mara, facendo la ruota dinanzi a lei; e dopo che i fuochi furono cessati si accompagnò con loro, e li condusse al ballo, e al cosmorama, dove si vedeva il mondo vecchio e il mondo nuovo, pagando lui per tutti, anche per Jeli il quale andava dietro la comitiva come un cane senza padrone, a veder ballare il figlio di massaro Neri colla Mara, la quale girava in tondo e si accoccolava come una colombella sulle tegole, e teneva tesa con bel garbo una cocca del grembiale, e il figlio di massaro Neri saltava come un puledro, tanto che la gnà Lia piangeva come una bimba dalla consolazione, e massaro Agrippino faceva cenno di sì col capo, che la cosa andava bene.

Infine, quando furono stanchi, se ne andarono di qua e di là *nel passeggio,* trascinati dalla folla come fossero in mezzo a una fiumana, a vedere i trasparenti illuminati, dove tagliavano il collo a San Giovanni, che avrebbe fatto pietà agli stessi turchi, e il santo sgambettava come un capriuolo sotto la mannaja. Lì vicino c'era la banda che suonava, sotto un gran paracqua di legno tutto illuminato, e nella piazza c'era una folla tanto grande che mai s'erano visti alla fiera tanti cristiani.

Mara andava al braccio del figlio di massaro Neri come una signorina, e gli parlava nell'orecchio, e rideva che pareva si divertisse assai. Jeli non ne poteva più dalla stanchezza, e si mise a dormire seduto sul marciapiede fin quando lo svegliarono i primi petardi del fuoco d'artifizio. In quel momento Mara era sempre al fianco del figlio di massaro Neri, gli si appoggiava colle due mani intrecciate sulla spalla, e al lume dei fuochi colorati sembrava ora tutta bianca ed ora tutta rossa. Quando scapparono pel cielo gli ultimi razzi in folla, il figlio di massaro Neri si voltò verso di lei, verde in viso, e le diede un bacio.

Jeli non disse nulla, ma in quel punto gli si cambiò in veleno tutta la festa che aveva goduto sin allora, e tornò a pensare a tutte le sue

eyes bulging out of her head, who was also lighting rockets, and a hatless priest in a black cassock who seemed obsessed with piety.

"There's the son of farmer Neri, the steward at Salonia; he's offering more than ten *lire*'s worth of rockets!" Mis' Lia, pointing to a young man who was walking around the square holding two rockets at once, like two candles, so that all the women were gobbling him up with their eyes and shouting to him: "Long live St. John!"

"His father is rich and owns over twenty head of cattle," farmer Agrippino added.

Mara also knew that he had carried the big banner in the procession, holding it up as straight as a spindle, he was such a strong, well-built lad.

Farmer Neri's son seemed to hear them and to be lighting his rockets for Mara, showing off in front of her. After the fireworks were over, he joined their party and led them to the dance and the cosmorama, with its views of the Old and the New World; he paid for everyone, including Jeli, who followed behind the group like a dog without a master, watching farmer Neri's son dance with Mara, who spun around and plumped down, like a little dove on the rooftiles, smartly holding out one corner of her pinafore, while farmer Neri's son bounded like a colt, so that Mis' Lia wept like a baby from contentment, and farmer Agrippino nodded his head approvingly to see matters going so well.

Finally, when they were tired, they strolled to and fro on the "promenade," carried along by the crowd as if in midcurrent of a river, looking at the illuminated transparencies in which St. John was depicted having his head cut off, in such a way that even the Turks themselves would pity him, while he was kicking up his legs like a young deer beneath the axe. Nearby the band was playing under a big wooden rainshed that was all lit up, and the square contained such a big crowd that never before had so many people been seen at the fair.

Mara gave her arm to farmer Neri's son like a fine young lady, whispered in his ear, and laughed so much that she seemed to be enjoying herself immensely. Jeli was worn out with fatigue, and fell asleep sitting on the sidewalk until he was awakened by the first bursts of the fireworks. At that moment Mara was still by the side of farmer Neri's son, leaning on him with her two hands joined on his shoulder; in the light of the multicolored fireworks she looked now all white, now all red. When the final mass of rockets soared into the sky, farmer Neri's son turned toward her, his face in a green glow, and kissed her.

Jeli said nothing, but at that moment all the enjoyment of the feast up till then turned into poison for him, and his mind reverted to all

disgrazie che gli erano uscite di mente, e che era rimasto senza padrone, e non sapeva più che fare, né dove andare, e non aveva più né pane né tetto, che potevano mangiarselo i cani al pari dello *stellato* il quale era rimasto in fondo al burrone, scuoiato sino agli zoccoli.

Intanto attorno a lui la gente faceva gazzarra ancora nel buio che si era fatto, Mara colle compagne saltava, e cantava per la stradicciola sassosa, mentre tornavano a casa.

– Buona notte! buona notte! andavano dicendo le compagne a misura che si lasciavano per la strada.

Mara dava la buona notte, che pareva che cantasse, tanta contentezza ci aveva nella voce e il figlio di massaro Neri poi sembrava proprio che non volesse lasciarla andare più, mentre massaro Agrippino e la gnà Lia litigavano nell'aprire l'uscio di casa. Nessuno badava a Jeli, soltanto massaro Agrippino si rammentò di lui, e gli chiese:

– Ed ora dove andrai?

– Non lo so – disse Jeli.

– Domani vieni a trovarmi, e t'aiuterò a cercar dall'allogarti. Per stanotte torna in piazza dove siamo stati a sentir suonar la banda; un posto su qualche panchetta lo troverai, e a dormire allo scoperto tu devi esserci avvezzo.

Jeli c'era avvezzo, ma quello che gli faceva pena era che Mara non gli diceva nulla, e lo lasciasse a quel modo sull'uscio come un pezzente; e il domani, tornando a cercar di massaro Agrippino, appena furono soli colla ragazza le disse:

– Oh gnà Mara! come li scordate gli amici!

– Oh, sei tu Jeli? disse Mara. No, io non ti ho scordato. Ma ero così stanca dopo i fuochi!

– Gli volete bene almeno, al figlio di massaro Neri? chiese lui voltando e rivoltando il bastone fra le mani.

– Che discorsi andate facendo! rispose bruscamente la gnà Mara. Mia madre è di là che sente tutto.

Massaro Agrippino gli trovò da allogarlo come pecoraio alla Salonia, dov'era fattore massaro Neri, ma siccome Jeli era poco pratico del mestiere si dovette contentare di una grossa diminuzione di salario.

Adesso badava alle sue pecore, e ad imparare come si fa il formaggio, e la ricotta, e il caciocavallo, e ogni altro frutto di mandra, ma fra le chiacchiere che si facevano alla sera nel cortile cogli altri pastori e contadini, mentre le donne sbucciavano le fave della minestra, se si veniva a parlare del figlio di massaro Neri, il quale si prendeva in moglie Mara di massaro Agrippino, Jeli non diceva più nulla, e nemmeno osava di aprir bocca. Una volta che il campajo lo motteggiò

the disasters he had temporarily forgotten: that he was unemployed, and didn't know what to do or where to go; that he had no means of support or any roof over his head now; that the dogs could come and eat him the way they'd eat Blaze, who was still at the bottom of the gorge, skinned to his hooves.

Meanwhile, in the darkness that had set in around him, people were still raising a hubbub; Mara was dancing with her girlfriends and singing as they returned home over the stony path.

"Good night! Good night!" her friends would say as they took their leave along the way.

Mara said good night as if she were singing, there was so much satisfaction in her voice, and then farmer Neri's son seemed really unwilling to let her proceed, while farmer Agrippino and Mis' Lia argued as they opened the house door. No one paid any attention to Jeli; only farmer Agrippino remembered him, and asked him:

"So where will you go now?"

"I don't know," Jeli said.

"Come and see me tomorrow, and I'll help you find a situation. For tonight, go back to the square where we were listening to the band; you'll find a place on some bench, and you must be used to sleeping in the open air."

Jeli *was* used to it, but the thing that saddened him was that Mara said nothing to him, but left him on the doorstep that way like a pauper. The next day, when he returned to look for farmer Agrippino, as soon as he was alone with the girl he said:

"Oh, Mis' Mara, how you forget your friends!"

"Oh, is that you, Jeli?" Mara said. "No, I haven't forgotten you. But I was so tired after the fireworks!"

"Do you love him at least, farmer Neri's son?" he asked, turning his staff around and around in his hands.

"What guff you do talk!" Mara replied brusquely. "My mother's over there and can hear everything."

Farmer Agrippino found him a situation as shepherd at Salonia, where farmer Neri was the steward, but since Jeli was inexperienced at the job, he had to be content with a big cut in pay.

Now he looked after his sheep, learning how cheese, ricotta, caciocavallo, and all other sheep-milk products are made. But amid the evening gossip of the other herdsmen and peasants in the courtyard, while the women were shelling the beans for the soup, whenever the subject of conversation turned to farmer Neri's son, who was going to marry farmer Agrippino's Mara, Jeli stopped talking, and didn't even venture to open his mouth. Once, when the chief shepherd laughed

dicendogli che Mara non aveva voluto saperne più di lui, dopo che
tutti avevano detto che sarebbero stati marito e moglie, Jeli che badava alla pentola in cui bolliva il latte, rispose facendo sciogliere il
caglio adagio adagio:

– Ora Mara si è fatta più bella col crescere, che sembra una
signora.

Però siccome egli era paziente e laborioso, imparò presto ogni cosa
del mestiere meglio di uno che ci fosse nato, e siccome era avvezzo a
star colle bestie amava le sue pecore come se le avesse fatte lui, e
quindi il *male* alla Salonia non faceva tanta strage, e la mandra pro-
sperava ch'era un piacere per massaro Neri tutte le volte che veniva
alla fattoria, tanto che ad anno nuovo si persuase ad indurre il
padrone perché aumentasse il salario di Jeli, sicché costui venne ad
avere quasi quello che prendeva col fare il guardiano dei cavalli. Ed
erano danari bene spesi, ché Jeli non badava a contar le miglia e
miglia per cercare i migliori pascoli ai suoi animali, e se le pecore
figliavano o erano malate se le portava a pascolare dentro le bisaccie
dell'asinello, e si recava in collo gli agnelli che gli belavano sulla faccia col muso fuori del sacco, e gli poppavano le orecchie. Nella nevi-
cata famosa della notte di Santa Lucia la neve cadde alta quattro
palmi nel *lago morto* alla Salonia, e tutto all'intorno per miglia e
miglia che non si vedeva altro per tutta la campagna, come venne il
giorno, – e delle pecore non sarebbero rimaste nemmeno le orecchie,
se Jeli non si fosse alzato nella notte tre o quattro volte a cacciare le
pecore pel chiuso, così le povere bestie si scuotevano la neve di
dosso, e non rimasero seppellite come tante ce ne furono nelle mandre vicine – a quel che disse Massaro Agrippino quando venne a
dare un'occhiata ad un campicello di fave che ci aveva alla Salonia, e
disse pure che di quell'altra storia del figlio di massaro Neri, il quale
doveva sposare sua figlia Mara, non era vero niente, ché Mara aveva
tutt'altro per il capo.

– Se avevano detto che dovevano sposarsi a Natale, disse Jeli.

– Non è vero niente, non dovevano sposare nessuno; tutte chiacchiere di gente invidiosa che si immischia negli affari altrui; rispose
massaro Agrippino.

Però il campajo, il quale la sapeva più lunga, per averne sentito parlare in piazza, quando andava in paese la domenica, raccontò invece la
cosa tale e quale com'era, dopo che massaro Agrippino se ne fu
andato. Non si sposavano più perché il figlio di massaro Neri aveva

at him, saying that Mara hadn't wanted to have anything more to do with him, after everyone had said they'd be man and wife one day, Jeli, who was watching the pot in which the milk was boiling, answered as he slowly separated out the curds:

"Now that she's grown up, Mara has become more beautiful, and she looks like a fine young lady."

But, since he was patient and diligent, he quickly learned all the details of his job better than some people who are born to it; and since he was accustomed to be around animals, he loved his sheep as though they were his children; therefore the sheep disease wasn't as deadly at Salonia, and the flock prospered so well that farmer Neri was pleased every time he visited the farmhouse—until, at the new year, he decided to persuade the proprietor to raise Jeli's pay. Thus he came to earn nearly as much as he had when he herded the horses. And it was money well spent, because Jeli didn't trouble to count the miles and miles he covered in quest of the best grazing for his flock, and when the ewes lambed or were sick he'd transport them to the pasture in the donkey's saddlebags, and would carry on his shoulders the lambs, which bleated in his face, their noses protruding from the sack, and sucked at his ears. In the unforgettable snowstorm on St. Lucy's night,[8] when the snow fell to a depth of four spans on the Dead Lake at Salonia, and for miles and miles around, so that nothing else could be seen in the whole countryside when day came, not even the ears of the sheep would have been left showing if Jeli hadn't gotten up three or four times during the night to drive the flock into the fold, so that the poor animals could shake off the snow that was on them, and weren't buried as so many others were in the neighboring flocks, according to what farmer Agrippino said when he came to inspect a small beanfield he had at Salonia. He also said that that other story about farmer Neri's son going to marry his daughter Mara hadn't a grain of truth in it, since Mara had quite other plans in her head.

"But people said they were to be married at Christmas," Jeli said.

"It's not true at all, they weren't getting married to anybody; it was all the gossip of envious people butting into other folks' business," farmer Agrippino replied.

But the chief shepherd, who knew better because he had heard the matter discussed in the square when he visited the village on Sunday, told the events exactly as they had occurred, after farmer Agrippino had left. They were no longer getting married because it had come to

---

8. December 13.

risaputo che Mara di massaro Agrippino se la intendeva con don Alfonso, il signorino, il quale aveva conosciuta Mara da piccola; e massaro Neri aveva detto che il suo ragazzo voleva che fosse onorato come suo padre, e delle corna in casa non ne voleva altre che quelle dei suoi buoi.

Jeli era lì presente anche lui, seduto in circolo cogli altri a colezione, e in quel momento stava affettando il pane. Egli non disse nulla, ma l'appetito gli andò via per quel giorno.

Mentre conduceva al pascolo le pecore tornò a pensare a Mara quando era ragazzina, che stavano insieme tutto il giorno e andavano nella *valle del Jacitano* e sul *poggio alla Croce,* ed ella stava a guardarlo col mento in aria mentre egli si arrampicava a prendere i nidi sulle cime degli alberi; e pensava anche a don Alfonso il quale veniva a trovarlo dalla villa vicina e si sdraiavano bocconi sull'erba a stuzzicare con un fuscellino i nidi di grilli. Tutte quelle cose andava rimuginando per ore ed ore, seduto sull'orlo del fossato, tenendosi i ginocchi fra le braccia, e i noci alti di Tebidi, e le folte macchie dei valloni, e le pendici delle colline verdi di sommacchi, e gli ulivi grigi che si addossavano nella valle come nebbia, e i tetti rossi del casamento, e il campanile «che sembrava un manico di saliera» fra gli aranci del giardino. – Qui la campagna gli si stendeva dinanzi brulla, deserta, chiazzata dall'erba riarsa, sfumando silenziosa nell'afa lontana.

In primavera, appena i baccelli delle fave cominciavano a piegare il capo, Mara venne alla Salonia col babbo e la mamma, e il ragazzo e l'asinello, a raccogliere le fave, e tutti insieme venivano a dormire alla fattoria per quei due o tre giorni che durò la raccolta. Jeli in tal modo vedeva la ragazza mattina e sera, e spesso sedevano accanto sul muricciuolo dell'ovile, a discorrere insieme, mentre il ragazzo contava le pecore. – Mi pare d'essere a Tebidi, diceva Mara, quando eravamo piccoli, e stavamo sul ponticello della viottola.

Jeli si rammentava di ogni cosa anche lui, sebbene non dicesse nulla perché era stato sempre un ragazzo giudizioso e di poche parole.

Finita la raccolta, alla vigilia della partenza, Mara venne a salutare il giovanotto, nel tempo che ei stava facendo la ricotta, ed era tutto intento a raccogliere il siero colla cazza. – Ora ti dico addio, gli disse ella, perché domani torniamo a Vizzini.

– Come sono andate le fave?

– Male sono andate! la *lupa* le ha mangiate tutte quest'anno.

the attention of farmer Neri's son that farmer Agrippino's Mara had an "understanding" with Don Alfonso, the young gentleman, who had known Mara since she was little; and farmer Neri had said that his boy wanted to be respected like his father and didn't want any horns in his house except those of his oxen.

Jeli was also present, seated in the lunch circle with the rest. At that moment he was slicing the bread. He said nothing, but he lost his appetite for the rest of that day.

While he was leading his flock to the pasture, his thoughts turned back to Mara as a little girl, when they kept each other company all day long, going to the Valley of Jacitano and Cross Hill, and she'd stand there looking at him with her chin in the air while he climbed up to gather nests in the treetops. He also thought back to Don Alfonso, who used to come from the nearby country house to meet him, and how they'd stretch out on their bellies in the grass and poke crickets' nests with a twig. He kept on ruminating over all those things for hours and hours, sitting on the edge of the ditch, his knees clasped in his arms: the tall walnut trees at Tebidi, the dense shrubbery in the ravines, the hillsides green with sumac, the gray olive trees clustering in the valley like mist, the red roofs of the housing compound, and the bell tower that "resembled the handle of a saltcellar" amid the orange trees in the orchard. Here, the countryside that spread out in front of him was bleak, deserted, dotted with parched grass, fading away silently into the sultry distance.

In spring, as soon as the beanpods began to bend their heads, Mara came to Salonia with her father and mother, the boy and the donkey, to pick the beans, and they'd all come to sleep in the farmhouse for the two or three days that the picking lasted. In that way Jeli saw the girl morning and evening, and they frequently sat next to the low wall of the sheepfold, talking to each other while the boy counted the sheep. "I feel as if I were at Tebidi, when we were small," Mara said, "and we stood on the little bridge on the path."

Jeli, too, remembered everything, though he said nothing about it because he had always been a judicious lad, and one of few words.

After the beanpicking, on the eve of departure, Mara came to take her leave of the young man, at a time when he was making ricotta and was fully concentrated on collecting the whey with the big iron spoon. "I'm saying good-bye now," she said, "because tomorrow we're going back to Vizzini."

"How did the beans turn out?"

"Badly! The 'wolf' weed[9] ate them all up this year."

---

9. Or: "dry rot."

– Dipende dalla pioggia che è stata scarsa, disse Jeli, noi siamo stati costretti ad uccidere anche le agnelle perché non avevano da mangiare; su tutta la Salonia non è venuta tre dita di erba.

– Ma a te poco te ne importa. Il salario l'hai sempre, buona o mal'annata!

– Sì, è vero, disse lui: ma mi rincresce dare quelle povere bestie in mano al beccajo.

– Ti ricordi quando sei venuto per la festa di San Giovanni, ed eri rimasto senza padrone?

– Sì, me ne ricordo.

– Fu mio padre che ti allogò qui, da massaro Neri.

– E tu perché non l'hai sposato il figlio di massaro Neri?

– Perché non c'era la volontà di Dio. Mio padre è stato sfortunato, riprese di lì a poco. Dacché ce ne siamo andati a Marineo ogni cosa ci è riescita male. La fava, il seminato, quel pezzetto di vigna che ci abbiamo lassù. Poi mio fratello è andato soldato, e ci è morta pure una mula che valeva quarant'onze.

– Lo so, rispose Jeli, la mula baia!

– Ora che abbiamo perso la roba, chi vuoi che mi sposi?

Mara andava sminuzzando uno sterpolino di pruno, mentre parlava, col mento sul seno, e gli occhi bassi, e col gomito stuzzicava un po' il gomito di Jeli, senza badarci. Ma Jeli cogli occhi sulla zangola anche lui non rispondeva nulla; ed ella riprese:

– A Tebidi dicevano che saremmo stati marito e moglie, lo rammenti?

– Sì, disse Jeli, e posò la cazza sull'orlo della zangola. Ma io sono un povero pecoraio e non posso pretendere alla figlia di un massaro come sei tu.

La Mara rimase un pochino zitta e poi disse:

– Se tu mi vuoi, io per me ti piglio volentieri.

– Davvero?

– Sì, davvero.

– E massaro Agrippino che cosa dirà?

– Mio padre dice che ora il mestiere lo sai, e tu non sei di quelli che vanno a spendere il loro salario, ma di un soldo ne fai due, e non mangi per non consumare il pane, così arriverai ad aver delle pecore anche tu, e ti farai ricco.

– Se è così, conchiuse Jeli, ti piglio volentieri anch'io.

– To'! gli disse Mara come si era fatto buio, e le pecore andavano tacendosi a poco a poco. Se vuoi un bacio adesso te lo dò, perché saremo marito e moglie.

"It's a matter of the rainfall, which has been sparse," Jeli said. "We were forced to slaughter even the ewe lambs because they had nothing to eat. On all of Salonia the grass didn't get three fingers high."

"But you don't care much about that. You always get paid whether the year is good or bad!"

"Yes, that's true," he said, "but I don't enjoy handing those poor creatures over to the butcher."

"Remember when you came for the feast of St. John, and you had lost your job?"

"Yes, I remember."

"It was my father who found you this situation with farmer Neri."

"Why didn't you marry farmer Neri's son?"

"Because it wasn't the will of God! . . . My father has been unlucky," she resumed shortly afterward. "Ever since we moved to Marineo, everything has turned out badly for us. The beans, the grain, that tiny vineyard we have up there. Then my brother went into the army, and on top of that a mule worth forty *onze* died on us."

"I know," Jeli replied, "the bay mule."

"Now that we've lost our possessions, who do you expect would marry me?"

Mara was breaking a thornbush twig into little pieces while she spoke, her chin on her bosom and her eyes cast down; with her elbow she was poking Jeli's elbow a little without paying attention. But Jeli, whose eyes were on the ricotta vessel, didn't make any reply, and she continued:

"At Tebidi people used to say we'd be man and wife, remember?"

"Yes," Jeli said, placing the iron spoon on the rim of the vessel. "But I'm just a poor shepherd, and I can't ask the hand of a tenant farmer's daughter like you."

Mara remained silent for a bit, then said:

"If you'll have me, *I'd* gladly take *you*."

"Really?"

"Yes, really."

"And what will farmer Agrippino say?"

"My father says that by now you know your new job, and you're not one of those who squander their pay; rather, you make two *soldi* out of every one, and you eat sparingly to save bread, so that one day you'll have sheep of your own and get rich."

"If that's how things are," Jeli concluded, "I'll gladly take you, too."

"A deal!" said Mara. It had gotten dark, and the sheep were gradually growing quiet. "If you want a kiss now, I'll give you one, because we're going to be married."

Jeli se lo prese in santa pace, e non sapendo che dire soggiunse:

– Io t'ho sempre voluto bene, anche quando volevi lasciarmi pel figlio di massaro Neri; ma non ebbe cuore di dirgli di quell'altro.

– Non lo vedi? eravamo destinati! conchiuse Mara.

Massaro Agrippino infatti disse di sì, e la gnà Lia mise insieme presto presto un giubbone nuovo, e un paio di brache di velluto per il genero. Mara era bella e fresca come una rosa, con quella mantellina bianca che sembrava l'agnello pasquale, e quella collana d'ambra che le faceva il collo bianco; sicché Jeli quando andava per le strade al fianco di lei, camminava impalato, tutto vestito di panno e di velluto nuovo, e non osava soffiarsi il naso, col fazzoletto di seta rosso, per non farsi scorgere, e i vicini e tutti quelli che sapevano la storia di Don Alfonso gli ridevano sul naso. Quando Mara disse *sissignore,* e il prete gliela diede in moglie con un gran crocione, Jeli se la condusse a casa, e gli parve che gli avessero dato tutto l'oro della Madonna, e tutte le terre che aveva visto cogli occhi.

– Ora che siamo marito e moglie, – le disse giunti a casa, seduto di faccia a lei e facendosi piccino piccino, – ora che siamo marito e moglie posso dirtelo che non mi par vero come tu m'abbia voluto . . . mentre avresti potuto prenderne tanti meglio di me . . . così bella e graziosa come sei! . . .

Il poveraccio non sapeva dirle altro, e non capiva nei panni nuovi dalla contentezza di vedersi Mara per la casa, che rassettava e toccava ogni cosa, e faceva la padrona. Egli non trovava il verso di spicciarsi dall'uscio per tornarsene alla Salonia; quando fu venuto il lunedì, indugiava nell'assettare sul basto dell'asinello le bisacce e il tabarro e il paracqua incerato. – Tu dovresti venirtene alla Salonia anche te! diceva alla moglie che stava a guardarlo dalla soglia. Tu dovresti venirtene con me. – Ma la donna si mise a ridere, e gli rispose che ella non era nata a far la pecoraia, e non aveva nulla da andare a farci alla Salonia.

Infatti Mara non era nata a far la pecoraia, e non ci era avvezza alla tramontana di gennaio quando le mani si irrigidiscono sul bastone, e sembra che vi caschino le unghie, e ai furiosi acquazzoni, in cui l'acqua vi penetra fino alle ossa, e alla polvere soffocante delle strade, quando le pecore camminano sotto il sole cocente, e al giaciglio duro e al pane muffito, e alle lunghe giornate silenziose e solitarie, in cui per la campagna arsa non si vede altro di lontano, rare volte, che qualche contadino nero dal sole, il quale si spinge innanzi silenzioso l'asinello, per la strada bianca e interminabile.

Jeli took the kiss with calm pleasure. Not knowing what to say, he added: "I've always loved you, even when you wanted to leave me for farmer Neri's son." But he didn't have the courage to mention the other man to her.

"Don't you see? We were meant for each other," Mara said in conclusion.

Indeed, farmer Agrippino gave his consent, and Mis' Lia quickly put together a new jacket and a pair of velvet trousers for her son-in-law. Mara was as beautiful and bright as a rose; in her white shoulder cape she looked like an Easter lamb, and her amber necklace made her throat look white, so that when Jeli went down the roads beside her he walked stiffly, dressed up in broadcloth and new velvet. He didn't dare blow his nose with his red silk handkerchief, to avoid being noticed; the neighbors and everyone else who knew the story of Don Alfonso laughed in his face. When Mara said: "I do" and the priest made a big cross over her as he pronounced her a married woman, Jeli led her home; he felt as if he had been given all the gold of the Madonna and all the land his eyes had ever seen.

"Now that we're man and wife," he said when they had arrived home, and he was sitting face to face with her, making himself inconspicuous, "now that we're man and wife, I can tell you that I just can't believe that you've accepted me . . . when you could have chosen so many better men . . . beautiful and graceful as you are! . . ."

The poor fellow didn't know what else to say to her; he felt that he would burst his new finery, he was so pleased to see Mara in his house, handling and straightening out everything, and acting the housewife. He couldn't tear himself away from the door to return to Salonia. When Monday came, he lingered over the task of arranging the saddlebags, heavy cloak, and waxed umbrella on the donkey's packsaddle. "You ought to come to Salonia, too!" he said to his wife, who was standing on the threshold watching him. "You ought to come with me." But the woman started laughing, and replied that she wasn't cut out to be a shepherdess and had no business at Salonia.

Mara was indeed not born to be a shepherdess; she wasn't used to the January north wind, when your hands grow numb on the staff and your nails seem to be falling off; or to the furious downpours in which the rain soaks you to the bones; or to the choking dust on the roads when the sheep walk beneath the broiling sun; or to the hard sleeping places and the moldy bread, and the long days of lonely silence in which nothing is seen in the distance in the scorched countryside except, very occasionally, some deeply suntanned peasant silently driving

Almeno Jeli sapeva che Mara stava al caldo sotto le coltri, o filava davanti al fuoco, in crocchio colle vicine, o si godeva il sole sul ballatojo, mentre egli tornava dal pascolo stanco ed assetato, o fradicio di pioggia, o quando il vento spingeva la neve dentro il casolare, e spegneva il fuoco di sarmenti. Ogni mese Mara andava a riscuotere il salario dal padrone, e non le mancavano né le uova nel pollaio, né l'olio nella lucerna, né il vino nel fiasco. Due volte al mese poi Jeli andava a trovarla, ed ella lo aspettava sul ballatojo, col fuso in mano; e dopo che egli avea legato l'asino nella stalla e toltogli il basto, messogli la biada nella greppia, e riposta la legna sotto la tettoja nel cortile, o quel che portava in cucina, Mara l'aiutava ad appendere il tabarro al chiodo, e a togliersi le gambiere di pelle, davanti al focolare, e gli versava il vino, metteva a bollire la minestra, apparecchiava il desco, cheta cheta e previdente come una brava massaia, nel tempo stesso che gli parlava di questo e di quello, della chioccia che aveva messo a covare, della tela che era sul telajo, del vitello che allevavano, senza dimenticare una sola delle faccenduole che andava facendo. Jeli quando si trovava in casa sua, si sentiva d'essere di più del papa.

Ma la notte di Santa Barbara tornò a casa ad ora insolita, che tutti i lumi erano spenti nella stradicciuola, e l'orologio della città suonava la mezzanotte. Egli veniva perché la cavalla che il padrone aveva lasciata al pascolo s'era ammalata all'improvviso, e si vedeva chiaro che quella era cosa che ci voleva il maniscalco subito subito, e ce n'era voluto per condurla sino in paese, colla pioggia che cadeva come una fiumara, e colle strade dove si sprofondava sino a mezza gamba. Tuttavia ebbe un bel bussare e chiamar Mara da dietro l'uscio, gli toccò d'aspettare mezzora sotto la grondaja, sicché l'acqua gli usciva dalle calcagna. Sua moglie venne ad aprirgli finalmente, e cominciò a strapazzarlo peggio che se fosse stata lei a scorazzare per i campi con quel tempaccio. – O cos'hai? gli domandava lui.

– Ho che m'hai fatto paura a quest'ora! che ti par ora da cristiani questa? Domani sarò ammalata!

– Va' a coricarti, il fuoco l'accenderò io.

– No, bisogna che vada a prender la legna.

– Andrò io.

– No, ti dico!

Quando Mara ritornò colla legna nelle braccia Jeli le disse:

his donkey ahead of him along the endless white road. At least Jeli knew that Mara was lying warmly under her blankets, or spinning in front of the fire, amid a group of neighbor women, or enjoying the sun on the veranda, while he was returning from the pasture weary and parched, or sopping with rain, or the wind was driving the snow into his hut and blowing out the vine-runner fire. Every month Mara would go to collect his pay from his master, and she didn't lack eggs in her henhouse, oil in her lamp, or wine in her flask. Then, twice a month Jeli would come to see her; she'd be waiting on the veranda, spindle in hand. After he had tied up the donkey in the stable and removed its packsaddle, placed fodder in its manger, and put the firewood under the lean-to in the yard or carried some into the kitchen, Mara would help him hang his cloak on its nail and take off his leather leggings in front of the hearth, and would pour wine for him, start the soup boiling, and set the table, doing all this very quietly and prudently like a good housekeeper, while she spoke to him about this and that, about the hen that had started to brood, the cloth she had on the loom, and the calf they were raising, not forgetting a single one of the chores she was busy with. When Jeli was at home, he felt grander than the Pope.

But on St. Barbara's night[10] he came home at an unusual hour, when all the lights were out on the little street and the city clock was striking midnight. He was coming then because the mare that his master had left out to graze had suddenly fallen ill, and he could see clearly that it was a matter demanding the immediate attention of the veterinarian. It had been a hard job to get her all the way to the village in the rain that was falling in torrents and over roads in which your legs sank in halfway. Nevertheless, he had to keep on knocking and calling Mara as he waited at the door; he had to stand a half-hour under the gutter, until the water was running out at his heels. Finally his wife came to open up, and began to scold him worse than if *she* had been the one roaming the countryside in that terrible weather. "What's wrong with you?" he asked.

"It's because you frightened me at this time of night! Do you think this is an hour for Christians to be up and about? Tomorrow I'll be sick!"

"Go back to bed, *I'll* light the fire."

"No, I have to go get the firewood."

"*I'll* go."

"No, I tell you!"

When Mara got back with the firewood in her arms, Jeli said:

---

10. December 4.

– Perché hai aperto l'uscio del cortile? Non ce n'era più di legna in cucina?

– No, sono andata a prenderla sotto la tettoja.

Ella si lasciò baciare, fredda fredda, e volse il capo dall'altra parte.

– Sua moglie lo lascia a infradiciare dietro l'uscio, dicevano i vicini, quando in casa c'è il tordo!

Ma Jeli non sapeva nulla, ch'era becco, né gli altri si curavano di dirglielo, perché a lui non gliene importava niente, e s'era accollata la donna col danno, dopo che il figlio di massaro Neri l'aveva piantata per aver saputo la storia di don Alfonso. Jeli invece ci viveva beato e contento nel vituperio, e s'ingrassava come un majale, «ché le corna sono magre, ma mantengono la casa grassa!».

Una volta infine il ragazzo della mandra glielo disse in faccia, mentre si abbaruffavano per le pezze di formaggio che si trovavano tosate.

– Ora che don Alfonso vi ha preso la moglie, vi pare di essere suo cognato, e avete messo superbia che vi par di essere un re di corona con quelle corna che avete in testa.

Il fattore e il campajo si aspettavano di veder scorrere il sangue a quelle parole; ma invece Jeli rimase istupidito come se non le avesse udite, o come se non fosse stato fatto suo, con una faccia da bue che le corna gli stavano bene davvero.

Ora si avvicinava la Pasqua e il fattore mandava tutti gli uomini della fattoria a confessarsi, colla speranza che pel timor di Dio non rubassero più. Jeli andò anche lui e all'uscir di chiesa cercò del ragazzo con cui erano corse quelle parole e gli buttò le braccia al collo dicendogli:

– Il confessore mi ha detto di perdonarti; ma io non sono in collera con te per quelle chiacchiere; e se tu non toserai più il formaggio a me non me ne importa nulla di quello che mi hai detto nella collera.

Fu da quel momento che lo chiamarono per soprannome *Corna d'oro,* e il soprannome gli rimase, a lui e tutti i suoi, anche dopo che ei si lavò le corna nel sangue.

La Mara era andata a confessarsi anche lei, e tornava di chiesa tutta raccolta nella mantellina, e cogli occhi bassi che sembrava una santa Maria Maddalena. Jeli il quale l'aspettava taciturno sul ballatojo, come la vide venire a quel modo, che si vedeva come ci avesse il Signore in corpo, la stava a guardare pallido pallido dai piedi alla testa, come la vedesse per la prima volta, o gliela avessero cambiata la sua Mara, e quasi non osava alzare gli occhi su di lei, mentre ella

"Why did you open the door to the yard? Wasn't there any more wood in the kitchen?"

"No, I went to the shed to get it."

She allowed him to kiss her, acting very frigid, and turned her head away.

"His wife lets him get soaked at the door," the neighbors said, "when her fancy man is in the house!"

But Jeli was completely unaware of being a cuckold, and no one else bothered to inform him, because he hadn't objected to the situation but had taken the woman onto his hands as "damaged goods" after farmer Neri's son had jilted her because he knew about her affair with Don Alfonso. On the contrary, Jeli was living blissfully and contentedly in his shame (they said) and battening on it like a pig, "because horns are thin, but they keep the household fat!"

One time his shepherd boy finally said it to his face in the course of a squabble over hunks of cheese that had been secretly pared. "Now that Don Alfonso has taken your wife, you act as if you were his brother-in-law, and you've grown so high and mighty that you think those horns on your head are a royal crown."

The steward and the chief shepherd expected to see blood flowing after that speech; instead, Jeli remained dazed, as if he hadn't heard it, or as if the matter didn't pertain to him; his facial expression was so bovine that his horns really suited him.

Now Easter was approaching, and the steward was sending all the farmhands to Confession, in hopes that the fear of God would keep them from further pilfering. Jeli went, too, and when he left the church he looked for the boy with whom he had had that argument. He threw his arms around his neck and said:

"The priest I confessed to told me to forgive you, but I'm not angry with you over that gossip, and if you stop paring the cheese on me, I don't care at all about what you said to me in the heat of anger."

From that time on, he received the nickname "Golden Horns," a nickname that stuck to him and all his kindred, even after he had washed his horns in blood.

Mara had gone to Confession also, and she was returning from church all wrapped up in her shoulder cape, with her eyes cast down so that she resembled a Mary Magdalene. Jeli was silently waiting for her on the veranda, and when he saw her arriving that way, looking as if she had the Lord within her, he ran his eyes over her from head to foot (he was all pale), as if he were seeing her for the first time or as if someone had foisted a different Mara on him. He hardly dared raise

sciorinava la tovaglia, e metteva in tavola le scodelle, tranquilla e pulita al suo solito.

Poi dopo averci pensato un gran pezzo le domandò:

– È vero che te la intendi con don Alfonso?

Mara gli piantò in faccia i suoi occhioni neri neri, e si fece il segno della croce. – Perché volete farmi far peccato in questo giorno! esclamò.

– Io non ci ho creduto, perché con don Alfonso eravamo sempre insieme, quando eravamo ragazzi, e non passava giorno ch'ei non venisse a Tebidi, quand'era in campagna lì vicino. E poi egli è ricco che i denari li ha a palate, e se volesse delle donne potrebbe maritarsi, né gli mancherebbe la roba, o il pane da mangiare.

Mara però andavasi riscaldando, e cominciò a strapazzarlo in mal modo, sicché il poveraccio non osava alzare il naso dal piatto.

Infine perché quella grazia di Dio che stavano mangiando non andasse in tossico Mara cambiò discorso, e gli domandò se ci avesse pensato a far zappare quel po' di lino che avevano seminato nel campo delle fave.

– Sì, rispose Jeli, e il lino verrà bene.

– Se è così, disse Mara, in questo inverno ti farò due camicie nuove che ti terranno caldo.

Insomma Jeli non lo capiva quello che vuol dire becco, e non sapeva cosa fosse la gelosia; ogni cosa nuova stentava ad entrargli in capo, e questa poi gli riesciva così grossa che addirittura faceva una fatica del diavolo ad entrarci; massime allorché si vedeva dinanzi la sua Mara, tanto bella, e bianca, e pulita, che l'aveva voluto ella stessa, ed alla quale egli aveva pensato tanti anni e tanti anni, fin da quando era ragazzo, che il giorno in cui gli avevano detto com'ella volesse sposarne un altro non aveva avuto più cuore di mangiare o di bere tutto il giorno – ed anche se pensava a don Alfonso, col quale erano stati tante volte insieme, ed ei gli portava ogni volta dei dolci e del pane bianco, gli pareva di averlo tuttora dinanzi agli occhi con quei vestitini nuovi, e i capelli ricciuti, e il viso bianco e liscio come una fanciulla, e dacché non lo aveva più visto, perché egli era un povero pecoraio, e stava tutto l'anno in campagna, gli era sempre rimasto in cuore a quel modo. Ma la prima volta che per sua disgrazia rivide don Alfonso, dopo tanti anni, Jeli si sentì dentro come se lo cuocessero. Don Alfonso s'era fatto grande, da non sembrare più quello; ed ora aveva una bella barba ricciuta al pari dei capelli, e una giacchetta di velluto, e una catenella d'oro sul panciotto. Però riconobbe Jeli, e gli batté anche sulle spalle salutandolo. Era venuto

his eyes to her while she was spreading out the tablecloth and placing their bowls on the table, calmly and neatly as always.

Then, after a long period of reflection, he asked:

"Is it true that you're carrying on with Don Alfonso?"

Mara looked him in the face with her big, very dark eyes, and crossed herself. "Why do you want to accuse me of a sin on this day of all days?" she exclaimed.

"I didn't believe it, because Don Alfonso and I were always together when we were boys, and a day didn't go by that he didn't come to Tebidi when he was vacationing in the country nearby. Besides, he's rich, with bundles of money, and if he wanted women he could get married, and he wouldn't lack for possessions or bread to eat."

But Mara was getting heated and began scolding him severely, so that the poor fellow didn't dare lift his nose from his plate.

Finally, so that the food they were eating, a gift from God, wouldn't turn into poison, Mara changed the topic and asked him whether he had thought about getting someone to hoe the bit of flax they had planted in the beanfield.

"Yes," Jeli replied, "and the flax will do well."

"If it does," Mara said, "this winter I'll make you two new shirts that will keep you warm."

In short, Jeli didn't understand the meaning of the word "cuckold," and he didn't know what jealousy was. It was difficult for him to get any new concept into his head, and this one was so enormous for him that it was really the devil's own job to make him comprehend it, especially when he was face to face with his Mara, who was so beautiful, white-skinned, and tidy, who had chosen him herself, and who had been in his mind all those years, ever since he was a boy, so that on the day he had been told she wanted to marry someone else, he didn't feel like eating or drinking the rest of the day. It was the same when he thought about Don Alfonso, with whom he had been together so many times, and each time Alfonso would bring him candy or white bread. Alfonso seemed to be in front of him always, with his new little suits, his curly hair, and his face white and smooth as a girl's; since he hadn't seen him anymore, because he was just a poor shepherd who remained out in the fields all year long, he had always remembered him that way. But the first time he saw Don Alfonso again (to his misfortune) after all those years, Jeli felt as if he were being burned inside. Don Alfonso had become tall, so that he no longer looked like the same person; now he had a beautiful beard, which curled like his hair, and a velvet jacket, and a gold chain across his vest. But he recognized Jeli, and even

col padrone della fattoria insieme a una brigata d'amici, a fare una scampagnata nel tempo che si tosavano le pecore; ed era venuta pure Mara all'improvviso col pretesto che era incinta e aveva voglia di ricotta fresca.

Era una bella giornata calda, nei campi biondi, colle siepi in fiore, e i lunghi filari verdi delle vigne, le pecore saltellavano e belavano dal piacere, al sentirsi spogliate da tutta quella lana, e nella cucina le donne facevano un gran fuoco per cuocere la gran roba che il padrone aveva portato per il desinare. I signori intanto che aspettavano si erano messi all'ombra, sotto i carrubi, e facevano suonare i tamburelli e le cornamuse, e ballavano colle donne della fattoria che parevano tutt'una cosa. Jeli mentre andava tosando le pecore, si sentiva qualcosa dentro di sé, senza sapere perché, come uno spino, come un chiodo, come una forbice che gli lavorasse internamente minuta minuta, come un veleno. Il padrone aveva ordinato che gli sgozzassero due capretti, e il castrato di un anno, e dei polli, e un tacchino. Insomma voleva fare le cose in grande, e senza risparmio, per farsi onore coi suoi amici, e mentre tutte quelle bestie schiamazzavano dal dolore, e i capretti strillavano sotto il coltello, Jeli si sentiva tremare le ginocchia e di tratto in tratto gli pareva che la lana che andava tosando e l'erba in cui le pecore saltellavano avvampassero di sangue.

– Non andare! disse egli a Mara, come don Alfonso la chiamava perché venisse a ballare cogli altri. Non andare, Mara!

– Perché?

– Non voglio che tu vada. Non andare!

– Lo senti che mi chiamano.

Egli non profferiva più alcuna parola intelligibile, mentre stava curvo sulle pecore che tosava. Mara si strinse nelle spalle, e se ne andò a ballare. Ella era rossa ed allegra cogli occhi neri che sembravano due stelle, e rideva che le si vedevano i denti bianchi, e tutto l'oro che aveva indosso le sbatteva e le scintillava sulle guancie e sul petto che pareva la Madonna tale e quale. Jeli s'era rizzato sulla vita, colla lunga forbice in pugno, e così bianco in viso, così bianco come aveva visto una volta suo padre il vaccajo, quando tremava di febbre accanto al fuoco, nel casolare. Tutt'a un tratto come vide che don Alfonso, colla bella barba ricciuta, e la giacchetta di velluto e la catenella d'oro sul panciotto, prese Mara per

thumped him on the back when he said hello. He had come with the owner of the farm and a group of friends for a country outing during sheep-shearing season. Mara had also arrived unexpectedly under the pretext that she was pregnant and had a hankering for fresh ricotta.

It was a beautiful warm day in the fields that were yellow with grain, with the blossoming hedges and the long green rows of grapevines; the sheep were gamboling and bleating with joy to be relieved of all that wool, and in the kitchen the women were making a big fire to cook all the things the proprietor had brought along for the luncheon. Meanwhile, the gentlemen had sat down to wait in the shade, beneath the carob-trees, and were listening to the music of tambourines and bagpipes, and dancing with the farm women to everyone's content-ment.[11] While Jeli was shearing the sheep, he felt something inside him, without knowing why, something like a thorn, like a nail, like a pair of shears digging all the way into his vitals, like poison. The pro-prietor had ordered his people to slaughter two kids, the yearling wether, some chickens, and a turkey. In short, he wanted to do things on a grand scale, sparing no expense, to do himself proud with his friends; and while all those animals were calling out in pain, and the kids were squealing under the knife, Jeli felt his knees trembling, and at moments he felt as if the wool he was shearing and the grass on which the sheep were gamboling were blazing with blood.

"Don't go!" he said to Mara while Don Alfonso was calling her to come and dance with the others. "Don't go, Mara!"

"Why not?"

"I don't want you to go. Don't go!"

"You hear them calling me."

He no longer uttered any intelligible word while he leaned over the sheep he was shearing. Mara shrugged her shoulders and went to dance. She was ruddy and merry, with those dark eyes that were like two stars, and laughed so gaily that you could see her white teeth; all the gold jewelry she was wearing flapped and sparkled against her cheeks and her bosom, so that she looked exactly like pictures of the Madonna. Jeli had stood up straight, the long shears in his fist, and very white in the face, as white as his father the cowherd had once been when he was trembling with fever beside the fire in their cot-tage. All at once, when he saw Don Alfonso, with his curly beard, his velvet jacket, and his gold chain across his vest, take Mara by the hand

---

11. "To everyone's contentment" is just a guess at the meaning of the odd Italian phrase *che parevano tutt'una cosa*, which would mean literally "who seemed one and the same thing." In a previous translation the phrase is simply omitted.

la mano per ballare, solo allora, come vide che la toccava, si slanciò su di lui, e gli tagliò la gola di un sol colpo, proprio come un capretto.

Più tardi, mentre lo conducevano dinanzi al giudice, legato, disfatto, senza che avesse osato opporre la menoma resistenza.

– Come! – diceva – Non dovevo ucciderlo nemmeno? . . . Se mi aveva preso la Mara! . . .

to dance with her, only then, when he saw him touch her, did he dash over to him and cut his throat with a single slash, just the way you slaughter a kid.

Later, when he was brought before the judge, his hands tied, disheveled, without having dared to offer the least resistance, he kept saying:

"What? I shouldn't even have killed him? But he stole Mara from me! . . ."

ROSSO MALPELO

Malpelo si chiamava così perché aveva i capelli rossi; ed aveva i capelli rossi perché era un ragazzo malizioso e cattivo, che prometteva di riescire un fior di birbone. Sicché tutti alla cava della rena rossa lo chiamavano Malpelo; e persino sua madre col sentirgli dir sempre a quel modo aveva quasi dimenticato il suo nome di battesimo.

Del resto, ella lo vedeva soltanto il sabato sera, quando tornava a casa con quei pochi soldi della settimana; e siccome era *malpelo* c'era anche a temere che ne sottraesse un paio di quei soldi; e nel dubbio, per non sbagliare, la sorella maggiore gli faceva la ricevuta a scapaccioni.

Però il padrone della cava aveva confermato che i soldi erano tanti e non più; e in coscienza erano anche troppi per Malpelo, un monellaccio che nessuno avrebbe voluto vedersi davanti, e che tutti schivavano come un can rognoso, e lo accarezzavano coi piedi, allorché se lo trovavano a tiro.

Egli era davvero un brutto ceffo, torvo, ringhioso, e selvatico. Al mezzogiorno, mentre tutti gli altri operai della cava si mangiavano in crocchio la loro minestra, e facevano un po' di ricreazione, egli andava a rincantucciarsi col suo corbello fra le gambe, per rosicchiarsi quel suo pane di otto giorni, come fanno le bestie sue pari; e ciascuno gli diceva la sua motteggiandolo, e gli tiravan dei sassi, finché il soprastante lo rimandava al lavoro con una pedata. Ei c'ingrassava fra i calci e si lasciava caricare meglio dell'asino grigio, senza osar di lagnarsi. Era sempre cencioso e lordo di rena rossa, ché la sua sorella s'era fatta sposa, e aveva altro pel capo: nondimeno era conosciuto come la bettonica per tutto Monserrato e la Carvana, tanto che la cava dove lavorava la chiamavano «la cava di Malpelo», e cotesto al padrone gli seccava assai. Insomma lo tenevano addirittura per carità e perché mastro Misciu, suo padre, era morto nella cava.

Era morto così, che un sabato aveva voluto terminare certo lavoro preso a cottimo, di un pilastro lasciato altra volta per

NASTY REDHEAD

Nasty Redhead got his name from his red hair, and he had red hair because he was a spiteful, mean boy who gave every sign that he'd grow up to be a first-class scoundrel. So that everyone in the red sandpit called him Nasty Redhead, and even his mother, hearing him called nothing but that, had almost forgotten the name he'd been baptized with.

Anyway, she only saw him on Saturday evenings, when he came home with his meager week's pay. Since he was a nasty redhead, there was also reason to suspect he was secretly pocketing some of the money; being in doubt, and to avoid making a mistake, his older sister would give him a receipt in the form of blows on the head.

But the owner of the pit had assured them that the pay was just that amount, and no more; and, truthfully, even that was too much for Nasty Redhead, a rotten little brat whom people didn't want to have around, and whom everyone avoided like a mangy dog, "caressing" him with their feet whenever he got within range.

He really was an ugly customer, surly, bad-tempered, and savage. At noon, while all the other pit hands were eating their chow in a group and relaxing a little, he would huddle in a corner with his basket between his legs, nibbling away at his week-old bread, just the way animals do (he was like an animal, in general); everyone would make some mocking remark to him, and they'd throw stones at him, until the foreman sent him back to work with a kick. He would thrive on the kicks, and he'd accept loads heavier than the gray donkey would carry, without daring to complain. He was always in tatters and filthy with red sand, because his sister had gotten engaged and had other things on her mind: all the same, he was extremely well known all over Monserrato and Carvana, so much so that the pit where he worked was called "Nasty Redhead's pit," which annoyed the owner no end. In short, he was kept on as an outright charity case, and because master Misciu, his father, had died in the pit.

He had died when, one Saturday, he had tried to finish a job he had taken on for a flat-sum payment, working on a pillar-prop that had been

111

sostegno nella cava, e che ora non serviva più, e s'era calcolato così ad occhio col padrone per 35 o 40 carra di rena. Invece mastro Misciu sterrava da tre giorni e ne avanzava ancora per la mezza giornata del lunedì. Era stato un magro affare e solo un minchione come mastro Misciu aveva potuto lasciarsi gabbare a questo modo dal padrone; perciò appunto lo chiamavano mastro Misciu Bestia, ed era l'asino da basto di tutta la cava. Ei, povero diavolaccio, lasciava dire e si contentava di buscarsi il pane colle sue braccia, invece di menarle addosso ai compagni, e attaccar brighe. Malpelo faceva un visaccio come se quelle soperchierie cascassero sulle sue spalle, e così piccolo com'era aveva di quelle occhiate che facevano dire agli altri: – Va' là, che tu non ci morrai nel tuo letto, come tuo padre.

Invece nemmen suo padre ci morì nel suo letto, tuttoché fosse una buona bestia. Zio Mommu lo sciancato, aveva detto che quel pilastro lì ei non l'avrebbe tolto per venti onze, tanto era pericoloso; ma d'altra parte tutto è pericoloso nelle cave, e se si sta a badare al pericolo, è meglio andare a fare l'avvocato.

Adunque il sabato sera mastro Misciu raschiava ancora il suo pilastro che l'avemaria era suonata da un pezzo, e tutti i suoi compagni avevano accesa la pipa e se n'erano andati dicendogli di divertirsi a grattarsi la pancia per amor del padrone, e raccomandandogli di non fare *la morte del sorcio*. Ei, che c'era avvezzo alle beffe, non dava retta, e rispondeva soltanto cogli ah! ah! dei suoi bei colpi di zappa in pieno; e intanto borbottava: – Questo è per il pane! questo pel vino! questo per la gonnella di Nunziata! – e così andava facendo il conto del come avrebbe speso i denari del suo *appalto* – il cottimante!

Fuori della cava il cielo formicolava di stelle, e laggiù la lanterna fumava e girava al pari di un arcolaio; ed il grosso pilastro rosso, sventrato a colpi di zappa, contorcevasi e si piegava in arco come se avesse il mal di pancia, e dicesse: *ohi! ohi!* anch'esso. Malpelo andava sgomberando il terreno, e metteva al sicuro il piccone, il sacco vuoto ed il fiasco del vino. Il padre che gli voleva bene, poveretto, andava dicendogli: «Tirati indietro!» oppure «Sta' attento! Sta' attento se cascano dall'alto dei sassolini o della rena grossa». Tutt'a un tratto non disse più nulla, e Malpelo, che si era voltato a riporre i ferri nel corbello, udì un rumore sordo e soffocato, come fa la rena allorché si rovescia tutta in una volta; ed il lume si spense.

Quella sera in cui vennero a cercare in tutta fretta l'ingegnere che dirigeva i lavori della cava ei si trovava a teatro, e non avrebbe cambiato la sua poltrona con un trono, perch'era gran dilettante.

left there earlier to support the pit but was now no longer needed. He had made a deal with the owner based on his own rough estimate that the prop would yield 35 or 40 cartloads of sand. But, instead, master Misciu had been excavating for three days and there was still enough left for half of Monday. It had been an unprofitable arrangement, and only a naïve man like master Misciu could have let himself be fooled by the owner that way; it was for that very reason that he was called master Misciu the Dumb Animal, and served as beast of burden to the whole pit. He, poor devil, let them talk and was content to use the strength of his arms to earn his bread instead of to attack his fellow workers and start fights. Nasty Redhead would always make a horrible grimace, as if those outrages were being aimed at *him;* small as he was, he darted glances that made the others say: "You there, you won't die in bed like your father!"

But his father didn't die in bed, either, despite being a serviceable animal. "Uncle" Mommu, the cripple, had said that *he* wouldn't have removed that prop for twenty *onze,* it was so dangerous; but, on the other hand, everything is dangerous in sand pits, and if your mind dwells on danger, you'd do better to go and be a lawyer.

And so, on Saturday evening master Misciu was still scraping away at his pillar after Angelus had already rung a while back; all his fellow workers had lit their pipes and gone away, telling him to have fun hanging around for the owner's sake and advising him not to "die like a rat." Being accustomed to jokes, he paid them no mind, answering merely with the "Ah! ah!" with which he accompanied the strong, well-aimed blows of his spade. Meanwhile he'd mutter: "This one is for the bread! This one for the wine! This one for Nunziata's skirt!" And he kept on reckoning up how he'd spend the money from the flat-sum job he'd undertaken!

Outside the pit the sky teemed with stars, and down there the lantern smoked and turned like a wool-winder. The thick red pillar, emptied out by spade strokes, twisted and bent into an arc as if it had a bellyache and as if it, too, were saying: "Ooh, ooh!" Nasty Redhead moved along clearing the terrain and putting the pickaxe, the empty sack, and the wine flask in a safe place. His father, poor fellow, who loved him, kept saying: "Move back!" or "Watch out! Watch out in case pebbles or coarse sand falls from above!" All of a sudden his remarks came to a stop, and Nasty Redhead, who had turned around to put the tools back in the basket, heard a dull, muffled sound, the kind that sand makes when it subsides all at once; and the light went out.

That evening when they hurriedly went to fetch the engineer who directed the work in the pit, he was at the theater and wouldn't have given up his orchestra seat for a throne, because he was a great fan.

Rossi rappresentava l'*Amleto*, e c'era un bellissimo teatro. Sulla porta si vide accerchiato da tutte le femminucce di Monserrato, che strillavano e si picchiavano il petto per annunziare la gran disgrazia ch'era toccata a comare Santa, la sola, poveretta, che non dicesse nulla, e sbatteva i denti quasi fosse in gennaio. L'ingegnere, quando gli ebbero detto che il caso era accaduto da circa quattro ore, domandò cosa venissero a fare da lui dopo quattro ore. Nondimeno ci andò con scale e torcie a vento, ma passarono altre due ore, e fecero sei, e lo sciancato disse che a sgomberare il sotterraneo dal materiale caduto ci voleva una settimana.

Altro che quaranta carra di rena! Della rena ne era caduta una montagna, tutta fina e ben bruciata dalla lava, che si sarebbe impastata colle mani e dovea prendere il doppio di calce. Ce n'era da riempire delle carra per delle settimane. Il bell'affare di mastro Bestia!

L'ingegnere se ne tornò a veder seppellire Ofelia; e gli altri minatori si strinsero nelle spalle, e se ne tornarono a casa ad uno ad uno. Nella ressa e nel gran chiacchierìo non badarono a una voce di fanciullo, la quale non aveva più nulla di umano, e strillava: – Scavate! scavate qui! presto! – To'! – disse lo sciancato – è Malpelo! – Da dove è venuto fuori Malpelo? – Se tu non fossi stato Malpelo, non te la saresti scappata, no! – Gli altri si misero a ridere, e chi diceva che Malpelo avea il diavolo dalla sua, un altro che avea il cuoio duro a mo' dei gatti. Malpelo non rispondeva nulla, non piangeva nemmeno, scavava colle unghie colà nella rena, dentro la buca, sicché nessuno s'era accorto di lui; e quando si accostarono col lume gli videro tal viso stravolto, e tali occhiacci invetrati, e tale schiuma alla bocca da far paura; le unghie gli si erano strappate e gli pendevano dalle mani tutte in sangue. Poi quando vollero toglierlo di là fu un affar serio; non potendo più graffiare, mordeva come un cane arrabbiato e dovettero afferrarlo pei capelli, per tirarlo via a viva forza.

Però infine tornò alla cava dopo qualche giorno, quando sua madre piagnuccolando ve lo condusse per mano; giacché, alle volte il pane che si mangia non si può andare a cercarlo di qua e di là. Anzi non volle più allontanarsi da quella galleria, e sterrava con accanimento, quasi ogni corbello di rena lo levasse di sul petto a suo padre. Alle volte, mentre zappava, si fermava bruscamente, colla zappa in aria, il viso torvo e gli occhi stralunati, e sembrava che stesse ad

Rossi[1] was playing Hamlet, and there was a huge crowd. At the door the engineer found himself besieged by all the poor women of Monserrato, who were keening and beating their breasts to announce the great misfortune that had befallen neighbor Santa; she, poor woman, was the only one who remained silent, her teeth chattering as if it were January. When the engineer was told that the accident had occurred about four hours earlier, he asked what they wanted of him four hours too late. All the same, he went to the spot with ladders and windproof torches, but another two hours went by, making six, and the cripple said that it would take a week to clear the underground passage of all the material that had fallen.

Speak of forty cartloads of sand! A mountain of sand had fallen, fine sand that was thoroughly lava-burnt, sand that you could knead in your hands and that could absorb twice its weight in lime for making mortar. There was enough to fill carts for weeks. A clever deal master Animal had made!

The engineer went back to see Ophelia buried; the other miners shrugged their shoulders and went home one by one. Amid the crowd and the loud conversations no one heeded a boy's voice that had no human quality left in it, but was shrieking: "Dig! Dig here! Quick!" "What do you know," said the cripple, "it's Nasty Redhead!" "Where did Nasty Redhead come from?" "If you hadn't been Nasty Redhead, you wouldn't have escaped, no!" The others started laughing, one saying that Nasty Redhead had the devil on his side, another that he had nine lives like a cat. Nasty Redhead made no reply, he wasn't even crying; he had been digging in the sand there, inside the excavation, so that no one had noticed him. When they approached him with a light, they saw that his face was so twisted, his eyes so wide and glazed, and his mouth so full of froth that he was frightening. His nails had been torn off, and were hanging from his hands full of blood. Then, when they tried to take him away from there, it was a tough job; he couldn't scratch anymore, but he bit like a mad dog, and they had to grab him by the hair and pull him out by main strength.

But finally, after several days, he returned to the pit, when his mother, whimpering, led him there by the hand; because, at times, you can't run all around looking for the bread you have to eat. In fact, he didn't want to go away from that very passage; he'd dig there doggedly, as if every basketful of sand were being removed from his father's chest. At times while digging he'd halt suddenly, his spade in the air, his face sullen and his eyes bulging, seeming to be listening to

---

1. The outstanding actor Ernesto Rossi (1827–1896).

ascoltare qualche cosa che il suo diavolo gli susurrava negli orecchi, dall'altra parte della montagna di rena caduta. In quei giorni era più tristo e cattivo del solito, talmente che non mangiava quasi, e il pane lo buttava al cane, come se non fosse *grazia di Dio*. Il cane gli voleva bene, perché i cani non guardano altro che la mano la quale dà loro il pane. Ma l'asino grigio, povera bestia, sbilenca e macilenta, sopportava tutto lo sfogo della cattiveria di Malpelo; ei lo picchiava senza pietà, col manico della zappa, e borbottava: – Così creperai più presto!

Dopo la morte del babbo pareva che gli fosse entrato il diavolo in corpo, e lavorava al pari di quei bufali feroci che si tengono coll'anello di ferro al naso. Sapendo che era *malpelo*, ei si acconciava ad esserlo il peggio che fosse possibile, e se accadeva una disgrazia, o che un operaio smarriva i ferri, o che un asino si rompeva una gamba, o che crollava un pezzo di galleria, si sapeva sempre che era stato lui; e infatti ei si pigliava le busse senza protestare, proprio come se le pigliano gli asini che curvano la schiena, ma seguitano a fare a modo loro. Cogli altri ragazzi poi era addirittura crudele, e sembrava che si volesse vendicare sui deboli di tutto il male che s'immaginava gli avessero fatto, a lui e al suo babbo. Certo ei provava uno strano diletto a rammentare ad uno ad uno tutti i maltrattamenti ed i soprusi che avevano fatto subire a suo padre, e del modo in cui l'avevano lasciato crepare. E quando era solo borbottava: «Anche con me fanno così! e a mio padre gli dicevano Bestia, perché ei non faceva così!». E una volta che passava il padrone, accompagnandolo con un'occhiata torva: «È stato lui, per trentacinque tarì!». E un'altra volta, dietro allo sciancato: «E anche lui! e si metteva a ridere! Io l'ho udito, quella sera!».

Per un raffinamento di malignità sembrava aver preso a proteggere un povero ragazzetto, venuto a lavorare da poco tempo nella cava, il quale per una caduta da un ponte s'era lussato il femore, e non poteva far più il manovale. Il poveretto, quando portava il suo corbello di rena in spalla, arrancava in modo che sembrava ballasse la tarantella, e aveva fatto ridere tutti quelli della cava, così che gli avevano messo nome Ranocchio; ma lavorando sotterra, così ranocchio com'era, il suo pane se lo buscava; e Malpelo gliene dava anche del suo, per prendersi il gusto di tiranneggiarlo, dicevano.

Infatti egli lo tormentava in cento modi. Ora lo batteva senza un motivo e senza misericordia, e se Ranocchio non si difendeva, lo picchiava più forte, con maggiore accanimento, e gli diceva: – To'! Bestia! Bestia sei! Se non ti senti l'animo di difenderti da me che non

something that his devil was whispering in his ear from the other side
of the mountain of fallen sand. During those days he was meaner and
more malevolent than usual, so much so that he hardly ate, but would
throw his bread to the dog, just as if it weren't "the gift of God." The
dog loved him, because dogs don't look at anything but the hand that
gives them bread. But the gray donkey, poor animal, misshapen and
emaciated, bore the whole brunt of Nasty Redhead's viciousness; the
boy would beat him mercilessly with the spade handle, muttering:
"This way, you'll croak sooner!"

After his father's death, the devil seemed to have gotten into him,
and he did his work like those fierce buffaloes that have to be con-
trolled by an iron nose-ring. Aware that he was a "nasty redhead," he
resigned himself to be the worst possible kind of one; whenever an accident happened, or a workman couldn't find his tools, or a donkey
broke a leg, or part of a passage fell in, everyone always knew it was
his doing. And indeed he took the beatings without protesting, just as
donkeys do, bending their backs, though they continue to behave just
as they like. To the other boys he was downright cruel; it seemed as if
he wanted to take out on the weak all the wrongs that he imagined had
been done to himself and his father. Surely he took a strange pleasure
in recalling, one by one, all the bad treatments and outrages that his
father had undergone, and the way his father's fellow workers had let
him die like a dog. When he was alone, he'd mutter: "They do the
same to me! And they called my father Animal because he didn't act
that way!" Once, when the owner went by, he followed him with surly
eyes that said: "It was him, for a paltry thirty-five *tarì*!" And, another
time, as he followed the cripple: "It was him, too! And he started
laughing! I heard him, that evening!"

As a refining touch to his malevolence he seemed to have taken
under his wing a poor young boy who had recently come to work in
the pit. In a fall from a scaffold he had dislocated a thighbone, and
could no longer work in construction. When the poor boy carried a
basket of sand on his shoulder, he hobbled so badly he looked as if he
were dancing a tarantella, and he had made everyone in the pit laugh,
so that they had dubbed him Frog. But frog as he was, he was earning
his bread by working underground, and Nasty Redhead even gave
him some of his—to acquire a taste for lording it over him, they said.

And indeed he'd torment him in a hundred ways. Now he'd beat
him mercilessly for no reason, and if Frog didn't defend himself, he'd
hit harder, more doggedly, saying: "Take this! Animal! You're a dumb
animal! If you don't have the courage to defend yourself from

ti voglio male, vuol dire che ti lascerai pestare il viso da questo e da quello!

O se Ranocchio si asciugava il sangue che gli usciva dalla bocca o dalle narici: – Così, come ti cuocerà il dolore delle busse, imparerai a darne anche tu! – Quando cacciava un asino carico per la ripida salita del sotterraneo, e lo vedeva puntare gli zoccoli, rifinito, curvo sotto il peso, ansante e coll'occhio spento, ei lo batteva senza misericordia, col manico della zappa, e i colpi suonavano secchi sugli stinchi e sulle costole scoperte. Alle volte la bestia si piegava in due per le battiture, ma stremo di forze non poteva fare un passo, e cadeva sui ginocchi, e ce n'era uno il quale era caduto tante volte, che ci aveva due piaghe alle gambe; e Malpelo allora confidava a Ranocchio: – L'asino va picchiato, perché non può picchiar lui; e s'ei potesse picchiare, ci pesterebbe sotto i piedi e ci strapperebbe la carne a morsi.

Oppure: – Se ti accade di dar delle busse, procura di darle più forte che puoi; così coloro su cui cadranno ti terranno per da più di loro, e ne avrai tanti di meno addosso.

Lavorando di piccone o di zappa poi menava le mani con accanimento, a mo' di uno che l'avesse con la rena, e batteva e ribatteva coi denti stretti, e con quegli *ah! ah!* che aveva suo padre. – La rena è traditora, diceva a Ranocchio sottovoce; somiglia a tutti gli altri, che se sei più debole ti pestano la faccia, e se sei più forte, o siete in molti, come fa lo Sciancato, allora si lascia vincere. Mio padre la batteva sempre, ed egli non batteva altro che la rena, perciò lo chiamavano Bestia, e la rena se lo mangiò a tradimento, perché era più forte di lui.

Ogni volta che a Ranocchio toccava un lavoro troppo pesante, e Ranocchio piagnuccolava a guisa di una femminuccia, Malpelo lo picchiava sul dorso e lo sgridava: – Taci pulcino! – e se Ranocchio non la finiva più, ei gli dava un mano, dicendo con un certo orgoglio: – Lasciami fare; io sono più forte di te. – Oppure gli dava la sua mezza cipolla, e si contentava di mangiarsi il pane asciutto, e si stringeva nelle spalle, aggiungendo: – Io ci sono avvezzo.

Era avvezzo a tutto lui, agli scapaccioni, alle pedate, ai colpi di manico di badile, o di cinghia da basto, a vedersi ingiuriato e beffato da tutti, a dormire sui sassi, colle braccia e la schiena rotta da quattordici ore di lavoro; anche a digiunare era avvezzo, allorché il padrone lo puniva levandogli il pane o la minestra. Ei diceva che la razione di busse non gliela aveva levata mai il padrone; ma le busse non costavano nulla. Non si lamentava però, e si vendicava di soppiatto, a

someone who has nothing against you, like me, that means you'll let just anyone beat your face to a pulp!"

Or, if Frog wiped away the blood that was issuing from his mouth or nostrils: "This way, when you smart with the pain from my beating, you'll learn how to give a beating yourself!" When he was driving a laden donkey up the steep incline of the passage and saw it dig in its hooves, exhausted, bent beneath the weight, out of breath, its eyes glassy, he'd beat it mercilessly with the spade handle, and the blows made a dull sound against its shins and its protruding ribs. Sometimes the animal would bend in two under the blows, but, at the end of its strength, couldn't take another step and would fall on its knees; there was one that had fallen so often, it had two open sores on its legs. At such times, Nasty Redhead would tell Frog in confidence: "A donkey gets beaten because it can't *give* a beating. If it could, it would trample us under its feet and rip out our flesh by the mouthful."

Or else: "If it happens that you do give a beating, try to make it as hard as you can; that way, the people you give it to will consider you better than they are, and you'll have that many fewer bothering you."

Then, when working with pick or spade, he'd move his arms furiously like someone who had a grudge against the sand; he'd hit it again and again with his teeth clenched and the same cries of "Ah! Ah!" as his father. "The sand is treacherous," he'd say quietly to Frog, "it's like everyone else. If you're the weaker one, they beat your face in, but if you're the stronger one, or if you attack it in a group, the way the Cripple does, then it lets you overcome it. My father always hit it, but he never hit anything *but* the sand, and so they called him Animal, and the sand swallowed him up by surprise, because it was stronger than he was."

Every time that Frog was assigned a job that was beyond his powers, and whined like a weak woman, Nasty Redhead would hit him on the back and bawl him out: "Keep quiet, squirt!" But if Frog couldn't manage it, he'd lend him a hand, saying, a little pridefully: "Let me, I'm stronger than you." Or else he'd give him his half-onion and would be content to eat his dry bread; he'd shrug his shoulders, adding: "I'm used to it."

He was used to everything, to cuffs on the head, to kicks, to blows with a shovel handle or a packsaddle girth, to seeing himself insulted and laughed at by everyone, to sleeping on stones, his arms and back exhausted by fourteen hours of work. He was also used to going hungry, when his boss punished him by taking away his bread or his soup. He'd say that the boss had never taken away his portion of beatings; but beatings didn't cost anything. But he didn't complain, and he took his revenge

tradimento, con qualche tiro di quelli che sembrava ci avesse messo la coda il diavolo: perciò ei si pigliava sempre i castighi anche quando il colpevole non era stato lui; già se non era stato lui sarebbe stato capace di esserlo, e non si giustificava mai: per altro sarebbe stato inutile. E qualche volta come Ranocchio spaventato lo scongiurava piangendo di dire la verità e di scolparsi, ei ripeteva: – A che giova? Sono *malpelo*! – e nessuno avrebbe potuto dire se quel curvare il capo e le spalle sempre fosse effetto di bieco orgoglio o di disperata rassegnazione, e non si sapeva nemmeno se la sua fosse selvatichezza o timidità. Il certo era che nemmeno sua madre aveva avuta mai una carezza da lui, e quindi non gliene faceva mai.

Il sabato sera, appena arrivava a casa con quel suo visaccio imbrattato di lentiggini e di rena rossa, e quei cenci che gli piangevano addosso da ogni parte, la sorella afferrava il manico della scopa se si metteva sull'uscio in quell'arnese, ché avrebbe fatto scappare il suo damo se avesse visto che razza di cognato gli toccava sorbirsi; la madre era sempre da questa o da quella vicina, e quindi egli andava a rannicchiarsi sul suo saccone come un cane malato. Adunque, la domenica, in cui tutti gli altri ragazzi del vicinato si mettevano la camicia pulita per andare a messa o per ruzzare nel cortile, ei sembrava non avesse altro spasso che di andar randagio per le vie degli orti, a dar la caccia a sassate alle povere lucertole, le quali non gli avevano fatto nulla, oppure a sforacchiare le siepi dei fichidindia. Per altro le beffe e le sassate degli altri fanciulli non gli piacevano.

La vedova di mastro Misciu era disperata di aver per figlio quel malarnese, come dicevano tutti, ed egli era ridotto veramente come quei cani, che a furia di buscarsi dei calci e delle sassate da questo e da quello, finiscono col mettersi la coda fra le gambe e scappare alla prima anima viva che vedono, e diventano affamati, spelati e selvatici come lupi. Almeno sottoterra, nella cava della rena, brutto e cencioso e sbracato com'era, non lo beffavano più, e sembrava fatto apposta per quel mestiere persin nel colore dei capelli, e in quegli occhiacci di gatto che ammiccavano se vedevano il sole. Così ci sono degli asini che lavorano nelle cave per anni ed anni senza uscirne mai più, ed in quei sotterranei, dove il pozzo di ingresso è verticale, ci si calan colle funi, e ci restano finché vivono. Sono asini vecchi, è vero, comprati dodici o tredici lire, quando stanno per portarli alla Plaja, a strangolarli; ma pel lavoro che hanno da fare laggiù sono ancora buoni; e Malpelo, certo, non valeva di più, e se veniva fuori dalla cava il sabato sera,

sneakily, underhandedly, playing some sort of trick in which the devil seemed to have a hand. And so he always received the punishment even when he hadn't been the guilty party—if he hadn't done it, he would have been capable of it!—and he never made an excuse for himself: it would have been useless, anyway. At times, when Frog got scared and tearfully begged him to tell the truth and avoid the blame, he'd repeat: "What's the use? I'm a nasty redhead!" And no one could have said whether that constant bending of his head and shoulders was the result of sullen pride or of despairing resignation; they didn't even know whether it was wildness in him, or timidity. What was certain was that not even his mother had ever received a caress from him, and thus never gave him any.

On Saturday evenings, when he came home with his face splashed with freckles and red sand, and those rags hanging on every side of him pathetically, his sister gripped the broom handle if he appeared in the doorway looking like that, because he would have made her fiancé run away to see what sort of brother-in-law he'd have to put up with. His mother was always in the house of some neighbor woman or another, and so he'd go and curl up on his straw mattress like a sick dog. Then, on Sunday, when all the other boys in the neighborhood put on a clean shirt to go to Mass or to romp in the yard, he seemed to have no other pastime than to wander over the paths to the vegetable gardens, to chase the poor lizards by flinging stones at them, though they hadn't done anything to him, or to make holes in the hedges of prickly pear. Anyway, he didn't like the mockery and stone throwing of the other boys.

Master Misciu's widow was in despair at having that rascal for a son, everyone said, and really he had been reduced to the state of those dogs which, by dint of receiving kicks and stonings on all sides, finally put their tails between their legs and run away the minute they see a living soul, and become as hungry, mangy, and savage as wolves. At least underground, in the sandpit, ugly, ragged, and slovenly as he was, they no longer laughed at him; he seemed perfectly adapted to that line of work, even in the color of his hair and those mean cat's eyes which blinked if they saw sunlight. It's the same with the donkeys that work in the pits for years and years without ever coming out again; they're lowered by ropes into those passages where the entrance shaft is vertical, and they remain there as long as they live. It's true, we're talking about old donkeys, bought for twelve or thirteen *lire* when they're about to be brought to the Seashore slaughterhouse to be put to death; but they're still good enough for the work they have to do down there, and truly Nasty Redhead wasn't worth more than that. If he still came up out of the pit on Saturday evenings, it was

era perché aveva anche le mani per aiutarsi colla fune, e doveva andare a portare a sua madre la paga della settimana.

Certamente egli avrebbe preferito di fare il manovale, come Ranocchio, e lavorare cantando sui ponti, in alto, in mezzo all'azzurro del cielo, col sole sulla schiena – o il carrettiere, come compare Gaspare che veniva a prendersi la rena della cava, dondolandosi sonnacchioso sulle stanghe, colla pipa in bocca, e andava tutto il giorno per le belle strade di campagna – o meglio ancora avrebbe voluto fare il contadino che passa la vita fra i campi, in mezzo al verde, sotto i folti carrubi, e il mare turchino là in fondo, e il canto degli uccelli sulla testa. Ma quello era stato il mestiere di suo padre, e in quel mestiere era nato lui. E pensando a tutto ciò, indicava a Ranocchio il pilastro che era caduto addosso al genitore, e dava ancora della rena fina e bruciata che il carrettiere veniva a caricare colla pipa in bocca, e dondolandosi sulle stanghe, e gli diceva che quando avrebbero finito di sterrare si sarebbe trovato il cadavere di suo padre, il quale doveva avere dei calzoni di fustagno quasi nuovi. Ranocchio aveva paura, ma egli no. Ei narrava che era stato sempre là, da bambino, e aveva sempre visto quel buco nero, che si sprofondava sotterra, dove il padre soleva condurlo per mano. Allora stendeva le braccia a destra e a sinistra, e descriveva come l'intricato laberinto delle gallerie si stendesse sotto i loro piedi dappertutto, di qua e di là, sin dove potevano vedere la sciara nera e desolata, sporca di ginestre riarse, e come degli uomini ce n'erano rimasti tanti, o schiacciati, o smarriti nel buio, e che camminano da anni e camminano ancora, senza poter scorgere lo spiraglio del pozzo pel quale sono entrati, e senza poter udire le strida disperate dei figli, e quali li cercano inutilmente.

Ma una volta in cui riempiendo i corbelli si rinvenne una delle scarpe di mastro Misciu, ei fu colto da tal tremito che dovettero tirarlo all'aria aperta colle funi, proprio come un asino che stesse per dar dei calci al vento. Però non si poterono trovare né i calzoni quasi nuovi, né il rimanente di mastro Misciu; sebbene i pratici asserissero che quello dovea essere il luogo preciso dove il pilastro gli si era rovesciato addosso; e qualche operaio, nuovo del mestiere, osservava curiosamente come fosse capricciosa la rena, che aveva sbattacchiato il Bestia di qua e di là, le scarpe da una parte e i piedi dall'altra.

Dacché poi fu trovata quella scarpa, Malpelo fu colto da tal paura di veder comparire fra la rena anche il piede nudo del babbo, che non volle mai più darvi un colpo di zappa; gliela dessero a lui sul capo, la zappa. Egli andò a lavorare in un altro punto della galleria e non volle

because he still had hands to hoist himself up the rope, and because he had to bring his week's pay to his mother.

He would surely have preferred to be a construction worker like Frog, to sing at his work on scaffolds, up in the air, amid the blue of the sky, with the sunshine on his back—or a carter like neighbor Gaspare, who came to pick up the sand from the pit, swaying sleepily over the shafts, his pipe in his mouth, and who traveled the beautiful country roads all day long. Or, even better, he'd have liked to be a peasant, spending his life in the fields, amid the green, beneath the thick foliage of the carob-trees, with the deep blue sea in the distance and birdsong overhead. But this had been his father's occupation, and he had been born into it. Reflecting on all this, he'd point out to Frog the pillar that had fallen onto his father, and was still yielding fine, well-baked sand which the carter came to take away, pipe in mouth and swaying over the shafts. He told him that when the spot was completely excavated, they'd find the body of his father, who should be wearing fustian trousers that were practically new. Frog was afraid, but not him. He told him that he had always been there, since childhood, and had always seen that black hole, which extended deep into the earth; his father used to lead him by the hand there. Then he stretched out his arms to the right and to the left, and he'd describe how the intricate labyrinth of passages extended everywhere below their feet, in every direction, up to the point where they could see the black and desolate lava field, littered with parched bushes of broom; he'd tell him of all the men who had never come back from there, either crushed or lost in the dark, wandering for years and wandering still, without being able to catch sight of the gleam of light from the shaft by which they had entered, and without being able to hear the desperate cries of their sons, who were seeking them in vain.

But once, when, in the course of filling their baskets, workers found one of master Misciu's shoes, Nasty Redhead was seized with such trembling that he had to be pulled into the open air with ropes, just like a donkey giving kicks in the air. But they couldn't find either the almost-new trousers or the rest of master Misciu, even though the experts assured them that that had to be the precise place where the pillar had collapsed onto him. One workman, new to the job, remarked, in his curiosity, about how capricious the sand was, slamming the Animal here and there, his shoes on one side and his feet on another.

After that shoe was found, Nasty Redhead was seized with such fear of seeing his father's bare foot appearing amid the sand, as well, that he refused to give another stroke of the spade there, even if they were to hit him on the head with it. He went to work in a different area of the passage, and

più tornare da quelle parti. Due o tre giorni dopo scopersero infatti il cadavere di mastro Misciu, coi calzoni indosso, e steso bocconi che sembrava imbalsamato. Lo zio Mommu osservò che aveva dovuto stentar molto a morire, perché il pilastro gli si era piegato in arco addosso, e l'aveva seppellito vivo; si poteva persino vedere tuttora che mastro Bestia avea tentato istintivamente di liberarsi scavando nella rena, e avea le mani lacerate e le unghie rotte. – Proprio come suo figlio Malpelo! – ripeteva lo sciancato – ei scavava di qua, mentre suo figlio scavava di là. – Però non dissero nulla al ragazzo per la ragione che lo sapevano maligno e vendicativo.

Il carrettiere sbarazzò il sotterraneo dal cadavere al modo istesso che lo sbarazzava della rena caduta e dagli asini morti, ché stavolta oltre al lezzo del carcame, c'era che il carcame era *di carne battezzata;* e la vedova rimpiccolì i calzoni e la camicia, e li adattò a Malpelo, il quale così fu vestito quasi a nuovo per la prima volta, e le scarpe furono messe in serbo per quando ei fosse cresciuto, giacché rimpiccolirsi le scarpe non si potevano, e il fidanzato della sorella non ne avea volute di scarpe del morto.

Malpelo se li lisciava sulle gambe quei calzoni di fustagno quasi nuovo, gli pareva che fossero dolci e lisci come le mani del babbo che solevano accarezzargli i capelli, così ruvidi e rossi com'erano. Quelle scarpe le teneva appese ad un chiodo, sul saccone, quasi fossero state le pantofole del papa, e la domenica se le pigliava in mano, le lustrava e se le provava; poi le metteva per terra, l'una accanto all'altra, e stava a contemplarsele coi gomiti sui ginocchi, e il mento nelle palme per delle ore intere, rimugginando chi sa quali idee in quel cervellaccio.

Ei possedeva delle idee strane, Malpelo! Siccome aveva ereditato anche il piccone e la zappa del padre, se ne serviva, quantunque fossero troppo pesanti per l'età sua; e quando gli aveano chiesto se voleva venderli, che glieli avrebbero pagati come nuovi, egli aveva risposto di no; suo padre li ha resi così lisci e lucenti nel manico colle sue mani, ed ei non avrebbe potuto farsene degli altri più lisci e lucenti di quelli, se ci avesse lavorato cento e poi cento anni.

In quel tempo era crepato di stenti e di vecchiaia l'asino grigio; e il carrettiere era andato a buttarlo lontano nella sciara. – Così si fa, brontolava Malpelo; gli arnesi che non servono più si buttano lontano. – Ei andava a visitare il carcame del *grigio* in fondo al burrone, e vi conduceva a forza anche Ranocchio, il quale non avrebbe voluto andarci; e Malpelo gli diceva che a questo mondo bisogna avvezzarsi a vedere in faccia ogni cosa bella o brutta; e stava a

refused to return to the former one. Two or three days later, they did actually find master Misciu's body, wearing the trousers, and stretched out face downward, looking as if it were embalmed. "Uncle" Mommu remarked that he must have suffered greatly before dying, because the pillar had bent into an arc over him and had buried him alive; in fact, there still were visible signs that master Animal had instinctively tried to get free by digging in the sand; his hands were torn up, and his nails broken. "Just like his son Nasty Redhead!" the cripple repeated. "He was digging on this end while his son was digging on that end." But they said nothing to the boy, because they knew him to be vicious and vindictive.

The carter cleared the passage of the corpse in the same way he used to clear it of fallen sand and dead donkeys, because this time, in addition to the stench from the body, it was a question of "flesh that had been baptized." The widow shortened the trousers and the shirt, altering them for Nasty Redhead, who thus was dressed for the first time in nearly new clothes. The shoes were stored away until he grew up, because shoes can't be made smaller, and his sister's fiancé hadn't wanted a dead man's shoes.

Nasty Redhead smoothed out those nearly new fustian trousers on his legs. They seemed to him as soft and smooth as his father's hands, which used to caress his hair, rough and red as it was. He kept those shoes hanging from a nail over his straw mattress, as if they had been the Pope's slippers; on Sundays he'd handle them, polish them, and try them on. Then he'd put them on the floor, one next to the other, and study them for hours at a time, his elbows on his knees and his chin in his palms; who knows what ideas he was ruminating in that wicked brain of his?

And he did have odd ideas, that Nasty Redhead! Since he had inherited his father's pick and spade, also, he used them even though they were too heavy for a boy his age; when asked whether he wanted to sell them, at the same price as if they were new, he had refused. His father's own hands had made their handles that smooth and shiny, and he couldn't have gotten any others to be smoother or shinier even if he worked at it for a hundred years and then another hundred.

By that time the gray donkey had died of overwork and old age, and the carter had gone off and dumped him far away on the lava field. "That's how it goes," Nasty Redhead grumbled, "the equipment that's no good anymore is dumped far away." He'd go to visit Gray's body at the bottom of the gorge, and he'd force Frog to come along, though he wouldn't have wanted to go. Nasty Redhead would tell him that, in this world, you must get used to looking everything in the face, whether it was beautiful or

considerare con l'avida curiosità di un monellaccio i cani che accorrevano da tutte le fattorie dei dintorni a disputarsi le carni del *grigio*. I cani scappavano guaendo, come comparivano i ragazzi, e si aggiravano ustolando sui greppi dirimpetto, ma il Rosso non lasciava che Ranocchio li scacciasse a sassate. – Vedi quella cagna nera, gli diceva, che non ha paura delle tue sassate; non ha paura perché ha più fame degli altri. Gliele vedi quelle costole! Adesso non soffriva più, l'asino grigio, e se ne stava tranquillo colle quattro zampe distese, e lasciava che i cani si divertissero a vuotargli le occhiaie profonde e a spolpargli le ossa bianche e i denti che gli laceravano le viscere non gli avrebbero fatto piegar la schiena come il più semplice colpo di badile che solevano dargli onde mettergli in corpo un po' di vigore quando saliva la ripida viuzza. Ecco come vanno le cose! Anche il *grigio* ha avuto dei colpi di zappa e delle guidalesche, e anch'esso quando piegava sotto il peso e gli mancava il fiato per andare innanzi, aveva di quelle occhiate, mentre lo battevano, che sembrava dicesse: Non più! non più! Ma ora gli occhi se li mangiano i cani, ed esso se ne ride dei colpi e delle guidalesche con quella bocca spolpata e tutta denti. E se non fosse mai nato sarebbe stato meglio.

La sciara si stendeva malinconica e deserta fin dove giungeva la vista, e saliva e scendeva in picchi e burroni, nera e rugosa, senza un grillo che vi trillasse, o un uccello che vi volasse su. Non si udiva nulla, nemmeno i colpi di piccone di coloro che lavoravano sotterra. E ogni volta Malpelo ripeteva che al di sotto era tutta scavata dalle gallerie, per ogni dove, verso il monte e verso la valle; tanto che una volta un minatore c'era entrato coi capelli neri, e n'era uscito coi capelli bianchi, e un altro cui s'era spenta la torcia aveva invano gridato aiuto ma nessuno poteva udirlo. Egli solo ode le sue stesse grida! diceva, e a quell'idea, sebbene avesse il cuore più duro della sciara, trasaliva.

– Il padrone mi manda spesso lontano, dove gli altri hanno paura d'andare. Ma io sono Malpelo, e se io non torno più, nessuno mi cercherà.

Pure, durante le belle notti d'estate, le stelle splendevano lucenti anche sulla sciara, e la campagna circostante era nera anch'essa, come la sciara, ma Malpelo stanco della lunga giornata di lavoro, si sdraiava sul sacco, col viso verso il cielo, a godersi quella quiete e quella luminaria dell'alto; perciò odiava le notti di luna, in cui il mare formicola di scintille, e la campagna si disegna qua e là vagamente – allora la sciara sembra più brulla e desolata. – Per noi che

ugly. He would stand and observe with the eager curiosity of a young urchin the dogs that came running from every farmhouse in the vicinity to fight over Gray's remains. The dogs would run away yelping when the boys appeared, and would circle around the ridges opposite, howling, but Red wouldn't allow Frog to chase them away with stones. "You see that black bitch," he'd say, "who isn't afraid of your stones? She's not afraid because she's hungrier than the rest. Look at those ribs on her!" Now the gray donkey wasn't suffering anymore; it lay there calmly with its four legs outstretched, and let the dogs have a good time emptying its deep eye sockets and tearing the flesh from its white bones; the teeth that ripped into its bowels wouldn't make it bend its back the way the simplest blow with a shovel used to—those blows they used to give it to put a little energy into its body when it was climbing up the steep little path. That's how things are! Gray, also, had had spade strokes and harness sores, and, when he was bent beneath a load and didn't have enough breath to take another step, he, too, while being beaten, would give one of those looks that seem to say: "No more! No more!" But now those eyes are being eaten by the dogs, and Gray is laughing at the blows and the harness sores with that fleshless mouth that is all teeth. And if he had never been born, he would have been better off.

The lava field, melancholy and deserted, extended as far as the eye could see; it rose and fell in peaks and gorges, black and wrinkled, without a cricket to chirp in it or a bird to fly over it. There was nothing to be heard, not even the pickaxe strokes of the men working underground. And, each time, Nasty Redhead repeated that it was all dug out into passages down below, in every direction, toward the mountain and toward the valley—to such an extent that a miner had once gone in with black hair and had come out with white hair; and another man, whose torch had gone out, had shouted for help in vain, but no one could hear him. "He alone hears his own shouts!" he'd say, and at that idea, even though his heart was tougher than the lava field, he'd give a start.

"The boss frequently sends me to a great distance, where the others are afraid to go. But I'm Nasty Redhead, and if I don't come back, no one will go looking for me."

And yet, during the beautiful summer nights, the stars shone brightly even over the lava field, and the surrounding countryside was dark, too, like the lava, but Nasty Redhead, weary from his long day's work, would stretch out on his sack, his face to the sky, and enjoy that calm and that lofty light display; for that reason he hated moonlit nights, in which the sea teems with sparkles and the countryside can be made out vaguely here and there; at such times the lava field seems more barren and

siamo fatti per vivere sotterra, pensava Malpelo, ci dovrebbe essere buio sempre e dappertutto. – La civetta strideva sulla sciara, e ramingava di qua e di là; ei pensava: – Anche la civetta sente i morti che son qua sotterra e si dispera perché non può andare a trovarli.

Ranocchio aveva paura delle civette e dei pipistrelli; ma il Rosso lo sgridava perché chi è costretto a star solo non deve aver paura di nulla, e nemmeno l'asino grigio aveva paura dei cani che se lo spolpavano, ora che le sue carni non sentivano più il dolore di esser mangiate.

– Tu eri avvezzo a lavorar sui tetti come i gatti – gli diceva – e allora era tutt'altra cosa. Ma adesso che ti tocca a viver sotterra, come i topi, non bisogna più aver paura dei topi, né dei pipistrelli, che son topi vecchi con le ali, e i topi ci stanno volentieri in compagnia dei morti.

Ranocchio invece provava una tale compiacenza a spiegargli quel che ci stessero a far le stelle lassù in alto; e gli raccontava che lassù c'era il paradiso, dove vanno a stare i morti che sono stati buoni e non hanno dato dispiaceri ai loro genitori. – Chi te l'ha detto? – domandava Malpelo, e Ranocchio rispondeva che glielo aveva detto la mamma.

Allora Malpelo si grattava il capo, e sorridendo gli faceva un certo verso da monellaccio malizioso che la sa lunga. – Tua madre ti dice così perché, invece dei calzoni, tu dovresti portar la gonnella. –

E dopo averci pensato su un po':

– Mio padre era buono e non faceva male a nessuno, tanto che gli dicevano Bestia. Invece è là sotto, ed hanno persino trovato i ferri e le scarpe e questi calzoni qui che ho indosso io. –

Da lì a poco, Ranocchio il quale deperiva da qualche tempo, si ammalò in modo che la sera dovevano portarlo fuori dalla cava sull'asino, disteso fra le corbe, tremante di febbre come un pulcin bagnato. Un operaio disse che quel ragazzo *non ne avrebbe fatto osso duro* a quel mestiere, e che per lavorare in una miniera senza lasciarvi la pelle bisognava nascervi. Malpelo allora si sentiva orgoglioso di esserci nato e di mantenersi così sano e vigoroso in quell'aria malsana, e con tutti quegli stenti. Ei si caricava Ranocchio sulle spalle, e gli faceva animo alla sua maniera, sgridandolo e picchiandolo. Ma una volta nel picchiarlo sul dorso Ranocchio fu colto da uno sbocco di sangue, allora Malpelo spaventato si affannò a cercargli nel naso e dentro la bocca cosa gli avesse fatto, e giurava che non avea potuto fargli quel gran male, così come l'aveva battuto, e a dimostrarglielo, si dava dei gran pugni sul petto e sulla schiena con un sasso; anzi un operaio, lì presente, gli sferrò un gran calcio sulle spalle, un calcio che risuonò come

desolate. "For us who are born to live below ground," Nasty Redhead would reflect, "there ought to be darkness always and everywhere." The little-owl hooted on the lava, roaming here and there, and he reflected: "Even the owl senses the dead men who are below ground here, and it's in despair because it can't go and find them."

Frog was afraid of owls and bats, but Red used to bawl him out, because people who are compelled to be alone shouldn't be afraid of anything; not even the gray donkey was afraid of the dogs that were eating it up, now that its flesh no longer felt the pain of being devoured.

"You were accustomed to working on roofs like a cat," he'd say to him, "and then it was a completely different matter. But now that it's your fate to live underground like a rat, you no longer need to be afraid of rats, or of bats, which are just old rats with wings, and rats like to keep company with the dead."

For his part, Frog derived great pleasure from explaining to him what the stars were doing up in the sky; he'd tell him that Heaven was up there, where dead people went who were good and never grieved their parents. "Who told you so?" Nasty Redhead would ask, and Frog would reply that his mother had told him that.

Then Nasty Redhead would scratch his head and, with a smile, would repeat a saying typical of a spiteful, know-it-all brat: "Your mother tells you that because, instead of pants, you should be wearing skirts."

And, after thinking it over a little:

"My father was good and never did harm to anyone, so much so that they called him Dumb Animal. But he's down there, and they even found his tools and shoes, and these trousers that I'm wearing right now."

Not long afterward, Frog, who had been in a decline for some time, became so ill that every evening he had to be carried out of the pit on the donkey's back, sprawling among the big baskets of sand and shaking with fever like a wet chick. One workman said that that boy "would never stick it out" at that job; to work in a mine and not lose your life there, you've got to be born to it. At such times Nasty Redhead felt proud of being born to it and of remaining so healthy and vigorous in that bad air and with all those privations. He'd carry Frog on his back, encouraging him in his own way, by yelling at him and hitting him. But one time, when he hit him on the back, Frog spat blood; Nasty Redhead was frightened and desperately examined his nose and mouth to see what he had done to him; he swore that he couldn't have caused such a serious injury, the way he had struck him; to prove it to him, he gave himself heavy blows on the chest and the back with a stone. In fact, a workman who was present gave Red a big kick in the back, a kick

su di un tamburo, eppure Malpelo non si mosse, e soltanto dopo che l'operaio se ne fu andato, aggiunse: – Lo vedi? Non mi ha fatto nulla! E ha picchiato più forte di me, ti giuro!

Intanto Ranocchio non guariva e seguitava a sputar sangue, e ad aver la febbre tutti i giorni. Allora Malpelo rubò dei soldi della paga della settimana, per comperargli del vino e della minestra calda, e gli diede i suoi calzoni quasi nuovi che lo coprivano meglio. Ma Ranocchio tossiva sempre e alcune volte sembrava soffocasse, e la sera non c'era modo di vincere il ribrezzo della febbre, né con sacchi, né coprendolo di paglia, né mettendolo dinanzi alla fiammata. Malpelo se ne stava zitto ed immobile chino su di lui, colle mani sui ginocchi, fissandolo con quei suoi occhiacci spalancati come se volesse fargli il ritratto, e allorché lo udiva gemere sottovoce, e gli vedeva il viso trafelato e l'occhio spento, preciso come quello dell'asino grigio allorché ansava rifinito sotto il carico nel salire la viottola, ei gli borbottava: – È meglio che tu crepi presto! Se devi soffrire in tal modo, è meglio che tu crepi! – E il padrone diceva che Malpelo era capace di schiacciargli il capo a quel ragazzo, e bisognava sorvegliarlo.

Finalmente un lunedì Ranocchio non venne più alla cava, e il padrone se ne lavò le mani, perché allo stato in cui era ridotto oramai era più di impiccio che d'altro. Malpelo si informò dove stesse di casa, e il sabato andò a trovarlo. Il povero Ranocchio era più di là che di qua, e sua madre piangeva e si disperava come se il suo figliolo fosse di quelli che guadagnano dieci lire la settimana.

Cotesto non arrivava a comprendere Malpelo, e domandò a Ranocchio perché sua madre strillasse a quel modo, mentre che da due mesi ei non guadagnava nemmeno quel che si mangiava. Ma il povero Ranocchio non gli dava retta e sembrava che badasse a contare quanti travicelli c'erano sul tetto. Allora il Rosso si diede ad almanaccare che la madre di Ranocchio strillasse a quel modo perché il suo figliuolo era sempre stato debole e malaticcio, e l'aveva tenuto come quei marmocchi che non si slattano mai. Egli invece era stato sano e robusto, ed era *malpelo,* e sua madre non aveva mai pianto per lui perché non aveva mai avuto timore di perderlo.

Poco dopo, alla cava dissero che Ranocchio era morto, ed ei pensò che la civetta adesso strideva anche per lui nella notte, e tornò a visitare le ossa spolpate del *grigio,* nel burrone dove solevano andare insieme con Ranocchio. Ora del *grigio* non rimanevano più che le ossa sgangherate, ed anche di Ranocchio sarebbe stato così, e sua madre si sarebbe asciugati gli occhi, poiché anche la madre di Malpelo s'era

that made a noise like a drum, but Nasty Redhead didn't budge. It was only after the workman went away that he added: "See? He didn't do a thing to me! And he hit harder than I did, I swear to you!"

Meanwhile Frog didn't get better; he continued to spit blood, and to be feverish every day. Then Nasty Redhead stole a little money from his week's pay to buy him wine and hot soup, and gave him his almost-new trousers, which covered him better. But Frog was always coughing; sometimes he seemed to be choking; and in the evenings there was no way to prevent him from shuddering with fever, neither by piling sacks on him, nor by covering him with straw, nor by putting him in front of a blazing fire. Nasty Redhead would stay bent over him, in silence and motionless, hands on knees, staring at him with those malicious eyes of his wide open, as if he wanted to do a portrait of him; whenever he heard him moan quietly, or saw his breathless face and glassy eyes—just like those of the gray donkey when it panted in exhaustion beneath its load while climbing the incline—he'd murmur to him: "You're better off croaking quickly! If you have to suffer this way, you're better off croaking!" And the pit owner used to say that Nasty Redhead was capable of crushing that boy's skull, and that it was necessary to keep an eye on him.

Finally one Monday Frog didn't show up at the pit, and the owner washed his hands of him, because in the condition to which he was now reduced he was more of a hindrance than anything else. Nasty Redhead inquired as to where he lived, and on Saturday he went to visit him. Poor Frog was more dead than alive, and his mother was weeping and lamenting as if her son were one of those who earn ten *lire* a week.

Nasty Redhead couldn't manage to comprehend this, and he asked Frog why his mother was shrieking like that, seeing that for two months he hadn't even been earning the cost of his food. But poor Frog paid no attention to him; he seemed to be intent on counting the number of rafters in the roof. Then Red, puzzling it out, decided that Frog's mother was shrieking that way because her son had always been weak and sickly, and she had maintained him like those babies that can never be weaned. He, on the other hand, had been healthy and sturdy, and he was a nasty redhead, so that his mother had never cried over him because she had never been afraid of losing him.

Shortly afterward, they said in the pit that Frog had died. It seemed to Red that the owl was hooting for him, too, at night, and he went to revisit the fleshless bones of Gray in the gorge where he had been accustomed to go with Frog. All that was now left of Gray was his scattered, smashed bones; it would be that way with Frog, too, and his mother would dry her eyes, since even Nasty Redhead's mother had

asciugati i suoi dopo che mastro Misciu era morto, e adesso si era maritata un'altra volta, ed era andata a stare a Cifali; anche la sorella si era
maritata e avevano chiusa la casa. D'ora in poi, se lo battevano, a loro
non importava più nulla, e a lui nemmeno, e quando sarebbe divenuto
come il *grigio* o come Ranocchio, non avrebbe sentito più nulla.

Verso quell'epoca venne a lavorare nella cava uno che non s'era mai
visto, e si teneva nascosto il più che poteva; gli altri operai dicevano fra
di loro che era scappato dalla prigione, e se lo pigliavano ce lo tornavano a chiudere per degli anni e degli anni. Malpelo seppe in quel-
l'occasione che la prigione era un luogo dove si mettevano i ladri, e i
malarnesi come lui, e si tenevano sempre chiusi là dentro e guardati a
vista.

Da quel momento provò una malsana curiosità per quell'uomo che
aveva provata la prigione e n'era scappato. Dopo poche settimane
però il fuggitivo dichiarò chiaro e tondo che era stanco di quella vi-
taccia da talpa e piuttosto si contentava di stare in galera tutta la vita,
ché la prigione, in confronto, era un paradiso e preferiva tornarci coi
suoi piedi. – Allora perché tutti quelli che lavorano nella cava non si
fanno mettere in prigione? – domandò Malpelo.

– Perché non sono *malpelo* come te! – rispose lo sciancato. – Ma
non temere, che tu ci andrai e ci lascerai le ossa.

Invece le ossa le lasciò nella cava, Malpelo, come suo padre, ma in
modo diverso. Una volta si doveva esplorare un passaggio che si
riteneva comunicasse col pozzo grande a sinistra, verso la valle, e se la
cosa era vera, si sarebbe risparmiata una buona metà di mano d'opera
nel cavar fuori la rena. Ma se non era vero, c'era il pericolo di smar-
rirsi e di non tornare mai più. Sicché nessun padre di famiglia voleva
avventurarvisi, né avrebbe permesso che ci si arrischiasse il sangue
suo per tutto l'oro del mondo.

Ma Malpelo non aveva nemmeno chi si prendesse tutto l'ora del
mondo per la sua pelle, se pure la sua pelle valeva tutto l'oro del
mondo; sua madre si era rimaritata e se n'era andata a stare a Cifali,
e sua sorella s'era maritata anch'essa. La porta della casa era chiusa,
ed ei non aveva altro che le scarpe di suo padre appese al chiodo; perciò gli commettevano sempre i lavori più pericolosi, e le imprese più
arrischiate, e s'ei non si aveva riguardo alcuno, gli altri non ne avevano certamente per lui. Quando lo mandarono per quella esplo-
razione si risovvenne del minatore, il quale si era smarrito, da anni ed
anni, e cammina e cammina ancora al buio gridando aiuto, senza che
nessuno possa udirlo; ma non disse nulla. Del resto a che sarebbe
giovato? Prese gli arnesi di suo padre, il piccone, la zappa, la lanterna,

dried her eyes after master Misciu had died, and had now remarried and gone to live in Cifali. His sister had married, too, and the house had been shut up. From now on, if he was beaten, it was of no more concern to them, and not to him, either; and when he had become like Gray or Frog, he wouldn't feel anything any longer.

Around that time a man came to work in the pit who had never been seen there; he kept hidden as much as he could. The other workmen said among themselves that he had escaped from prison, and that if he was recaptured, he'd be locked up again for years and years. On that occasion Nasty Redhead learned that prison was a place where they put thieves, and scoundrels like himself, keeping them constantly locked up in there under surveillance.

From that moment on, he felt an unhealthy curiosity about that man who had experienced prison and had escaped from it. A few weeks later, however, the fugitive declared outright that he was tired of that rotten mole's existence and would prefer to stay in jail for the rest of his life, because prison was a paradise by comparison, and he'd rather go back there on his own feet. "Then, why doesn't everyone who works in the pit get himself put in prison?" Nasty Redhead asked.

"Because they aren't nasty redheads like you!" the cripple replied. "But have no fear, you'll go there and you'll never come out again."

But instead, it was the pit that Nasty Redhead never came out of, like his father, but in a different way. Once, it became necessary to explore a passage that was thought to communicate with the big shaft on the left, toward the valley. If that was true, a good half of the labor that was needed to excavate the sand could be saved. But if it wasn't true, there was danger of getting lost and never returning. And so, no man who was father of a family wanted to venture on that assignment, or would have allowed any of his relatives to risk their lives there for all the money in the world.

But Nasty Redhead didn't even have anyone who would take all the money in the world as compensation for his loss, even imagining that his life was worth all the money in the world. His mother had remarried and had gone to live in Cifali, and his sister had married, too. The door to his house was shut, and he owned nothing but his father's shoes hanging on the nail. For that reason they always assigned him the most dangerous tasks, and the riskiest endeavors; if he didn't look out for himself, certainly no one else was going to look out for him. When they sent him on that exploration, he recalled the miner who had gotten lost all those years ago, the one who was still walking and walking in the dark calling for help without the possibility of being heard by anyone. But he said nothing. What good would it have done,

il sacco col pane, e il fiasco del vino, e se ne andò: né più si seppe nulla di lui.

Così si persero persin le ossa di Malpelo, e i ragazzi della cava abbassano la voce quando parlano di lui nel sotterraneo, ché hanno paura di vederselo comparire dinanzi, coi capelli rossi e gli occhiacci grigi.

anyway? He took his father's equipment, the pick, the spade, the lantern, the sack with the bread, and the flask of wine, and he set out. Nothing more was ever heard of him.

And so, even the bones of Nasty Redhead were lost, and the boys in the pit lower their voices when they talk about him in the underground passage, because they're afraid they might see him appear before them, with his red hair, and his malicious gray eyes.

CAVALLERIA RUSTICANA

Turiddu Macca, il figlio della gnà Nunzia, come tornò da fare il soldato, ogni domenica si pavoneggiava in piazza coll'uniforme da bersagliere e il berretto rosso, che sembrava quello della buona ventura, quando metté su banco colla gabbia dei canarini. Le ragazze se lo rubavano cogli occhi, mentre andavano a messa col naso dentro la mantellina, e i monelli gli ronzavano attorno come le mosche. Egli aveva portato anche una pipa col re a cavallo che pareva vivo, e accendeva gli zolfanelli sul dietro dei calzoni, levando la gamba, come se desse una pedata. Ma con tutto ciò Lola di massaro Angelo non si era fatta vedere né alla messa, né sul ballatoio ché si era fatta sposa con uno di Licodia, il quale faceva il carrettiere e aveva quattro muli di Sortino in stalla. Dapprima Turiddu come lo seppe, santo diavolone! voleva trargli fuori le budella dalla pancia, voleva trargli, a quel di Licodia! però non ne fece nulla, e si sfogò coll'andare a cantare tutte le canzoni di sdegno che sapeva sotto la finestra della bella.

– Che non ha nulla da fare Turiddu della gnà Nunzia, dicevano i vicini, che passa le notti a cantare come una passera solitaria?

Finalmente s'imbatté in Lola che tornava dal *viaggio* alla Madonna del Pericolo, e al vederlo, non si fece né bianca né rossa quasi non fosse stato fatto suo.

– Beato chi vi vede! le disse.

– Oh, compare Turiddu, me l'avevano detto che siete tornato al primo del mese.

– A me mi hanno detto delle altre cose ancora! rispose lui. Che è vero che vi maritate con compare Alfio, il carrettiere?

– Se c'è la volontà di Dio! rispose Lola tirandosi sul mento le due cocche del fazzoletto.

RUSTIC CHIVALRY

When Turiddu Macca, the son of Mis' Nunzia, returned from his stint in the army, he'd show off in the village square every Sunday in his bersagliere[1] uniform and his red cap, which seemed like the one the fortune teller wears when he sets up his stand with its cage of canaries. The girls would steal him away from one another with their eyes, while they went to Mass with their noses buried in their shoulder capes; and the urchins would buzz around him like flies. He had also brought home a tobacco pipe with a carving of the king on horseback that looked real, and he used to strike matches on the seat of his trousers, lifting his leg as if he were kicking somebody. But despite all that, Lola, farmer Angelo's daughter, hadn't showed up either at Mass or on her veranda, because she had become engaged to a man from Licodia who made his living as a carter and had four mules from Sortino in his stable. When Turiddu first learned of this, damnation! He'd have liked to disembowel that fellow from Licodia, that's what he would have liked! But he did nothing of the sort, and he vented his feelings by singing all the sarcastic songs he knew beneath the beautiful girl's window.

"Doesn't Mis' Nunzia's son Turiddu have anything to do," the neighbors said, "if he can spend his nights singing like a lonely hen sparrow?"

Finally he ran into Lola as she was returning from a pilgrimage to Our Lady of Peril. When she saw him, her face turned neither white nor red; it was as if it were none of her business.

"Lucky the man who sees you!" he said to her.

"Oh, neighbor Turiddu, I was told you had come home on the first of the month."

"And *I* was told plenty of other things!" he replied. "Is it true that you're marrying neighbor Alfio, the carter?"

"What do you want? It's the will of God!" replied Lola, drawing the two corners of her kerchief over her chin.

---

1. Literally, "sharpshooter, target man," but actually a member of a corps of light infantry instituted in 1836. The bersagliere uniform featured feathers in the cap.

– La volontà di Dio la fate col tira e molla come vi torna conto! E la volontà di Dio fu che dovevo tornare da tanto lontano per trovare ste belle notizie, gnà Lola!

Il poveraccio tentava di fare ancora il bravo, ma la voce gli si era fatta roca; ed egli andava dietro alla ragazza dondolandosi colla nappa del berretto che gli ballava di qua e di là sulle spalle. A lei, in coscienza, rincresceva di vederlo così col viso lungo, però non aveva cuore di lusingarlo con belle parole.

– Sentite, compare Turiddu, gli disse alfine, lasciatemi raggiungere le mie compagne. Che direbbero in paese se mi vedessero con voi? . . .

– È giusto, rispose Turiddu; ora che sposate compare Alfio, che ci ha quattro muli in stalla, non bisogna farla chiacchierare la gente. Mia madre invece, poveretta, la dovette vendere la nostra mula baia, e quel pezzetto di vigna sullo stradone, nel tempo ch'ero soldato. Passò quel tempo che Berta filava, e voi non ci pensate più al tempo in cui ci parlavamo dalla finestra sul cortile, e mi regalaste quel fazzoletto, prima d'andarmene, che Dio sa quante lagrime ci ho pianto dentro nell'andar via lontano tanto che si perdeva persino il nome del nostro paese. Ora addio, gnà Lola, *facemu cuntu ca chioppi e scampau, e la nostra amicizia finiu.*

La gnà Lola si maritò col carrettiere; e la domenica si metteva sul ballatoio, colle mani sul ventre per far vedere tutti i grossi anelli d'oro che le aveva regalati suo marito. Turiddu seguitava a passare e ripassare per la stradicciuola, colla pipa in bocca e le mani in tasca, in aria d'indifferenza, e occhieggiando le ragazze; ma dentro ci si rodeva che il marito di Lola avesse tutto quell'oro, e che ella fingesse di non accorgersi di lui quando passava. – Voglio fargliela proprio sotto gli occhi a quella cagnaccia! borbottava.

Di faccia a compare Alfio ci stava massaro Cola, il vignaiuolo, il quale era ricco come un maiale, dicevano, e aveva una figliuola in casa. Turiddu tanto disse e tanto fece che entrò camparo da massaro Cola, e cominciò a bazzicare per la casa e a dire le paroline dolci alla ragazza.

– Perché non andate a dirle alla gnà Lola ste belle cose? rispondeva Santa.

"You do the will of God any old way, just as it suits your purpose! And the will of God was that I should come home from so far away to learn this fine news, Mis' Lola!"

The poor fellow tried to go on playing the hero, but his voice had become hoarse, and he swayed as he walked after the girl, with the tassel of his cap bouncing here and there on his back. She was genuinely sorry to see him with such a long face, but she couldn't bring herself to flatter his hopes with fine words.

"Listen, neighbor Turiddu," she finally said, "let me rejoin my girlfriends. What would the people in the village say if they saw me with you? . . ."

"You're right," Turiddu answered; "now that you're marrying neighbor Alfio, who has four mules in his stable, you mustn't make people gossip. But my mother, poor woman, had to sell our bay she-mule, and that tiny vineyard on the highroad, while I was in the army. The good old days[2] are over, and you no longer remember the times when we'd speak to each other through the window overlooking the yard, and you made me a present of that handkerchief before I went away, which I cried God knows how many tears into when I traveled so far that no one even knew the name of our village. Well, good-bye now, Mis' Lola; let's just imagine that it rained and stopped raining, and our friendship is over."[3]

Mis' Lola married the carter, and on Sundays she appeared on her veranda, her hands on her stomach to display all the big gold rings her husband had given her. Turiddu continued to walk up and down the lane, his pipe in his mouth and his hands in his pockets, acting nonchalant and leering at the girls; but inside he was eating himself up because Lola's husband had all that money and she pretended not to notice him when he passed by. "I want to take it out on that dirty bitch right in front of her eyes!" he'd mutter.

Just opposite neighbor Alfio lived farmer Cola, the vineyard owner, who was said to be as rich as a pig and who had a daughter at home. Turiddu, by various ways and means, got a job as field watchman for farmer Cola, and he started hanging around the house and saying sweet nothings to the girl.

"Why don't you go and say these fine things to Mis' Lola?" Santa would reply.

---

2. Literally, "the time when Bertha span." This centuries-old Italian expression may refer to Bertha (Bertrada), the mother of Charlemagne, the first Holy Roman Emperor, crowned in 800.   3. A standard Italian version of the Sicilian text would be: "Facciamo conto che sia piovuto e poi spiovuto, e la nostra amicizia è finita."

– La gnà Lola è una signorona! La gnà Lola ha sposato un re di corona, ora!

– Io non me li merito i re di corona.

– Voi ne valete cento delle Lole, e conosco uno che non guarderebbe la gnà Lola, né il suo santo, quando ci siete voi, ché la gnà Lola, non è degna di portarvi le scarpe, non è degna.

– La volpe quando all'uva non ci poté arrivare . . .

– Disse: come sei bella, *racinedda* mia!

– Ohé! quelle mani, compare Turiddu.

– Avete paura che vi mangi?

– Paura non ho né di voi, né del vostro Dio.

– Eh! vostra madre era di Licodia, lo sappiamo! Avete il sangue rissoso! Uh! che vi mangerei cogli occhi!

– Mangiatemi pure cogli occhi, che briciole non ne faremo; ma intanto tiratemi su quel fascio.

– Per voi tirerei su tutta la casa, tirerei!

Ella, per non farsi rossa, gli tirò un ceppo che aveva sottomano, e non lo colse per miracolo.

– Spicciamoci, che le chiacchiere non ne affastellano sarmenti.

– Se fossi ricco, vorrei cercarmi una moglie come voi, gnà Santa.

– Io non sposerò un re di corona come la gnà Lola, ma la mia dote ce l'ho anch'io, quando il Signore mi manderà qualcheduno.

– Lo sappiamo che siete ricca, lo sappiamo!

– Se lo sapete allora spicciatevi, ché il babbo sta per venire, e non vorrei farmi trovare nel cortile.

Il babbo cominciava a torcere il muso, ma la ragazza fingeva di non accorgersi, poiché la nappa del berretto del bersagliere gli aveva fatto il solletico dentro il cuore, e le ballava sempre dinanzi gli occhi. Come il babbo mise Turiddu fuori dell'uscio, la figliuola gli aprì la finestra, e stava a chiacchierare con lui tutta la sera, che tutto il vicinato non parlava d'altro.

– Per te impazzisco, diceva Turiddu, e perdo il sonno e l'appetito.

– Chiacchiere.

– Vorrei essere il figlio di Vittorio Emanuele per sposarti!

– Chiacchiere.

– Per la madonna che ti mangerei come il pane!

– Chiacchiere!

– Ah! sull'onor mio!

"Mis' Lola is a high and mighty lady! Mis' Lola has married a king with a crown now!"

"*I* don't rate kings with crowns."

"You're worth a hundred women like Lola, and I know a man who wouldn't even look at Mis' Lola, or at her patron saint, when you're here, because Mis' Lola isn't worthy of carrying your shoes, no, she's not."

"When the fox couldn't reach the grapes . . ."

"It said: 'How beautiful you are, my bunch of grapes!'"

"Oh, ho! Hands to yourself, neighbor Turiddu!"

"Afraid I'll eat you up?"

"I'm not afraid of you or of your God."

"Ha! Your mother was from Licodia, we know! You've got quarrelsome blood! Ooh! I could eat you up with my eyes!"

"Go ahead and eat me up with your eyes, and there still won't be any crumbs. But in the meantime carry up that bundle of wood for me."

"For you I'd carry up the whole house, I would!"

To keep from blushing, she threw a hunk of wood at him that was ready to her hand, and missed him by a miracle.

"Let's get moving, because chitchat doesn't tie up vine runners in bundles."

"If I were rich, I'd look for a wife like you, Mis' Santa."

"I won't marry a king with a crown, the way Mis' Lola did, but I do have a dowry of my own, for the day that the Lord sends somebody my way."

"We know that you're rich, we know!"

"If you know it, get a move on, because my father will arrive any minute, and I don't want him to find me out here in the yard."

Her father was beginning to make grimaces, but the girl pretended not to notice, because the tassel of that bersagliere cap had tickled her heart and was always bouncing in front of her eyes. When her father showed Turiddu the door, the girl opened the window for him; she'd stay there conversing with him all evening long, so that all the neighbors were talking about nothing else.

"I'm going crazy for you," Turiddu would say. "I can't sleep and I have no appetite."

"Stuff and nonsense."

"I'd like to be the son of King Vittorio Emmanuele, so I could marry you!"

"Nonsense."

"By the Madonna, I could eat you up like bread!"

"Nonsense!"

"No, on my honor!"

– Ah! mamma mia!

Lola che ascoltava ogni sera, nascosta dietro il vaso di basilico, e si faceva pallida e rossa, un giorno chiamò Turiddu.

– E così, compare Turiddu, gli amici vecchi non si salutano più?

– Ma! sospirò il giovinotto, beato chi può salutarvi!

– Se avete intenzione di salutarmi, lo sapete dove sto di casa! rispose Lola.

Turiddu tornò a salutarla così spesso che Santa se ne avvide, e gli batté la finestra sul muso. I vicini se lo mostravano con un sorriso, o con un moto del capo, quando passava il bersagliere. Il marito di Lola era in giro per le fiere con le sue mule.

– Domenica voglio andare a confessarmi, ché stanotte ho sognato dell'uva nera, disse Lola.

– Lascia stare! lascia stare! supplicava Turiddu.

– No, ora che s'avvicina la Pasqua, mio marito lo vorrebbe sapere il perché non sono andata a confessarmi.

– Ah! mormorava Santa di massaro Cola, aspettando ginocchioni il suo turno dinanzi al confessionario dove Lola stava facendo il bucato dei suoi peccati. Sull'anima mia non voglio mandarti a Roma per la penitenza!

Compare Alfio tornò colle sue mule, carico di soldoni, e portò in regalo alla moglie una bella veste nuova per le feste.

– Avete ragione di portarle dei regali, gli disse la vicina Santa, perché mentre voi siete via vostra moglie vi adorna la casa!

Compare Alfio era di quei carrettieri che portano il berretto sull'orecchio, e a sentir parlare in tal modo di sua moglie cambiò di colore come se l'avessero accoltellato. – Santo diavolone! esclamò, se non avete visto bene, non vi lascierò gli occhi per piangere! a voi e a tutto il vostro parentado!

– Non son usa a piangere! rispose Santa; non ho pianto nemmeno quando ho visto con questi occhi Turiddu della gnà Nunzia entrare di notte in casa di vostra moglie.

– Va bene, rispose compare Alfio, grazie tante.

Turiddu, adesso che era tornato il gatto, non bazzicava più di giorno per la stradicciuola, e smaltiva l'uggia all'osteria, cogli amici; e la vigilia di Pasqua avevano sul desco un piatto di salsiccia. Come entrò compare Alfio, soltanto dal modo in cui gli piantò gli occhi addosso,

"Oh, Lord!"

Lola, who was listening every evening, hidden behind her pot of basil,[4] and who turned both pale and red, called to Turiddu one day.

"And so, neighbor Turiddu, old friends don't say hello anymore?"

"What do you mean?" the young man sighed. "Lucky the man who can say hello to you!"

"If you have any intention of saying hello, you know where I live!" Lola replied.

Turiddu kept saying hello to her so often that Santa came to notice it and slammed her window in his face. The neighbors would point to him with a smile, or a movement of their head, whenever the bersagliere passed by. Lola's husband was making the rounds of the animal fairs with his she-mules.

"On Sunday I want to go to Confession, because last night I dreamt about black grapes," Lola said.

"Let it go! Let it go!" Turiddu begged her.

"No, now that Easter is nearly here, my husband would be curious about why I didn't go to Confession."

"Ah!" murmured farmer Cola's daughter Santa, as she knelt awaiting her turn at the confessional where Lola was washing out her sins. "By my soul, it isn't to Rome I want to send you to do your penance!"

Neighbor Alfio came home with his she-mules, loaded with money, and brought as a present for his wife a beautiful new dress for the holiday.

"You're right to bring her presents," his neighbor Santa told him, "because while you're away, your wife decorates your house!"

Neighbor Alfio was one of those carters who fly off the handle easily,[5] and when he heard his wife talked about in such terms, he changed color as if he had been stabbed. "Hell and damnation!" he exclaimed, "if you've seen incorrectly, I won't leave you with any eyes to cry over it, you and your whole family!"

"I'm not the crying kind," Santa replied. "I didn't cry even when I saw with my own eyes how Mis' Nunzia's son Turiddu went into your wife's house at night."

"All right," neighbor Alfio replied, "many thanks!"

Now that the cat was no longer away, Turiddu didn't loiter in the lane during the day anymore; he chased away his boredom at the inn with his friends. On Easter Eve, they had a platter of sausages on the table. When neighbor Alfio entered, merely the way Alfio fixed his

---

4. See "Fantasticheria," footnote 2.   5. Literally: "who wear their cap over their ear."

Turiddu comprese che era venuto per quell'affare e posò la forchetta sul piatto.

– Avete comandi da darmi, compare Alfio? gli disse.

– Nessuna preghiera, compare Turiddu, era un pezzo che non vi vedevo, e voleva parlarvi di quella cosa che sapete voi.

Turiddu da prima gli aveva presentato il bicchiere, ma compare Alfio lo scansò colla mano. Allora Turiddu si alzò e gli disse:

– Son qui, compar Alfio.

Il carrettiere gli buttò le braccia al collo.

– Se domattina volete venire nei fichidindia della Canziria potremo parlare di quell'affare, compare.

– Aspettatemi sullo stradone allo spuntar del sole, e ci andremo insieme.

Con queste parole si scambiarono il bacio della sfida. Turiddu strinse fra i denti l'orecchio del carrettiere, e così gli fece promessa solenne di non mancare.

Gli amici avevano lasciato la salciccia zitti zitti, e accompagnarono Turiddu sino a casa. La gnà Nunzia, poveretta, l'aspettava sin tardi ogni sera.

– Mamma, le disse Turiddu, vi rammentate quando sono andato soldato, che credevate non avessi a tornar più? Datemi un bel bacio come allora, perché domattina andrò lontano.

Prima di giorno si prese il suo coltello a molla, che aveva nascosto sotto il fieno quando era andato coscritto, e si mise in cammino pei fichidindia della Canziria.

– Oh! Gesummaria! dove andate con quella furia? piagnucolava Lola sgomenta, mentre suo marito stava per uscire.

– Vado qui vicino, rispose compar Alfio, ma per te sarebbe meglio che io non tornassi più.

Lola, in camicia, pregava ai piedi del letto e si stringeva sulle labbra il rosario che le aveva portato fra Bernardino dai Luoghi Santi, e recitava tutte le avemarie che potevano capirvi.

– Compare Alfio, cominciò Turiddu dopo che ebbe fatto un pezzo di strada accanto al suo compagno, il quale stava zitto, e col berretto sugli occhi. Come è vero Iddio so che ho torto e mi lascierei ammazzare. Ma prima di venir qui ho visto la mia vecchia che si era alzata per vedermi partire, col pretesto di governare il pollaio, quasi il cuore le parlasse, e quant'è vero Iddio vi ammazzerò come un cane per non far piangere la mia vecchierella.

– Così va bene, rispose compare Alfio, spogliandosi del farsetto, e picchieremo sodo tutt'e due.

eyes on him made Turiddu understand that he had come in reference to that business, and he put his fork down on the platter.

"Do you have any services to ask of me, neighbor Alfio?" he asked.

"Not a thing, neighbor Turiddu; it's been a while since I've seen you, and I wanted to talk to you about that matter you know of."

At first Turiddu had offered him his glass of wine, but neighbor Alfio shunted it aside with his hand. Then Turiddu stood up and said:

"Here I am, neighbor Alfio."

The carter threw his arms around his neck.

"If you want to come to the prickly-pear thicket in Canziria tomorrow morning, we'll be able to talk this matter over, neighbor."

"Wait for me on the highroad when the sun comes up, and we'll go there together."

Having said this, they exchanged the kiss of challenge. Turiddu gripped the carter's ear in his teeth, thus making a solemn promise that he wouldn't fail to appear.

Turiddu's friends had left their sausages in complete silence, and they accompanied him home. Mis' Nunzia, poor woman, waited up for him till a late hour every night.

"Mother," Turiddu said, "do you remember when I went into the army and you thought I'd never come back? Give me a good kiss the way you did that time, because tomorrow morning I'm taking a long trip."

Before daybreak he took his claspknife, which he had hidden beneath the hay when he had been conscripted, and set out for the Canziria prickly pears.

"Oh, Jesus and Mary, where are you going in such hot haste?" Lola whimpered in alarm when her husband was about to leave the house.

"I'm going somewhere close by," neighbor Alfio replied, "but it would be better for you if I never came back."

Lola, in her nightgown, prayed at the foot of her bed, pressing to her lips the rosary that Friar Bernardino had brought back for her from the Holy Land, and she recited all the Hail Marys that it could accommodate.

"Neighbor Alfio," Turiddu began after walking for a stretch alongside his fellow wayfarer, who remained silent, his cap pulled down over his eyes. "As truly as God exists, I know I'm in the wrong, and I'd let myself be killed. But before coming here, I saw my old mother, who had gotten out of bed to see me off, pretending she had chores in the henhouse, as if her heart told her something, and, as sure as there's a God, I'm going to kill you like a dog to keep my poor old mother from weeping."

"That's all right," neighbor Alfio replied, taking off his vest. "Both of us will fight hard."

Entrambi erano bravi tiratori; Turiddu toccò la prima botta, e fu a tempo a prenderla nel braccio; come la rese, la rese buona, e tirò all'inguinaia.

– Ah! compare Turiddu! avete proprio intenzione di ammazzarmi!

– Sì, ve l'ho detto; ora che ho visto la mia vecchia nel pollaio, mi pare di averla sempre dinanzi agli occhi.

– Apriteli bene, gli occhi! gli gridò compar Alfio, che sto per rendervi la buona misura.

Come egli stava in guardia tutto raccolto per tenersi la sinistra sulla ferita, che gli doleva, e quasi strisciava per terra col gomito, acchiappò rapidamente una manata di polvere e la gettò negli occhi dell'avversario.

– Ah! urlò Turiddu accecato, son morto.

Ei cercava di salvarsi facendo salti disperati all'indietro; ma compar Alfio lo raggiunse con un'altra botta nello stomaco e una terza nella gola.

–E tre! questa è per la casa che tu m'hai adornato. Ora tua madre lascierà stare le galline.

Turiddu annaspò un pezzo di qua e di là fra i fichidindia e poi cadde come un masso. Il sangue gli gorgogliava spumeggiando nella gola, e non poté profferire nemmeno: – Ah! mamma mia!

They were both skillful at knife fighting. Turiddu was the first to be wounded, but he deftly managed to receive the blow on his arm. When he returned it, he returned it adroitly, and struck Alfio in the groin.

"Oh, neighbor Turiddu! You seriously intend to kill me!"

"Yes, I told you so. Now that I've seen my old mother in the hen-house, she seems to be constantly before my eyes."

"Open those eyes wide," neighbor Alfio shouted, "because I'm going to give you measure for measure!"

As he stood on his guard, hunched up because he was keeping his left hand on his wound, which hurt, his elbow nearly grazed the ground. He rapidly seized a handful of dust and threw it into his opponent's eyes.

"Oh!" howled Turiddu, blinded, "I'm a dead man!"

He tried to escape by jumping backward desperately, but neighbor Alfio caught up with him, planting a second blow in his stomach and a third in his throat.

"That makes three! This one is for my house, which you 'decorated.' Now your mother will leave the chickens alone."

Turiddu groped around a little here and there among the prickly pears, then fell like a rock. The blood was foaming as it bubbled out of his throat, and he didn't even have time to utter: "Oh, Mother!"

LA LUPA

Era alta, magra; aveva soltanto un seno fermo e vigoroso da bruna e pure non era più giovane; era pallida come se avesse sempre addosso la malaria, e su quel pallore due occhi grandi così, e delle labbra fresche e rosse, che vi mangiavano.

Al villaggio la chiamavano *la Lupa* perché non era sazia giammai – di nulla. Le donne si facevano la croce quando la vedevano passare, sola come una cagnaccia, con quell'andare randagio e sospettoso della lupa affamata; ella si spolpava i loro figliuoli e i loro mariti in un batter d'occhio, con le sue labbra rosse, e se li tirava dietro alla gonnella solamente a guardarli con quegli occhi da satanasso, fossero stati davanti all'altare di Santa Agrippina. Per fortuna *la Lupa* non veniva mai in chiesa né a Pasqua, né a Natale, né per ascoltar messa, né per confessarsi. – Padre Angiolino di Santa Maria di Gesù, un vero servo di Dio, aveva persa l'anima per lei.

Maricchia, poveretta, buona e brava ragazza, piangeva di nascosto, perché era figlia della *Lupa,* e nessuno l'avrebbe tolta in moglie, sebbene ci avesse la sua bella roba nel cassettone, e la sua buona terra al sole, come ogni altra ragazza del villaggio.

Una volta *la Lupa* si innamorò di un bel ragazzo che era tornato da soldato, e mieteva il fieno con lei nelle chiuse del notaro, ma proprio quello che si dice innamorarsi, sentirsene ardere le carni sotto al fustagno del corpetto, e provare, fissandolo negli occhi, la sete che si ha nelle ore calde di giugno, in fondo alla pianura. Ma colui seguitava a mietere tranquillamente col naso sui manipoli, e le diceva: – O che avete, gnà Pina? Nei campi immensi, dove scoppiettava soltanto il volo dei grilli, quando il sole batteva a piombo, *la Lupa* affastellava manipoli su manipoli, e covoni su covoni, senza stancarsi

THE SHE-WOLF

She was tall and thin; her only advantageous feature was a swarthy woman's firm and vigorous bosom, though she was no longer young. She was as pale as if she were constantly suffering from malaria, and amid that pallor were two enormous eyes and bright red lips that devoured you.

In the village they called her "the She-wolf" because she never had her fill—of anything.[1] The women used to cross themselves when they saw her go by, as all alone as a vicious bitch, with that vagrant, mistrustful gait of a starving wolf. She would bleed their sons and husbands dry in the twinkling of an eye, with her red lips, and make them follow her skirt merely by looking at them with those devil's eyes, even if they were standing in front of St. Agrippina's[2] altar. Fortunately, the She-wolf never came to church, neither at Easter, nor at Christmas, nor to hear Mass, nor to go to Confession.—Father Angiolino of St. Mary of Jesus, a true servant of God, had lost his soul for her.

Maricchia, poor thing, a good and proper girl, used to weep in secret because she was the She-wolf's daughter and no one would marry her, even though she had lovely belongings in her chest of drawers and a piece of landed property, like any other girl in the village.

One time, the She-wolf fell in love with a handsome youngster who had come home from the army, and was mowing hay with her in the notary's fields. This was a true case of falling in love: feeling your flesh burn beneath your fustian bodice and, as you stare at him, suffering the thirst that you feel on hot June days deep in the lowlands. But the man went on mowing calmly, with his nose to the bundles of hay, saying to her: "What's wrong, Mis' Pina?" In the vast fields, where only the crackle of the flying crickets could be heard, when the sun beat down from directly overhead, the She-wolf was tying up one bundle after

---

1. The word *lupa* can also connote, or even denote, a nymphomaniac or a prostitute.
2. Patron saint of Mineo, whose feast fell around the third Sunday in August.

mai, senza rizzarsi un momento sulla vita, senza accostare le labbra
al fiasco, pur di stare sempre alle calcagna di Nanni, che mieteva e
mieteva, e le domandava di quando in quando: – Che volete, gnà
Pina?

Una sera ella glielo disse, mentre gli uomini sonnecchiavano nel-
l'aia, stanchi della lunga giornata, ed i cani uggiolavano per la vasta
campagna nera: – Te voglio! Te che sei bello come il sole, e dolce
come il miele. Voglio te!

– Ed io invece voglio vostra figlia, che è zitella, rispose Nanni
ridendo.

La Lupa si cacciò le mani nei capelli, grattandosi le tempie senza
dir parola, e se ne andò, né più comparve nell'aia. Ma in ottobre
rivide Nanni, al tempo che cavavano l'olio, perché egli lavorava accanto alla sua casa, e lo scricchiolìo del torchio non la faceva formire
tutta notte.

– Prendi il sacco delle ulive, disse alla figliuola, e vieni con me.

Nanni spingeva colla pala le ulive sotto la macina, e gridava ohi! alla
mula perché non si arrestasse. – La vuoi mia figlia Maricchia? gli domandò la gnà Pina. – Cosa gli date a vostra figlia Maricchia? rispose
Nanni. – Essa ha la roba di suo padre, e dippiù io le dò la mia casa; a
me mi basterà che mi lasciate un cantuccio nella cucina, per stendervi
un po' di pagliericcio. – Se è così se ne può parlare a Natale, disse
Nanni. – Nanni era tutto unto e sudicio dell'olio e delle ulive messe a
fermentare, e Maricchia non lo voleva a nessun patto; ma sua madre
l'afferrò pe' capelli, davanti al focolare, e le disse co' denti stretti: – Se
non lo pigli ti ammazzo!

La Lupa era quasi malata, e la gente andava dicendo che il diavolo
quando invecchia si fa eremita. Non andava più in qua e in là; non si
metteva più sull'uscio, con quegli occhi da spiritata. Suo genero,
quando ella glieli piantava in faccia quegli occhi, si metteva a ridere,
e cavava fuori l'abitino della Madonna per segnarsi. Maricchia stava
in casa ad allattare i figliuoli, e sua madre andava nei campi, a lavorare cogli uomini, proprio come un uomo, a sarchiare, a zappare, a
governare le bestie, a potare le viti, fosse stato greco e levante di
gennaio, oppure scirocco di agosto, allorquando i muli lasciavano
cader la testa penzoloni, e gli uomini dormivano bocconi a ridosso
del muro a tramontana. *In quell'ora fra vespero e nona, in cui non
ne va in volta femmina buona*, la gnà Pina era la sola anima viva che

another, one sheaf after another, without ever getting tired, without straightening up for a moment, without putting her lips to the flask, just so she could remain constantly at Nanni's heels, as he continued to mow, merely asking occasionally: "What is it you want, Mis' Pina?"

One evening she told him, while the men were dozing on the threshing floor, tired from their long day's work, and the dogs were howling in the vast dark countryside: "It's you I want! You're handsome as the sun and sweet as honey. I want *you*!"

"And I, on the other hand, want your daughter, who's never been married," Nanni replied with a laugh.

The She-wolf thrust her hands into her hair, scratching her temples but saying nothing; she went away and didn't show up on the threshing floor after that. But in October she saw Nanni again at oilpressing time, because he was working next to her house, and the creaking of the press kept her awake all night.

"Take the sack of olives," she said to her daughter, "and come with me." Nanni was shoveling the olives under the millstone, calling out "Hey!" to the she-mule to keep her from stopping. "You want my daughter Maricchia?" Mis' Pina asked him. "What do you intend to give to your daughter Maricchia?" Nanni replied. "She's got what her father left her, and on top of that I'll give her my house. It'll be enough for me if you leave me a corner in the kitchen to make a straw pallet there." "If that's the case, we can talk it over at Christmas," Nanni said. Nanni was all greasy and dirty with the oil and the olives that had been set aside to ferment, and Maricchia didn't want him on any terms; but her mother grabbed her by the hair, in front of the hearth, and said through her clenched teeth: "If you don't accept him, I'll kill you!"

The She-wolf was practically ill, and people were saying that "when the devil grows old, he becomes a hermit." She no longer roamed about; she no longer planted herself in her doorway with those lunatic's eyes. Whenever she directed those eyes at her son-in-law's face, he'd start to laugh, and he'd pull out his *abitino della Madonna*[3] to bless himself with. Maricchia would stay home nursing her babies, and her mother would go to the fields to work alongside the men, and just as hard as a man, weeding, hoeing, tending livestock, or pruning vines, whether the northeast and east winds were blowing in January or the scirocco in August, when the mules would let their heads hang down and the men slept on their stomachs in the shelter of a

---

3. Literally: "the Virgin's little garment." This is an amulet, worn around the neck, made up of two sewn-together squares of cloth enclosing a holy image.

si vedesse errare per la campagna, sui sassi infuocati delle viottole, fra le stoppie riarse dei campi immensi, che si perdevano nell'afa, lontan lontano, verso l'Etna nebbioso, dove il cielo si aggravava sull'orizzonte.

– Svegliati! disse *la Lupa* a Nanni che dormiva nel fosso, accanto alla siepe polverosa, col capo fra le braccia. Svegliati, ché ti ho portato il vino per rinfrescarti la gola.

Nanni spalancò gli occhi imbambolati, fra veglia e sonno, trovandosela dinanzi ritta, pallida, col petto prepotente, e gli occhi neri come il carbone, e stese brancolando le mani.

– No! non ne va in volta femmina buona nell'ora fra vespero e nona! singhiozzava Nanni, ricacciando la faccia contro l'erba secca del fossato, in fondo in fondo, colle unghie nei capelli. – Andatevene! Andatevene! non ci venite più nell'aia!

Ella se ne andava infatti, *la Lupa*, riannodando le trecce superbe, guardando fisso dinanzi ai suoi passi nelle stoppie calde, cogli occhi neri come il carbone.

Ma nell'aia ci tornò delle altre volte, e Nanni non le disse nulla; e quando tardava a venire, nell'ora fra vespero e nona, egli andava ad aspettarla in cima alla viottola bianca e deserta, col sudore sulla fronte; – e dopo si cacciava le mani nei capelli, e le ripeteva ogni volta: Andatevene! andatevene! Non ci tornate più nell'aia! – Maricchia piangeva notte e giorno, e alla madre le piantava in faccia gli occhi ardenti di lagrime e di gelosia, come una lupacchiotta anch'essa, quando la vedeva tornare da' campi pallida e muta ogni volta. – Scellerata! le diceva. Mamma scellerata!

– Taci!

– Ladra! ladra!

– Taci!

– Andrò dal brigadiere, andrò!

– Vacci!

E ci andò davvero, coi figli in collo, senza temere di nulla, e senza versare una lagrima, come una pazza, perché adesso l'amava anche lei quel marito che le avevano dato per forza, unto e sudicio dalle ulive messe a fermentare.

northward-facing wall. "During those hours between Vespers and Nones, in which no decent woman walks abroad,"[4] Mis' Pina was the only living soul who could be seen wandering across the countryside, over the sun-baked stones in the paths, amid the dried-up stubble in the vast fields that were lost to the view in the sultry haze, far, far off toward mist-shrouded Etna, where the sky weighed heavily on the horizon.

"Wake up!" the She-wolf said to Nanni, who was sleeping in the ditch alongside the dusty hedge, his head cradled on his arms. "Wake up, I've brought you wine to soothe your throat."

Nanni opened his bewildered eyes wide, still half-asleep, to find her standing erect in front of him, pale, with her prominent bosom and eyes black as coal, and he held out his hands waveringly.

"No! Decent women don't go around between Vespers and Nones!" Nanni sobbed, burying his face in the dry grass of the ditch, deep into it, with his nails in his hair. "Go away! Go away! Don't come back to the threshing floor!"

She did actually go away, the She-wolf did, tying up her magnificent tresses again, looking straight ahead of her, as she walked through the hot stubble, with those eyes black as coal.

But she returned to the threshing floor on other occasions, and Nanni didn't say anything. When she was late showing up, in those hours between Vespers and Nones, he'd go to wait for her at the top of the white, deserted path, his forehead all sweaty. Afterwards, he'd thrust his hands into his hair, and repeat to her on each occasion: "Go away! Go away! Don't come back to the threshing floor!" Maricchia wept day and night; she stared into her mother's face, her eyes burning with tears and jealousy, herself like a female wolf cub, whenever she saw her coming back from the fields, pale and silent each time. "Criminal!" she said to her. "Criminal mother!"

"Be quiet!"

"Thief! Thief!"

"Be quiet!"

"I'll go to the police sergeant, I will!"

"Well, go!"

And she did go, carrying her babies, afraid of nothing, not shedding a tear, like a madwoman, because by this time she, too, loved that husband who had been forced on her, greasy and dirty from the olives that had been set aside to ferment.

---

4. This rhymed saying, in standard Italian in the original text, is adapted and somewhat altered from a Sicilian equivalent. Nones and Vespers are ecclesiastical hours corresponding roughly to three P.M. and six P.M.

Il brigadiere fece chiamare Nanni, e lo minacciò della galera, e della forca. Nanni si diede a singhiozzare ed a strapparsi i capelli; non negò nulla, non tentò scolparsi. – È la tentazione! diceva; è la tentazione dell'inferno! si buttò ai piedi del brigadiere supplicandolo di mandarlo in galera.

– Per carità, signor brigadiere, levatemi da questo inferno! fatemi ammazzare, mandatemi in prigione; non me la lasciate veder più, mai! mai!

– No! rispose però *la Lupa* al brigadiere. Io mi son riserbato un cantuccio della cucina per dormirvi, quando gli ho data la mia casa in dote. La casa è mia. Non voglio andarmene!

Poco dopo, Nanni s'ebbe nel petto un calcio dal mulo e fu per morire; ma il parroco ricusò di portargli il Signore se *la Lupa* non usciva di casa. *La Lupa* se ne andò, e suo genero allora si poté preparare ad andarsene anche lui da buon cristiano; si confessò e comunicò con tali segni di pentimento e di contrizione che tutti i vicini e i curiosi piangevano davanti al letto del moribondo. E meglio sarebbe stato per lui che fosse morto in quel tempo, prima che il diavolo tornasse a tentarlo e a ficcarglisi nell'anima e nel corpo quando fu guarito. – Lasciatemi stare! diceva alla *Lupa;* per carità, lasciatemi in pace! Io ho visto la morte cogli occhi! La povera Maricchia non fa che disperarsi. Ora tutto il paese lo sa! Quando non vi vedo è meglio per voi e per me . . .

Ed avrebbe voluto strapparsi gli occhi per non vedere quelli della *Lupa,* che quando gli si ficcavano ne' suoi gli facevano perdere l'anima ed il corpo. Non sapeva più che fare per svincolarsi dall'incantesimo. Pagò delle messe alle anime del Purgatorio e andò a chiedere aiuto al parroco e al brigadiere. A Pasqua andò a confessarsi, e fece pubblicamente sei palmi di lingua a strasciconi sui ciottoli del sacrato innanzi alla chiesa, in penitenza, e poi, come *la Lupa* tornava a tentarlo:

– Sentite! le disse, non ci venite più nell'aia, perché se tornate a cercarmi, com'è vero Iddio, vi ammazzo!

– Ammazzami, rispose *la Lupa,* ché non me ne importa; ma senza di te non voglio starci.

Ei come la scorse da lontano, in mezzo a' seminati verdi, lasciò di zappare la vigna, e andò a staccare la scure dall'olmo. *La Lupa* lo vide venire, pallido e stralunato, colla scure che luccicava al sole, e non si arretrò di un sol passo, non chinò gli occhi, seguitò ad andargli incontro, con le mani piene di manipoli di papaveri rossi, e mangiandoselo con gli occhi neri. – Ah! malanno all'anima vostra! balbettò Nanni.

The sergeant summoned Nanni and threatened to put him in jail or hang him. Nanni started sobbing and pulling out his hair. He denied nothing, he made no attempt to evade his guilt. "It's temptation!" he kept saying, "it's devilish temptation!" He threw himself at the sergeant's feet, begging him to send him to jail.

"Please, sergeant, take me out of this hell! Have me killed, send me to prison, but don't let me see her again, never, never!"

"No!" the She-wolf replied to the sergeant, however. "I stipulated that I would have a corner of the kitchen to sleep in when I gave him my house as a dowry. The house is legally mine. I don't want to leave!"

Not long afterward, Nanni received a kick in the chest from a mule and was close to death, but the parish priest refused to take him the Lord's body and blood unless the She-wolf was out of the house. The She-wolf departed, and then her son-in-law was able to prepare to take his own departure as a good Christian; he made Confession and took Communion with such signs of repentance and contrition that all the neighbors and gawkers wept in front of the dying man's bed. And he would have been better off dying at that time, before the devil started tempting him again and embedding himself in his body and soul, once he had recovered. "Let me alone!" he'd say to the She-wolf. "Please leave me in peace! I've seen death with my eyes! Poor Maricchia is in total despair. Now the whole village knows! If I don't see you, it will be better for you and for me. . . ."

And he'd have liked to tear out his eyes to avoid seeing those of the She-wolf, because when they stared into his they made him lose body and soul. He no longer knew what to do to free himself from the enchantment. He paid for Masses for the souls in Purgatory, and he went to the parish priest and the police sergeant to ask for help. At Easter he went to Confession, and he performed a public penance, dragging himself along and licking the stones in the churchyard in front of the church. Then, when the She-wolf tempted him again, he said:

"Listen! Don't come back to the threshing floor, because if you come looking for me again, as there's a God in Heaven, I'll kill you!"

"Kill me," the She-wolf said, "because I don't care; but I don't want to go on living without you."

When he spotted her in the distance, amid the green fields of grain, he stopped hoeing the vineyard and went to pull his axe out of the elm-tree. The She-wolf saw him coming, looking pale and distracted, the axe gleaming in the sunlight; but she didn't retreat a single step, she didn't lower her eyes; she continued walking toward him, her hands full of bunches of red poppies and her dark eyes devouring him. "Oh, God damn your soul!" Nanni stammered.

L'AMANTE DI GRAMIGNA

Caro Farina, eccoti non un racconto ma l'abbozzo di un racconto. Esso almeno avrà il merito di esser brevissimo, e di esser storico – un documento umano, come dicono oggi; interessante forse per te, e per tutti coloro che studiano nel gran libro del cuore. Io te lo ripeterò così come l'ho raccolto pei viottoli dei campi, press'a poco colle medesime parole semplici e pittoresche della narrazione popolare, e tu veramente preferirai di trovarti faccia a faccia col fatto nudo e schietto, senza stare a cercarlo fra le linee del libro, attraverso la lente dello scrittore. Il semplice fatto umano farà pensare sempre; avrà sempre l'efficacia dell'*essere stato,* delle lagrime vere, delle febbri e delle sensazioni che sono passate per la carne; il misterioso processo per cui le passioni si annodano, si intrecciano, maturano, si svolgono nel loro cammino sotterraneo nei loro andirivieni che spesso sembrano contradditorî, costituirà per lungo tempo ancora la possente attrattiva di quel fenomeno psicologico che dicesi l'argomento di un racconto, e che l'analisi moderna si studia di seguire con scrupolo scientifico. Di questo che ti narro oggi ti dirò soltanto il punto di partenza e quello d'arrivo, e per te basterà, e un giorno forse basterà per tutti.

Noi rifacciamo il processo artistico al quale dobbiamo tanti monumenti gloriosi, con metodo diverso, più minuzioso e più intimo; sacrifichiamo volentieri l'effetto della catastrofe, del risultato psicologico, intravvisto con intuizione quasi divina dai grandi artisti del passato, allo sviluppo logico, necessario di esso, ridotto meno imprevisto, meno drammatico, ma non meno fatale; siamo più modesti, se non più umili; ma le conquiste che facciamo delle verità psicologiche non saranno un fatto meno utile all'arte dell'avvenire. Si arriverà mai a tal perfezionamento nello studio delle passioni, che

GRAMIGNA'S MISTRESS

Dear Farina,[1] I am submitting to you, not a story, but the sketch of a story. At least it will have the merit of being very brief, and based on true facts— a human document, as the saying goes nowadays. It may be interesting to you and all those whose studies are in the great book of the heart. I shall repeat it to you just as I collected it on the country lanes, practically in the same simple but picturesque phrasing of folk narrative, and you'll really enjoy finding yourself face to face with the clean, bare events, without needing to search for them between the lines, as seen through the writer's distorting lens. Simple human events will always make people reflect, they will always have the effectiveness of a real occurrence, of genuine tears, of fevers and emotions that have been actually lived. The mysterious process by which passions are linked and intertwined, by which they mature and develop on their underground journey, in their comings and goings that often appear self-contradictory, will constitute for a long time to come the strong attraction exerted by that psychological phenomenon known as the plot of a story, one that modern analysis is intent on pursuing with scientific scrupulosity. Of the story I am telling you today, I shall state merely the point of departure and the endpoint; that will be enough for you, and some day, perhaps, it will be enough for everybody.

We are remaking the artistic process to which we owe so many glorious treasures, using a different method, one that is more detailed and more infinite. We are gladly sacrificing climactic effects and psychological conclusions, which were glimpsed with all but godlike intuition by the great artists of the past, in favor of the logical, inevitable development of such effects, which we render less surprising and less dramatic, but no less ordained by fate. We are more modest, if not more humble; but the conquests of psychological truths that we achieve will not be an attainment less useful to the art of the future. Will such great perfection

---

1. Salvatore Farina was the editor of the Milanese periodical *La rivista minima,* in which this story was first published.

diventerà inutile il proseguire in cotesto studio dell'uomo interiore? La scienza del cuore umano, che sarà il frutto della nuova arte, svilupperà talmente e così generalmente tutte le risorse dell'immaginazione che nell'avvenire i soli romanzi che si scriveranno saranno *i fatti diversi?*

Intanto io credo che il trionfo del romanzo, la più completa e la più umana delle opere d'arte, si raggiungerà allorché l'affinità e la coesione di ogni sua parte sarà così completa che il processo della creazione rimarrà un mistero, come lo svolgersi delle passioni umane; e che l'armonia delle sue forme sarà così perfetta, la sincerità della sua realtà così evidente, il suo modo e la sua ragione di essere così necessarie, che la mano dell'artista rimarrà assolutamente invisibile, e il romanzo avrà l'impronta dell'avvenimento reale, e l'opera d'arte sembrerà *essersi fatta da sé,* aver maturato ed esser sorta spontanea come un fatto naturale, senza serbare alcun punto di contatto col suo autore; che essa non serbi nelle sue forme viventi alcuna impronta della mente in cui germogliò, alcuna ombra dell'occhio che la intravvide, alcuna traccia delle labbra che ne mormorarono le prime parole come il *fiat* creatore; ch'essa stia per ragion propria, pel solo fatto che è come dev'essere, ed è necessario che sia, palpitante di vita ed immutabile al pari di una statua di bronzo, di cui l'autore abbia avuto il coraggio divino di eclissarsi e sparire nella sua opera immortale.

Parecchi anni or sono, laggiù lungo il Simeto, davano la caccia a un brigante, certo Gramigna, se non erro, un nome maledetto come l'erba che lo porta, il quale da un capo all'altro della provincia s'era lasciato dietro il terrore della sua fama. Carabinieri, soldati, e militi a cavallo lo inseguivano da due mesi, senza esser riesciti a mettergli le unghie addosso: era solo, ma valeva per dieci, e la malapianta minacciava di abbarbicare. Per giunta si approssimava il tempo della messe, il fieno era già steso pei campi, le spighe chinavano il capo e dicevano di sì ai mietitori che avevano già la falce in pugno, e nonostante nessun proprietario osava affacciare il naso al disopra della siepe del suo podere, per timore di incontrarvi Gramigna che se ne stesse sdraiato fra i solchi, colla carabina fra le gambe, pronto a far saltare il capo al primo che venisse a guardare nei fatti suoi. Sicché le lagnanze erano generali. Allora il prefetto si fece chiamare tutti quei signori della questura,

in the study of the passions ever be reached that it will become need-less to proceed with this study of the inner man? Will the knowledge of the human heart that results from this new art expand all the resources of the imagination so greatly and so universally that in the future the only novels people write will be like sensational news items?

Meanwhile, my own belief is that the triumph of the novel, that most complete and most human of all works of art, will arrive when the interrelationship and cohesiveness of all parts of it will be so com-plete that the process of creation will remain a mystery, like the un-folding of human passions; and that the harmony of its forms will be so perfect, the sincerity of its realism so evident, its style and its reason-for-being so preordained that the hand of the artist will remain altogether invisible: the novel will bear the imprint of the real occur-rence, and the work of art will seem "to have created itself," to have matured and emerged spontaneously like an event in nature, without retaining any point of contact with its author. Let the work of art not retain in its living forms any mark of the mind from which it sprang, any shadow of the eye that glimpsed it, any trace of the lips that mur-mured its opening words like a creator's *fiat*.[2] Let the work of art stand on its own feet, by the mere fact that it is the way it ought to be and the way it must necessarily be, throbbing with life and as changeless as a bronze statue, its author having had the godlike courage to with-draw from view and submerge himself in his immortal work.

Several years ago, down there along the Simeto river, a manhunt was under way for an outlaw, a certain Gramigna if I'm not mistaken, a name as cursed as the couchgrass weed that bears it. From one end of the province to the other he had left behind the terror of his notoriety. National police, soldiers, and mounted militiamen had been pursuing him for two months without managing to get their hands on him. He was alone, but he was as resourceful as any ten men, and the weed threatened to take root. Besides, the grain harvest was drawing near, the hay was already spread out in the fields, the ear-laden stalks were bending their heads and inviting the reapers, who already had their scythes in their hands—and nevertheless no landowner dared to show his nose above his boundary hedges for fear of finding Gramigna there, sprawling between the furrows, his carbine between his legs, ready to blow the head off the first man who meddled in his business. And so, the complaints were universal. Then the governor of the province

---

2. That is, like God's repeated commands of "Let there be . . ." in the story of Creation in Genesis.

dei carabinieri, e dei compagni d'armi, e disse loro due paroline di quelle che fanno drizzar le orecchie. Il giorno dopo un terremoto per ogni dove; pattuglie, squadriglie, vedette per ogni fossato, e dietro ogni muricciolo; se lo cacciavano dinanzi come una mala bestia per tutta la provincia, di giorno, di notte, a piedi, a cavallo, col telegrafo. Gramigna sgusciava loro di mano, e rispondeva a schioppettate se gli camminavano un po' troppo sulle calcagna. Nelle campagne, nei villaggi, per le fattorie, sotto le frasche delle osterie, nei luoghi di ritrovo, non si parlava d'altro che di lui, di Gramigna, di quella caccia accanita, di quella fuga disperata; i cavalli dei carabinieri cascavano stanchi morti; i compagni d'armi si buttavano rifiniti per terra in tutte le stalle, le pattuglie dormivano all'impiedi; egli solo, Gramigna, non era stanco mai, non dormiva mai, fuggiva sempre, s'arrampicava sui precipizi, strisciava fra le messi, correva carponi nel folto dei fichidindia, sgattajolava come un lupo nel letto asciutto dei torrenti. Il principale argomento di ogni discorso, nei crocchi, davanti agli usci del villaggio, era la sete divorante che doveva soffrire il perseguitato, nella pianura immensa, arsa, sotto il sole di giugno. I fannulloni spalancavano gli occhi.

Peppa, una delle più belle ragazze di Licodia, doveva sposare in quel tempo compare Finu «candela di sego» che aveva terre al sole e una mula baia in stalla, ed era un giovanotto grande e bello come il sole, che portava lo stendardo di Santa Margherita come fosse un pilastro, senza piegare le reni.

La madre di Peppa piangeva dalla contentezza per la gran fortuna toccata alla figliuola, e passava il tempo a voltare e rivoltare nel baule il corredo della sposa, «tutto di roba bianca a quattro» come quella di una regina, e orecchini che le arrivavano alle spalle, e anelli d'oro per le dieci dita delle mani; dell'oro ne aveva quanto ne poteva avere Santa Margherita, e dovevano sposarsi giusto per santa Margherita, che cadeva in giugno, dopo la mietitura del fieno. «Candela di sego» nel tornare ogni sera dalla campagna, lasciava la mula all'uscio della Peppa, e veniva a dirle che i seminati erano un incanto, se Gramigna non vi appiccava il fuoco, e il graticcio di contro al letto non sarebbe bastato a contenere tutto il grano della raccolta, che gli pareva mill'anni di condursi la sposa in casa, in groppa alla mula baia. Ma Peppa un bel giorno gli disse: – La vostra mula lasciatela stare, perché non voglio maritarmi.

summoned all the top brass of the local police, the national police, and the national guard, and made them a short speech of the type that makes you prick up your ears. The next day there was a sort of earthquake everywhere: patrols, squads, lookouts alongside every ditch and behind every wall. They were beating the bushes for him like a dangerous beast all over the province, by day, by night, on foot, on horseback, with the telegraph. Gramigna kept slipping out of their hands, replying with gunshots whenever they trod too closely on his heels. In the countryside, villages, and farmhouses, beneath the inn-sign bushes, wherever people met, the talk was of him alone, Gramigna, that relentless hunt, that desperate flight. The horses of the national police dropped in their tracks from exhaustion; the militiamen threw themselves to the ground in every stable, all worn out; the patrols slept standing up. Only he, Gramigna, was never tired, never slept, constantly fled, climbing cliffs, gliding through the harvested crops, running on all fours through the thick of the prickly pears, sneaking away like a wolf down the dry streambeds. The main subject of every conversation in familiar circles and in front of village doors was the devouring thirst that the hunted man must be suffering on the vast, parched lowlands beneath the June sun. The loafers opened wide eyes.

Peppa, one of the most beautiful girls in Licodia, was due around that time to marry neighbor Finu, the "tallow candle," who owned land and had a bay mule in his stable. He was a tall young man as handsome as the sun, and he used to carry St. Margaret's banner in processions as if he were a stone pillar, without bending his back.

Peppa's mother used to weep for joy at the good luck that had befallen her daughter; she spent her time constantly turning over the fiancée's trousseau in the trunk. It was "all white linens, and plenty of it," like a queen's, and earrings that reached down to the shoulders, and gold rings for the ten fingers of the hands; there was as much gold as St. Margaret herself could have. The wedding was set for the very feast day of St. Margaret, which fell in June, after the haycutting.[3] When Tallow Candle came back from the fields every evening, he left his she-mule at Peppa's door and came to tell her that the crops were marvelous, if only Gramigna didn't set fire to them, and the wicker receptacle opposite the bed wouldn't be big enough to hold all the grain from the harvest; he said he just couldn't wait to lead his bride home, riding behind him on the bay mule. But one fine day Peppa told him: "Let your mule relax, because I don't want to get married."

---

3. Reference books give July 20 as St. Margaret's Day.

Il povero «candela di sego» rimase sbalordito e la vecchia si mise a strapparsi i capelli come udì che sua figlia rifiutava il miglior partito del villaggio. – Io voglio bene a Gramigna, le disse la ragazza, e non voglio sposare altri che lui!

– Ah! gridava la mamma per la casa, coi capelli grigi al vento, che pareva una strega. – Ah! quel demonio è venuto sin qui a stregarmi la mia figliuola!

– No! rispondeva Peppa coll'occhio fisso che pareva d'acciajo. – No, non è venuto qui.

– Dove l'hai visto dunque?

– Io non l'ho visto. Ne ho sentito parlare. Sentite! ma lo sento qui, che mi brucia!

In paese la cosa fece rumore, per quanto la tenessero nascosta. Le comari che avevano invidiato a Peppa il seminato prosperoso, la mula baia, e il bel giovanotto che portava lo stendardo di Santa Margherita senza piegar le reni, andavano dicendo ogni sorta di brutte storie, che Gramigna veniva a trovarla di notte nella cucina, e che glielo avevano visto nascosto sotto il letto. La povera madre aveva acceso una lampada alle anime del purgatorio, e persino il curato era andato in casa di Peppa, a toccarle il cuore colla stola, onde scacciare quel diavolo di Gramigna che ne aveva preso possesso. Però ella seguitava a dire che non lo conosceva neanche di vista quel cristiano; ma che la notte lo vedeva in sogno, e alla mattina si levava colle labbra arse quasi avesse provato anch'essa tutta la sete ch'ei doveva soffrire.

Allora la vecchia la chiuse in casa, perché non sentisse più parlare di Gramigna; e tappò tutte le fessure dell'uscio con immagini di santi. Peppa ascoltava quello che dicevano nella strada dietro le immagini benedette, e si faceva pallida e rossa, come se il diavolo le soffiasse tutto l'inferno nella faccia.

Finalmente sentì dire che avevano scovato Gramigna nei fichidindia di Palagonia. – Ha fatto due ore di fuoco! dicevano, c'è un carabiniere morto, e più di tre compagni d'armi feriti. Ma gli hanno tirato addosso tal gragnuola di fucilate che stavolta hanno trovato un lago di sangue dove egli si trovava.

Allora Peppa si fece la croce dinanzi al capezzale della vecchia, e fuggì dalla finestra.

Gramigna era nei fichidindia di Palagonia, che non avevano potuto scovarlo in quel forteto da conigli, lacero, insanguinato, pallido per due giorni di fame, arso dalla febbre, e colla carabina spianata: come la vide venire, risoluta, in mezzo alle macchie dei fichidindia, nel fosco

Poor Tallow Candle was dumbfounded, and Peppa's mother started tearing out her hair when she heard that her daughter was turning down the best match in the village. "I love Gramigna," the girl told her, "and I don't want to marry anyone but him!"

"Oh!" her mother went around the house shouting, her gray hair disheveled, so that she resembled a witch. "Oh! What demon has come all the way here to cast a spell on my daughter?!"

"No!" Peppa would answer, with a firm glance that might have been of steel. "No, he hasn't come here."

"Then, where did you see him?"

"I haven't seen him. I've heard people talk about him. Feel me! I feel him here, burning me!"

In the village the news got abroad, try as they would to keep it secret. The neighbor women who had envied Peppa the thriving grainfield, the bay she-mule, and the handsome young man who carried St. Margaret's banner without bending his back, went around telling all sorts of ugly stories: that Gramigna came to see her in the kitchen at night, and that he'd been seen hiding under the bed. The poor mother had burned a lamp for the souls in Purgatory, and even the priest had gone to Peppa's house to touch her heart with his surplice and thus drive out that devil Gramigna who had taken possession of it. But she continued to say that she didn't know that man even by sight, but saw him in her dreams at night; in the mornings she'd get up with lips as parched as if she, too, had experienced all the thirst that he must be suffering.

Then her mother locked her in the house to keep her from hearing any more about Gramigna; and she blocked up all the chinks in the door with pictures of saints. Peppa would stand behind the consecrated images, listening to what was being said in the street, and she'd become pale and flushed by turns, as if the devil were blowing all of Hell in her face.

Finally she heard that Gramigna had been unearthed in the prickly-pear thickets of Palagonia. "He was firing for two hours!" people said: "A national policeman was killed, and more than three soldiers wounded. But they fired such a hail of bullets at him that this time they found a pool of blood where he was standing."

Then Peppa crossed herself in front of her mother's bolster, and escaped through the window.

Gramigna was in the Palagonia prickly-pear thickets; they hadn't been able to rout him out of that dense scrub fit only for rabbits; though he was tattered, bloodstained, pale from two days of fasting, and burning up with fever, he kept his carbine aimed. When he saw her approaching resolutely amid the prickly-pear bushes, in the hazy

chiarore dell'alba, ci pensò un momento, se dovesse lasciare partire il colpo. – Che vuoi? le chiese. Che vieni a far qui?

– Vengo a star con te; gli disse lei guardandolo fisso. Sei tu Gramigna?

– Sì, son io Gramigna. Se vieni a buscarti quelle venti oncie della taglia, hai sbagliato il conto.

– No, vengo a star con te! rispose lei.

– Vattene! diss'egli. Con me non puoi starci, ed io non voglio nessuno con me! Se vieni a cercar denaro hai sbagliato il conto ti dico, io non ho nulla, guarda! Sono due giorni che non ho nemmeno un pezzo di pane.

– Adesso non posso più tornare a casa, disse lei; la strada è tutta piena di soldati.

– Vattene! cosa m'importa? ciascuno per la sua pelle!

Mentre ella voltava le spalle, come un cane scacciato a pedate, Gramigna la chiamò. – Senti, va' a prendermi un fiasco d'acqua, laggiù nel torrente, se vuoi stare con me bisogna rischiar la pelle.

Peppa andò senza dir nulla, e quando Gramigna udì la fucilata si mise a sghignazzare, e disse fra sé: – Questa era per me. – Ma come la vide comparire poco dopo, col fiasco al braccio, pallida e insanguinata, prima le si buttò addosso, per strapparle il fiasco, e poi quando ebbe bevuto che pareva il fiato le mancasse le chiese – L'hai scappata? Come hai fatto?

– I soldati erano sull'altra riva, e c'era una macchia folta da questa parte.

– Però t'hanno bucata la pelle. Hai del sangue nelle vesti?

– Sì.

– Dove sei ferita?

– Sulla spalla.

– Non fa nulla. Potrai camminare.

Così le permise di stare con lui. Ella lo seguiva tutta lacera, colla febbre della ferita, senza scarpe, e andava a cercargli un fiasco d'acqua o un tozzo di pane, e quando tornava colle mani vuote, in mezzo alle fucilate, il suo amante, divorato dalla fame e dalla sete, la batteva. Finalmente una notte in cui brillava la luna nei fichidindia, Gramigna le disse – Vengono! e la fece addossare alla rupe, in fondo al crepaccio, poi fuggì dall'altra parte. Fra le macchie si udivano spesseggiare le fucilate, e l'ombra avvampava qua e là di brevi fiamme. Ad un tratto Peppa udì un calpestìo vicino a sé e vide tornar Gramigna che si strascinava con una gamba rotta, e si appoggiava ai ceppi dei fichidindia per ricaricare la carabina. – È

gleam of dawn, he thought for a moment about whether to fire. "What do you want?" he asked. "What have you come here for?"

"I've come to be with you," she said, gazing steadily at him. "Are you Gramigna?"

"Yes, I'm Gramigna. If you've come in order to collect those twenty *onze* in taxes, you've got another guess coming."

"No, I've come to be with you!" she replied.

"Go away!" he said. "You can't be with me, and I don't want anybody with me! If you've come after money, you've made a mistake, I tell you. I have nothing, look! For two days I haven't even had a piece of bread."

"I can't go back home anymore," she said. "The road is full of soldiers."

"Go away! What's it to me? It's every man for himself!"

While she was turning around, like a dog driven away with kicks, Gramigna called to her: "Listen, go bring me a flaskful of water from the stream down there. If you want to be with me, you've got to risk your skin."

Peppa went without saying a word. When Gramigna heard the gunshots, he began to guffaw, and said to himself: "That was meant for me." But when he saw her appear shortly afterward, carrying the flask, pale and bloodstained, first he jumped on her to tear the flask away from her; then, after drinking so much he seemed to have lost his breath, he asked her: "You got away? How did you do it?"

"The soldiers were on the opposite bank, and there was a dense thicket on this side."

"But they made a hole in your hide. Do you have blood on your clothes?"

"Yes."

"Where are you wounded?"

"In the shoulder."

"That's not serious. You'll be able to walk."

And so he allowed her to be with him. She followed him, all tattered, feverish from her wound, shoeless; she'd go fetch him a flask of water or a hunk of bread, and when she returned empty-handed, amid flying bullets, her lover, consumed with hunger and thirst, would beat her. Finally, one night when the moon was shining on the prickly pears, Gramigna said: "They're coming!" and he made her stand with her back to the rock face deep inside the crevice, while he ran in another direction. Amid the scrub the gunshots could be heard becoming more frequent, and the darkness was lit up here and there by brief flashes. All at once, Peppa heard footsteps near her, and saw Gramigna coming back, dragging

finita! gli disse lui. Ora mi prendono; – e quello che le agghiacciò il sangue più di ogni cosa fu il luccicare che ci aveva negli occhi, da sembrare un pazzo. Poi quando cadde sui rami secchi come un fascio di legna, i compagni d'armi gli furono addosso tutti in una volta.

Il giorno dopo lo strascinarono per le vie del villaggio, su di un carro, tutto lacero e sanguinoso. La gente che si accalcava per vederlo, si metteva a ridere trovandolo così piccolo, pallido e brutto, che pareva un pulcinella. Era per lui che Peppa aveva lasciato compare Finu «candela di sego»! Il povero «candela di sego» andò a nascondersi quasi toccasse a lui di vergognarsi, e Peppa la condussero fra i soldati, ammanettata, come una ladra anche lei, lei che ci aveva dell'oro quanto Santa Margherita! La povera madre di Peppa dovette vendere «tutta la roba bianca» del corredo, e gli orecchini d'oro, e gli anelli per le dieci dita, onde pagare gli avvocati di sua figlia, e tirarsela di nuovo in casa, povera, malata, svergognata, brutta anche lei come Gramigna, e col figlio di Gramigna in collo. Ma quando gliela diedero, alla fine del processo, recitò l'avemaria, nella casermeria nuda e già scura, in mezzo ai carabinieri; le parve che le dessero un tesoro, alla povera vecchia, che non possedeva più nulla e piangeva come una fontana dalla consolazione. Peppa invece sembrava che non ne avesse più di lagrime, e non diceva nulla, né in paese nessuno la vide più mai, nonostante che le due donne andassero a buscarsi il pane colle loro braccia. La gente diceva che Peppa aveva imparato il mestiere, nel bosco, e andava di notte a rubare. Il fatto era che stava rincantucciata nella cucina come una bestia feroce, e ne uscì soltanto allorché la sua vecchia fu morta di stenti, e dovette vendere la casa.

– Vedete! le diceva «candela di sego» che pure le voleva sempre bene. – Vi schiaccierei la testa fra due sassi pel male che avete fatto a voi e agli altri.

– È vero! rispondeva Peppa, lo so! Questa è stata la volontà di Dio.

Dopo che fu venduta la casa e quei pochi arnesi che le restavano se ne andò via dal paese, di notte come era venuta, senza voltarsi indietro a guardare il tetto sotto cui aveva dormito tanto tempo, e se ne andò a fare la volontà di Dio in città, col suo ragazzo, vicino al carcere dove era rinchiuso Gramigna. Ella non vedeva altro che le gelosie tetre, sulla gran facciata muta, e le sentinelle la scacciavano se si fermava a cercare cogli occhi dove potesse esser lui. Finalmente le dissero che egli non ci era più da un pezzo, che l'avevano condotto via, di là del

himself along with a broken leg and leaning on the prickly-pear stumps to reload his carbine. "This is the end!" he said. "Now they'll capture me." But what froze her blood more than anything else was the glittering in his eyes that made him look crazy. Then, when he fell onto the dry branches like a bundle of firewood, the soldiers were on top of him all at the same time.

The next day, they dragged him through the village streets on a cart, all tattered and bloodstained. The people who crowded around to see him started laughing to find him so small of stature, pallid, and ugly, looking like a Punchinello puppet. It was for him that Peppa had jilted neighbor Finu, the "tallow candle"! Poor Tallow Candle went and hid himself, as if it were he who ought to be ashamed. Peppa was led among the soldiers, in handcuffs, she, too, like a thief, she who had as much gold jewelry as St. Margaret! Peppa's poor mother had to sell "all the white linens" in the trousseau, and the gold earrings, and the rings for all ten fingers, in order to pay her daughter's lawyers and get her back home again, though Peppa was impoverished, sick, shameless, and just as ugly as Gramigna, and was carrying Gramigna's son in her arms. But when her daughter was restored to her after the trial, she recited a Hail Mary right there in the bare and already dark barracks, in the midst of the national policemen. The poor old woman felt as if she were being given a treasure; she now possessed nothing else, and she wept like a fountain from consolation. Peppa, on the other hand, seemed to have no tears left to shed; she said nothing, and no one in the village saw her again, even though the two women went out to earn their bread with the strength of their arms. People said that, in the woods, Peppa had learned the trade and went around robbing at night. The fact was that she remained huddled up in her kitchen like a wild animal, leaving it only when her mother had died of her hardships, and she was compelled to sell the house.

"You see!" Tallow Candle, who still loved her in spite of all, used to say to her. "I'd like to crush your head between two rocks for the harm you've done yourself and the others."

"It's true!" Peppa would reply. "I know! It was the will of God."

After the house and the few belongings she had left were sold, she departed from the village, at night as she had come, without turning back to look at the roof beneath which she had slept for so long, and she went to do the will of God in the city, with her boy, near the prison in which Gramigna was confined. All she could see was the gloomy shutters on the big, silent facade; the sentries drove her away whenever she stopped to look, trying to discover where he might be. Finally she was told that he hadn't been there for some time, but had been

mare, ammanettato e colla sporta al collo. Ella non disse nulla. Non si mosse più di là, perché non sapeva dove andare, e non l'aspettava più nessuno. Vivacchiava facendo dei servizii ai soldati, ai carcerieri, come facesse parte ella stessa di quel gran fabbricato tetro e silenzioso, e pei carabinieri poi che le avevano preso Gramigna nel folto dei fichidindia, e gli avevano rotto la gamba a fucilate, sentiva una specie di tenerezza rispettosa, come l'ammirazione bruta della forza. La festa, quando li vedeva col pennacchio, e gli spallini lucenti, rigidi ed impettiti nell'uniforme di gala, se li mangiava cogli occhi, ed era sempre per la caserma spazzando i cameroni e lustrando gli stivali, tanto che la chiamavano «lo strofinacciolo dei carabinieri». Soltanto allorché li vedeva caricare le armi a notte fatta, e partire a due a due, coi calzoni rimboccati, il revolver sullo stomaco, o quando montavano a cavallo, sotto il lampione che faceva luccicare la carabina, e udiva perdersi nelle tenebre lo scalpito dei cavalli, e il tintinnìo della sciabola, diventava pallida ogni volta, e mentre chiudeva la porta della stalla rabbrividiva; e quando il suo marmocchio giocherellava cogli altri monelli nella spianata davanti al carcere, correndo fra le gambe dei soldati, e i monelli gli dicevano «il figlio di Gramigna, il figlio di Gramigna!» ella si metteva in collera, e li inseguiva a sassate.

taken away overseas, handcuffed and with his big basket on his back. She said nothing. She no longer left that place, because she didn't know where to go, and no one else was awaiting her. She eked out her existence doing chores for the soldiers and jailers, as if she herself were a part of that gloomy, silent pile; even for the national policemen who had taken Gramigna away from her in the prickly-pear thicket and had broken his leg with their shots, she felt a sort of respectful tenderness, an animal's admiration for strength, as it were. On holidays, when she saw them with their plumes and gleaming epaulets, stiff and proud in their dress uniforms, she devoured them with her eyes. She was always in the barracks, sweeping out the rooms and polishing boots, so that she got the nickname "policemen's cleaning woman." Only when she saw them load their weapons after nightfall and leave two by two with their trousers turned up and a revolver stuck in their belt, or when they mounted their horses beneath the big lamp that made their carbines gleam, and she heard the horses' hoofbeats and the clinking of the sabers growing fainter in the darkness, she turned pale every time and shuddered while she shut the stable door. And when her youngster played with the other urchins in the yard in front of the prison, running among the soldiers' legs, and the urchins called at him: "Son of Gramigna! Son of Gramigna!" she would get angry and chase them with stones.

MALARIA

E' vi par di toccarla colle mani – come della terra grassa che fumi, là, dappertutto, torno torno alle montagne che la chiudono, da Agnone al Mongibello incappucciato di neve – stagnante nella pianura, a guisa dell'afa pesante di luglio. Vi nasce e vi muore il sole di brace, e la luna smorta, e la *Puddara*, che sembra navigare in un mare che svapori, e gli uccelli e le margherite bianche della primavera, e l'estate arsa; e vi passano in lunghe file nere le anitre nel nuvolo dell'autunno, e il fiume che luccica quasi fosse di metallo, fra le rive larghe e abbandonate, bianche, slabbrate, sparse di ciottoli; e in fondo il lago di Lentini, come uno stagno, colle sponde piatte, senza una barca, senza un albero sulla riva, liscio ed immobile. Sul greto pascolano svogliatamente i buoi, rari, infangati sino al petto, col pelo irsuto. Quando risuona il campanaccio della mandra, nel gran silenzio, volan via le cutrettole, silenziose, e il pastore istesso, giallo di febbre, e bianco di polvere anche lui, schiude un istante le palpebre gonfie, levando il capo all'ombra dei giunchi secchi.

È che la malaria v'entra nelle ossa col pane che mangiate, e se aprite bocca per parlare, mentre camminate lungo le strade soffocanti di polvere e di sole, e vi sentite mancar le ginocchia, o vi accasciate sul basto della mula che va all'ambio, colla testa bassa. Invano Lentini, e Francofonte, e Paternò, cercano di arrampicarsi come pecore sbrancate sulle prime colline che scappano dalla pianura, e si circondano di aranceti, di vigne, di orti sempre verdi; la malaria acchiappa gli abitanti per le vie spopolate, e li inchioda dinanzi agli usci delle case scalcinate dal sole, tremanti di febbre sotto il pastrano, e con tutte le coperte del letto sulle spalle.

Laggiù, nella pianura, le case sono rare e di aspetto malinconico, lungo le strade mangiate dal sole, fra due mucchi di concime fumante, appoggiate alle tettoie crollanti, dove aspettano coll'occhio spento, legati alla mangiatoia vuota, i cavalli di ricambio. – O sulla

PESTILENTIAL AIR

You feel as if you could touch it with your hands—like rich, steaming soil, there, everywhere, all around the mountains that enclose it, from Agnone to Mount Etna with its hood of snow—stagnant in the lowlands, like the heavy sultriness of July. The blazing sun is born in it and dies in it, and so does the wan moon, and the Pleiades, which seem to be floating on an evaporating sea, and the birds and the white daisies in the spring, and the parched summer. The ducks fly through it in long black rows in the overcast sky of autumn, and the river traverses it, glittering as though made of metal, between its wide, deserted, white, irregular, pebble-strewn banks. And in the distance is the lake of Lentini, like a pond, with a level shoreline, without a boat on it, without a tree alongside it, smooth and motionless. On the gravelly shore the oxen graze listlessly, just a few here and there, muddied up to their breast, long-haired. When the herd bell rings in that deep silence, the wagtails fly away silently, and the oxherd himself, he, too, yellow with fever and white with dust, closes his swollen eyelids for a moment, raising his head in the shade of the dry bulrushes.

It's because that pestilential air gets into your bones along with the bread you eat, whenever you open your mouth to speak, while you walk down the dust-choked, sun-baked roads, feeling your knees buckle, or slump over the packsaddle of your she-mule as she ambles with her head down. It's to no purpose that Lentini, Francofonte, and Paternò try to climb, like stray sheep, up the first hills that emerge from the plain and surround themselves with orange gloves, vineyards, and vegetable gardens that are always green; the pestilential air seizes their inhabitants in the deserted streets and nails them down in front of the doors of their houses which peel in the sun, and they tremble with fever beneath their topcoats and under all the blankets on their beds.

Down there, in the lowlands, the houses are few and far between and have a melancholy air, along the roads devoured by the sun, between two heaps of smoking manure, leaning against collapsing sheds in which the spare horses, tied to the empty manger, are waiting glassy-eyed.—

171

sponda del lago, colla frasca decrepita dell'osteria appesa all'uscio, le grandi stanzaccie vuote, e l'oste che sonnecchia accoccolato sul limitare, colla testa stretta nel fazzoletto, spiando ad ogni svegliarsi, nella campagna deserta, se arriva un passeggiero assetato. – Oppure come cassette di legno bianco, impennacchiate da quattro eucalipti magri e grigi, lungo la ferrovia che taglia in due la pianura come un colpo d'accetta, dove vola la macchina fischiando al pari di un vento d'autunno, e la notte corruscano scintille infuocate. – O infine qua e là, sul limite dei poderi segnato da un pilastrino appena squadrato, coi tetti appuntellati dal di fuori, colle imposte sconquassate, dinanzi all'aia screpolata, all'ombra delle alte biche di paglia dove dormono le galline colla testa sotto l'ala, e l'asino lascia cascare il capo, colla bocca ancora piena di paglia, e il cane si rizza sospettoso, e abbaia roco al sasso che si stacca dall'intonaco, alla lucertola che striscia, alla foglia che si muove nella campagna inerte.

La sera, appena cade il sole, si affacciano sull'uscio uomini arsi dal sole, sotto il cappellaccio di paglia e colle larghe mutande di tela, sbadigliando e stirandosi le braccia; e donne seminude, colle spalle nere, allattando dei bambini già pallidi e disfatti, che non si sa come si faranno grandi e neri, e come ruzzeranno sull'erba quando tornerà l'inverno, e l'aia diverrà verde un'altra volta, e il cielo azzurro e tutt'intorno la campagna riderà al sole. E non si sa neppure dove stia e perché ci stia tutta quella gente che alla domenica corre per la messa alle chiesuole solitarie, circondate dalle siepi di fichidindia, a dieci miglia in giro, sin dove si ode squillare la campanella fessa nella pianura che non finisce mai.

Però dov'è la malaria è terra benedetta da Dio. In giugno le spighe si coricano dal peso, e i solchi fumano quasi avessero sangue nelle vene appena c'entra il vomero in novembre. Allora bisogna pure che chi semina e chi raccoglie caschi come una spiga matura, perché il Signore ha detto: «Il pane che si mangia bisogna sudarlo». Come il sudore della febbre lascia qualcheduno stecchito sul pagliericcio di granoturco, e non c'è più bisogno di solfato né di decotto d'eucalipto, lo si carica sulla carretta del fieno, o attraverso il basto dell'asino, o su di una scala, come si può, con un sacco sulla faccia, e si va a deporlo alla chiesuola solitaria, sotto i fichidindia spinosi di cui nessuno perciò mangia i frutti. Le donne piangono in crocchio, e gli uomini stanno a guardare, fumando.

Così s'erano portato il camparo di Valsavoia, che si chiamava

Or, on the shores of the lake, with the decrepit bush hanging on the inn door as its sign, the big, empty public rooms, and the innkeeper dozing as he squats on the threshold, his head tied up in his bandanna, searching the deserted countryside every time he wakes up to see whether some thirsty wayfarer will arrive.—Or else, those houses like white wooden boxes, shaded by four thin, gray eucalyptuses, alongside the railroad track that chops the plain in two like a hatchet cut, where the train flies by whistling like an autumn wind, and fiery sparks gleam at night.—Or, finally, those houses here and there, at the farm boundary marked by a little column of roughly dressed stone, with their roofs propped up outside and their rickety shutters, in front of the cracked threshing floor, in the shade of the tall ricks of straw where the chickens sleep with their heads under their wings and the donkey lets its head droop, its mouth still full of straw, and the dog stands up mistrustfully, barking hoarsely at the stone falling out of the plastered wall, or the lizard scuttling by, or the leaf stirring in the sluggish countryside.

In the evening, as soon as the sun goes down, suntanned men appear in the doorway, wearing big straw hats and wide canvas shorts, yawning and stretching; and half-naked women, with swarthy shoulders, nursing babies that are already pale and haggard, so that no one can tell how they'll become big and dark, or how they'll romp in the grass when winter returns and the threshing floor will become green again, and the blue sky and the countryside all around will laugh in the sunshine. No one knows, either, where all those people come from (or why they live there) who come to Mass on Sundays in the lonely little churches surrounded by prickly-pear hedges, from ten miles around, from as far as you can hear the little cracked bell ringing over the endless plain.

But, where pestilential air prevails, the soil is blessed by God. In June the grain stalks bend over flat under their own weight, and the furrows steam, as if they had blood in their veins, the moment that the plowshare bites into them in November. Then, it's necessary for the sower and the reaper to fall like a ripe ear, too, because the Lord said: "You must eat your bread in the sweat of your brow." When the sweat of fever leaves someone dried up on his maize-straw pallet, and he has no more need of sulphur or of eucalyptus infusion, he's loaded onto the haywagon or slung across the donkey's packsaddle, or onto a ladder, whatever is available, with a sack over his face, and they go and bury him at the lonely little church, beneath the thorny prickly pears, of which no one eats the fruit for that reason. The women gather in a group to weep, and the men stand looking on, smoking.

In that way they had carried out the field watchman at Valsavoia,

Massaro Croce, ed erano trent'anni che inghiottiva solfato e decotto d'eucalipto. In primavera stava meglio, ma d'autunno, come ripassavano le anitre, egli si metteva il fazzoletto in testa, e non si faceva più vedere sull'uscio che ogni due giorni; tanto che si era ridotto pelle ed ossa, e aveva una pancia grossa come un tamburo, che lo chiamavano *il Rospo* anche pel suo fare rozzo e selvatico, e perché gli erano diventati gli occhi smorti e a fior di testa. Egli diceva sempre prima di morire: – Non temete, che pei miei figli il padrone ci penserà – E con quegli occhiacci attoniti guardava in faccia ad uno ad uno coloro che gli stavano attorno al letto, l'ultima sera, e gli mettevano la candela sotto il naso. Lo zio Menico, il capraio, che se ne intendeva, disse che doveva avere il fegato duro come un sasso e pesante un rotolo e mezzo. Qualcuno aggiungeva pure:

– Adesso se ne impipa! ché s'è ingrassato e fatto ricco a spese del padrone, e i suoi figli non hanno bisogno di nessuno! Credete che l'abbia preso soltanto pei begli occhi del padrone tutto quel solfato e tutta quella malaria per trent'anni?

Compare Carmine, l'oste del lago, aveva persi allo stesso modo i suoi figliuoli tutt'e cinque, l'un dopo l'altro, tre maschi e due femmine. Pazienza le femmine! Ma i maschi morivano appunto quando erano grandi, nell'età di guadagnarsi il pane. Oramai egli lo sapeva; e come le febbri vincevano il ragazzo, dopo averlo travagliato due o tre anni, non spendeva più un soldo, né per solfato né per decotti, spillava del buon vino e si metteva ad ammannire tutti gli intingoli di pesce che sapeva, onde stuzzicare l'appetito al malato. Andava apposta colla barca a pescare la mattina, tornava carico di cefali, di anguille grosse come il braccio, e poi diceva al figliuolo, ritto dinanzi al letto e colle lagrime agli occhi: – Te'! mangia! – Il resto lo pigliava Nanni, il carrettiere per andare a venderlo in città. – Il lago vi dà e il lago vi piglia – Gli diceva Nanni, vedendo piangere di nascosto compare Carmine. – Che volete farci, fratel mio? – Il lago gli aveva dato dei bei guadagni. E a Natale, quando le anguille si vendono bene, nella casa in riva al lago, cenavano allegramente dinanzi al fuoco, maccheroni, salsiccia e ogni ben di Dio, mentre il vento urlava di fuori come un lupo che abbia fame e freddo. In tal modo coloro che restavano si consolavano dei morti. Ma a poco a poco andavano assottigliandosi così che la madre divenne curva come un gancio dai crepacuori, e il padre che era grosso e grasso, stava sempre sull'uscio, onde non vedere quelle stanzaccie vuote, dove prima cantavano e lavoravano i suoi ragazzi. L'ultimo rimasto non voleva morire assolutamente, e piangeva e si disperava allorché lo coglieva

who was called farmer Croce, and had been swallowing sulphur and eucalyptus infusion for thirty years. In the spring he'd felt better, but in autumn, when the ducks flew over, he had put his bandanna on his head and was only seen at his doorway every two days, until he shrank to skin and bones and had a belly big as a drum, so that they called him Toad, both because of his crude and primitive behavior, and because his eyes had become glassy and bulging. He kept saying, before he died: "Have no fear, because the landowner will take care of my children." And with those ugly, astonished eyes he would look in the face of everyone around his bed, one by one, that last evening, as they held the candle to his face. "Uncle" Menico, the goatherd, who knew all about such things, said that his stomach must be hard as a rock, and must weigh a *rotolo* and a half. Somebody added:

"Now he doesn't give a damn, because he's grown fat and rich at the proprietor's expense, and his children don't need anybody's help! Do you think he took all that sulphur and all that bad air for thirty years just because he liked the proprietor's looks?"

Neighbor Carmine, the innkeeper at the lake, had lost all five of his children, one after another, in the same way, three boys and two girls. As for the females, oh, well! But the boys died off just when they were growing up and were old enough to earn a living. Now he knew better, and, when the fever overcame the last boy after he had suffered from it for two or three years, he didn't spend another cent, either on sulphur or on infusions; he tapped good wine and started preparing all the tasty fish dishes he knew how to make, in order to stimulate the patient's appetite. He purposely went out fishing in his boat in the morning, returning loaded down with mullets and eels as big around as your arm, and then he'd say to his son, as he stood in front of his bed with tears in his eyes: "Here! Eat!" The fish that remained was taken by Nanni the carter to be sold in town. "The lake gives and the lake takes away," Nanni would say to neighbor Carmine when he saw him crying in secret. "What can you do about it, brother?" The lake had given him good earnings. And at Christmas, when eels sell well, they'd dine merrily in front of the fire in the house by the lake—macaroni, sausage, and all the good things God gives—while the wind howled outside like a cold, hungry wolf. In such manner the survivors comforted themselves for their dead. But gradually their numbers were so reduced that the mother became as bent-over as a fishhook from her sorrows, and the father, who was big and fat, always stood in the doorway so he wouldn't see those empty rooms in which his boys once sang and worked. The last remaining one absolutely didn't want to die; he'd weep and fall into

la febbre, e persino andò a buttarsi nel lago dalla paura della morte. Ma il padre che sapeva nuotare lo ripescò, e lo sgridava che quel bagno freddo gli avrebbe fatto tornare la febbre peggio di prima. – Ah! singhiozzava il giovanetto colle mani nei capelli, – per me non c'è più speranza! per me non c'è più speranza! — Tutto sua sorella Agata, che non voleva morire perché era sposa – osservava compare Carmine di faccia a sua moglie, seduta accanto al letto; e lei, che non piangeva più da un pezzo, confermava col capo, curva al pari di un gancio.

Lei, ridotta a quel modo, e suo marito grasso e grosso avevano il cuoio duro, e rimasero soli a guardar la casa. La malaria non ce l'ha contro di tutti. Alle volte uno vi campa cent'anni, come Cirino lo scimunito, il quale non aveva né re né regno, né arte né parte, né padre né madre, né casa per dormire, né pane da mangiare, e tutti lo conoscevano a quaranta miglia intorno, siccome andava da una fattoria all'altra, aiutando a governare i buoi, a trasportare il concime, a scorticare le bestie morte, a fare gli uffici vili; e pigliava delle pedate e un tozzo di pane; dormiva nei fossati, sul ciglione dei campi, a ridosso delle siepi, sotto le tettoie degli stallazzi; e viveva di carità, errando come un cane senza padrone, scamiciato e scalzo, con due lembi di mutande tenuti insieme da una funicella sulle gambe magre e nere; e andava cantando a squarciagola sotto il sole che gli martellava sulla testa nuda, giallo come lo zafferano. Egli non prendeva più né solfato, né medicine, né pigliava le febbri. Cento volte l'avevano raccolto disteso, quasi fosse morto, attraverso la strada; infine la malaria l'aveva lasciato, perché non sapeva più che farsene di lui. Dopo che gli aveva mangiato il cervello e la polpa delle gambe, e gli era entrata tutta nella pancia gonfia come un otre, l'aveva lasciato contento come una pasqua, a cantare al sole meglio di un grillo. Di preferenza lo scimunito soleva stare dinanzi lo stallatico di Valsavoja, perché ci passava della gente, ed egli correva loro dietro per delle miglia, gridando, uuh! uuh! finché gli buttavano due centesimi. L'oste gli prendeva i centesimi e lo teneva a dormire sotto la tettoia, sullo strame dei cavalli, che quando si tiravano dei calci, Cirino correva a svegliare il padrone gridando uuh! e la mattina li strigliava e li governava.

Più tardi era stato attratto dalla ferrovia che costrussero lì vicino. I vetturali e i viandanti erano diventati più rari sulla strada, e lo scimunito non sapeva che pensare, guardando in aria delle ore le rondini che volavano, e batteva le palpebre al sole per capacitarsene. La prima volta, al vedere tutta quella gente insaccata nei carrozzoni che

despair whenever the fever assailed him, and finally jumped into the lake out of fear of dying. But his father, who knew how to swim, pulled him out, scolding him because that cold plunge would make his fever come back worse than before. "Oh," the young man would sigh, his hands in his hair, "there's no more hope for me! There's no more hope for me!" "Just like his sister Agata, who didn't want to die because she was engaged," remarked neighbor Carmine to his wife, who was sitting beside the bed; and she, who hadn't wept for some time, agreed with a nod of the head perched on that body as bent-over as a fishhook.

She, shrunken that way, and her husband, big and fat, had a thick skin, and remained alone to oversee the house. The pestilential air doesn't have it in for everyone. At times a person will live in it for a hundred years, like Cirino the halfwit, who had "neither king nor kingdom, neither a trade nor income," neither father nor mother, no house to sleep in, no bread to eat. He was known to everyone for forty miles around, as he wandered from one farmhouse to another, helping to tend the oxen, carry manure, skin dead animals, and do the dirtiest work; he received kicks and a hunk of bread; he slept in ditches, on the ridges between fields, in the shelter of hedges, under stable sheds; he lived on charity, roaming about like a dog without a master, shirtless and barefoot, with two scraps of shorts held together with a string on his thin, dark legs. He'd go around singing at the top of his lungs beneath the sun that hammered down on his bare head; he was yellow as saffron. He no longer took sulphur or medicines, but didn't catch fevers. A hundred times he'd been picked up as he lay sprawled across the road like a corpse; the pestilential air had finally left him alone because it no longer knew what to do with him. After it had eaten away his brain and the fleshy part of his legs, and had settled entirely in his stomach, which was swollen like a wineskin, it had left him as happy as a king, singing in the sunlight more merrily than a cricket. The halfwit preferred standing in front of the Valsavoia stables, because people passed by there; he'd run after them for miles, yelling: "Ooh, ooh!" until they threw two *centesimi* to him. The innkeeper would take the coins and let him sleep under the shed, on the horses' straw. When they kicked one another, Cirino would run and awaken the innkeeper with shouts of "Ooh!" and in the morning he'd currycomb them and tend to them.

Later on, he had been attracted by the railroad being constructed nearby. The carriers and pedestrians had become less often seen on the road, and the halfwit didn't know what to make of this; for hours he'd look up in the sky at the flying swallows, blinking his eyes in the sun to try to understand. The first time he saw all those people

passavano dalla stazione, parve che indovinasse. E d'allora in poi ogni giorno aspettava il treno, senza sbagliare di un minuto, quasi avesse l'orologio in testa; e mentre gli fuggiva dinanzi, gettandogli contro la faccia il fumo e lo strepito, egli si dava a corrergli dietro, colle braccia in aria, urlando in tuono di collera e di minaccia: uuh! uuh! . . .

L'oste, anche lui, ogni volta che da lontano vedeva passare il treno sbuffante nella malaria, non diceva nulla, ma gli sputava contro il fatto suo scrollando il capo, davanti alla tettoia deserta e ai boccali vuoti. Prima gli affari andavano così bene che egli aveva preso quattro mogli, l'una dopo l'altra, tanto che lo chiamavano «Ammazzamogli» e dicevano che ci aveva fatto il callo, e tirava a pigliarsi la quinta, se la figlia di massaro Turi Oricchiazza non gli faceva rispondere: – Dio ne liberi! nemmeno se fosse d'oro, quel cristiano! Ei si mangia il prossimo suo come un coccodrillo! – Ma non era vero che ci avesse fatto il callo, perché quando gli era morta comare Santa, ed era la terza, egli sino all'ora di colezione non ci aveva messo un boccone di pane in bocca, né un sorso d'acqua, e piangeva per davvero dietro il banco dell'osteria. – Stavolta voglio pigliarmi una che è avvezza alla malaria – aveva detto dopo quel fatto. – Non voglio più soffrirne di questi dispiaceri.

Le mogli gliele ammazzava la malaria, ad una ad una, ma lui lo lasciava tal quale, vecchio e grinzoso, che non avreste immaginato come quell'uomo lì ci avesse anche lui il suo bravo omicidio sulle spalle, quantunque tirasse a prendere la quarta moglie. Pure la moglie ogni volta la cercava giovane e appetitosa, ché senza moglie l'osteria non può andare, e per questo gli avventori s'erano diradati. Ora non restava altri che compare Mommu, il cantoniere della ferrovia lì vicino, un uomo che non parlava mai, e veniva a bere il suo bicchiere fra un treno e l'altro, mettendosi a sedere sulla panchetta accanto all'uscio, colle scarpe in mano, per lasciare riposare i piedi. – Questi qui non li coglie la malaria! – pensava «Ammazzamogli» senza aprir bocca nemmeno lui, ché se la malaria li avesse fatti cadere come le mosche non ci sarebbe stato chi facesse andare quella ferrovia là. Il poveraccio, dacché s'era levato dinanzi agli occhi il solo uomo che gli avvelenava l'esistenza, non ci aveva più che due nemici al mondo: la ferrovia che gli rubava gli avventori, e la malaria che gli portava via le mogli. Tutti gli altri nella pianura, sin dove arrivavano gli occhi, provavano un momento di contentezza, anche se nel lettuccio ci avevano qualcuno che se ne andava a poco a poco, o se la febbre li abbatteva sull'uscio, col fazzoletto in testa e il tabarro addosso. Si ricreavano guardando il

enclosed in the big coaches that passed by the station, he seemed to have guessed. And from then on, he'd wait for the train every day, never off by a minute, as if he had a clock in his head; while it raced away before his eyes, flinging its smoke and clatter into his face, he'd run after it, his arms in the air, howling in angry, menacing tones: "Ooh! Ooh! . . ."

The innkeeper,[1] too, whenever he saw the train go by in the distance, puffing through the pestilential air, never said a word, but expressed his opinion by spitting at it while shaking his head, in front of the deserted shed and the empty tankards. Earlier, his business had been so good that he had married four women in succession, so that people called him "Wife Killer" and said he had grown used to losing them. He was aiming at a fifth marriage, but the daughter of farmer Turi Ugly-Ears greeted his suit with: "God forbid! Not even if that man were made of gold! He eats up his fellow man like a crocodile!" But it wasn't true that he was callous about the death of his wives, because when neighbor Santa, who was his third, died on him, he hadn't put a morsel of bread or a sip of water in his mouth until lunchtime, and he shed real tears behind the bar of the inn. "This time I want to marry one who's accustomed to the bad air," he had said after that occurrence. "I don't want to undergo this chagrin anymore."

The bad air killed off his wives one by one, but left him just as he was, old and wrinkled, so that you wouldn't imagine that that man, too, had a man's blood on his hands, even though he had his heart set on a fourth wife. And yet, each time, he looked out for a young, charming woman, because an inn can't run without a woman, and that's why his custom had fallen off. Now there was no one left but neighbor Mommu, the nearby stationmaster, a man who never spoke, but would come to drain a glass in between trains, sitting down on the bench beside the doorway, holding his shoes in his hand to give his feet a rest. "This fellow won't be carried off by the bad air!" thought Wife Killer, without opening *his* mouth, either, because if the bad air made them drop like flies, there wouldn't be anyone to make that railroad operate. The poor fellow, once he had rid himself of the one man who poisoned his existence, now had only two enemies in the world: the railroad, which was stealing his customers, and the bad air, which was taking away his wives. Everyone else in the lowlands, as far as the eye could see, was experiencing a moment of contentment, even if they had some bedridden relative who was gradually slipping away, or even if fever struck them down at their doorway, their bandannas on

---

1. Not the same person as neighbor Carmine.

seminato che veniva su prosperoso e verde come il velluto, o le biade che ondeggiavano al par di un mare, e ascoltavano la cantilena lunga dei mietitori, distesi come una fila di soldati, e in ogni viottolo si udiva la cornamusa, dietro la quale arrivavano dalla Calabria degli sciami di contadini per la messe, polverosi, curvi sotto la bisaccia pesante, gli uomini avanti e le donne in coda, zoppicanti e guardando la strada che si allungava con la faccia arsa e stanca. E sull'orlo di ogni fossato, dietro ogni macchia d'aloe, nell'ora in cui cala la sera come un velo grigio, fischiava lo zufolo del guardiano, in mezzo alle spighe mature che tacevano, immobili al cascare del vento, invase anch'esse dal silenzio della notte. – Ecco! – pensava «Ammazzamogli». – Tutta quella gente là se fa tanto di non lasciarci la pelle e di tornare a casa, ci torna con dei denari in tasca.

Ma lui no! lui non aspettava né la raccolta né altro, e non aveva animo di cantare. La sera calava tanto triste, nello stallazzo vuoto e nell'osteria buia. A quell'ora il treno passava da lontano fischiando, e compare Mommu stava accanto al suo casotto colla bandieruola in mano; ma fin lassù, dopo che il treno era svanito nelle tenebre, si udiva Cirino lo scimunito che gli correva dietro urlando, uuh! . . . E «Ammazzamogli» sulla porta dell'osteria buia e deserta pensava che per quelli lì la malaria non ci era.

Infine quando non poté pagar più l'affitto dell'osteria e dello stallazzo, il padrone lo mandò via dopo 57 anni che c'era stato, e «Ammazzamogli» si ridusse a cercare impiego nella ferrovia anche lui, e a tenere in mano la bandieruola quando passava il treno.

Allora stanco di correre tutto il giorno su e giù lungo le rotaie, rifinito dagli anni e dai malanni, vedeva passare due volte al giorno la lunga fila dei carrozzoni stipati di gente; le allegre brigate di cacciatori che si sparpagliavano per la pianura; alle volte un contadinello che suonava l'organetto a capo chino, rincantucciato su di una panchetta di terza classe; le belle signore che affacciavano allo sportello il capo avvolto nel velo; l'argento e l'acciaio brunito dei sacchi e delle borse da viaggio che luccicavano sotto i lampioni smerigliati; le alte spalliere imbottite e coperte di trina. Ah, come si doveva viaggiar bene lì dentro, schiacciando un sonnellino! Sembrava che un pezzo di città sfilasse lì davanti, colla luminaria delle strade, e le botteghe sfavillanti. Poi il treno si perdeva nella vasta nebbia della sera, e il poveraccio, cavandosi un momento le scarpe, seduto sulla panchina, borbottava: – Ah! per questi qui non c'è proprio la malaria!

their heads and their cloaks on their backs. They consoled themselves at the sight of their thriving fields, velvety green, or the stalks of grain rippling like an ocean. They'd listen to the prolonged chanting of the reapers, lined up like soldiers; in every lane could be heard a bagpipe, and behind it, arriving from Calabria, were swarms of farm laborers coming for the harvest, dusty, bent under their heavy knapsacks, the men in front and the women in the rear, all of them walking shakily and looking at the road, which stretched into the distance, with sunburnt, weary faces. And on the rim of every ditch, behind every aloes bush, at the hour when evening falls like a gray veil, the watchman's pipe whistled amid the ripe ears, which were silent and motionless when the wind dropped, they, too, engulfed in the silence of the night. "There!" thought Wife Killer. "If all these people manage to stay alive and get back home, they'll get back with money in their pockets."

But not he! *He* wasn't expecting a good harvest or anything else, and he didn't feel like singing. Evening was falling so sadly on the empty stable and the dark inn. At that hour the train went by whistling in the distance, and neighbor Mommu was standing beside his lodge, flag in hand. But at all that distance, after the train had vanished into the darkness, you could hear Cirino the halfwit running after it howling: "Ooh! . . ." And Wife Killer, at the door of his dark, deserted inn, reflected that for those two the bad air didn't exist.

Finally, when he could no longer pay the rent on the inn and the stable, the owner sent him packing after 57 years' tenure, and Wife Killer, too, was reduced to seeking work on the railroad, holding the flag when the train passed by.

Then, tired of running back and forth along the tracks all day, exhausted by old age and ailments, he'd watch the long line of coaches crammed with people pass by twice a day: the jolly hunting parties, which would soon scatter over the plain; sometimes a young peasant who played the accordion with head bowed, huddled on a third-class bench; the beautiful ladies who showed their veil-draped heads at the window; the silver and burnished steel of the suitcases and traveling bags gleaming beneath the frosted lights; the high-backed seats, upholstered and covered with lace. Oh, how nice it must be to ride in there, catching a nap! It was like a bit of the city roaring by in front of him, with its streetlamps and its glittering shops. Then the train would be lost in the immense mist of evening, and the poor man, taking off his shoes for a moment, as he sat on his bench, would mutter: "Oh, for *them* the bad air definitely doesn't exist!"

LA ROBA

Il viandante che andava lungo il Biviere di Lentini, steso là come un pezzo di mare morto, e le stoppie riarse della Piana di Catania, e gli aranci sempre verdi di Francofonte, e i sugheri grigi di Resecone, e i pascoli deserti di Passaneto e di Passanitello, se domandava, per ingannare la noia della lunga strada polverosa, sotto il cielo fosco dal caldo, nell'ora in cui i campanelli della lettiga suonano tristamente nell'immensa campagna, e i muli lasciano ciondolare il capo e la coda, e il lettighiere canta la sua canzone malinconica per non lasciarsi vincere dal sonno della malaria: – Qui di chi è? – sentiva rispondersi: – Di Mazzarò. – E passando vicino a una fattoria grande quanto un paese, coi magazzini che sembrano chiese, e le galline a stormi accoccolate all'ombra del pozzo, e le donne che si mettevano la mano sugli occhi per vedere chi passava: – E qui? – Di Mazzarò. – E cammina e cammina, mentre la malaria vi pesava sugli occhi, e vi scuoteva all'improvviso l'abbaiare di un cane, passando per una vigna che non finiva più, e si allargava sul colle e sul piano, immobile, come gli pesasse addosso la polvere, e il guardiano sdraiato bocconi sullo schioppo, accanto al vallone, levava il capo sonnacchioso, e apriva un occhio per vedere chi fosse: – Di Mazzarò. – Poi veniva un uliveto folto come un bosco, dove l'erba non spuntava mai, e la raccolta durava fino a marzo. Erano gli ulivi di Mazzarò. E verso sera, allorché il sole tramontava rosso come il fuoco, e la campagna si velava di tristezza, si incontravano le lunghe file degli aratri di Mazzarò che tornavano adagio adagio dal maggese, e i buoi che passavano il guado lentamente, col muso nell'acqua scura; e si vedevano nei pascoli lontani della Canziria, sulla pendice brulla, le immense macchie biancastre delle mandre di Mazzarò; e si udiva il fischio del pastore echeggiare nelle gole, e il campanaccio che risuonava ora sì ed ora no, e il canto solitario perduto nella valle. – Tutta roba di Mazzarò. Pareva che fosse di Mazzarò perfino il sole che tramontava, e le cicale che ronzavano, e gli uccelli che andavano a rannicchiarsi col volo

POSSESSIONS

Say you were a wayfarer passing alongside the Lake of Lentini, which lies there like a small dead sea, and alongside the parched stubble of the Plain of Catania, and the evergreen orange trees of Francofonte, and the gray cork-oaks of Resecone, and the deserted pastures of Passaneto and Passanitello. And say you wanted to overcome the boredom of the long, dusty road, beneath a sky hazy with heat, at the hour when the bells of the litter-driver ring cheerlessly through the vast countryside, while his mules let their heads and tails hang down, and the driver sings his melancholy song to keep from dropping into a malarial slumber. If, in order to do so, you asked: "Who owns all this?," you'd hear the answer: "Mazzarò." And, passing by a farmhouse as large as a village, with storehouses that looked like churches, and flocks of chickens squatting in the shade of the well, and women putting their hands to their eyes to see who was going by: "And this?" "Mazzarò." As your journey continued, while the bad air weighed down your eyes, and you were suddenly startled by the barking of a dog, while passing through an interminable vineyard that spread over hill and plain as motionless as if the dust were weighing it down, and the watchman, stretched out on his stomach over his gun, next to the ravine, raised his sleepy head and opened one eye to see who was there: "Mazzarò." Next came an olive grove as dense as a forest, in which no grass ever grew and the harvesting lasted till March. They were Mazzarò's olive trees. And toward evening, when the sun was setting as red as fire, and the countryside was being mantled in gloom, you would run across the long rows of Mazzarò's plows returning slowly from the fallow field, and the oxen calmly wading through the ford, their muzzles in the dark water. And you'd see, in the distant pastures of Canziria, on the barren slope, the vast whitish spots that indicated Mazzarò's flocks; and you could hear the shepherd's pipe echoing in the gorges, and the flock bell ringing at intervals, and the lonely singing lost in the valley. "All possessions of Mazzarò." Mazzarò seemed to own even the setting sun, and the buzzing cicadas, and the birds

breve dietro le zolle, e il sibilo dell'assiolo nel bosco. Pareva che Mazzarò fosse disteso tutto grande per quanto era grande la terra, e che gli si camminasse sulla pancia. – Invece egli era un omiciattolo, diceva il lettighiere, che non gli avreste dato un baiocco, a vederlo; e di grasso non aveva altro che la pancia, e non si sapeva come facesse a riempirla, perché non mangiava altro che due soldi di pane; e sì ch'era ricco come un maiale; ma aveva la testa ch'era un brillante, quell'uomo.

Infatti, colla testa come un brillante, aveva accumulato tutta quella roba, dove prima veniva da mattina a sera a zappare, a potare, a mietere; col sole, coll'acqua, col vento; senza scarpe ai piedi, e senza uno straccio di cappotto; che tutti si rammentavano di avergli dato dei calci nel di dietro, quelli che ora gli davano dell'*eccellenza*, e gli parlavano col berretto in mano. Né per questo egli era montato in superbia, adesso che tutte le eccellenze del paese erano suoi debitori; e diceva che eccellenza vuol dire povero diavolo e cattivo pagatore; ma egli portava ancora il berretto, soltanto lo portava di seta nera, era la sua sola grandezza, e da ultimo era anche arrivato a mettere il cappello di feltro, perché costava meno del berretto di seta. Della roba ne possedeva fin dove arrivava la vista, ed egli aveva la vista lunga – dappertutto, a destra e a sinistra, davanti e di dietro, nel monte e nella pianura. Più di cinquemila bocche, senza contare gli uccelli del cielo e gli animali della terra, che mangiavano sulla sua terra, e senza contare la sua bocca la quale mangiava meno di tutte, e si contentava di due soldi di pane e un pezzo di formaggio, ingozzato in fretta e in furia, all'impiedi, in un cantuccio del magazzino grande come una chiesa, in mezzo alla polvere del grano, che non ci si vedeva, mentre i contadini scaricavano i sacchi, o a ridosso di un pagliaio, quando il vento spazzava la campagna gelata, al tempo del seminare, o colla testa dentro un corbello nelle calde giornate della messe. Egli non beveva vino, non fumava, non usava tabacco, e sì che del tabacco ne producevano i suoi orti lungo il fiume, colle foglie larghe ed alte come un fanciullo, di quelle che si vendevano a 95 lire. Non aveva il vizio del giuoco, né quello delle donne. Di donne non aveva mai avuto sulle spalle che sua madre, la quale gli era costata anche 12 tarì, quando aveva dovuto farla portare al camposanto.

Era che ci aveva pensato e ripensato tanto a quel che vuol dire la roba, quando andava senza scarpe a lavorare nella terra che adesso era sua, ed aveva provato quel che ci vuole a fare i tre tarì della giornata, nel mese di luglio, a star colla schiena curva 14 ore, col soprastante a cavallo dietro, che vi piglia a nerbate se fate di rizzarvi un momento.

returning to their nests behind the sods in a brief flight, and the hooting of the scops owl in the woods. Mazzarò seemed to be spread out
over the whole extent of the earth; it was as if you were traveling over
his belly. But actually, the litter-driver would say, he was a tiny man that
you wouldn't give a penny for if you saw him; the only thing fat about
him was his stomach, and no one knew how he managed to fill it, because he never ate more than two *soldi's* worth of bread. Yes, he was as
rich as a pig, but he had a head that was a diamond, that man.

Indeed, with that head like a diamond he had amassed all those possessions, whereas in earlier days he had been out from morning to
evening hoeing, pruning, reaping, in sun, rain, or wind, without shoes
on his feet or a shred of overcoat. Everyone recalled giving him kicks
in the behind, the same people who now called him "your excellence"
and held their hats in their hands when they spoke to him. Nor had all
this made him haughty, now that all the gentry in the vicinity were in
debt to him; he used to say that an "excellence" was a poor devil who
was slow to pay his debts. As for him, he still wore a cap, not a gentleman's hat, but his cap was of black silk (that was his only form of os-
tentation). Lately he had come to wear a felt hat, but only because it
cost less than a silk cap. His possessions stretched as far as the eye
could see, and he had keen sight—everywhere, left and right, before
and behind, on mountain and plain. More than five thousand mouths,
not counting the birds in the sky or the beasts in the field, were fed on
his property, and that didn't include his own mouth, which ate less than
any of the others and was satisfied with two *soldi's* worth of bread and
a piece of cheese, gulped down at top speed, while he was on his feet,
in a corner of one of the church-sized storehouses, or amid the dust of
the grain that hid everything from sight when the farmhands were un-
loading their sacks, or in the lee of a straw rick when the wind was
sweeping the frozen countryside at sowing time, or with his head inside a basket for shade in the hot days of harvest time. He didn't drink
wine, he didn't smoke, he didn't take snuff, even though his riverside
plots produced tobacco with leaves as broad and tall as a child, the sort
that is sold for 95 *lire.* He wasn't addicted to gambling or women. The
only woman he ever had to take care of was his mother, and she had
cost him 12 *tarì* when he had had to have her carried to the cemetery.

You see, he had thought so very often about what it means to have
possessions, in those days when he labored without shoes on the land
that was now his; he had experienced what it means to earn three *tarì*
a day in the month of July, bending your back for fourteen hours, with
the overseer riding behind you, whipping you if you straightened up

Per questo non aveva lasciato passare un minuto della sua vita che non fosse stato impiegato a fare della roba; e adesso i suoi aratri erano numerosi come le lunghe file dei corvi che arrivano in novembre; e altre file di muli, che non finivano più, portavano le sementi; le donne che stavano accoccolate nel fango, da ottobre a marzo, per raccogliere le sue olive, non si potevano contare, come non si possono contare le gazze che vengono a rubarle; e al tempo della vendemmia accorrevano dei villaggi interi alle sue vigne, e fin dove sentivasi cantare, nella campagna, era per la vendemmia di Mazzarò. Alla messe poi i mietitori di Mazzarò sembravano un esercito di soldati, che per mantenere tutta quella gente, col biscotto alla mattina e il pane e l'arancia amara a colazione, e la merenda, e le lasagne alla sera, ci volevano dei denari a manate, e le lasagne si scodellavano nelle madie larghe come tinozze. Perciò adesso, quando andava a cavallo dietro la fila dei suoi mietitori, col nerbo in mano, non ne perdeva d'occhio uno solo, e badava a ripetere: – Curviamoci, ragazzi! – Egli era tutto l'anno colle mani in tasca a spendere, e per la sola fondiaria il re si pigliava tanto che a Mazzarò gli veniva la febbre, ogni volta.

Però ciascun anno tutti quei magazzini grandi come chiese si riempivano di grano che bisognava scoperchiare il tetto per farcelo capire tutto; e ogni volta che Mazzarò vendeva il vino, ci voleva più di un giorno per contare il denaro, tutto di 12 tarì d'argento, ché lui non ne voleva di carta sudicia per la sua roba, e andava a comprare la carta sudicia soltanto quando aveva da pagare il re, o gli altri; e alle fiere gli armenti di Mazzarò coprivano tutto il campo, e ingombravano le strade, che ci voleva mezza giornata per lasciarli sfilare, e il santo, colla banda, alle volte dovevano mutar strada, e cedere il passo.

Tutta quella roba se l'era fatta lui, colle sue mani e colla sua testa, col non dormire la notte, col prendere la febbre dal batticuore o dalla malaria, coll'affaticarsi dall'alba a sera, e andare in giro, sotto il sole e sotto la pioggia, col logorare i suoi stivali e le sue mule – egli solo non si logorava, pensando alla sua roba, ch'era tutto quello ch'ei avesse al mondo; perché non aveva né figli, né nipoti, né parenti; non aveva altro che la sua roba. Quando uno è fatto così, vuol dire che è fatto per la roba.

Ed anche la roba era fatta per lui, che pareva ci avesse la calamita, perché la roba vuol stare con chi sa tenerla, e non la sciupa come quel barone che prima era stato il padrone di Mazzarò, e l'aveva raccolto per carità nudo e crudo ne' suoi campi, ed era stato il padrone di tutti quei prati, e di tutti quei boschi, e di tutte quelle vigne e tutti quegli armenti, che quando veniva nelle sue terre a

for a minute. That's why he hadn't let a moment of his life go by without using it to gain possessions. And now his plows were as numerous as the long strings of crows that arrive in November, while other, endless strings of mules carried the seed grain. The women who crouched in the mud from October to March gathering his olives couldn't be counted, nor could the magpies that came to steal them. At grape harvest, entire villages showed up at his vineyards, and wherever you heard singing in the countryside, it was for Mazzarò's vintaging. Then, at grain harvest, Mazzarò's reapers were like an army of soldiers; to feed all those people—biscuits in the morning, bread and bitter oranges at lunch, and an afternoon snack, and lasagna in the evening— took heaps of money, and the lasagna was dished out into platters as big as troughs. And so now, when he rode his horse behind the line of his reapers, whip in hand, he kept his eye on every last one of them, and made sure to repeat: "Let's bend our backs, men!" All year long his expenses made him dig into his pockets, and in land tax alone the king took so much that Mazzarò became feverish each time.

But every year all those church-sized granaries were so full of grain that you'd almost have to remove their roofs to make it all fit; and every time Mazzarò sold wine, it took over a day to count the money, all in 12-*tarì* silver coins, because he wouldn't accept any dirty paper in exchange for his possessions; he went and bought dirty paper only when he had to pay the king or someone else. At the animal fairs Mazzarò's herds and flocks covered the whole grounds and blocked the roads; it took half a day to let them go by, and sometimes the saint's procession and the musicians had to take a different path and yield their ground.

He had amassed all those possessions with his own head and hands, not sleeping at night, becoming feverish with palpitations or from the bad air, tiring himself out from dawn to dusk, going around in sun and rain, wearing out his boots and his she-mules—only he himself didn't wear out, as he thought about his possessions, which were all he had in the world; because he had neither sons, nor grandsons, nor relatives; he had nothing but his possessions. When a man is of that nature, it means that he is meant to own property.

And, in turn, property was meant for him; he seemed to attract it with a magnet; because property tends to remain with a man who can retain it and doesn't squander it like that baron who had once been Mazzarò's master, and who had taken him in, as an absolute pauper, out of charity, to work in his fields. He had been the owner of all those meadows, and all those forests, and all those vineyards and all those herds; when he

cavallo coi campieri dietro, pareva il re, e gli preparavano anche
l'alloggio e il pranzo, al minchione, sicché ognuno sapeva l'ora e il
momento in cui doveva arrivare, e non si faceva sorprendere colle
mani nel sacco. – Costui vuol essere rubato per forza! diceva
Mazzarò, e schiattava dalle risa quando il barone gli dava dei calci
nel di dietro, e si fregava la schiena colle mani, borbottando: «Chi
è minchione se ne stia a casa», – «la roba non è di chi l'ha, ma di
chi la sa fare». Invece egli, dopo che ebbe fatta la sua roba, non
mandava certo a dire se veniva a sorvegliare la messe, o la vendemmia, e quando, e come; ma capitava all'improvviso, a piedi o a
cavallo alla mula, senza campieri, con un pezzo di pane in tasca; e
dormiva accanto ai suoi covoni, cogli occhi aperti, e lo schioppo fra
le gambe.

In tal modo a poco a poco Mazzarò divenne il padrone di tutta
la roba del barone; e costui uscì prima dall'uliveto, e poi dalle
vigne, e poi dai pascoli, e poi dalle fattorie e infine dal suo palazzo
istesso, che non passava giorno che non firmasse delle carte bol-
late, e Mazzarò ci metteva sotto la sua brava croce. Al barone non
rimase altro che lo scudo di pietra ch'era prima sul portone, ed era
la sola cosa che non avesse voluto vendere, dicendo a Mazzarò: –
Questo solo, di tutta la mia roba, non fa per te. – Ed era vero;
Mazzarò non sapeva che farsene, e non l'avrebbe pagato due baioc-
chi. Il barone gli dava ancora del tu, ma non gli dava più calci nel
di dietro.

– Questa è una bella cosa, d'avere la fortuna che ha Mazzarò!
diceva la gente; e non sapeva quel che ci era voluto ad acchiappare
quella fortuna: quanti pensieri, quante fatiche, quante menzogne,
quanti pericoli di andare in galera, e come quella testa che era un
brillante avesse lavorato giorno e notte, meglio di una macina del
mulino, per fare la roba; e se il proprietario di una chiusa limitrofa si
ostinava a non cedergliela, e voleva prendere pel collo Mazzarò,
dover trovare uno stratagemma per costringerlo a vendere, e farcelo
cascare, malgrado la diffidenza contadinesca. Ei gli andava a vantare,
per esempio, la fertilità di una tenuta la quale non produceva nemmeno lupini, e arrivava a fargliela credere una terra promessa, sinché
il povero diavolo si lasciava indurre a prenderla in affitto, per specu-
larci sopra, e ci perdeva poi il fitto, la casa e la chiusa, che Mazzarò
se l'acchiappava – per un pezzo di pane. – E quante seccature
Mazzarò doveva sopportare! – I mezzadri che venivano a lagnarsi
delle malannate, i debitori che mandavano in processione le loro
donne a strapparsi i capelli e picchiarsi il petto per scongiurarlo di

rode onto his lands with the field watchmen behind him, he resembled the king, and they'd prepare lodgings and dinner for the poor ninny in advance, because everyone knew the precise moment when he was due to arrive, so no one was caught with his hand in the till. "He insists on being robbed!" Mazzarò used to say, and he'd burst with laughter when the baron kicked him in the behind; he'd rub the spot with his hands, muttering: "If you're a ninny, you should stay home," or else: "Property doesn't belong to the man who has it, but to the man who can amass it." He, on the other hand, once he had amassed his property, certainly didn't send out announcements that he was coming to inspect the grain harvest or the vintaging, or at what time, or how; he'd show up unexpectedly, on foot or riding his she-mule, without watchmen, with a piece of bread in his pocket, and he'd sleep alongside his sheaves, with his eyes open and his gun between his legs.

In that way Mazzarò gradually became owner of all the baron's possessions; first the baron lost his olive grove, then his vineyards, then his pastures, then his farmhouses, and finally his manor house itself; not a day went by when he didn't put his signature to legal documents and Mazzarò signed below with his bold cross. All the baron had left was the stone coat-of-arms that used to be affixed over the main gateway; it was the only thing he had refused to sell, as he said to Mazzarò: "This alone of all my possessions doesn't suit you." And that was true; Mazzarò had no use for it, and wouldn't have given two cents for it. The baron still addressed him as *tu*, but no longer kicked him in the behind.

"It's a wonderful thing to have Mazzarò's good luck!" people would say, not knowing what it had taken to seize upon that good luck: all the planning, all the labors, all the lies, all the risks of going to jail. They didn't know how hard that head "like a diamond" had worked night and day, harder than a millstone, to amass those possessions. Whenever the owner of an adjacent plot of land persisted in his refusal to yield it, and wanted to put the squeeze on Mazzarò, he had had to invent a stratagem to force him to sell and make him fall into the trap in spite of the mistrustfulness of rural folk. For example, he would praise the fertility of a holding that didn't even produce lupins, and finally made the man believe it was the promised land, until the poor devil let himself be induced into renting it as a speculation. He then lost the rent, his house, and the plot of land, which Mazzarò would get his hands on "for a song." And all the annoyances Mazzarò had to put up with! Tenant farmers who came to complain about bad crops; debtors who sent their wives in a parade to pull out their hair and beat their breasts, beseeching him not to put them out on the

non metterli in mezzo alla strada, col pigliarsi il mulo o l'asinello, che non avevano da mangiare.

– Lo vedete quel che mangio io? rispondeva lui, – pane e cipolla! e sì che ho i magazzini pieni zeppi, e sono il padrone di tutta questa roba. – E se gli domandavano un pugno di fave, di tutta quella roba, ei diceva: – Che, vi pare che l'abbia rubata? Non sapete quanto costano per seminarle, e zapparle, e raccoglierle? – E se gli domandavano un soldo rispondeva che non l'aveva.

E non l'aveva davvero. Che in tasca non teneva mai 12 tarì, tanti ce ne volevano per far fruttare tutta quella roba, e il denaro entrava ed usciva come un fiume dalla sua casa. Del resto a lui non gliene importava del denaro; diceva che non era roba, e appena metteva insieme una certa somma, comprava subito un pezzo di terra; perché voleva arrivare ad avere della terra quanta ne ha il re, ed esser meglio del re, ché il re non può né venderla, né dire ch'è sua.

Di una cosa sola gli doleva, che cominciasse a farsi vecchio, e la terra doveva lasciarla là dov'era. Questa è una ingiustizia di Dio, che dopo di essersi logorata la vita ad acquistare della roba, quando arrivate ad averla, che ne vorreste ancora, dovete lasciarla! E stava delle ore seduto sul corbello, col mento nelle mani, a guardare le sue vigne che gli verdeggiavano sotto gli occhi, e i campi che ondeggiavano di spighe come un mare, e gli oliveti che velavano la montagna come una nebbia, e se un ragazzo seminudo gli passava dinanzi, curvo sotto il peso come un asino stanco, gli lanciava il suo bastone fra le gambe, per invidia, e borbottava: – Guardate chi ha i giorni lunghi! costui che non ha niente!

Sicché quando gli dissero che era tempo di lasciare la sua roba, per pensare all'anima, uscì nel cortile come un pazzo, barcollando, e andava ammazzando a colpi di bastone le sue anitre e i suoi tacchini, e strillava: – Roba mia, vientene con me!

street by taking away their mule or donkey, because they had nothing to eat.

"Do you see what *I* eat?" he'd reply. "Bread and onions! Yes, my storehouses are chockfull, and I'm the owner of all these possessions." And if they asked him for a handful of beans, out of all those possessions, he'd say: "What? Do you think I stole all of this? Don't you know how much beans cost to sow, and hoe, and pick?" And if they asked him for a *soldo,* he said he didn't have one.

And he really didn't. Because he didn't keep even 12 *tarì* in his pocket, he needed so much money to exploit all his property; his money came in and went out of his house like a river. Anyway, he didn't care about money; he said it wasn't property, and no sooner had he put together a given sum than he immediately bought a piece of land, because he wanted to end up owning as much land as the king does. He'd actually be better off than the king, because the king can't sell his land, or say that he owns it outright.

Just one thing saddened him, that he was starting to grow old, and would have to leave his land behind. God is unfair; after using up your life acquiring possessions, when you manage to get them, and would like even more, you've got to leave them! He would remain seated on a basket for hours, his chin in his hands, watching his vineyards grow green before his eyes, and his fields rippling with grain like an ocean, and his olive groves spreading over the mountain like a mist. If a half-naked boy went by, bent under his load like a tired donkey, he'd fling his walking-stick at his legs, out of envy, muttering: "Look who has his life ahead of him! An absolute pauper!"

And so, when he was told that it was time to leave his possessions behind, and think about his soul, he walked out of the yard like a madman, staggering, and went around killing his ducks and turkeys with blows of his stick, shrieking: "My possessions, come along with me!"

STORIA DELL'ASINO DI S. GIUSEPPE

L'avevano comperato alla fiera di Buccheri ch'era ancor puledro, e appena vedeva una ciuca, andava a frugarle le poppe; per questo si buscava testate e botte da orbi sul groppone, e avevano un bel gridargli: «Arriccà!». Compare Neli, come lo vide vispo e cocciuto a quel modo, che si leccava il muso alle legnate, mettendoci su una scrollatina d'orecchie, disse: «Questo è il fatto mio». E andò diritto al padrone, tenendo nella tasca la mano colle trentacinque lire.

– Il puledro è bello – diceva il padrone – e val più di trentacinque lire. Non ci badate se ha quel pelame bianco e nero come una gazza. Ora vi faccio vedere sua madre, che la teniamo lì nel boschetto perché il puledro ha sempre la testa alla poppa. Vedrete la bella bestia morella! che mi lavora meglio di una mula e mi ha fatti più figli che non abbia peli addosso. In coscienza mia! non so d'onde sia venuto quel mantello di gazza al puledro. Ma l'ossatura è buona, ve lo dico io! Già gli uomini non valgono pel mostaccio. Guardate che petto! e che pilastri di gambe! Guardate come tiene le orecchie! Un asino che tiene le orecchie ritte a quel modo lo potete mettere sotto il carro o sotto l'aratro come volete, e fargli portare quattro tumoli di farro meglio di un mulo, per la santa giornata che corre oggi! Sentite questa coda, che vi ci potete appendere voi con tutto il vostro parentado!

Compare Neli lo sapeva meglio di lui; ma non era minchione per dir di sì, e stava sulla sua colla mano in tasca, alzando le spalle e arricciando il naso, mentre il padrone gli faceva girare il puledro dinanzi.

– Uhm! – borbottava compare Neli. – Con quel pelame lì, che par l'asino di san Giuseppe! Le bestie di quel colore sono tutte *vigliacche*, e quando passate a cavallo pel paese, la gente vi ride in faccia. Cosa devo regalarvi per l'asino di san Giuseppe?

Il padrone allora gli voltò le spalle infuriato, gridando che se non conoscevano le bestie, o se non avevano denari per comprare, era

THE HISTORY OF ST. JOSEPH'S DONKEY

They had bought him at the animal fair in Buccheri when he was still a colt; as soon as he saw a female donkey, he'd go over and nuzzle her dugs. For doing so, he received butts with the head and a hail of blows on his crupper. It was no use to shout "Giddy-up!" at him. Neighbor Neli, seeing him so spry and stubborn, licking his muzzle when he was beaten and wiggling his ears, as well, said: "This one suits me." And he went straight to the donkey's owner, keeping in his pocket his hand that was clutching the thirty-five *lire*.

"The colt's a pretty one," said his owner, "and he's worth more than thirty-five *lire*. Pay no attention to his coat, which is black-and-white like a magpie. Now I'll show you his dam; we keep her in that patch of woods over there because the colt always has his head at her dugs. You'll see what a nice all-over dark color she has! She works harder than a she-mule for me, and she's given me more colts than she has hairs on her. Believe me, I don't know where the colt got that magpie coat from. But his bones are strong, let me tell you! Even men aren't to be judged by their mustaches. Look at that chest on him! And what legs like columns! Look at the way he holds his ears! A donkey that holds his ears up straight that way can be put behind a cart or a plow, whichever you like, and you can expect him to carry four *tumoli* of spelt better than a mule, I swear by the saint whose day it is! Feel this tail; you can hang from it, along with all your relatives!"

Neighbor Neli knew this better than he, but he wasn't such a ninny as to agree out loud; he stood his ground, his hand in his pocket, shrugging his shoulders and wrinkling his nose, while the donkey's owner had the colt walk around in front of him.

"Mmm," neighbor Neli muttered. "With that coat, which makes him look like St. Joseph's donkey! Animals that color are all bad workers, and when you ride one through the village, people laugh in your face. What are you asking for St. Joseph's donkey?"

Then the owner turned his back on him in a rage, shouting that, if he didn't know anything about animals, or didn't have the money to

193

meglio non venire alla fiera, e non far perdere il tempo ai cristiani, nella santa giornata che era.

Compare Neli lo lasciò a bestemmiare, e se ne andò con suo fratello, il quale lo tirava per la manica del giubbone, e gli diceva che se voleva buttare i denari per quella brutta bestia, l'avrebbe preso a pedate.

Però di sottecchi non perdevano di vista l'asino di san Giuseppe, e il suo padrone che fingeva di sbucciare delle fave verdi, colla fune della cavezza fra le gambe, mentre compare Neli andava girandolando fra le groppe dei muli e dei cavalli, e si fermava a guardare, e contrattava ora questa ed ora quella delle bestie migliori, senza aprire il pugno che teneva in tasca colle trentacinque lire, come se ci avesse avuto da comprare mezza fiera. Ma suo fratello gli diceva all'orecchio, accennandogli l'asino di san Giuseppe:

– Quello è il fatto nostro.

La padrona dell'asino di tanto in tanto correva a vedere cosa s'era fatto, e al trovare suo marito colla cavezza in mano, gli diceva:

– Che non lo manda oggi la Madonna uno che compri il puledro?

E il marito rispondeva ogni volta:

– Ancora niente! C'è stato uno a contrattare, e gli piaceva. Ma è tirato allo spendere, e se n'è andato coi suoi denari. Vedi, quello là, colla berretta bianca, dietro il branco delle pecore. Però sinora non ha comperato nulla, e vuol dire che tornerà.

La donna avrebbe voluto mettersi a sedere su due sassi, là vicino al suo asino, per vedere se si vendeva. Ma il marito le disse:

– Vattene! Se vedono che aspetti, non conchiudono il negozio.

Il puledro intanto badava a frugare col muso fra le gambe delle somare che passavano, massime che aveva fame, tanto che il padrone, appena apriva bocca per ragliare, lo faceva tacere a bastonate, perché non l'avevano voluto.

– È ancora là! – diceva compare Neli all'orecchio del fratello, fingendo di tornare a passare per cercare quello dei ceci abbrustoliti. – Se aspettiamo sino all'avemaria, potremo averlo per cinque lire meno del prezzo che abbiamo offerto.

Il sole di maggio era caldo, sicché di tratto in tratto, in mezzo al vocìo e al brulichìo della fiera, succedeva per tutto il campo un gran silenzio, come non ci fosse più nessuno; e allora la padrona dell'asino tornava a dire a suo marito:

– Non ti ostinare per cinque lire di più o di meno; che stasera non c'è da far la spesa; e poi sai che cinque lire il puledro se le mangia in un mese, se ci resta sulla pancia.

buy them, he would have done better to stay away from the fair, wasting decent people's time on that holy day.

Neighbor Neli left him to his cursing, and departed with his brother, who had been tugging him by his jacket sleeve and saying that, if he had thrown out his money on that ugly animal, he'd have kicked him.

But they secretly kept an eye on St. Joseph's donkey, and on his owner, who pretended to be shelling green broad beans, the halter rope between his legs, while neighbor Neli was rambling amid the cruppers of the mules and horses, stopping to look and negotiating for a few of the better animals, never opening his fist that held the thirty-five *lire* in his pocket, as if he intended to buy out half the fair. But his brother kept saying in his ear, as he indicated St. Joseph's donkey:

"That's the one we really can use."

The wife of the donkey's owner ran over every so often to see what had happened; finding her husband with the halter in his hand, she'd say:

"Why doesn't the Madonna send us someone today to buy the colt?"

And, each time, her husband answered:

"Nothing yet! One man came by to haggle, and he liked the animal. But he's tight with his money, and he took it away with him. See? That fellow there, in the white cap, behind the flock of sheep. But so far he hasn't bought a thing, which means he'll be back."

The woman would have liked to sit down on two stones, close to her donkey, to see whether he'd be sold. But her husband said:

"Go away! If they see you waiting, they won't conclude the deal."

Meanwhile the colt was busy nuzzling between the legs of every female donkey that went by, especially since he was hungry; he did that so often that, the moment he opened his mouth to bray, his owner shut him up with blows of his stick, because no one had wanted to buy him.

"He's still there!" neighbor Neli kept saying in his brother's ear, as he pretended to be coming back that way in search of the roast-chick-pea vendor. "If we wait until the Angelus, we can get him for five *lire* under the price we offered."

The May sun was hot, so that from time to time, amid the shouting and the crowding at the fair, a deep silence would fall over the whole field, as if no one were there any longer. At such moments, the wife of the donkey's owner would say again to her husband:

"Don't be stubborn over five *lire* more or less. We don't have the money to go shopping this evening. Besides, you know that the colt will eat five *lire*'s worth of fodder in a month, if he's left on our hands."

– Se non te ne vai – rispondeva suo marito – ti assesto una pedata di quelle buone!

Così passavano le ore alla fiera; ma nessuno di coloro che passavano davanti all'asino di san Giuseppe si fermava a guardarlo; e sì che il padrone aveva scelto il posto più umile, accanto alle bestie di poco prezzo, onde non farlo sfigurare col suo pelame di gazza accanto alle belle mule baie ed ai cavalli lucenti! Ci voleva uno come compare Neli per andare a contrattare l'asino di san Giuseppe, che tutta la fiera si metteva a ridere al vederlo. Il puledro, dal tanto aspettare al sole, lasciava ciondolare il capo e le orecchie, e il suo padrone s'era messo a sedere tristamente sui sassi, colle mani penzoloni anch'esso fra le ginocchia e la cavezza nelle mani, guardando di qua e di là le ombre lunghe che cominciavano a fare nel piano, al sole che tramontava, le gambe di tutte quelle bestie che non avevano trovato un compratore. Compare Neli allora e suo fratello, e un altro amico che avevano raccattato per la circostanza, vennero a passare di là, guardando in aria, che il padrone dell'asino torse il capo anche lui per non far vedere di star lì ad aspettarli; e l'amico di compare Neli disse così, stralunato come l'idea fosse venuta a lui:

– O guarda l'asino di san Giuseppe! Perché non comprate questo qui, compare Neli?

– L'ho contrattato stamattina; ma è troppo caro. Poi farei ridere la gente con quell'asino bianco e nero. Vedete che nessuno l'ha voluto fino adesso!

– È vero, ma il colore non fa nulla, per quello che vi serve.

E domandò al padrone:

– Quanto vi dobbiamo regalare per l'asino di san Giuseppe?

La padrona dell'asino di san Giuseppe, vedendo che si ripigliava il negozio, andava riaccostandosi quatta, quatta, colle mani giunte sotto la mantellina.

– Non me ne parlate! – cominciò a gridare compare Neli, scappando per il piano. – Non me ne parlate che non ne voglio sentir parlare!

– Se non lo vuole, lasciatelo stare – rispose il padrone. – Se non lo piglia lui, lo piglierà un altro. «Tristo chi non ha più nulla da vendere dopo la fiera!»

– Ed io voglio essere ascoltato, santo diavolone! – strillava l'amico. – Che non posso dire la mia bestialità anch'io?

E correva ad afferrare compare Neli pel giubbone; poi tornava a parlare all'orecchio del padrone dell'asino, il quale voleva tornarsene

"If you don't go away," her husband replied, "I'll give you a kick, and a real hard one!"

That's how the hours went by at the fair; but none of those who passed in front of St. Joseph's donkey stopped to look at him. For one thing, his owner had picked out the most undesirable location, next to the low-priced animals, so that the donkey's magpie coat wouldn't be too conspicuous next to the beautiful bay she-mules and the shining horses! It took a man like neighbor Neli to bargain for St. Joseph's donkey, while everyone at the fair started laughing at the sight of him. From waiting in the sun so long, the colt had let his head hang and his ears droop, and his owner had sat down gloomily on the stones, he, too, with his hands dangling between his knees, and with the halter in his hands, looking to and fro at the long shadows that the legs of all those animals that hadn't found a buyer were beginning to cast on the plain as the sun went down. Then neighbor Neli, his brother, and another friend they had picked up for the occasion passed by, looking up in the air; the owner of the donkey turned his head away so he wouldn't seem to have been waiting for them there. Neighbor Neli's friend looked dumbfounded and said, as if *he* had had the idea:

"Oh, look at St. Joseph's donkey! Why don't you buy this one, neighbor Neli?"

"I bargained for it this morning, but it's too expensive. Besides, I'd make people laugh with that black-and-white donkey. You see that nobody has been interested in him up to now!"

"True, but his color doesn't matter, for the use you'll make of him."

And he inquired of the owner:

"What are you asking for St. Joseph's donkey?"

The wife of the owner of St. Joseph's donkey, seeing that negotiations had resumed, approached again very quietly, her hands clasped under her shoulder cape.

"Don't talk to me about it!" neighbor Neli started yelling, running away along the level ground. "Don't talk to me about it, because I don't want to hear about it!"

"If he doesn't want him, let him go," the owner replied. "If *he* doesn't buy him, someone else will. 'It's too bad about the man who has nothing left to sell after the fair!'"

"But I want to be listened to, damn it!" the friend shrieked. "Why am I not entitled to make my stupid remarks, too?"

And he ran over and grabbed neighbor Neli by the jacket; then he came back and whispered in the ear of the donkey's owner, who was

a casa per forza coll'asinello, e gli buttava le braccia al collo, susurrandogli:

– Sentite! cinque lire più o meno, se non lo vendete oggi, un minchione come mio compare non lo trovate più da comprarvi la vostra bestia che non vale un sigaro.

Ed abbracciava anche la padrona dell'asino, le parlava all'orecchio, per tirarla dalla sua. Ma ella si stringeva nelle spalle, e rispondeva col viso torvo:

– Sono affari del mio uomo. Io non c'entro. Ma se ve lo dà per meno di quaranta lire è un minchione, in coscienza! Ci costa di più a noi!

– Stamattina ero pazzo ad offrire trentacinque lire! – ripicchiava compare Neli. – Vedete se ha trovato un altro compratore per quel prezzo? In tutta la fiera non c'è più che quattro montoni rognosi e l'asino di san Giuseppe. Adesso trenta lire, se li vuole!

– Pigliatele! – suggeriva piano al marito la padrona dell'asino colle lagrime agli occhi. – Stasera non abbiamo da far la spesa, e a Turiddu gli è tornata la febbre; ci vuole il solfato.

– Santo diavolone! – strillava suo marito. – Se non te ne vai, ti faccio assaggiare la cavezza! – Trentadue e mezzo, via! – gridò infine l'amico, scuotendoli forte per il colletto. – Né voi, né io! Stavolta deve valere la mia parola, per i santi del paradiso! e non voglio neppure un bicchiere di vino! Vedete che il sole è tramontato? Cosa aspettate ancora tutt'e due?

E strappò di mano al padrone la cavezza, mentre compare Neli, bestemmiando, tirava fuori dalla tasca il pugno colle trentacinque lire, e gliele dava senza guardarle, come gli strappassero il fegato. L'amico si tirò in disparte colla padrona dell'asino, a contare i denari su di un sasso, mentre il padrone dell'asino scappava per la fiera come un puledro, bestemmiando e dandosi dei pugni.

Ma poi si lasciò raggiungere dalla moglie, la quale adagio adagio andava contando di nuovo i denari nel fazzoletto, e domandò:

– Ci sono?

– Sì, ci son tutti; sia lodato san Gaetano! Ora vado dallo speziale.

– Li ho minchionati! Io glielo avrei dato anche per venti lire; gli asini di quel colore lì sono *vigliacchi*.

E compare Neli, tirandosi dietro il ciuco per la scesa, diceva:

– Com'è vero Dio, glie l'ho rubato il puledro! Il colore non fa niente. Vedete che pilastri di gambe, compare? Questo vale quaranta lire ad occhi chiusi.

adamant about going back home with the donkey colt. Throwing his arms around the man's neck, he said softly:

"Listen! What's five *lire* more or less? If you don't sell him today, you won't find another ninny as big as my neighbor to buy your animal, which isn't worth a cigar!"

And he also embraced the owner's wife around the neck, whispering in her ear in order to bring her over to his side. But she shrugged her shoulders and replied with a sullen face:

"It's my husband's business. I have nothing to do with it. But if he sells it to you for less than forty *lire*, he's a fool, take my word for it! The donkey costs *us* more!"

"This morning it was crazy of me to offer thirty-five *lire!*" neighbor Neli retorted. "See, has he found another buyer at that price? There's nothing left in the fair but a few mangy wethers and St. Joseph's donkey. Now, thirty *lire,* if he wants it!"

"Take it!" the wife of the donkey's owner prompted her husband quietly, with tears in her eyes. "We have no money for shopping this evening, and Turiddu's fever is back; we need sulphur for it."

"Damn it!" her husband shrieked. "If you don't go away, I'll give you a taste of the halter!" "Thirty-two and a half, and that's it!" the friend finally shouted, shaking them hard by the collar. "That's final! This time, what *I* say has to count, by all the saints in Paradise! And I'm not even asking for a glass of wine for brokering the deal! Can't you see that the sun has gone down? What are the two of you still waiting for?"

And he yanked the halter out of the owner's hand, while neighbor Neli, cursing, drew out of his pocket his hand that was clutching the thirty-five *lire,* and handed over the money without looking at it, as if his liver were being torn out. His friend stepped off to one side with the wife of the donkey's owner to count the money on a rock, while the donkey's owner dashed away through the fair like a colt, cursing and punching himself.

But then he let himself be overtaken by his wife, who was slowly counting the money again in her kerchief. He asked:

"Is it all there?"

"Yes, all of it, thanks to St. Gaetano! Now I'm going to the pharmacist's."

"I fooled them! I would have given him to them for even twenty *lire!* Donkeys that color are bad workers."

But neighbor Neli, pulling the donkey behind him down the slope, was saying:

"As true as there's a God in Heaven, I stole the colt from him! The color doesn't matter. See what legs like columns he has, neighbor? This one's worth forty *lire* easily."

– Se non c'ero io – rispose l'amico – non ne facevate nulla. Qui ci ho ancora due lire e mezzo di vostro. E se volete, andremo a berle alla salute dell'asino.

Adesso al puledro gli toccava di aver la salute per guadagnarsi le trentadue lire e cinquanta che era costato, e la paglia che si mangiava. Intanto badava a saltellare dietro a compare Neli, cercando di addentargli il giubbone per giuoco, quasi sapesse che era il giubbone del padrone nuovo, e non gliene importasse di lasciare per sempre la stalla dov'era stato al caldo, accanto alla madre, a fregarsi il muso sulla sponda della mangiatoia, o a fare a testate e a capriole col montone, e andare a stuzzicare il maiale nel suo cantuccio. E la padrona, che contava di nuovo i denari nel fazzoletto davanti al banco dello speziale, non pensava nemmen lei che aveva visto nascere il puledro, tutto bianco e nero colla pelle lucida come seta, che non si reggeva ancora sulle gambe, e stava accovacciato al sole nel cortile, e tutta l'erba con cui s'era fatto grande e grosso le era passata per le mani. La sola che si rammentasse del puledro era la ciuca, che allungava il collo ragliando verso l'uscio della stalla; ma quando non ebbe più le poppe gonfie di latte, si scordò del puledro anch'essa.

– Ora questo qui – diceva compare Neli – vedrete che mi porta quattro tumoli di farro meglio di un mulo. E alla messe lo metto a trebbiare.

Alla trebbiatura il puledro, legato in fila per il collo colle altre bestie, muli vecchi e cavalli sciancati, trotterellava sui covoni da mattina a sera, tanto che si riduceva stanco e senza voglia di abboccare nel mucchio della paglia, dove lo mettevano a riposare all'ombra, come si levava il venticello, mentre i contadini spagliavano, gridando: Viva Maria!

Allora lasciava cascare il muso e le orecchie ciondoloni, come un asino fatto, coll'occhio spento, quasi fosse stanco di guardare quella vasta campagna bianca la quale fumava qua e là della polvere delle aie, e pareva non fosse fatta per altro che per lasciar morire di sete e far trottare sui covoni. Alla sera tornava al villaggio colle bisacce piene, e il ragazzo del padrone seguitava a pungerlo nel garrese, lungo le siepi del sentiero che parevano vive dal cinguettìo delle cingallegre e dall'odor di nepitella e di ramerino, e l'asino avrebbe voluto darci una boccata, se non l'avessero fatto trottare sempre, tanto che gli calò il sangue alle gambe, e dovettero portarlo dal maniscalco; ma al padrone non gliene importava nulla, perché la raccolta era stata buona, e il

"If I hadn't been there," his friend replied, "you wouldn't have accomplished a thing. I still have here two and a half *lire* belonging to you. If you like, let's go and spend it drinking to the donkey's health."

Now the donkey needed all the health he could get in order to work off the thirty-two and a half *lire* he had cost and the straw he ate. Meanwhile, he attentively trotted behind neighbor Neli, trying to bite his jacket in fun, as if he knew it was the jacket of his new owner, and as if it didn't matter to him that he was leaving behind forever the stable where he had felt warm, next to his mother, rubbing his muzzle on the rim of the manger, playing with the wether with capers and butts of the head, and prodding the pig in its corner. And the wife of his first owner, counting out the money in her kerchief again in front of the pharmacist's counter, didn't even recall that she had seen the colt being born, all black-and-white with his skin shiny as silk, still unable to stand up, curled up in the sunshine in the yard; and that all the grass on which he had grown big and fat had passed through her hands. The only one who remembered the colt was his mother, who brayed as she stretched out her neck toward the stable door; but when her dugs were no longer swollen with milk, she, too, forgot about the colt.

"Now this one here," neighbor Neli was saying, "see if he doesn't carry four *tumoli* of spelt better than a mule. And at harvest time I'll make him thresh."

At the threshing the colt, tied by the neck in line with the other animals, old mules and crippled horses, trotted on the sheaves from morning till evening, until he was so tired he didn't feel like snapping up straw from the stack, where they placed him to rest in the shade, when the breeze sprang up, while the farmhands were separating the grain from the straw, shouting: "Long live the Blessed Virgin Mary!"

Then he lowered his muzzle and let his ears droop, just like an adult donkey, his eyes glassy as if he were tired of looking at that vast white countryside, which seemed to be emitting smoke here and there—it was the dust from the threshing floors—and seemed to have been created for nothing else but letting you die of thirst as you trotted on the sheaves. In the evening he'd return to the village with his saddlebags full, as his owner's boy followed, jabbing him in the withers with the goad, alongside the hedges bordering the path, which seemed alive with the twittering of the titmice and the fragrance of the calamint and rosemary. The donkey would have liked to take a bite out of the hedges, but they made him keep trotting, until the blood was flowing down his legs and he had to be taken to the veterinarian. But none of that mattered to his owner,

puledro si era buscate le sue trentadue lire e cinquanta. Il padrone diceva: «Ora il lavoro l'ha fatto, e se lo vendo anche per venti lire, ci ho sempre il mio guadagno».

Il solo che volesse bene al puledro era il ragazzo che lo faceva trotterellare pel sentiero, quando tornavano dall'aia; e piangeva mentre il maniscalco gli bruciava le gambe coi ferri roventi, che il puledro si contorceva, colla coda in aria, e le orecchie ritte come quando scorazzava pel campo della fiera, e tentava divincolarsi dalla fune attorcigliata che gli stringeva il labbro, e stralunava gli occhi dallo spasimo quasi avesse il giudizio, quando il garzone del maniscalco veniva a cambiare i ferri rossi qual fuoco, e la pelle fumava e friggeva come il pesce nella padella. Ma compare Neli gridava al suo ragazzo: – Bestia! perché piangi? Ora il suo lavoro l'ha fatto, e giacché la raccolta è andata bene lo venderemo e compreremo un mulo, che è meglio.

I ragazzi certe cose non le capiscono, e dopo che vendettero il puledro a massaro Cirino il Licodiano, il figlio di compare Neli andava a fargli visita nella stalla e ad accarezzarlo nel muso e sul collo, ché l'asino si voltava a fiutarlo come se gli fosse rimasto attaccato il cuore a lui, mentre gli asini son fatti per essere legati dove vuole il padrone, e mutano di sorte come cambiano di stalla. Massaro Cirino il Licodiano aveva comprato l'asino di san Giuseppe per poco, giacché aveva ancora la cicatrice al pasturale, che la moglie di compare Neli, quando vedeva passare l'asino col padrone nuovo, diceva: «Quello era la nostra sorte; quel pelame bianco e nero porta allegria nell'aia; e adesso le annate vanno di male in peggio, talché abbiamo venduto anche il mulo».

Massaro Cirino aveva aggiogato l'asino all'aratro, colla cavalla vecchia che ci andava come una pietra d'anello, e tirava via il suo bravo solco tutto il giorno per miglia e miglia, dacché le lodole cominciano a trillare nel cielo bianco dell'alba, sino a quando i pettirossi correvano a rannicchiarsi dietro gli sterpi nudi che tremavano di freddo, col volo breve e il sibilo malinconico, nella nebbia che montava come un mare. Soltanto, siccome l'asino era più piccolo della cavalla, ci avevano messo un cuscinetto di strame sul basto, sotto il giogo, e stentava di più a strappare le zolle indurite dal gelo, a furia di spallate: «Questo mi risparmia la cavalla che è vecchia, diceva massaro Cirino. Ha il cuore grande come la Piana di Catania, quell'asino di san Giuseppe! e non si direbbe».

because the harvest had been good, and the colt had earned back his thirty-two and a half *lire*. His owner said: "Now he's done his work, and if I sell him for even twenty *lire*, I'll still have made a profit."

The only one who loved the colt was the boy who made him trot down the path on the way back from the threshing floor. He wept while the blacksmith-vet burned the donkey's legs with red-hot irons and the donkey writhed, his tail in the air and his ears as erect as when he was running around the fairgrounds. He was trying to work himself loose from the twisted rope that was pressing into his lips; and his eyes popped out with the pain, as if he had sense like a human being, when the blacksmith's assistant came over with new irons red as fire, and his skin was smoking and frying like a fish in the pan. But neighbor Neli shouted to his boy: "Idiot! What are you crying for? Now he's done his work, and, since the harvest has been good, we'll sell him and buy a mule, which is better."

Boys just don't understand certain things. After they sold the colt to farmer Cirino, the man from Licodia, neighbor Neli's son would visit him in his stable and pat his muzzle and neck, while the donkey turned around to sniff him as if his heart had remained attached to him, whereas donkeys were created to be tied up wherever their owner wants, and change their destiny the way they change stables. Farmer Cirino from Licodia had bought St. Joseph's donkey at a low price because he already had scars on his pasterns. Whenever neighbor Neli's wife saw the donkey pass by with his new master, she'd say: "He was our good-luck charm. That black-and-white coat brings happiness to the threshing floor. Now our crops are getting worse all the time, so that we've had to sell the mule, too."

Farmer Cirino had yoked the donkey to the plow along with the old mare, who worked like a gem, and he plowed a good furrow all day long for miles and miles, from the hour when the larks began to warble in the white dawn sky, until the hour when the robins hastened back, with a brief flutter and a melancholy whistling call, to their nests behind the bare brambles that shook in the cold wind, amid the fog that rose like a sea. Only, because the donkey was shorter than the mare, they had placed a cushion of straw on top of his packsaddle, beneath the yoke, and it was a greater effort for him to pull out the sods, which were hardened by the frost, by dint of vigorous thrusts of the shoulders. "This one is saving my old mare for me," farmer Cirino would say. "He's got a heart as big as the Plain of Catania, that St. Joseph's donkey! And you wouldn't think it, to look at him."

E diceva pure a sua moglie, la quale gli veniva dietro raggomitolata nella mantellina, a spargere la semente con parsimonia:

– Se gli accadesse una disgrazia, mai sia! siamo rovinati, coll'annata che si prepara.

La donna guardava l'annata che si preparava, nel campicello sassoso e desolato, dove la terra era bianca e screpolata, da tanto che non ci pioveva, e l'acqua veniva tutta in nebbia, di quella che si mangia la semente; e quando fu l'ora di zappare il seminato pareva la barba del diavolo, tanto era rado e giallo, come se l'avessero bruciato coi fiammiferi. «Malgrado quel maggese che ci avevo preparato!» piagnucolava massaro Cirino strappandosi di dosso il giubbone. «Che quell'asino ci ha rimesso la pelle come un mulo! Quello è l'asino della malannata!»

La sua donna aveva un gruppo alla gola dinanzi al seminato arso, e rispondeva coi goccioloni che le venivano giù dagli occhi:

– L'asino non fa nulla. A compare Neli gli ha portato la buon'annata. Ma noi siamo sfortunati.

Così l'asino di san Giuseppe cambiò di padrone un'altra volta, come massaro Cirino se ne tornò colla falce in spalla dal seminato, che non ci fu bisogno di mieterlo quell'anno, malgrado ci avessero messo le immagini dei santi infilate alle cannucce, e avessero speso due tarì per farlo benedire dal prete. «Il diavolo ci vuole!» andava bestemmiando massaro Cirino di faccia a quelle spighe tutte ritte come pennacchi, che non ne voleva neppur l'asino; e sputava in aria verso quel cielo turchino senza una goccia d'acqua. Allora compare Luciano il carrettiere, incontrando massaro Cirino il quale si tirava dietro l'asino colle bisacce vuote, gli chiese:

– Cosa volete che vi regali per l'asino di san Giuseppe?

– Datemi quel che volete. Maledetto sia lui e il santo che l'ha fatto! – rispose massaro Cirino. – Ora non abbiamo più pane da mangiare, né orzo da dare alle bestie.

– Io vi do quindici lire perché siete rovinato; ma l'asino non val tanto, che non tira avanti ancora più di sei mesi. Vedete com'è ridotto?

– Avreste potuto chieder di più! – si mise a brontolare la moglie di massaro Cirino dopo che il negozio fu conchiuso. – A compare Luciano gli è morta la mula, e non ha denari da comprarne un'altra. Adesso se non comprava quell'asino di san Giuseppe, non sapeva che farne del suo carro e degli arnesi; e vedrete che quell'asino sarà la sua ricchezza!

L'asino imparò anche a tirare il carro, che era troppo alto di stanghe per lui, e gli pesava tutto sulle spalle, sicché non avrebbe durato

And he'd also say to his wife, who followed behind him, wrapped up in her shoulder cape, sowing the seed frugally:

"If anything happened to him, God forbid, we'd be ruined, with the weather the way it's been."

The woman observed the outlook for that year's crop, in her little stony, desolate field, in which the ground was white and cracked, it hadn't rained for so long, and the only water that came was in the shape of fog, the kind that ruins the seed. When the time came to weed the grainfield, it looked like the devil's beard, it was so sparse and yellow, as if it had been burned with matches. "In spite of my leaving it fallow!" farmer Cirino whined, tearing off his jacket. "That donkey worked his heart out on it like a mule! He's a bad-luck donkey!"

His wife had a lump in her throat when she saw the parched field, and replied, with big teardrops falling from her eyes:

"It's not the donkey's fault. He brought good luck to neighbor Neli. But we're jinxed."

And so, St. Joseph's donkey changed owners again when farmer Cirino returned from his grainfield, his scythe on his shoulder, because there was no need to reap it that year, even though they had stuck pictures of saints onto reeds and placed them in the field, and had spent two *tarì* to have the priest bless it. "What we need is the devil!" farmer Cirino went around cursing at the sight of those ears of grain, so light that the stalks remained as upright as plumes, and even the donkey refused them. He'd spit in the air, in the direction of that deep-blue sky that held not even a drop of water. Then neighbor Luciano the carter, meeting farmer Cirino, who was tugging the donkey behind him with empty saddlebags, asked him:

"What would you take for your St. Joseph's donkey?"

"Give me whatever you like. A curse on him and the saint on whose day he was born!" farmer Cirino replied. "Now we have no more bread to eat, or barley to give to the animals."

"I'll give you fifteen *lire* because you're ruined, but the donkey isn't worth that much, because he doesn't have more than six months left in him. Do you see what a state he's in?"

"You could have asked for more!" farmer Cirino's wife began to grumble after the deal was concluded. "Neighbor Luciano's she-mule died and he doesn't have enough money to buy another one. If he didn't buy that St. Joseph's donkey now, he wouldn't be able to use his cart and harness. You'll see: that donkey will make him rich!"

The donkey learned how to draw the cart, too. Its shafts were too high off the ground for him and the whole cart weighed down on his

nemmeno sei mesi, arrancando per le salite, che ci volevano le legnate
di compare Luciano per mettergli un po' di fiato in corpo; e quando
andava per la discesa era peggio, perché tutto il carico gli cascava addosso, e lo spingeva in modo che doveva far forza colla schiena in arco,
e con quelle povere gambe rose dal fuoco, che la gente vedendolo si
metteva a ridere, a quando cascava ci volevano tutti gli angeli del paradiso a farlo rialzare. Ma compare Luciano sapeva che gli portava tre
quintali di roba meglio di un mulo, e il carico glielo pagavano a cinque
tarì il quintale. – Ogni giorno che campa l'asino di san Giuseppe son
quindici tarì guadagnati, diceva, e quanto a mangiare mi costa meno
d'un mulo. – Alle volte la gente che saliva a piedi lemme lemme dietro il carro, vedendo quella povera bestia che puntava le zampe senza
forza, e inarcava la schiena, col fiato spesso e l'occhio scoraggiato, suggeriva: – Metteteci un sasso sotto le ruote, e lasciategli ripigliar lena a
quella povera bestia. – Ma compare Luciano rispondeva: – Se lo lascio
fare, quindici tarì al giorno non li guadagno. Col suo cuoio devo rifare
il mio. Quando non ne potrà più del tutto lo venderò a quello del
gesso, che la bestia è buona e fa per lui; e non è mica vero che gli asini
di san Giuseppe sieno *vigliacchi*. Gliel'ho preso per un pezzo di pane
a massaro Cirino, ora che è impoverito.

In tal modo l'asino di san Giuseppe capitò in mano di quello del
gesso, il quale ne aveva una ventina di asini, tutti macilenti e mori-
bondi, che gli portavano i suoi saccarelli di gesso, e campavano di
quelle boccate di erbacce che potevano strappare lungo il cammino. Quello del gesso non lo voleva perché era tutto coperto di ci-
catrici peggio delle altre sue bestie, colle gambe solcate dal fuoco,
e le spalle logore dal pettorale, e il garrese roso dal basto dell'aratro, e i ginocchi rotti dalle cadute, e poi quel pelame bianco e nero
gli pareva che non dicesse in mezzo alle altre sue bestie morelle: –
Questo non fa niente, rispose compare Luciano. Anzi vi servirà a riconoscere i vostri asini da lontano. – E ribassò ancora due tarì sulle
sette lire che aveva domandato, per conchiudere il negozio. Ma
l'asino di san Giuseppe non l'avrebbe riconosciuto più nemmeno la
padrona che l'aveva visto nascere, tanto era mutato, quando andava
col muso a terra e le orecchie a paracqua sotto i saccarelli del gesso,
torcendo il groppone alle legnate del ragazzo che guidava il branco.
Pure anche la padrona stessa era mutata a quell'ora, colla malannata che c'era stata, e la fame che aveva avuta, e le febbri che avevano preso tutti alla pianura, lei, suo marito e il suo Turiddu, senza
denari per comprare il solfato, ché degli asini di san Giuseppe non

shoulders, so that he wouldn't have lasted even six months, plodding up the hillsides. It took beatings by neighbor Luciano to put a little energy in his body. And it was worse going downhill, because the entire load weighed upon him, oppressing him in such a way that he had to bend his back like a bow, making great efforts; and his poor legs had been scorched by fire. When people saw him, they started to laugh, and when he fell it took all the angels in Heaven to get him back on his feet. But neighbor Luciano knew that he was drawing a three-*quintali* load for him better than a mule could, and he was getting paid five *tarì* a *quintale*. "Every day that St. Joseph's donkey stays alive, I earn fifteen *tarì*," he said, "and as for feed he costs me less than a mule." At times the people walking uphill slowly behind the cart, seeing that poor animal dig in his hooves, his strength gone, bending his back, breathing heavily, and looking hopeless, would suggest: "Put a stone under the wheels, and let that poor animal catch his breath." But neighbor Luciano would reply: "If I give him his way, I won't make my fifteen *tarì* a day. I need his hide to save mine. When he's unable to work at all, I'll sell him to the plaster man, because the animal is good and suitable for him. It's not at all true that St. Joseph's donkeys are bad workers. I bought him from farmer Cirino for a song after he became poor."

And so, St. Joseph's donkey fell into the hands of the plaster man, who owned some twenty donkeys, all emaciated and moribund, which carried his sacks of plaster of Paris and lived off the mouthfuls of weeds they were able to snatch along the road. The plaster man hadn't wanted him, because he was more covered with scars than his other animals, his legs were flame-furrowed, his shoulders sore from the breast strap, his withers abraded by the plow packsaddle, and his knees broken from his falls. Besides, that black-and-white coat seemed out of place among his other donkeys, which were of a uniform dark color. "That doesn't matter," neighbor Luciano replied. "In fact, he'll help you recognize your group of donkeys at a distance." And, to conclude the deal, he lowered the seven-*lire* price he had asked by two *tarì*. But even the woman who had seen St. Joseph's donkey at his birth wouldn't have recognized him, he had changed so, when he went along laden with the sacks of plaster of Paris, his muzzle to the ground and his ears forming an umbrella, twisting his crupper under the blows of the boy who was leading the herd. Of course, the woman had also changed by that time, what with the bad crops she'd had, the hunger she'd suffered, and the fever that had attacked everyone in the lowlands, her, her husband, and her Turiddu, with no

se ne hanno da vendere tutti i giorni, nemmeno per trentacinque lire.

L'inverno, che il lavoro era più scarso, e la legna da far cuocere il gesso più rara e lontana, e i sentieri gelati non avevano una foglia nelle siepi, o una boccata di stoppia lungo il fossatello gelato, la vita era più dura per quelle povere bestie; e il padrone lo sapeva che l'inverno se ne mangiava la metà; sicché soleva comperarne una buona provvista in primavera. La notte il branco restava allo scoperto, accanto alla fornace, e le bestie si facevano schermo stringendosi fra di loro. Ma quelle stelle che luccicavano come spade li passavano da parte a parte, malgrado il loro cuoio duro, e tutti quei guidaleschi rabbrividivano e tremavano al freddo come avessero la parola.

Pure c'è tanti cristiani che non stanno meglio, e non hanno nemmeno quel cencio di tabarro nel quale il ragazzo che custodiva il branco dormiva raggomitolato davanti la fornace. Lì vicino abitava una povera vedova, in un casolare più sgangherato della fornace del gesso, dove le stelle penetravano dal tetto come spade, quasi fosse all'aperto, e il vento faceva svolazzare quei quattro cenci di coperta. Prima faceva la lavandaia, ma quello era un magro mestiere, ché la gente i suoi stracci se li lava da sé, quando li lava, ed ora che gli era cresciuto il suo ragazzo campava andando a vendere della legna al villaggio. Ma nessuno aveva conosciuto suo marito, e nessuno sapeva d'onde prendesse la legna che vendeva; lo sapeva il suo ragazzo che andava a racimolarla di qua e di là, a rischio di buscarsi una schioppettata dai campieri. – Se aveste un asino – gli diceva quello del gesso per vendere l'asino di san Giuseppe che non ne poteva più – potreste portare al villaggio dei fasci più grossi, ora che il vostro ragazzo è cresciuto. – La povera donna aveva qualche lira in un nodo del fazzoletto, e se la lasciò beccare da quello del gesso, perché si dice che «la roba vecchia muore in casa del pazzo».

Almeno così il povero asino di san Giuseppe visse meglio gli ultimi giorni; giacché la vedova lo teneva come un tesoro, in grazia di quei soldi che gli era costato, e gli andava a buscare della paglia e del fieno di notte, e lo teneva nel casolare accanto al letto, che scaldava come un focherello anche lui, e a questo mondo una mano lava l'altra. La donna spingendosi innanzi l'asino carico di legna come una montagna, che non gli si vedevano le orecchie, andava facendo dei castelli in aria; e il ragazzo sforacchiava le siepi e si avventurava nel limite del bosco per ammassare il carico, che madre e figlio credevano farsi ricchi a

money left for buying sulphur, because it isn't every day that you have St. Joseph's donkeys you can sell, not even for thirty-five *lire*.

In the winter, when less work was available, when firewood for heating the gypsum and producing the plaster of Paris was scarcer and farther afield, and the frozen paths no longer offered a leaf on their hedges or a mouthful of stubble along the frozen side-ditch, life was harder for those poor animals; and their owner knew that winter destroyed half of them, so that it was his practice to buy a large number of them in the spring. At night the herd was left outdoors, next to the gypsum furnace, and the animals snuggled against one another to ward off the cold. But those stars that glittered like swords pierced them through and through, despite their tough hides, and all those harness sores shuddered and trembled in the cold as if they could speak.

And yet, there are many human beings who aren't better off, and don't even possess the scrap of cloak in which the boy who tended the herd was wrapped as he slept curled up in front of the furnace. Nearby there lived a poor widow, in a hut more rickety than the gypsum furnace, where the stars pierced the roof like swords, making the interior feel like outdoors, and where the wind made the few shreds of blanket flutter. Earlier, she had worked as a laundress, but that was an unprofitable trade, because people there wash out their own ragged clothes, if they wash them at all; and, now that her boy had gotten bigger, she lived by selling firewood door to door in the village. But no one had ever known her to have a husband, and no one knew where she got the wood she sold. Her boy knew, because he went around scraping it together here and there, at the risk of being shot by the field watchmen. "If you had a donkey," the plaster man would tell her, in hopes of selling her his St. Joseph's donkey, which could no longer do the work, "you could carry bigger bundles to the village, now that your boy has gotten bigger." The poor woman had a few *lire* knotted up in her kerchief, and allowed the plaster man to worm the money out of her, because, as the saying goes, "old possessions die in the madman's house."

That way, at least, the poor St. Joseph's donkey lived his final days more comfortably; because the widow looked after him like a treasure, on account of the money he had cost her. She'd go out looking for straw and hay for him at night; she kept him in her cottage next to her bed, because he gave off warmth like a little fire, and in this world one hand washes the other. As she drove the donkey ahead of her, loaded down with a mountain of wood, so you couldn't see his ears, the woman would build castles in Spain; her boy would break through boundary hedges and venture to the edge of the woods to accumulate a load. Both

quel mestiere, tanto che finalmente il campiere del barone colse il ragazzo sul fatto a rubar frasche, e lo conciò per le feste dalle legnate. Il medico per curare il ragazzo si mangiò i soldi del fazzoletto, la provvista della legna, e tutto quello che c'era da vendere, e non era molto; sicché la madre una notte che il suo ragazzo farneticava dalla febbre, col viso acceso contro il muro, e non c'era un boccone di pane in casa, uscì fuori smaniando e parlando da sola come avesse la febbre anche lei, e andò a scavezzare un mandorlo lì vicino, che non pareva vero come ci fosse arrivata, e all'alba lo caricò sull'asino per andare a venderlo. Ma l'asino, dal peso, nella salita s'inginocchiò tale e quale come l'asino di san Giuseppe davanti al Bambino Gesù, e non volle più alzarsi.

– Anime sante! – borbottava la donna – portatemelo voialtre quel carico di legna!

E i passanti tiravano l'asino per la coda e gli mordevano gli orecchi per farlo rialzare.

– Non vedete che sta per morire? – disse infine un carrettiere; e così gli altri lo lasciarono in pace, ché l'asino aveva l'occhio di pesce morto, il muso freddo, e per la pelle gli correva un brivido.

La donna intanto pensava al suo ragazzo che farneticava, col viso rosso dalla febbre, e balbettava:

– Ora come faremo? Ora come faremo?

– Se volete venderlo con tutta la legna ve ne do cinque tarì – disse il carrettiere, il quale aveva il carro scarico. E come la donna lo guardava cogli occhi stralunati, soggiunse: – Compro soltanto la legna, perché l'asino ecco cosa vale! – E diede una pedata sul carcame, che suonò come un tamburo sfondato.

mother and son thought they'd get rich at that trade, until finally the baron's watchman caught the boy redhanded stealing branches, and gave him a severe beating. To cure the boy, the doctor devoured all the money in the kerchief, all their stock of firewood, and everything they had to sell, which wasn't much. And so, one night, while her boy was raving with fever, his flushed face turned to the wall, and there wasn't a bite of bread in the house, the woman went out in great agitation, talking to herself as if she had fever, too, and broke off the top of a nearby almond tree—it seemed impossible that she had managed to do it—and at dawn she loaded it on the donkey to go and sell it. But the weight made the donkey kneel going up the slope, exactly like St. Joseph's donkey in front of the Christ Child, and he couldn't get up again.

"Blessed saints!" the woman muttered. "*You* carry this load of wood for me!"

And passersby pulled the donkey by the tail and bit his ears to make him get up again.

"Don't you see he's on the point of death?" a carter finally said. And so the others left him in peace, because the donkey's eyes were like those of a dead fish, his muzzle was cold, and a shudder was running through his skin.

Meanwhile the woman was thinking about her boy who was raving, his face hot with fever, and she kept stammering:

"What are we to do now? What are we to do now?"

"If you want to sell him with all the wood, I'll give you five *tarì*," said the carter, who had no load on his cart. While the woman looked at him wild-eyed, he added: "I'm actually buying only the wood, because here's what the donkey is worth!" And he planted a kick on the carcass, which reverberated like a torn drum.

PANE NERO

Appena chiuse gli occhi compare Nanni, e ci era ancora il prete colla stola, scoppiò subito la guerra tra i figliuoli, a chi toccasse pagare la spesa del mortorio, ché il reverendo lo mandarono via coll'aspersorio sotto l'ascella.

Perché la malattia di compare Nanni era stata lunga, di quelle che vi mangiano la carne addosso, e la roba della casa. Ogni volta che il medico spiegava il foglio di carta sul ginocchio, per scrivere la ricetta, compare Nanni gli guardava le mani con aria pietosa, e biascicava: – Almeno, vossignoria, scrivetela corta, per carità!

Il medico faceva il suo mestiere. Tutti a questo mondo fanno il loro mestiere. Massaro Nanni nel fare il proprio, aveva acchiappato quelle febbri lì, alla Lamia, terre benedette da Dio, che producevano seminati alti come un uomo. I vicini avevano un bel dirgli: – Compare Nanni, in quella mezzeria della Lamia voi ci lascierete la pelle! – Quasi fossi un barone – rispondeva lui – che può fare quello che gli pare e piace!

I fratelli, che erano come le dita della stessa mano finché viveva il padre, ora dovevano pensare ciascuno ai casi proprii. Santo aveva moglie e figliuoli sulle braccia; Lucia rimaneva senza dote, su di una strada; e Carmenio, se voleva mangiar del pane, bisognava che andasse a buscarselo fuori di casa, e trovarsi un padrone. La mamma poi, vecchia e malaticcia, non si sapeva a chi toccasse mantenerla, di tutti e tre che non avevano niente. L'è che è una bella cosa quando si può piangere i morti, senza pensare ad altro!

I buoi, le pecore, la provvista del granaio, se n'erano andati col padrone. Restava la casa nera, col letto vuoto, e le faccie degli orfani scure anch'esse. Santo vi trasportò le sue robe, colla *Rossa*, e disse che pigliava con sé la mamma. – Così non pagava più la pigione della casa – dicevano gli altri. Carmenio fece il suo fagotto, e andò pastore da curatolo Vito, che aveva un pezzetto di pascolo al Camemi; e Lucia, per non stare insieme alla cognata, minacciava che sarebbe andata a servizio piuttosto.

DARK BREAD

As soon as neighbor Nanni shut his eyes, while the priest in his surplice was still there, war suddenly broke out among his children over who was to pay the funeral expenses; as for the priest, they sent him packing with his holy-water sprinkler under his arm.

Because neighbor Nanni's illness had been a long one, of the sort that devours both the patient's flesh and his household goods. Every time the doctor unfolded his leaf of paper on his knee to write out the prescription, neighbor Nanni would look at his hands piteously and mumble: "Sir, at least write a short one, please!"

The doctor was following his trade. Everybody in this world follows his trade. While farmer Nanni was following his own, he had caught those fevers, at Lamia, farmland blessed by God, which produced grain stalks as tall as a man. In vain his neighbors told him: "Neighbor Nanni, in that tenant farm Lamia you'll lose your life!" "As if I were a baron," he'd reply, "who can do whatever he likes!"

The siblings, who had been as close as the fingers on one hand while their father was alive, now had to think about their individual situations. Santo had a wife and children on his hands; Lucia was left without a dowry, as if thrown out in the street; and Carmenio, if he wanted to eat bread, had to go and earn it outside of the house by finding a master. And then, their mother, old and sickly—who would support her, of those three who had nothing? You're really lucky if you can afford to lament your dead, with no other troubles on your mind!

The oxen, the sheep, the stored grain, all had departed along with their owner. All that was left was the dark house, with its empty bed, and the orphans' faces, equally gloomy. Santo brought in his belongings, along with his wife "Redhead," and said that he was keeping their mother with him. "That way he's no longer paying the rent that he used to," the others said. Carmenio tied up his things in a bundle, and left to be a shepherd for sheep farmer Vito, who had a tiny pasture at Camemi; and Lucia, to avoid living with her sister-in-law, said threateningly that she'd rather go into domestic service.

213

– No! – diceva Santo. – Non si dirà che mia sorella abbia a far la serva agli altri. – Ei vorrebbe che la facessi alla *Rossa*! – brontolava Lucia.

La quistione grossa era per questa cognata che s'era ficcata nella parentela come un chiodo. – Cosa posso farci, adesso che ce l'ho? – sospirava Santo stringendosi nelle spalle. E' bisognava dar retta alla buona anima di mio padre, quand'era tempo!

La buon'anima glielo aveva predicato: – Lascia star la Nena, che non ha dote, né tetto, né terra.

Ma la Nena gli era sempre alle costole, al Castelluccio, se zappava, se mieteva, a raccogliergli le spighe, o a levargli colle mani i sassi di sotto ai piedi; e quando si riposava, alla porta del casamento, colle spalle al muro, nell'ora che sui campi moriva il sole, e taceva ogni cosa:

– Compare Santo, se Dio vuole, quest'anno non le avrete perse le vostre fatiche!

– Compare Santo, se il raccolto vi va bene, dovete prendere la chiusa grande, quella del piano; che ci son state le pecore, e riposa da due anni.

– Compare Santo, quest'inverno, se avrò tempo, voglio farvi un par di calzeroni che vi terranno caldo.

Santo aveva conosciuta la Nena quando lavorava al Castelluccio, una ragazza dai capelli rossi, ch'era figlia del camparo, e nessuno la voleva. Essa, poveretta, per questo motivo faceva festa a ogni cane che passasse, e si levava il pan di bocca per regalare a compare Santo la berretta di seta nera, ogni anno a santa Agrippina, e per fargli trovare un fiasco di vino, o un pezzo di formaggio, allorché arrivava al Castelluccio. – Pigliate questo, per amor mio, compare Santo. È di quel che beve il padrone. – Oppure: – Ho pensato che l'altra settimana vi mancava il companatico.

Egli non sapeva dir di no, e intascava ogni cosa. Tutt'al più per gentilezza rispondeva: – Così non va bene, comare Nena, levarvelo di bocca voi, per darlo a me.

– Io son più contenta se l'avete voi.

Poi, ogni sabato sera, come Santo andava a casa, la buon'anima tornava a ripetere al figliuolo: – Lascia star la Nena, che non ha questo; lascia star la Nena, che non ha quest'altro.

– Io lo so che non ho nulla: – diceva la Nena, seduta sul muricciuolo verso il sole che tramontava. – Io non ho né terra, né case; e quel po'

"No!" Santo repeated. "People won't say that my sister has to be somebody else's servant." "He'd like me to be Redhead's!" Lucia would grumble.

The big problem concerned that sister-in-law, who had come between the siblings like a nail hammered in. "What can I do about it, now that I have her?" Santo would sigh, shrugging his shoulders. "I should have listened to my dear departed father while there was still time!"

His dear departed father had lectured him: "Leave Nena alone. She has no dowry, no house, no land."

But Nena was always at his side, at Castelluccio, whether he was hoeing or reaping; she'd gather up the ears of grain or lift the stones from under his feet with her hands. When he rested, at the gate to the housing compound, with his back against the wall, at the hour when the sun was dying over the fields, and everything was still, she'd say:

"Neighbor Santo, God willing, this year your work won't be thrown out." Or:

"Neighbor Santo, if your harvest is good, you ought to acquire that big enclosed plot on the plain. The sheep have grazed it, and it's lain fallow for two years." Or else:

"Neighbor Santo, this winter, if I have the time, I want to make you a pair of heavy trousers that will keep you warm."

Santo had met Nena when he was working at Castelluccio; she was a red-haired girl, the daughter of the livestock watchman, and no one wanted her. And so, she, poor thing, used to throw herself at any dog that passed by; she took the food out of her mouth to buy neighbor Santo a black silk cap every year for St. Agrippina's Day,[1] or to supply him with a flask of wine or a piece of cheese whenever he arrived at Castelluccio. "Take this for love of me, neighbor Santo. It's the kind that the proprietor drinks." Or: "It occurred to me that last week you had nothing to eat along with your bread."

He didn't know how to say no, and he'd pocket everything. The most he did was to reply politely: "It's not right, neighbor Nena, to deprive yourself and give presents to me."

"I'm happier when *you* have it."

Then, every Saturday evening, when Santo came home, his dear departed father had repeated to his son: "Leave Nena alone, she doesn't have this, that, or the other."

"I know I don't own a thing," Nena would say, as she sat on the low wall facing the setting sun. "I have no land or house; and I've had to

---

1. See footnote 2 in "La Lupa."

di roba bianca ho dovuto levarmela di bocca col pane che mi mangio.
Mio padre è un povero camparo, che vive alle spalle del padrone; e
nessuno vorrà togliersi addosso il peso della moglie senza dote.

Ella aveva però la nuca bianca, come l'hanno le rosse; e mentre
teneva il capo chino, con tutti quei pensieri dentro, il sole le indorava
dietro alle orecchie i capelli color d'oro, e le guance che ci avevano la
peluria fine come le pesche; e Santo le guardava gli occhi celesti come
il fiore del lino, e il petto che gli riempiva il busto, e faceva l'onda al
par del seminato. – Non vi angustiate, comare Nena – gli diceva. –
Mariti non ve ne mancheranno.

Ella scrollava il capo per dir di no; e gli orecchini rossi che sembravano di corallo gli accarezzavano le guance. – No, no, compare Santo.
Lo so che non son bella, e che non mi vuol nessuno.

– Guardate! – disse lui a un tratto, ché gli veniva quell'idea. –
Guardate come sono i pareri! . . . E' dicono che i capelli rossi sieno
brutti, e invece ora che li avete voi non mi fanno specie.

La buon'anima di suo padre, quando aveva visto Santo incapricciato
della Nena che voleva sposarla, gli aveva detto una domenica:

– Tu la vuoi per forza, la *Rossa*? Di' la vuoi per forza?

Santo, colle spalle al muro e le mani dietro la schiena, non osava
levare il capo; ma accennava di sì, di sì, che senza la *Rossa* non sapeva
come fare, e la volontà di Dio era quella.

– Ci hai a pensar tu, se ti senti di campare la moglie. Già sai che non
posso darti nulla. Una cosa sola abbiamo a dirti, io e tua madre qui
presente: pensaci prima di maritarti, che il pane è scarso, e i figliuoli
vengono presto.

La mamma, accoccolata sulla scranna, lo tirava pel giubbone, e gli
diceva sottovoce colla faccia lunga: – Cerca d'innamorarti della vedova
di massaro Mariano, che è ricca, e non avrà molte pretese, perché è
accidentata.

– Sì! – brontolava Santo. – Sì, che la vedova di massaro Mariano si
contenterà di un pezzente come me! . . .

Compare Nanni confermò anche lui che la vedova di massaro
Mariano cercava un marito ricco al par di lei, tuttoché fosse sciancata.
E poi ci sarebbe stato l'altro guaio, di vedersi nascere i nipoti zoppi.

– Tu ci hai a pensare – ripeteva al suo ragazzo. – Pensa che il pane
è sacro, e che i figliuoli vengono presto.

Poi, il giorno di Santa Brigida, verso sera, Santo aveva incontrato

put together the little linen trousseau I have by skimping on my food. My father is a poor livestock watchman who lives off our master; and no one is going to take on the burden of a wife without a dowry."

But she had a white nape, the way redheads do; and when she lowered her head, with all those thoughts in it, the sun would gild the auburn hair behind her ears, and her cheeks, with their down as fine as that on peaches; and Santo would look at her eyes, light blue like flax flowers, and her bosom, which filled out her bodice and throbbed like waving grain. "Don't fret, neighbor Nena," he'd say, "you won't go without a husband."

She'd shake her head to say no, and her red earrings, which looked like coral, would caress her cheeks. "No, no, neighbor Santo. I know that I'm not pretty, and that no one wants me."

"Just look!" he said all at once, as the idea struck him. "Just see how opinions differ! . . . They say that red hair is ugly, but now that I see it on you, it doesn't bother me."

When his dear departed father had seen Santo so infatuated with Nena that he wanted to marry her, he had said to him one Sunday:

"You insist on having Redhead? Tell me, you insist on it?"

Santo, his shoulders leaning on the wall and his hands behind his back, didn't dare raise his head, but he nodded yes, yes; he didn't know how to go on without Redhead; it was God's will.

"You've got to think it over, if you feel you can support a wife. You already know I can't give you any money. We've got just one thing to tell you, I and your mother here: think twice before getting married, because bread is hard to come by, and children arrive quickly."

His mother, huddled in the high-backed chair, would pull him by the jacket and tell him quietly, with a long face: "Try to fall in love with the widow of farmer Mariano. She's rich, and won't have many suitors, because she's paralyzed from a stroke."

"Sure!" Santo would grumble. "Sure, farmer Mariano's widow will be happy to get a pauper like me! . . ."

Neighbor Nanni, too, declared that farmer Mariano's widow was looking for a husband as rich as she was, even though she was crippled. And then, there'd be that other trouble, seeing their grandchildren born lame.

"You've got to think it over," he repeated to his boy. "Remember that bread is dear, and children arrive quickly."

Then, on St. Brigida's Day,[2] around evening, Santo had accidentally

---

2. Possibly St. Bridget of Sweden, St. Brigid of Ireland, or some more local saint. In any case, the dates of the feast have varied over the years.

a caso la *Rossa*, la quale coglieva asparagi lungo il sentiero, e arrossì
al vederlo, quasi non lo sapesse che doveva passare di là nel tornare
al paese, mentre lasciava ricadere il lembo della sottana che teneva
rimboccata alla cintura per andar carponi in mezzo ai fichidindia. Il
giovane la guardava, rosso in viso anche lui, e senza dir nulla. Infine
si mise a ciarlare che aveva terminata la settimana, e se ne andava a
casa. – Non avete a dirmi nulla pel paese, comare Nena?
Comandate.

– Se andassi a vendere gli asparagi verrei con voi, e si farebbe la
strada insieme – disse la *Rossa*. E come egli, ingrullito, rispondeva di
sì col capo, di sì: ella aggiunse, col mento sul petto che faceva l'onda:

– Ma voi non mi vorreste, ché le donne sono impicci.

– Io vi porterei sulle braccia, comare Nena, vi porterei.

Allora comare Nena si mise a masticare la cocca del fazzoletto rosso
che aveva in testa. E compare Santo non sapeva che dire nemmen lui;
e la guardava, la guardava, e si passava le bisacce da una spalla all'altra, quasi non trovasse il verso. La nepitella e il ramerino facevano
festa, e la costa del monte, lassù fra i fichidindia, era tutta rossa del
tramonto. – Ora andatevene, gli diceva Nena, andatevene, che è tardi.
– E poi si metteva ad ascoltare le cinciallegre che facevano gazzarra.
Ma Santo non si muoveva. – Andatevene, ché possono vederci, qui
soli.

Compare Santo, che stava per andarsene infine, tornò all'idea di
prima, con un'altra spallata per assestare le bisacce, che egli l'avrebbe
portata sulle braccia, l'avrebbe portata, se si faceva la strada insieme.
E guardava comare Nena negli occhi che lo fuggivano e cercavano gli
asparagi in mezzo ai sassi, e nel viso che era infocato come se il tramonto vi battesse sopra.

– No, compare Santo, andatevene solo, che io sono una povera
ragazza senza dote.

– Lasciamo fare alla Provvidenza, lasciamo fare . . .

Ella diceva sempre di no, che non era per lui, stavolta col viso scuro
ed imbronciato. Allora compare Santo scoraggiato si assestò la bisaccia sulle spalle e si mosse per andarsene a capo chino. La *Rossa* almeno voleva dargli gli asparagi che aveva colti per lui. Facevano una
bella pietanza, se accettava di mangiarli per amor suo. E gli stendeva
le due cocche del grembiale colmo. Santo le passò un braccio alla cin-
tola, e la baciò sulla guancia, col cuore che gli squagliava.

In quella arrivò il babbo, e la ragazza scappò via spaventata. Il camparo aveva il fucile ad armacollo, e non sapeva chi lo tenesse di far la
festa a compare Santo, che gli giuocava quel tradimento.

come across Redhead as she was picking asparagus beside the path. She blushed when she saw him, as if she didn't know he had to pass that way to get back to the village; at the same time, she let fall again the hem of her petticoat, which she had tucked into her belt so she could move through the prickly pears on all fours. The young man looked at her, he, too, red in the face, and remained silent. Finally he started chatting: his week's work was over, and he was on his way home. "Isn't there anything I can tell people for you in the village, neighbor Nena? Just say the word."

"If I were to sell the asparagus, I'd come with you and we could take the walk together," Redhead said. He was muddled, and when he nodded his head yes, yes, she added, with her chin on her throbbing bosom: "But you wouldn't want me along, because women are a hindrance."

"I'd carry you in my arms, neighbor Nena, so I would."

Then neighbor Nena started chewing the corner of the red kerchief she was wearing on her head. And neighbor Santo didn't know what to say, either; he looked and looked at her, shifting his bags from one shoulder to the other, as if he couldn't find the right way to carry them. The calamint and rosemary gave off a wonderful scent, and the mountainside, up there amid the prickly pears, was all red in the sunset. "Go now," Nena was saying, "go now, because it's late." And then she started listening to the titmice, which were making a racket. But Santo didn't budge. "Go, because we can be seen, standing alone here."

Neighbor Santo, who was finally about to leave, reverted to his earlier idea (with another jerk of his shoulder to adjust the bags): that he'd carry her in his arms, so he would, if they took the walk together. And he looked neighbor Nena in the eyes, the eyes that were avoiding him and looking for the asparagus among the rocks, and in the face, the face that was as fiery red as if the sunset were beaming onto it.

"No, neighbor Santo, go alone, because I'm a poor girl without a dowry."

"Let's leave it to Providence, let's . . ."

She kept saying no, that she wasn't for him, this time with a dark, sulky face. Then neighbor Santo, discouraged, adjusted the bags on his shoulders and prepared to depart, his head bowed. Redhead at least wanted to give him the asparagus she had picked for him. It would make a tasty dish, if he consented to eat it for her sake. And she held out to him the two corners of her filled apron. Santo put an arm around her waist and kissed her on the cheek, his heart melting.

At that moment her father arrived, and the girl ran off in alarm. The livestock watchman had his rifle slung over his shoulder, and didn't know what was keeping him from really giving it to neighbor Santo, who had gone behind his back that way.

– No! non ne faccio di queste cose! – rispondeva Santo colle mani
in croce. – Vostra figlia voglio sposarla per davvero. Non per la paura
del fucile; ma son figlio di un uomo dabbene, e la Provvidenza ci
aiuterà perché non facciamo il male.

Così la domenica appresso s'erano fatti gli sponsali, colla sposa
vestita da festa, e suo padre il camparo cogli stivali nuovi, che ci si
dondolava dentro come un'anitra domestica. Il vino e le fave tostate
misero in allegria anche compare Nanni, sebbene avesse già addosso
la malaria; e la mamma tirò fuori dalla cassapanca un rotolo di filato
che teneva da parte per la dote di Lucia, la quale aveva già diciot-
t'anni, e prima d'andare alla messa ogni domenica, si strigliava per
mezz'ora, specchiandosi nell'acqua del catino.

Santo, colla punta delle dieci dita ficcate nelle tasche del giubbone,
gongolava, guardando i capelli rossi della sposa, il filato, e tutta l'allegria che ci era per lui quella domenica. Il camparo, col naso rosso,
saltellava dentro gli stivaloni, e voleva baciare tutti quanti ad uno ad
uno.

– A me no! – diceva Lucia, imbronciata pel filato che le portavano
via. – Questa non è acqua per la mia bocca. – Essa restava in un cantuccio, con tanto di muso, quasi sapesse già quel che le toccava
quando avrebbe chiuso gli occhi il genitore.

Ora infatti le toccava cuocere il pane e scopar le stanze per la cognata, la quale come Dio faceva giorno andava al podere col marito,
tuttoché fosse gravida un'altra volta, ché per riempir la casa di figliuoli era peggio di una gatta. Adesso ci volevano altro che i rega-
lucci di Pasqua e di santa Agrippina, e le belle paroline che si
scambiavano con compare Santo quando si vedevano al Castelluccio.
Quel mariuolo del camparo aveva fatto il suo interesse a maritare la
figliuola senza dote, e doveva pensarci compare Santo a mantenerla.
Dacché aveva la Nena vedeva che gli mancava il pane per tutti e
due, e dovevano tirarlo fuori dalla terra di Licciardo, col sudore della
loro fronte.

Mentre andavano a Licciardo, colle bisacce in ispalla, asciugandosi
il sudore colla manica della camicia, avevano sempre nella testa e dinanzi agli occhi il seminato, ché non vedevano altro fra i sassi della
viottola. Gli era come il pensiero di un malato che vi sta sempre grave
in cuore, quel seminato: prima giallo, ammelmato dal gran piovere;
poi, quando ricominciava a pigliar fiato, le erbacce, che Nena ci si era
ridotte le due mani una pietà per strapparle ad una ad una, bocconi,

"No! I don't do such things!" Santo answered, making a cross with his hands to affirm his statement. "I genuinely want to marry your daughter. Not because I'm afraid of your gun, but because I'm the son of an honorable man, and Providence will help us, because we aren't doing any wrong."

And so, the following Sunday, the wedding was held, with the bride in holiday dress, and her father, the livestock watchman, in new boots, waddling in them like a barnyard duck. The wine and the roasted beans made even neighbor Nanni merry, though he was already suffering from malaria; and Santo's mother took out of the bench-chest a roll of yarn that she had set aside for Lucia's dowry; Lucia was already eighteen and, before going to Mass every Sunday, she'd spruce up for half an hour, looking at her reflection in the water of the basin.

Santo, his ten fingertips thrust into his jacket pockets, rejoiced at the sight of his bride's red hair, the yarn, and all the merriment on his account that Sunday. The livestock watchman, his nose red, went hopping around inside his big boots and wanted to kiss everyone individually.

"Not me!" said Lucia, sulking over the yarn they were taking away from her. "That's no water for *my* mouth." She remained in a corner, pulling a long face, as if she already knew what was in store for her after her father died.

And, in fact, she now had to bake the bread and sweep out the rooms for her sister-in-law, who would set out for the farm with her husband at daybreak, though she was pregnant again; because, when it came to filling the house with children, she was worse than a cat. Now it was no longer a question of little presents for Easter or St. Agrippina's Day, or of the sweet nothings she had exchanged with neighbor Santo when they used to meet at Castelluccio. That swindler of a livestock watchman had made a good deal, marrying off his daughter without a dowry, and it was up to Santo to support her. After winning Nena, he saw that both of them were short of bread, and they had to wring it out of the land at Licciardo, in the sweat of their brow.

While they walked to Licciardo, knapsacks on their backs, wiping away their sweat with their shirtsleeves, they constantly had the grain crop on their mind and before their eyes; they saw nothing else among the rocks on the path. That grain was like the thoughts of a sick man that are always heavy in his heart: first, it was yellow, muddied by the abundant rains; then, when it began to recover, came the weeds, which had made Nena's two hands a wreck to pull out one by one, face down, with

con tanto di pancia, tirando la gonnella sui ginocchi, onde non far danno. E non sentiva il peso della gravidanza, né il dolore delle reni, come se ad ogni filo verde che liberava dalle erbacce, facesse un figliuolo. E quando si accoccolava infine sul ciglione, col fiato ai denti, cacciandosi colle due mani i capelli dietro le orecchie, le sembrava di vedere le spighe alte nel giugno, curvandosi ad onda pel venticello l'una sull'altra; e facevano i conti col marito, nel tempo che egli slacciava i calzeroni fradici, e nettava la zappa sull'erba del ciglione. – Tanta era stata la semente; tanto avrebbe dato se la spiga veniva a 12, o a 10, od anche a 7; il gambo non era robusto ma il seminato era fitto. Bastava che il marzo non fosse troppo asciutto, e che piovesse soltanto quando bisognava. Santa Agrippina benedetta doveva pensarci lei! – Il cielo era netto, e il sole indugiava, color d'oro, sui prati verdi, dal ponente tutto in fuoco, d'onde le lodole calavano cantando sulle zolle, come punti neri. La primavera cominciava a spuntare dappertutto, nelle siepi di fichidindia, nelle macchie della viottola, fra i sassi, sul tetto dei casolari, verde come la speranza; e Santo, camminando pesantemente dietro la sua compagna, curva sotto il sacco dello strame per le bestie, e con tanto di pancia, sentivasi il cuore gonfio di tenerezza per la poveretta, e le andava chiaccherando, colla voce rotta dalla salita, di quel che si avrebbe fatto, se il Signore benediceva i seminati fino all'ultimo. Ora non avevano più a discorrere dei capelli rossi, s'erano belli o brutti, e di altre sciocchezze. E quando il maggio traditore venne a rubare tutte le fatiche e le speranze dell'annata, colle sue nebbie, marito e moglie, seduti un'altra volta sul ciglione a guardare il campo che ingialliva a vista d'occhio, come un malato che se ne va all'altro mondo, non dicevano una parola sola, coi gomiti sui ginocchi, e gli occhi impietriti nella faccia pallida.

– Questo è il castigo di Dio! – borbottava Santo. – La buon'anima di mio padre me l'aveva detto!

E nella casuccia del povero penetrava il malumore della stradicciuola nera e fangosa. Marito e moglie si voltavano le spalle ingrugnati, litigavano ogni volta che la Rossa domandava i denari per la spesa, e se il marito tornava a casa tardi, o se non c'era legna per l'inverno, o se la moglie diventava lenta e pigra per la gravidanza: musi lunghi, parolacce ed anche busse. Santo agguantava la Nena pei capelli rossi, e lei gli piantava le unghie sulla faccia; accorrevano i vicini, e la Rossa strillava che quello scomunicato voleva farla abortire, e non si curava di mandare un'anima al limbo. Poi, quando Nena partorì, fecero la pace, e compare Santo andava portando sulle braccia la bambina,

her big belly, pulling her skirt up over her knees to cause no damage to it. She didn't feel the burden of her pregnancy or the pain in her back, as if with every green shoot that she freed from the weeds she were giving birth to a child. And when she finally crouched down on the boundary ridge, out of breath, tucking her hair behind her ears with both hands, she seemed to see the stalks of grain as tall as they would be in June, bending and waving against one another in the breeze. She would do calculations with her husband while he undid his soaking-wet heavy trousers and cleaned off his hoe on the grass of the ridge. There had been this much seed grain; it would yield this much if there were 12, or 10, or even only 7 spikelets to an ear; the stalks weren't very strong, but they were densely planted. If only March weren't too dry, and it rained only when necessary! Blessed St. Agrippina had to look after it! The sky was clear, and the golden sun lingered over the green meadows in the fiery west, from which the larks descended onto the sods singing, like black specks. Spring was beginning to burgeon everywhere, in the prickly-pear hedges, in the bushes beside the lane, amid the rocks, on the cottage roofs, as green as hope. And Santo, walking heavily behind his wife, who was bent under the sack of straw for the animals, with her big belly, felt his heart swell with tenderness for the poor woman; he kept chatting with her, his voice impeded by the climb, about what they'd do if the Lord blessed the crops up to the last minute. Now they had no more time for such discussions as whether red hair was beautiful or ugly, and other nonsense like that. And when a treacherous May robbed them, with its fogs, of all the season's labors and hopes, husband and wife, seated once more on the ridge, looking at the field growing yellow as they watched, like a sick man departing for the next world, didn't say a single world, their elbows on their knees and their eyes turned to stone in their pallid faces.

"This is God's punishment!" Santo would mutter. "My dear departed father told me so!"

And the bad mood of the dark, muddy lane penetrated into the poor man's hut. Husband and wife turned their backs on each other grumpily, arguing each time that Redhead asked for money for expenses; and if the husband came home late, or there was no firewood for the winter, or the woman became slow and sluggish because she was pregnant, there were long faces, curses, and even blows. Santo would seize Nena by her red hair, and she would dig her nails into his face; the neighbors would come running, and Redhead would shriek that that monster wanted her to miscarry, and wasn't concerned about sending an infant's soul to Limbo. Then, when Nena gave birth, they made

come se avesse fatto una principessa, e correva a mostrarla ai parenti e agli amici, dalla contentezza. Alla moglie, sinché rimase in letto, le preparava il brodo, le scopava la casa, le mondava il riso, e le si piantava anche ritto dinanzi, acciò non le mancasse nulla. Poi si affacciava sulla porta colla bimba in collo, come una balia; e chi gli domandava, nel passare, rispondeva: – Femmina! compare mio. La disgrazia mi perseguita sin qui, e mi è nata una femmina. Mia moglie non sa far altro.

La *Rossa* quando si pigliava le busse dal marito, sfogavasi colla cognata, che non faceva nulla per aiutare in casa; e Lucia rimbeccava che senza aver marito gli erano toccati i guai dei figliuoli altrui. La suocera, poveretta, cercava di metter pace in quei litigi, e ripeteva:

– La colpa è mia che non son più buona a nulla. Io vi mangio il pane a tradimento.

Ella non era più buona che a sentire tutti quei guai, e a covarseli dentro di sé: le angustie di Santo, i piagnistei di sua moglie, il pensiero dell'altro figlio lontano, che le stava fitto in cuore come un chiodo, il malumore di Lucia, la quale non aveva uno straccio di vestito per la festa, e non vedeva passare un cane sotto la sua finestra. La domenica, se la chiamavano nel crocchio delle comari che chiaccheravano all'ombra, rispondeva, alzando le spalle:

– Cosa volete che ci venga a fare! Per far vedere il vestito di seta che non ho?

Nel crocchio delle vicine ci veniva pure qualche volta Pino il Tomo, quello delle rane, che non apriva bocca e stava ad ascoltare colle spalle al muro e le mani in tasca, sputacchiando di qua e di là. Nessuno sapeva cosa ci stesse a fare; ma quando s'affacciava all'uscio comare Lucia, Pino la guardava di soppiatto, fingendo di voltarsi per sputacchiare. La sera poi, come gli usci erano tutti chiusi, s'arrischiava sino a cantarle le canzonette dietro la porta, facendosi il basso da sé – huum! huum! huum! – Alle volte i giovinastri che tornavano a casa tardi, lo conoscevano alla voce, e gli rifacevano il verso della rana, per canzonarlo.

Lucia intanto fingeva di darsi da fare per la casa, colla testa bassa e lontana dal lume, onde non la vedessero in faccia. Ma se la cognata brontolava: – Ora comincia la musica! – si voltava come una vipera a rimbeccare:

– Anche la musica vi dà noia? Già in questa galera non ce ne deve essere né per gli occhi né per le orecchie!

peace, and neighbor Santo would carry the baby girl around in his arms, as if he had begotten a princess, and he'd run over to show her to relatives and friends in his joy. As long as his wife was confined to bed, he made the broth for her, swept the house for her, cleaned the rice for her, and stood there right in front of her, so she would lack nothing. Then he'd stand in the doorway holding the baby, like a wetnurse. To every passerby who asked, he'd reply: "A girl, neighbor. Misfortune pursues me even here, and my child is a girl. That's all my wife knows how to give me."

When Redhead was beaten by her husband, she let out her feelings on her sister-in-law, saying she was no help to her in the house. Lucia would retort that, though she had no husband, she had all the trouble of other people's children. The poor mother-in-law tried to make peace in those squabbles, repeating:

"It's my fault, because I can't do anything anymore. I eat my bread at your expense."

All she was still good for was to hear all those troubles and brood over them in silence: Santo's worries; his wife's whining; the thought of her other son being so far away, which stuck in her heart like a nail; the unhappiness of Lucia, who didn't have a shred of holiday clothing, and didn't see a dog go by under her window. On Sundays, if she was called to join the group of neighbor women chatting in the shade, she'd shrug her shoulders and reply:

"What do you expect me to do there? Show you the silk dress I don't own?"

The group of neighbor women was sometimes joined by Pino "the odd character," the frogcatcher, who didn't open his mouth, but just stood listening with his back against the wall and his hands in his pockets, spitting in different directions. No one knew what he was doing there, but when neighbor Lucia showed her face at the window, Pino would look at her furtively, pretending to be turning around to spit. Then, in the evening, when all the doors were closed, he even ventured to sing songs to her outside the door, supplying his own bass accompaniment: "Hmm, hmm, hmm!" Sometimes the young hooligans who were coming home late recognized him by his voice and imitated frog calls to make fun of him.

Meanwhile Lucia pretended to busy herself around the house, her head bowed, far from the light so that no one could see her face. But if her sister-in-law grumbled, "Now the music is starting!," she'd turn around like a viper and retort:

"Even the music bothers you? In this jail, nothing is supposed to please either the eyes or the ears!"

La mamma che vedeva tutto, e ascoltava anch'essa, guardando la figliuola, diceva che a lei invece quella musica gli metteva allegria dentro. Lucia fingeva di non saper nulla. Però ogni giorno nell'ora in cui passava quello delle rane, non mancava mai di affacciarsi all'uscio, col fuso in mano. Il Tomo appena tornava dal fiume, gira e rigira pel paese, era sempre in volta per quelle parti, colla sua resta di rane in mano, strillando: – Pesci-cantanti! pesci-cantanti! – come se i poveretti di quelle straduccie potessero comperare dei pesci-cantanti.

– E' devono essere buoni pei malati! – diceva la Lucia che si struggeva di mettersi a contrattare col Tomo. Ma la mamma non voleva che spendessero per lei.

Il Tomo, vedendo che Lucia lo guardava di soppiatto, col mento sul seno, rallentava il passo dinanzi all'uscio, e la domenica si faceva animo ad accostarsi un poco più, sino a mettersi a sedere sullo scalino del ballatoio accanto, colle mani penzoloni fra le cosce; e raccontava nel crocchio come si facesse a pescare le rane, che ci voleva una malizia del diavolo. Egli era malizioso peggio di un asino rosso, Pino il Tomo, e aspettava che le comari se ne andassero per dire alla gnà Lucia: – E' ci vuol la pioggia pei seminati! – oppure: – Le olive saranno scarse quest'anno.

– A voi cosa ve ne importa? che campate sulle rane – gli diceva Lucia.

– Sentite, sorella mia, siamo tutti come le dita della mano; e come gli embrici, che uno dà acqua all'altro. Se non si raccoglie né grano, né olio, non entrano denari in paese, e nessuno mi compra le mie rane. Vi capacita?

Alla ragazza quel «sorella mia» le scendeva al cuore dolce come il miele, e ci ripensava tutta la sera, mentre filava zitta accanto al lume; e ci mulinava, ci mulinava sopra, come il fuso che frullava.

La mamma, sembrava che glielo leggesse nel fuso, e come da un par di settimane non si udivano più ariette alla sera, né si vedeva passare quello che vendeva le rane, diceva colla nuora: – Com'è tristo l'inverno! Ora non si sente più un'anima pel vicinato.

Adesso bisognava tener l'uscio chiuso, pel freddo, e dallo sportello non si vedeva altro che la finestra di rimpetto, nera dalla pioggia, o qualche vicino che tornava a casa, sotto il cappotto fradicio. Ma Pino il Tomo non si faceva più vivo, che se un povero malato aveva bisogno di un po' di brodo di rane, diceva la Lucia, non sapeva come fare.

Her mother, who saw all this, and who was also listening, would look at her daughter and say that, as for *her*, the music cheered her up. Lucia pretended not to know anything about it. But every day, at the hour when the frogcatcher went by, she never failed to show herself at the window, spindle in hand. As soon as "the character" came back from the river, he'd wander up and down the village; he was always roaming around that area with his string of frogs in his hand, yelling: "Singing fish! Singing fish!"—as if the poor folk in those alleys were able to buy "singing fish."

"They should be good for sick people," Lucia used to say, dying to establish a rapport with "the character." But her mother didn't want them to spend money on her.

"The character," seeing Lucia watching him furtively, her chin on her bosom, would slacken his pace in front of her door; on Sundays he mustered up enough courage to come a little closer, even to the point of sitting on the adjacent veranda step, his hands hanging between his thighs. In the group of women he'd tell how he caught the frogs, which took infernal shrewdness. He, Pino "the character," was shrewder than a red-coated donkey, and he'd wait until the women had dispersed before going over and saying to Mis' Lucia: "We need rain for the crops!" or: "There won't be many olives this year."

"What does that matter to you? You make your living from the frogs," Lucia would say.

"Listen, my sister, we all depend on one another like the fingers of one hand, or like the rooftiles, each one passing along the water to the next. If grain isn't harvested and oil isn't pressed, no money comes into the village, and no one buys my frogs. Get it?"

That "my sister" sank into the girl's heart as sweetly as honey; she kept thinking about it all evening, while she was spinning silently beside the lamp. She meditated and meditated on it, like the whirring spindle.

Her mother seemed to have read her secret in the spindle. After a couple of weeks during which no more songs were heard in the evening, and the frog vendor wasn't seen passing by, she said to her daughter-in-law: "How gloomy winter is! Now you can't hear a soul in the neighborhood."

Now they had to keep the door shut because of the cold, and all they could see through the casement was the window opposite, black with rain, or some neighbor coming home in his sopping overcoat. But Pino "the character" wasn't to be seen, so that if a poor sick person needed a little frog broth, Lucia said, he didn't know what to do.

– Sarà andato a buscarsi il pane in qualche altro modo – rispondeva la cognata. – Quello è un mestiere povero, di chi non sa far altro.

Santo, che un sabato sera aveva inteso la chiacchiera, per amor della sorella, le faceva il predicozzo:

– A me non mi piace questa storia del Tomo. Bel partito che sarebbe per mia sorella! Uno che campa delle rane, e sta colle gambe in molle tutto il giorno! Tu devi cercarti un campagnuolo, ché se non ha roba, almeno è fatto della stessa pasta tua.

Lucia stava zitta, a capo basso e colle ciglia aggrottate, e alle volte si mordeva le labbra per non spiattellare: – Dove lo trovo il campagnuolo? – Come se stesse a lei a trovare! Quello solo che aveva trovato, ora non si faceva più vivo, forse perché la *Rossa* gli aveva fatto qualche partaccia, invidiosa e pettegola com'era. Già Santo parlava sempre per dettato di sua moglie, la quale andava dicendo che quello delle rane era un fannullone, e certo era arrivata all'orecchio di compare Pino.

Perciò ad ogni momento scoppiava la guerra tra le due cognate:

– Qui la padrona, non son io! – brontolava Lucia. – In questa casa la padrona è quella che ha saputo abbindolare mio fratello, e chiapparlo per marito.

– Se sapevo quel che veniva dopo, non l'abbindolavo, no, vostro fratello; ché se prima avevo bisogno di un pane, adesso ce ne vogliono cinque.

– A voi che ve ne importa se quello delle rane ha un mestiere o no? Quando fosse mio marito, ci avrebbe a pensar lui a mantenermi.

La mamma, poveretta, si metteva di mezzo, colle buone; ma era donna di poche parole, e non sapeva far altro che correre dall'una all'altra, colle mani nei capelli, balbettando: – Per carità! per carità! – Ma le donne non le davano retta nemmeno, piantandosi le unghie sulla faccia, dopo che la *Rossa* si lasciò scappare un parolaccia «Arrabbiata!».

– Arrabbiata tu! che m'hai rubato il fratello!

Allora sopravveniva Santo, e le picchiava tutte e due per metter pace, e la *Rossa*, piangendo, brontolava:

– Io dicevo per suo bene! ché quando una si marita senza roba, poi i guai vengono presto.

E alla sorella che strillava e si strappava i capelli, Santo per rabbonirla tornava a dire:

– Cosa vuoi che ci faccia, ora ch'è mia moglie? Ma ti vuol bene e parla pel tuo meglio. Lo vedi che bel guadagno ci abbiamo fatto noi due a maritarci?

"He's probably gone to earn his living in some other way," her sister-in-law replied. "The trade he's in is a poor one, just good enough for someone who can't do anything else."

Santo, who had heard that conversation one Saturday evening, gave his sister a scolding out of love for her:

"I don't like this business with 'the character.' A fine match he'd make for a sister of mine! A man who lives off frogs and stands with his legs in the water all day! You need to find yourself a field hand; even if he doesn't own anything, at least he'd be made of the same stuff as you."

Lucia kept quiet, her head bowed and her brow knitted; sometimes she bit her lips to keep from blurting out: "Where am I to find this field hand?" As if it were up to her to find him! The one man she *had* found didn't show up anymore, maybe because Redhead had given him a dressing down, she was so envious and scandal-mongering. By now Santo always spoke at his wife's dictation, and she kept saying that the frog fellow was a good-for-nothing. This must have reached neighbor Pino's ears.

And so, war broke out between the two sisters-in-law constantly:

"I'm not the woman of the house!" Lucia grumbled. "The woman of this house is the one who was able to hoodwink my brother and catch him as a husband."

"If I had known what was coming, I wouldn't have hoodwinked your brother, no, ma'am; because if I needed one loaf of bread before, now I need five."

"What does it matter to you whether the frog fellow has a proper trade or not? If he were my husband, *he'd* have to worry about supporting me."

Her mother, poor woman, tried to mediate with calming words; but she wasn't much of a talker, and all she could do was to run back and forth between them, her hands in her hair, stammering: "Please! Please!" But the women didn't even pay attention to her; they scratched each other's faces after Redhead let slip the insult: "Man crazy!"

"*You're* the one who's man crazy! You stole my brother from me!"

Then Santo would intervene and beat both of them to pacify them; and Redhead would weep and grumble:

"I said it for her own good! Because when a woman marries and there's no money, the troubles come fast."

To calm down his sister, who was shrieking and pulling out her hair, Santo would repeat:

"What can I do about it, now that she's my wife? She loves you and she says those things to help you. See what a great benefit we two have gained from getting married?"

Lucia si lagnava colla mamma.

– Io voglio farci il guadagno che ci han fatto loro! Piuttosto voglio andare a servire! Qui se si fa vedere un cristiano, ve lo scacciano via.

– E pensava a quello delle rane che non si lasciava più vedere.

Dopo si venne a conoscere che era andato a stare colla vedova di massaro Mariano; anzi volevano maritarsi: perché è vero che non aveva un mestiere, ma era un pezzo di giovanotto fatto senza risparmio, e bello come san Vito in carne e in ossa addirittura; e la sciancata aveva roba da pigliarsi il marito che gli pareva e piaceva.

– Guardate qua, compare Pino – gli diceva: – questa è tutta roba bianca, questi son tutti orecchini e collane d'oro; in questa giara qui ci son 12 cafisi d'olio; e quel graticcio è pieno di fave. Se voi siete contento, potete vivere colle mani sulla pancia, e non avrete più bisogno di stare a mezza gamba nel pantano per acchiappar le rane.

– Per me sarei contento – diceva il Tomo. Ma pensava agli occhi neri di Lucia, che lo cercavano di sotto all'impannata della finestra, e ai fianchi della sciancata, che si dimenavano come quelli delle rane, mentre andava di qua e di là per la casa, a fargli vedere tutta quella roba. Però una volta che non aveva potuto buscarsi un grano da tre giorni, e gli era toccato stare in casa della vedova, a mangiare e bere, e a veder piovere dall'uscio, si persuase a dir di sì, per amor del pane.

– È stato per amor del pane, vi giuro! – diceva egli colle mani in croce, quando tornò a cercar comare Lucia dinanzi all'uscio. – Se non fosse stato per la malannata, non sposavo la sciancata, comare Lucia!

– Andate a contarglielo alla sciancata! – gli rispondeva la ragazza, verde dalla bile. – Questo solo voglio dirvi: che qui non ci avete a metter più piede.

E la sciancata gli diceva anche lei che non ci mettesse più piede, se no lo scacciava di casa sua, nudo e affamato come l'aveva preso. – Non sai che, prima a Dio, mi hai obbligo del pane che ti mangi?

A suo marito non gli mancava nulla: lui ben vestito, ben pasciuto, colle scarpe ai piedi, senza aver altro da fare che bighellonare in piazza tutto il giorno, dall'ortolano, dal beccaio, dal pescatore, colle mani dietro la schiena, e il ventre pieno, a veder contrattare la roba. – Quello è il suo mestiere, di fare il vagabondo! – diceva la *Rossa*. E Lucia rimbeccava che non faceva nulla perché aveva la moglie ricca che lo campava. – Se sposava me avrebbe lavorato per campar la moglie. – Santo, colla testa sulle mani, rifletteva che sua madre gliel o

Lucia complained to her mother.

"I want to gain the benefit that they did! Rather than that, I want to become a servant! Here, if a man shows up, they chase him away." And she'd think about the frog fellow, who never came around anymore.

Then she found out that he had gone to live with farmer Mariano's widow; in fact, they intended to get married. Because, while it was true that he didn't have a proper trade, still he was a well-built young man with nothing lacking; really just as handsome as a flesh-and-blood St. Vitus, and not merely a picture; and the crippled woman was rich enough to choose any husband that appealed to her.

"Look at this, neighbor Pino," she'd say, "this is all white linen, these are all gold earrings and necklaces; this tall jar contains 12 *cafisi* of olive oil; and that wicker container is filled with beans. If it satisfies you, you can live with your hands folded, and you'll never again need to stand in the swamp up to mid-thigh catching frogs."

"I, for one, am satisfied," "the character" said. But he thought about Lucia's dark eyes, which were seeking him below her window frame, and about the crippled woman's sides, which jerked like those of frogs when she moved around the house showing him all those possessions. But on one occasion when he had been unable to earn a penny in three days, and had had the good fortune to stay in the widow's house eating, drinking, and watching the rain from the doorway, he finally determined to accept for the sake of a good living.

"It was for the sake of a good living, I swear!" he'd say, his hands crossed to confirm the statement, when he revisited neighbor Lucia at her door. "If it hadn't been for the bad year I was having, I wouldn't have married the cripple, neighbor Lucia!"

"Go tell it to the cripple!" the girl replied, green with bile. "I want to tell you just this: you needn't set foot in here anymore."

And the crippled woman, too, told him not to set foot there, or else she'd chase him out of her house just as naked and hungry as when she had taken him in. "Don't you know that, God excepted, it's to me that you owe the bread you eat?"

Her husband lacked for nothing; well dressed and fed, with shoes on his feet, he had nothing to do but loiter in the square all day, visiting the greengrocer, the butcher, and the fishseller, his hands behind his back and his stomach full, watching people haggling over merchandise. "That's his trade: being a bum!" Redhead would say. And Lucia would retort that he did nothing because he had a rich wife to support him. "If he had married me, he would have worked to support his wife." Santo, head in hands, recalled that his mother had advised

aveva consigliato, di pigliarsela lui la sciancata, e la colpa era sua di essersi lasciato sfuggire il pan di bocca.

– Quando siamo giovani – predicava alla sorella – ci abbiamo in capo gli stessi grilli che hai tu adesso, e cerchiamo soltanto quel che ci piace, senza pensare al poi. Domandalo ora alla *Rossa* se si dovesse tornare a fare quel che abbiamo fatto! . . .

La *Rossa*, accoccolata sulla soglia, approvava col capo, mentre i suoi marmocchi le strillavano intorno, tirandola per le vesti e pei capelli. – Almeno il Signore Iddio non dovrebbe mandarci la croce dei figliuoli! – piagnucolava.

Dei figliuoli quelli che poteva se li tirava dietro nel campo, ogni mattina, come una giumenta i suoi puledri; la piccina dentro le bisacce, sulla schiena, e la più grandicella per mano. Ma gli altri tre però era costretta lasciarli a casa, a far disperare la cognata. Quella della bisaccia, e quella che trotterellava dietro zoppicando, strillavano in concerto per la viottola, al freddo dell'alba bianca, e la mamma di tanto in tanto doveva fermarsi, grattandosi la testa e sospirando: – Oh, Signore Iddio! – e scaldava col fiato le manine pavonazze della piccina, o tirava fuori dal sacco la lattante per darle la poppa, seguitando a camminare. Suo marito andava innanzi, curvo sotto il carico, e si voltava appena per darle il tempo di raggiungerlo tutta affannata, tirandosi dietro la bambina per la mano, e col petto nudo – non era per guardare i capelli della *Rossa*, oppure il petto che facesse l'onda dentro il busto, come al Castelluccio. Adesso la *Rossa* lo buttava fuori al sole e al gelo, come roba la quale non serve ad altro che a dar latte, tale e quale come una giumenta. – Una vera bestia da lavoro – quanto a ciò non poteva lagnarsi suo marito – a zappare, a mietere e a seminare, meglio di un uomo, quando tirava su le gonnelle, colle gambe nere sino a metà, nel seminato. Ora ella aveva ventisette anni, e tutt'altro da fare che badare alle scarpette e alle calze turchine. – Siamo vecchi, diceva suo marito, e bisogna pensare ai figliuoli. – Almeno si aiutavano l'un l'altro come due buoi dello stesso aratro. Questo era adesso il matrimonio.

– Pur troppo lo so anch'io! – brontolava Lucia – che ho i guai dei figli, senza aver marito. Quando chiude gli occhi quella vecchierella, se vogliono darmi ancora un pezzo di pane me lo danno. Ma se no, mi mettono in mezzo a una strada.

La mamma, poveretta, non sapeva che rispondere, e stava a sentirla, seduta accanto al letto, col fazzoletto in testa, e la faccia gialla dalla malattia. Di giorno s'affacciava sull'uscio, al sole, e ci stava

him to marry the crippled woman; he was to blame for letting the bread escape from his mouth.

"When we're young," he would preach to his sister, "we have in our head the same foolish notions you have now, and we look only for what we like, without thinking about the future. Ask Redhead now if we would do the same thing over again! . . ."

Redhead, squatting on the threshold, nodded in confirmation, while her kids were screaming all around her, tugging her by her clothes and hair. "At least the Lord God shouldn't send us the cross of having children!" she'd whimper.

The children that were able to followed her to the fields every morning, like colts following a mare: the baby girl in the knapsack on her back and the somewhat bigger one holding her hand. But she was compelled to leave the other three at home, where they drove her sister-in-law to despair. The one in the knapsack, and the one toddling clumsily after her, would shriek in harmony along the path, in the chill of the white dawn; every so often their mother had to halt, scratching her head and sighing: "Oh, Lord God!" And she'd warm the little girl's purple hands with her breath, or she'd take the infant out of the bag to nurse her while she went on walking. Her husband went ahead, bent under his load and scarcely turning long enough for her to catch up, all out of breath, dragging the girl behind her by the hand, and with her bosom bare. He had no mind to look at Redhead's hair, or her bosom throbbing inside her bodice, as he had done at Castelluccio. Now Redhead pulled out those breasts in sunshine or frost, like objects whose only purpose is to supply milk, just like a mare. A real beast of burden—as for that, her husband couldn't complain—hoeing, reaping, and sowing harder than a man when she pulled up her skirts in the grainfield, revealing legs that were darkened halfway up. Now she was twenty-seven, and dainty shoes and dark-blue stockings were the last things on her mind. "We're old," her husband said, "and we've got to think about the children." At least they helped each other like two oxen yoked to the same plow. That was their marriage now.

"Unfortunately, I experience it, too," Lucia used to grumble, "I've got the headache of the children without having a husband. When my old mother dies, they'll go on giving me a crust of bread only if they feel like it. If not, they'll throw me out in the street."

Her mother, poor thing, had nothing to say in reply; she'd listen to her, sitting beside the bed, her kerchief on her head, and her face yellow with sickness. In the daytime she remained in the doorway, in the sun, staying there in peace and quiet until the hour when the sunset

quieta e zitta sino all'ora in cui il tramonto impallidiva sui tetti nerastri dirimpetto, e le comari chiamavano a raccolta le galline.

Soltanto, quando veniva il dottore a visitarla, e la figliuola le accostava alla faccia la candela, domandava al medico, con un sorriso timido:

– Per carità, vossignoria . . . È cosa lunga?

Santo, che aveva un cuor d'oro, rispondeva:

– Non me ne importa di spendere in medicine, finché quella povera vecchierella resta qui, e so di trovarla nel suo cantuccio tornando a casa. Poi ha lavorato anch'essa la sua parte, quand'era tempo; e allorché saremo vecchi, i nostri figli faranno altrettanto per noi.

E accadde pure che Carmenio al Camemi aveva acchiappato le febbri. Se il padrone fosse stato ricco gli avrebbe comperato le medicine; ma curatolo Vito era un povero diavolo che campava su di quel po' di mandra, e il ragazzo lo teneva proprio per carità, ché quelle quattro pecore avrebbe potuto guardarsele lui, se non fosse stata la paura della malaria. Poi voleva fare anche l'opera buona di dar pane all'orfanello di compare Nanni, per ingraziarsi la Provvidenza che doveva aiutarlo, doveva, se c'era giustizia in cielo. Che poteva farci se possedeva soltanto quel pezzetto di pascolo al Camemi, dove la malaria quagliava come la neve, e Carmenio aveva presa la terzana? Un dì che il ragazzo si sentiva le ossa rotte dalla febbre, e si lasciò vincere dal sonno a ridosso di un pietrone che stampava l'ombra nera sulla viottola polverosa, mentre i mosconi ronzavano nell'afa di maggio, le pecore irruppero nei seminati del vicino, un povero maggese grande quanto un fazzoletto da naso, che l'arsura s'era mezzo mangiato. Nonostante zio Cheli, rincantucciato sotto un tettuccio di frasche, lo guardava come la pupilla degli occhi suoi, quel seminato che gli costava tanti sudori, ed era la speranza dell'annata. Al vedere le pecore che scorazzavano. – Ah! che non ne mangiano pane, quei cristiani? – E Carmenio si svegliò alle busse ed ai calci dello zio Cheli, il quale si mise a correre come un pazzo dietro le pecore sbandate, piangendo ed urlando. Ci volevano proprio quelle legnate per Carmenio, colle ossa che gli aveva già rotte la terzana! Ma gli pagava forse il danno al vicino cogli strilli e cogli ahimè? – Un'annata persa, ed i miei figli senza pane quest'inverno! Ecco il danno che hai fatto, assassino! Se ti levassi la pelle non basterebbe!

Zio Cheli si cercò i testimonii per citarli dinanzi al giudice colle pecore di curatolo Vito. Questi, al giungergli della citazione, fu come un colpo d'accidente per lui e sua moglie. – Ah! quel birbante di Carmenio ci ha rovinati del tutto! Andate a far del bene, che ve lo rendono in tal maniera! Potevo forse stare nella malaria a guardare le

was growing pale on the blackish roofs across the way, and the neighbor women were calling in their chickens.

But when the doctor came to see her, and her daughter brought the candle close to her face, she'd ask the doctor, with a shy smile:

"Please, sir . . . Do I have much time?"

Santo, who had a heart of gold, would answer:

"I don't care how much I spend on medicine during the time my poor old mother is still with us and I know I can find her in her corner when I get back home. Besides, she did her share of work when she was able to, and when we're old, our children will do the same for us."

And it also came about that Carmenio had caught the fever at Camemi. If his master had been rich, he would have bought medicine for him; but sheep farmer Vito was a poor devil who lived off that small flock, and kept the boy on out of pure charity, because he could easily have looked after that handful of sheep himself, if he hadn't been afraid of malaria. Besides, he also wanted to do the good deed of feeding neighbor Nanni's orphan boy, to get into the good graces of Providence, which was bound to help him, it was bound to, if there was any justice in Heaven. What could he do if all he owned was that tiny pasture at Camemi, where the bad air condensed like snow, and Carmenio had caught a tertian fever? One day when the boy felt the fever breaking his bones, and let himself be overcome by sleep in the shelter of a big rock that imprinted its black shadow on the dusty lane while the horseflies were buzzing in the May sultriness, the sheep invaded the neighbor's grainfield, a poor patch of ground as big as a handkerchief and half-devoured by drought. All the same, "Uncle" Cheli, huddled up under an overhang of bushes, considered it the apple of his eye, that grainfield which cost him so many pains, and was his hope for that year. When he saw the sheep running around in it, he cried: "What! Don't those people eat bread?" And Carmenio awoke to the blows and kicks of "Uncle" Cheli, who started running after the stray sheep like a lunatic, weeping and howling. All that Carmenio needed was that beating, with his bones already broken by the tertian fever! But did his screams and moans pay for the loss his neighbor had sustained? "A year's crop lost, and my children without bread this winter! That's the damage you did, you murderer! Even if I skinned you, it wouldn't be enough!"

"Uncle" Cheli found witnesses to be summoned before the judge along with farmer Vito's sheep. When Vito got his summons, it was like a catastrophe for him and his wife. "Oh, that rascal Carmenio has ruined us completely! Go be good to people, and that's how they repay you! Could I be expected to stay out in the bad air watching the

pecore? Ora lo zio Cheli finisce di farci impoverire a spese! – Il
poveretto corse al Camemi nell'ora di mezzogiorno, che non ci vedeva
dagli occhi dalla disperazione, per tutte le disgrazie che gli piovevano
addosso, e ad ogni pedata e ad ogni sorgozzone che assestava a
Carmenio, balbettava ansante: – Tu ci hai ridotti sulla paglia! Tu ci hai
rovinato, brigante! – Non vedete come son ridotto? – cercava di
rispondere Carmenio parando le busse. – Che colpa ci ho se non
potevo stare in piedi dalla febbre? Mi colse a tradimento, là, sotto il
pietrone! – Ma tant'è dovette far fagotto su due piedi, dir addio al
credito di due onze che ci aveva con curatolo Vito, e lasciar la mandra.
Che curatolo Vito si contentava di pigliar lui le febbri un'altra volta,
tante erano le sue disgrazie.

A casa Carmenio non disse niente, tornando nudo e crudo, col
fagotto in spalla infilato al bastone. Solo la mamma si rammaricava di
vederlo così pallido e sparuto, e non sapeva che pensare. Lo seppe più
tardi da don Venerando, che stava di casa lì vicino, e aveva pure della
terra al Camemi, al limite del maggese dello zio Cheli.

– Non dire il motivo per cui lo zio Vito ti ha mandato via! – suggeriva la mamma al ragazzo – se no, nessuno ti piglia per garzone. –
E Santo aggiungeva pure:

– Non dir nulla che hai la terzana, se no nessuno ti vuole, sapendo
che sei malato.

Però don Venerando lo prese per la sua mandra di Santa
Margherita, dove il curatolo lo rubava a man salva, e gli faceva più
danno delle pecore nel seminato. – Ti darò io le medicine; così non
avrai il pretesto di metterti a dormire, e di lasciarmi scorazzare le
pecore dove vogliono. Don Venerando aveva preso a benvolere tutta
la famiglia per amor della Lucia, che la vedeva dal terrazzino quando
pigliava il fresco al dopopranzo. – Se volete darmi anche la ragazza
gli dò sei tarì al mese. – E diceva pure che Carmenio avrebbe potuto
andarsene colla madre a Santa Margherita, perché la vecchia
perdeva terreno di giorno in giorno, e almeno alla mandra non le
sarebbero mancate le ova, il latte e il brodo di carne di pecora,
quando ne moriva qualcuna. La *Rossa* si spogliò del meglio e del
buono per metterle insieme un fagottino di roba bianca. Ora veniva
il tempo della semina, loro non potevano andare e venire tutti i
giorni da Licciardo, e la scarsezza d'ogni cosa arrivava coll'inverno.
Lucia stavolta diceva davvero che voleva andarsene a servire in casa
di don Venerando.

Misero la vecchiarella sul somaro, Santo da un lato e Carmenio

sheep? Now 'Uncle' Cheli is taking away our last few cents in expenses!" The poor man ran to Camemi at midday, blinded by his despair and all the misfortunes that were raining down on him; and with every kick and every punch on the neck that he gave Carmenio, he'd pant and stammer: "You've made us paupers! You've ruined us, you crook!" "Can't you see what bad shape I'm in?" Carmenio tried to counter, warding off the blows. "Is it my fault if the fever didn't let me stay on my feet? It came over me unexpectedly there, behind the rock!" But, all the same, he had to pack up on the spot, lose the two *onze* that he had already earned working for farmer Vito, and leave the flock behind. Because farmer Vito was ready to catch the fever himself next time, his misfortunes had been so great.

At home Carmenio said nothing, when he returned penniless, his bundle tied to his staff over his shoulder. Only his mother regretted seeing him so pale and gaunt, and she didn't know what to make of it. Later she learned what had happened from Don Venerando, who lived nearby but owned land at Camemi adjoining "Uncle" Cheli's field.

"Don't tell the reason why 'Uncle' Vito discharged you," she recommended to her son, "or else no one will take you on as a hand." And Santo added:

"Don't let on that you have tertian fever, or else no one will want you, knowing that you're sick."

But Don Venerando engaged him for his flock at Santa Margherita, where his sheep farmer was robbing him openly and doing more damage than the sheep in the grainfield. "I'll give you the medicine you need, so you won't have the excuse of falling asleep while you let my sheep run around wherever they want." Don Venerando had taken the whole family under his wing for Lucia's sake, because he used to see her from his balcony when he sat in the open air during the afternoon. "If you want to let me have the girl, too, I'll give her six *tarì* a month." And he also said that Carmenio could take his mother along to Santa Margherita, because the old woman was sinking daily and, with the flock, she would at least not lack for eggs, milk, and mutton broth whenever a sheep died. Redhead deprived herself of her best possessions to put together a little bundle of linens for her. Now, sowing season was approaching, they couldn't go and come from Licciardo every day, and everything was getting scarce with winter coming. This time Lucia actually made up her mind to go and be a servant in Don Venerando's house.

They put the old lady on the donkey, Santo on one side and

dall'altro, colla roba in groppa; e la mamma, mentre si lasciava fare, diceva alla figliuola, guardandola cogli occhi grevi sulla faccia scialba:
– Chissà se ci vedremo? Chissà se ci vedremo? Hanno detto che tornerò in aprile. Tu statti col timor di Dio, in casa del padrone. Là almeno non ti mancherà nulla.

Lucia singhiozzava nel grembiale; ed anche la *Rossa,* poveretta. In quel momento avevano fatto la pace, e si tenevano abbracciate, piangendo insieme. – La *Rossa* ha il cuore buono – diceva suo marito. – Il guaio è che non siamo ricchi, per volerci sempre bene. Le galline quando non hanno nulla da beccare nella stia, si beccano fra di loro.

Lucia adesso era ben collocata, in casa di don Venerando, e diceva che voleva lasciarla soltanto dopo ch'era morta, come si suole, per dimostrare la gratitudine al padrone. Aveva pane e minestra quanta ne voleva, un bicchiere di vino al giorno, e il suo piatto di carne la domenica e le feste. Intanto la mesata le restava in tasca tale e quale, e la sera aveva tempo anche di filarsi la roba bianca della dote per suo conto. Il partito ce l'aveva già sotto gli occhi nella stessa casa: Brasi, lo sguattero che faceva la cucina, e aiutava anche nelle cose di campagna quando bisognava. Il padrone s'era arricchito allo stesso modo, stando al servizio del barone, ed ora aveva il don, e poderi e bestiami a bizzeffe. A Lucia, perché veniva da una famiglia benestante caduta in bassa fortuna, e si sapeva che era onesta, le avevano assegnate le faccende meno dure, lavare i piatti, scendere in cantina, e governare il pollaio; con un sottoscala per dormirvi che pareva uno stanzino, e il letto, il cassettone e ogni casa; talché Lucia voleva lasciarli soltanto dopo che era morta. In quel mentre faceva l'occhietto a Brasi, e gli confidava che fra due o tre anni ci avrebbe avuto un gruzzoletto, e poteva «andare al mondo», se il Signore la chiamava.

Brasi da quell'orecchio non ci sentiva. Ma gli piaceva la Lucia, coi suoi occhi di carbone, e la grazia di Dio che ci aveva addosso. A lei pure le piaceva Brasi, piccolo, ricciuto, col muso fino e malizioso di can volpino. Mentre lavavano i piatti o mettevano legna sotto il calderotto, egli inventava ogni monelleria per farla ridere, come se le facesse il solletico. Le spruzzava l'acqua sulla nuca e le ficcava delle foglie d'indivia fra le trecce. Lucia strillava sottovoce, perché non udissero i padroni; si rincantucciava nell'angolo del forno, rossa

Carmenio on the other, with her belongings behind her. While their mother was having this done, she said to her daughter, looking at her with eyes that were heavy in her wan face:

"Who knows if we'll meet again? Who knows if we'll meet again? They said I'd come back in April. Live in your master's house with the fear of God in your heart. There at least you won't want for anything."

Lucia was weeping into her apron, and so was Redhead, poor thing. By that time they had made peace, and were hugging each other and crying together. "Redhead has a good heart," her husband said. "The trouble is that we aren't rich so we can always love one another. When hens don't have anything to peck at in their coop, they peck at one another."

Lucia now had a good position in Don Venerando's house; she said she didn't want to leave it till she was dead (this was a customary expression of gratitude toward one's master). She had bread and soup whenever she wanted, a glass of wine daily, and a plate of meat on Sundays and holidays. Meanwhile her monthly pay remained in her pocket intact, and in the evenings she even had time of her own for spinning white linens for her dowry. She already had a prospective husband within view in the same house: Brasi, the scullion who worked in the kitchen and also helped out with outdoor chores when necessary. Her master had grown rich in the same way, as a servant to the baron; and now he had the title "Don" and farms and livestock galore. Because Lucia came from a family that had been well-to-do but had declined into poverty, and was known to be respectable, he had assigned her the less onerous chores, washing dishes, going to the cellar for wine, and tending the chickens; as sleeping quarters she had a space under the stairs that was like a small room, with a bed, a chest of drawers, and everything. So that Lucia wanted to hold on to all that as long as she lived. In the meantime she flirted with Brasi, and told him in confidence that in two or three years she would have accumulated a nest egg, and would be able to "set up as a married woman" if the Lord so chose.

Brasi was deaf to any talk of marriage, but he liked Lucia, with her coal-black eyes and her natural charm. She liked Brasi, too; he was short and curly-haired, and had the same kind of shrewd and mischievous face as a Pomeranian. While they were washing dishes or putting wood under the kettle, he'd invent all sorts of pranks to make her laugh, as if he were tickling her. He'd splash water on the back of her neck, and stick endive leaves[3] in her hair. Lucia would squeal quietly,

_____

3. A folk love-charm.

in viso al pari della bragia, e gli gettava in faccia gli strofinacci ed i sarmenti, mentre l'acqua gli sgocciolava nella schiena come una delizia.

– «E colla carne si fa le polpette – fate la vostra, ché la mia l'ho fatta».

– Io no! – rispondeva Lucia. – A me non mi piacciono questi scherzi.

Brasi fingeva di restare mortificato. Raccattava la foglia d'indivia che gli aveva buttato in faccia, e se la ficcava in petto, dentro la camicia, brontolando:

– Questa è roba mia. Io non vi tocco. È roba mia e ha da star qui. Se volete mettervi della roba mia allo stesso posto, a voi! – E faceva atto di strapparsi una manciata di capelli per offrirglieli, cacciando fuori tanto di lingua.

Ella lo picchiava con certi pugni sodi da contadina che lo facevano aggobbire, e gli davano dei cattivi sogni la notte, diceva lui. Lo pigliava pei capelli, come un cagnuolo, e sentiva un certo piacere a ficcare le dita in quella lana morbida e ricciuta.

– Sfogatevi! sfogatevi! Io non sono permaloso come voi, e mi lascierei pestare come la salsiccia dalle vostre mani.

Una volta don Venerando li sorprese in quei giuochetti e fece una casa del diavolo. Tresche non ne voleva in casa sua; se no li scacciava fuori a pedate tutt'e due. Piuttosto quando trovava la ragazza sola in cucina, le pigliava il ganascino, e voleva accarezzarla con due dita.

– No! no! – replicava Lucia. – A me questi scherzi non mi piacciono. Se no piglio la mia roba e me ne vado.

– Di lui ti piacciono, di lui! E di me che sono il padrone, no? Cosa vuol dire questa storia? Non sai che posso regalarti degli anelli e dei pendenti di oro, e farti la dote, se ne ho voglia?

Davvero poteva fargliela, confermava Brasi, che il padrone aveva denari quanti ne voleva, e sua moglie portava il manto di seta come una signora, adesso che era magra e vecchia peggio di una mummia; per questo suo marito scendeva in cucina a dir le barzellette colle ragazze. Poi ci veniva per guardarsi i suoi interessi, quanta legna ardeva e quanta carne mettevano al fuoco. Era ricco, sì, ma sapeva quel che ci vuole a far la roba, e litigava tutto il giorno con sua moglie, la quale aveva dei fumi in testa, ora che faceva la signora, e si lagnava del fumo dei sarmenti e del cattivo odore delle cipolle.

– La dote voglio farmela io colle mie mani – rimbeccava Lucia. – La figlia di mia madre vuol restare una ragazza onorata, se un cristiano la cerca in moglie.

so her employers wouldn't hear; she'd huddle up in the oven corner, as red in the face as the embers, and she'd throw the rags and vine runners in his face, while the water trickled down her back delightfully.

"Meatballs are made out of meat. Make yours, because I've made mine," he quoted, inviting her to keep up her end of the game.

"Not me!" Lucia would reply. "I don't like that kind of fun."

Brasi pretended to be abashed. He'd pick up the endive leaf she had thrown in his face, and would place it in his bosom, inside his shirt, grumbling:

"This is my property. I won't touch it. It's my property, and it's got to stay here. If you want to put something I own in the same place, it's up to you!" And he made the gesture of pulling out a handful of his hair and offering it to her, while sticking his tongue all the way out.

She'd punch him with her solid peasant girl's fists that made him hunch up and gave him bad dreams at night, he said. She'd seize him by the hair like a puppy, and she felt a sort of pleasure when she thrust her fingers into that soft, curly fuzz.

"Let yourself go! Let yourself go! I'm not as irritable as you are, and I'd let you pound me like sausage."

Once, Don Venerando caught them at such sport, and raised a terrible row. He said he didn't want romances in his house; if they didn't watch it, he'd kick both of them out. But when he found the girl alone in the kitchen, he'd pinch her cheek and try to caress her with two fingers.

"No! No!" Lucia would complain. "I don't like such games. If you keep it up, I'll pack my belongings and leave."

"You like it when *he* does it! And not when *I* do it, though I'm your master? What's the meaning of this nonsense? Don't you know I can give you gold rings and earrings, and furnish your dowry, if I feel like it?"

And in fact he could, Brasi said in confirmation, because the boss had all the money he wanted, and his wife wore a silk cape like a fine lady's, now that she was thinner and older than a mummy. Which was why her husband went down to the kitchen to crack jokes with the maids. In addition, he went there to look after his interests, to see how much firewood was burning and how much meat they were cooking. Yes, he was rich, but he knew how hard it was to amass a fortune, and he spatted with his wife all day long; now that she was playing the great lady, she had all kinds of idle fancies, and complained about the smoke from the vine runners and the bad smell from the onions.

"I want to put together my dowry with my own hands," Lucia would retort. "My mother's daughter wants to stay a decent girl, in case a good man asks for her hand."

– E tu restaci! – rispondeva il padrone. – Vedrai che bella dote! e quanti verranno a cercartela la tua onestà!

Se i maccheroni erano troppo cotti, se Lucia portava in tavola due ova al tegame che sentivano l'arsiccio, don Venerando la strapazzava per bene, al cospetto della moglie, tutto un altro uomo, col ventre avanti e la voce alta. – Che credevano di far l'intruglio pel maiale? Con due persone di servizio che se lo mangiavano vivo! Un'altra volta le buttava la grazia di Dio sulla faccia! – La signora, benedetta, non voleva quegli schiamazzi, per via dei vicini, e rimandava la serva strillando in falsetto:

– Vattene in cucina; levati di qua, sciamannona! paneperso!

Lucia andava a piangere nel cantuccio del forno, ma Brasi la consolava, con quella sua faccia da mariuolo:

– Cosa ve ne importa? Lasciateli cantare! Se si desse retta ai padroni, poveri noi! Le ova sentivano l'arsiccio? Peggio per loro! Non potevo spaccar la legna nel cortile, e rivoltar le ova nel tempo istesso. Mi fanno far da cuoco e da garzone, e vogliono essere serviti come il re! Che non si rammentano più quando lui mangiava pane e cipolla sotto un olivo, e lei gli coglieva le spighe nel campo?

Allora serva e cuoco si confidavano la loro «mala sorte» che nascevano di «gente rispettata» e i loro parenti erano stati più ricchi del padrone, già tempo. Il padre di Brasi era carradore, nientemeno! e la colpa era del figliuolo che non aveva voluto attendere al mestiere, e si era incapriccito a vagabondare per le fiere, dietro il carretto del merciaiuolo: con lui aveva imparato a cucinare e a governar le bestie.

Lucia ricominciava la litania dei suoi guai: – il babbo, il bestiame, la *Rossa,* le malannate: – tutt'e due gli stessi, lei e Brasi, in quella cucina; parevano fatti l'uno per l'altra.

– La storia di vostro fratello colla *Rossa*? – rispondeva Brasi. – Grazie tante! – Però non voleva darle quell'affronto lì sul mostaccio. Non gliene importava nulla che ella fosse una contadina. Non ricusava per superbia. Erano poveri tutti e due e sarebbe stato meglio buttarsi nella cisterna con un sasso al collo.

Lucia mandò giù tutto quell'amaro senza dir motto, e se voleva piangere andava a nascondersi nel sottoscala, o nel cantuccio del forno, quando non c'era Brasi. Ormai a quel cristiano gli voleva bene, collo stare insieme davanti al fuoco tutto il giorno. I rabbuffi, le sgridate del padrone, li pigliava per sé, e lasciava a lui il miglior piatto, il bicchier di vino più colmo, andava in corte a spaccar la legna per lui,

"Then stay one!" her master would reply. "You'll see what a fine dowry you'll have! And how many men will seek you out for being respectable!"

If the macaroni was overcooked, if Lucia brought to the table two fried eggs that had a burnt smell, Don Venerando gave her a good tongue-lashing; in his wife's presence he was altogether different, sticking out his stomach and talking loud. Did they think they were preparing slops for the pig? With two servants who were eating him out of house and home! If it happened again, he'd fling the food in her face! His wife, bless her, didn't like that uproar, on account of the neighbors, and she'd send away the servant girl with falsetto shrieks:

"Back to the kitchen! Get out of here, you sloven! You spendthrift!"

Lucia would go and cry in the oven corner, but Brasi would cheer her up with that swindler's face of his:

"What do you care? Let them yell! If we paid attention to our bosses, woe to us! The eggs had a burnt smell? Too bad for them! I couldn't split the wood in the yard and flip over the eggs at the same time. They make me be the cook and the man-of-all-work, and they want to be served like the king! Why don't they remember the days when he used to eat bread and onions underneath an olive tree and she gathered the reaped grain in the field?"

Then the servant girl and the cook confided in each other with regard to their "evil fate"; they had been born into "honorable families," and their parents had been richer than their master long ago. Brasi's father had been a cartwright, no less! The blame lay in his son, who hadn't wanted to learn the trade, but had taken it into his head to roam around fairs, following the peddler's wagon: in the peddler's company he had learned how to cook and tend to livestock.

Lucia would start the litany of her grievances all over again: her father, the livestock, Redhead, the ruined crops. They were both the same, she and Brasi, in that kitchen; they seemed made for each other.

"The way your brother and Redhead were?" Brasi would reply. "Thanks a lot!" But he didn't want to insult her to her face. It didn't matter to him at all that she was a peasant girl. He wasn't turning down marriage with her out of pride. Both of them were poor, and he would be better off throwing himself down a well with a rock tied to his neck.

Lucia swallowed all that bitterness without a murmur; if she wanted to cry, she went and hid in her space under the stairs, or in the oven corner when Brasi wasn't there. By now she loved that man, after standing in front of the fire with him all day long. Her master's scoldings and reproaches she took upon herself, and she'd leave Brasi the better portion of food and the fuller glass of wine; she went out to the yard to split

e aveva imparato a rivoltare le ova e a scodellare i maccheroni in punto. Brasi, come la vedeva fare la croce, colla scodella sulle ginocchia, prima d'accingersi a mangiare, le diceva:

– Che non avete visto mai grazia di Dio?

Egli si lamentava sempre e di ogni cosa: che era una galera, e che aveva soltanto tre ore alla sera da andare a spasso o all'osteria; e se Lucia qualche volta arrivava a dirgli, col capo basso, e facendosi rossa:

– Perché ci andate all'osteria? Lasciatela stare l'osteria, che non fa per voi.

– Si vede che siete una contadina! – rispondeva lui. – Voi altri credete che all'osteria ci sia il diavolo. Io son nato da maestri di bottega, mia cara. Non son mica un villano!

– Lo dico per vostro bene. Vi spendete i soldi, e poi c'è sempre il caso d'attaccar lite con qualcheduno.

Brasi si sentì molle a quelle parole e a quegli occhi che evitavano di guardarlo. E si godeva il solluchero:

– O a voi cosa ve ne importa?

– Nulla me ne importa. Lo dico per voi.

– O voi non vi seccate a star qui in casa tutto il giorno?

– No, ringrazio Iddio del come sto, e vorrei che i miei parenti fossero come me, che non mi manca nulla.

Ella stava spillando il vino, accoccolata colla mezzina fra le gambe, e Brasi era sceso con lei in cantina a farle lume. Come la cantina era grande e scura al pari di una chiesa, e non si udiva una mosca in quel sotterraneo, soli tutti e due, Brasi e Lucia, egli le mise un braccio al collo e la baciò su quella bocca rossa al pari del corallo.

La poveretta l'aspettava sgomenta, mentre stava china tenendo gli occhi sulla brocca, e tacevano entrambi, e udiva il fiato grosso di lui, e il gorgogliare del vino. Ma pure mise un grido soffocato, cacciandosi indietro tutta tremante, così che un po' di spuma rossa si versò per terra.

– O che è stato? – esclamò Brasi. – Come se v'avessi dato uno schiaffo? Dunque non è vero che mi volete bene?

Ella non osava guardarlo in faccia, e si struggeva dalla voglia. Badava al vino versato, imbarazzata, balbettando:

– O povera me! o povera me! che ho fatto? Il vino del padrone! . . .

– Eh! lasciate correre; ché ne ha tanto il padrone. Date retta a me piuttosto. Che non mi volete bene? Ditelo, sì o no!

Ella stavolta si lasciò prendere la mano, senza rispondere, e quando Brasi le chiese che gli restituisse il bacio, ella glielo diede, rossa di una cosa che non era vergogna soltanto.

wood for him, and she had learned how to turn over the eggs and dish out the macaroni when it was just right. When Brasi saw her cross herself, her bowl on her knees, before settling down to eat, he'd say:

"Haven't you ever seen food before?"

He used to complain about everything all the time: the place was a prison, and he had only three hours in the evening to go for a stroll or to the inn. If Lucia sometimes asked him, lowering her head and blushing:

"Why do you go to the inn? Leave the inn alone, it's not for you"—

"It's obvious you're a farmgirl," he'd reply. "You people think the devil's at the inn. I was born of workshop owners, my dear. I'm not a hayseed!"

"I only say it for your good. You waste your money there, and, besides, there's always the chance of getting into a fight with someone."

Brasi felt softened by those words and those eyes which avoided looking at him. He enjoyed the bliss of it:

"What's it to *you*?"

"Nothing at all. I say it for your sake."

"Don't *you* get bored staying here in the house all day?"

"No, I thank God for my situation, and I wish my relatives were as well off as I am, because I lack for nothing."

She was tapping wine, crouching with the jug between her legs; Brasi had gone down to the cellar with her to light her way. Since the cellar was as big and dark as a church, and not even a fly could be heard down there, seeing himself all alone with Lucia, Brasi put his arm around her neck and kissed her on that mouth as red as coral.

The poor girl had been expecting it in alarm, as she bent over with her eyes on the jug, and both of them were silent, while you could hear his heavy breathing and the gurgling of the wine. All the same, she emitted a muffled cry and darted backward all in a tremble, so that a little red foam spilled on the floor.

"What's the matter?" Brasi exclaimed. "You act as if I had slapped you! Then, it isn't true that you love me?"

She didn't dare look him in the face, though she was dying with the desire to do so. She noticed the spilled wine and stammered, ill at ease:

"Oh, woe is me! Oh, woe is me! What have I done? The master's wine! . . ."

"Ah, let it run. The master has plenty of it. Instead of that, pay attention to me. So, you don't love me? Tell me, yes or no?"

This time she let him take her hand, without replying; when Brasi asked her to return the kiss, she did, blushing with something that wasn't merely modesty.

– Che non ne avete avuti mai? – domandava Brasi ridendo. – O bella! siete tutta tremante come se avessi detto di ammazzarvi.

– Sì, vi voglio bene anch'io – rispose lei; – e mi struggevo di dirvelo. Se tremo ancora non ci badate. È stata per la paura del vino.

– O guarda! anche voi? E da quando! Perché non me lo avete detto?

– Da quando s'è parlato che eravamo fatti l'uno per l'altro.

– Ah! – disse Brasi, grattandosi il capo. – Andiamo di sopra, che può venire il padrone.

Lucia era tutta contenta dopo quel bacio, e le sembrava che Brasi le avesse suggellato sulla bocca la promessa di sposarla. Ma lui non ne parlava neppure, e se la ragazza gli toccava quel tasto, rispondeva:

– Che premura hai? Poi è inutile mettersi il giogo sul collo, quando possiamo stare insieme come se fossimo maritati.

– No, non è lo stesso. Ora voi state per conto vostro ed io per conto mio; ma quando ci sposeremo, saremo una cosa sola.

– Una bella cosa saremo! Poi non siamo fatti della stessa pasta. Pazienza, se tu avessi un po' di dote!

– Ah! che cuore nero avete voi! No! Voi non mi avete voluto bene mai!

– Sì, che ve n'ho voluto. E son qui tutto per voi; ma senza parlar di quella cosa.

– No! Non ne mangio di quel pane! lasciatemi stare, e non mi guardate più!

Ora lo sapeva com'erano fatti gli uomini. Tutti bugiardi e traditori. Non voleva sentirne più parlare. Voleva buttarsi nella cisterna piuttosto a capo in giù; voleva farsi *Figlia di Maria*; voleva prendere il suo buon nome e gettarlo dalla finestra! A che le serviva, senza dote? Voleva rompersi il collo con quel vecchiaccio del padrone, e procurarsi la dote colla sua vergogna. Ormai!… Ormai!… Don Venerando l'era sempre attorno, ora colle buone, ora colle cattive, per guardarsi i suoi interessi, se mettevano troppa legna al fuoco, quanto olio consumavano per la frittura, mandava via Brasi a comprargli un soldo di tabacco, e cercava di pigliare Lucia pel ganascino, correndole dietro per la cucina, in punta di piedi perché sua moglie non udisse, rimproverando la ragazza che gli mancava di rispetto, col farlo correre a quel modo! – No! no! – ella pareva una gatta inferocita. – Piuttosto pigliava la sua roba, e se ne andava via! – E che mangi? E dove lo trovi un marito senza dote? Guarda questi orecchini! Poi ti regalerei 20 onze per la tua dote. Brasi per 20 onze si fa cavare tutti e due gli occhi!

"You've never had a kiss?" Brasi asked with a laugh. "Oh, my! You're trembling as if I'd said I'd kill you."

"Yes, I love you, too," she replied, "and I was dying to let you know. If I'm still trembling, think nothing of it. It was because I was scared about the wine."

"Well, look at that! You, too? For how long? Why didn't you tell me?"

"Ever since that remark that we were made for each other."

"Oh!" said Brasi, scratching his head. "Let's go back upstairs, because the boss may come."

Lucia was very contented after that kiss; it seemed to her as if Brasi had sealed his promise to marry her with that kiss on her mouth. But he didn't even refer to it, and if the girl brought up the subject, he'd reply:

"What's your hurry? Anyway, it's pointless to put the yoke on our necks when we can be together like husband and wife."

"No, it's not the same thing. Now you're on your own and I'm on my own; but when we get married, we'll be one united pair."

"We'll be a fine pair! Anyway, we're not made of the same stuff. It would be different if you had even a little dowry!"

"Oh, how mean you are! No, you've never really loved me!"

"Yes, I have. And here I am, all yours. But let's not talk about *that*."

"No! I won't go along with such things! Leave me alone, and don't look at me anymore!"

Now she knew what men were like. All liars and cheats. She didn't want to hear any more about them. Sooner, she'd jump into the well head first; she thought about becoming a Daughter of Mary;[4] she wanted to take her good name and throw it out the window! What good was it to her without a dowry? She wanted to sell herself cheaply to that dirty old man, her master, and obtain a dowry shamefully. By this time! . . . By this time! . . . Don Venerando was always around her, now acting kindly, now acting nastily, looking out for his interests, seeing whether they were putting too much wood on the fire, how much oil they used for the fried dishes. He'd send Brasi out to buy him a *soldo*'s worth of snuff, and then he'd try to pinch Lucia's cheek, following her around the kitchen on tiptoe so his wife wouldn't hear, reproaching the girl for her lack of respect toward him, making him run around that way! "No! No!" She resembled a maddened cat. Rather than that, she said, she'd pack up her things and leave! "And what will you eat? And where will you find a husband without a dowry? Look at these earrings! Besides, I'd give you 20 *onze* for your dowry. For 20 *onze* Brasi will let both his eyes be gouged out!"

---

4. The Daughters of Mary are a lay society of religious young women.

Ah! quel cuore nero di Brasi! La lasciava nelle manacce del padrone, che la brancicavano tremanti! La lasciava col pensiero della mamma che poco poteva campare, della casa saccheggiata e piena di guai, di Pino il Tomo che l'aveva piantata per andare a mangiare il pane della vedova! La lasciava colla tentazione degli orecchini e delle 20 onze nella testa!

E un giorno entrò in cucina colla faccia tutta stravolta, e i pendenti d'oro che gli sbattevano sulle guance. Brasi sgranava gli occhi, e le diceva:

— Come siete bella così, comare Lucia!

— Ah! vi piaccio così? Va bene, va bene!

Brasi ora che vedeva gli orecchini e tutto il resto, si sbracciava a mostrarsi servizievole e premuroso quasi ella fosse diventata un'altra padrona. Le lasciava il piatto più colmo, e il posto migliore accanto al fuoco. Con lei si sfogava a cuore aperto, ché erano poverelli tutte e due, e faceva bene all'anima confidare i guai a una persona che si vuol bene. Se appena appena fosse arrivato a possedere 20 onze, egli metteva su una piccola bettola e prendeva moglie. Lui in cucina, e lei al banco. Così non si stava più al comando altrui. Il padrone se voleva far loro del bene, lo poteva fare senza scomodarsi, giacché 20 onze per lui erano come una presa di tabacco. E Brasi non sarebbe stato schizzinoso, no! Una mano lava l'altra a questo mondo. E non era sua colpa se cercava di guadagnarsi il pane come poteva. Povertà non è peccato.

Ma Lucia si faceva rossa, o pallida, o le si gonfiavano gli occhi di pianto, e si nascondeva il volto nel grembiale. Dopo qualche tempo non si lasciò più vedere nemmeno fuori di casa, né a messa, né a confessare, né a Pasqua, né a Natale.

In cucina si cacciava nell'angolo più scuro, col viso basso, infagottata nella veste nuova che le aveva regalato il padrone, larga di cintura.

Brasi la consolava con buone parole. Le metteva un braccio al collo, le palpava la stoffa fine del vestito, e gliela lodava. Quegli orecchini d'oro parevano fatti per lei. Uno che è ben vestito e ha denari in tasca non ha motivo di vergognarsi e di tenere gli occhi bassi; massime poi quando gli occhi son belli come quelli di comare Lucia. La poveretta si faceva animo a fissarglieli in viso, ancora sbigottita, e balbettava:

— Davvero, mastro Brasi? Mi volete ancora bene?

— Sì, sì, ve ne vorrei! rispondeva Brasi colla mano sulla coscienza. Ma che colpa ci ho se non sono ricco per sposarvi? Se aveste 20 onze di dote vi sposerei ad occhi chiusi.

Oh, that mean cur Brasi! He was leaving her in the dirty hands of their master, which were trembling as he pawed her! He was leaving her with the recollections of her mother, who couldn't live long; of her home that was cleared of its furnishings and full of troubles; of Pino "the character," who had jilted her so he could go eat the widow's bread! He was leaving her with that temptation of the earrings and the 20 *onze* in her head!

And one day she came into the kitchen in great agitation; the gold earrings bouncing on her cheeks. Brasi opened his eyes wide, and said:

"How beautiful you are like that, neighbor Lucia!"

"Oh, you like me this way? Good, good!"

Now that Brasi saw the earrings and all the rest, he went out of his way to be helpful and obliging, as if she had become a second lady of the house. He'd leave the fuller plate and the better seat by the fire for her. He opened up his heart to her entirely, because weren't both of them poor people, and didn't it do the soul good to confide your troubles to a person you love? If, by hook or by crook, he could manage to accumulate 20 *onze,* he'd open a little tavern and get married. He'd be in the kitchen, and his wife at the bar. That way he would no longer be at someone else's beck and call. If their master wanted to do something good for them, he could do it without inconvenience to himself, because to him a 20-*onze* sum was like a pinch of snuff. And Brasi wouldn't be finicky, no! In this world, one hand washes the other. And he wasn't to blame for trying to earn his bread however he could. Poverty is no sin.

But Lucia would blush or turn pale, or else her eyes would swell with tears, and she'd hide her face in her apron. After a while she wasn't even seen outside the house anymore, neither at Mass, nor Confession, nor Easter, nor Christmas.

In the kitchen, she'd hide in the darkest corner, her eyes lowered, wrapped up in the new, wide-waisted dress that her master had given her.

Brasi would console her with kind words. He'd put an arm around her neck, feel the elegant material of the dress, and tell her how much he liked it. Those gold earrings seemed made for her. When you're well dressed and you have money in your pocket, you have no cause to feel ashamed and cast your eyes down, especially when those eyes are as beautiful as neighbor Lucia's. The poor girl mustered up courage by gazing at his face with those eyes; still dismayed, she'd stammer:

"Really, master Brasi? You still love me?"

"Yes, yes, sure I do!" Brasi would reply, impressing her with his sense of honor. "But is it my fault that I'm not rich enough to marry you? If you had a dowry of 20 *onze*, I'd marry you with my eyes shut."

Don Venerando adesso aveva preso a ben volere anche lui, e gli regalava i vestiti smessi e gli stivali rotti. Allorché scendeva in cantina gli dava un bel gotto di vino, dicendogli:

– Te'! bevi alla mia salute.

E il pancione gli ballava dal tanto ridere, al vedere le smorfie che faceva Brasi, e al sentirlo barbugliare alla Lucia, pallido come un morto:

– Il padrone è un galantuomo, comare Lucia! lasciate ciarlare i vicini, tutta gente invidiosa, che muore di fame, e vorrebbero essere al vostro posto.

Santo, il fratello, udì la cosa in piazza qualche mese dopo. E corse dalla moglie trafelato. Poveri erano sempre stati, ma onorati. La *Rossa* allibì anch'essa, e corse dalla cognata tutta sottosopra, che non poteva spiccicar parola. Ma quando tornò a casa da suo marito, era tutt'altra, serena e colle rose in volto.

– Se tu vedessi! Un cassone alto così di roba bianca! anelli, pendenti e collane d'oro fine. Poi vi son anche 20 onze di danaro per la dote. Una vera provvidenza di Dio!

– Non monta! – Tornava a dire di tanto in tanto il fratello, il quale non sapeva capacitarsene. – Almeno avesse aspettato che chiudeva gli occhi nostra madre! . . .

Questo poi accadde l'anno della neve, che crollarono buon numero di tetti, e nel territorio ci fu una gran mortalità di bestiame, Dio liberi! Alla Lamia e per la montagna di Santa Margherita, come vedevano scendere quella sera smorta, carica di nuvoloni di malaugurio, che i buoi si voltavano indietro sospettosi, e muggivano, la gente si affacciava dinanzi ai casolari, a guardar lontano verso il mare, colla mano sugli occhi, senza dir nulla. La campana del Monastero Vecchio, in cima al paese, suonava per scongiurare la malanotte, e sul poggio del Castello c'era un gran brulichìo di comari, nere sull'orizzonte pallido, a vedere in cielo *la coda del drago,* una striscia color di pece, che puzzava di zolfo, dicevano, e voleva essere una brutta notte. Le donne gli facevano gli scongiuri colle dita, al drago, gli mostravano l'abitino della Madonna sul petto nudo, e gli sputavano in faccia, tirando giù la croce sull'ombelico, e pregavano Dio e le anime del purgatorio, e Santa Lucia, che era la sua vigilia, di proteggere i campi, e le bestie, e i loro uomini anch'essi, chi ce li avea fuori del paese. Carmenio al principio dell'inverno era andato colla

Now, Don Venerando had taken a liking to him, as well, and would give him his hand-me-down suits and torn boots. Whenever he came down to the cellar, he'd give him a big glass of wine, saying:

"There! Drink it to my health."

And his big belly would bounce up and down with his great laughter at seeing Brasi simper that way, and hearing him mumble to Lucia, as white as a ghost:

"The master is a true gentleman, neighbor Lucia! Let the neighbors gossip; they're all envious and dying of hunger, and they'd like to be in your shoes."

Her brother Santo heard the gossip in the square a few months later. And he ran home to his wife out of breath. They had always been poor, but respected. Redhead was also left speechless; she ran to see her sister-in-law, so upset she couldn't get a word out. But when she came back home to her husband, she was a different woman, calm and pink-cheeked.

"If you could only see! A trunk stacked so high with white linens! Rings, earrings, and bracelets of fine gold. And then, she has 20 *onze* in money for her dowry. It's truly God's providence!"

"That doesn't matter!" Lucia's brother repeated from time to time, unable to face the situation. "If she had at least waited until our mother had passed on! . . ."

That event finally occurred in the year of the snows, when so many roofs fell in, and so much livestock died off in the region, God forbid!

At Lamia and on Mount Santa Margherita, when people saw that evening falling, leaden, laden with inauspicious stormclouds, so that the oxen were turning back mistrustfully and lowing, they stood in front of their cottages, looking far off toward the sea, their hands over their eyes, wordlessly. The bell of the Old Monastery, at the highest point of the village, rang to drive away the "evil night," and on the castle hill there was a great swarm of women, silhouetted against the pale horizon, watching the "dragon's tail"[5] in the sky, a streak black as pitch, and smelling of sulphur, they said; it was going to be a terrible night. The women warded off the dragon with their fingers, showed it their *abitino della Madonna*[6] on their bare bosoms, and spat in its face, pulling their crosses down over their navels and praying to God, the souls in Purgatory, and St. Lucy (it was the eve of her feast)[7] to protect their fields, their livestock, and their husbands, too, if any of them were away from the village. At the beginning of the winter Carmenio had gone

5. Variously interpreted as a comet or a waterspout.   6. See footnote 3 in "La Lupa."
7. Which falls on December 13. Also mentioned in "Jeli il pastore" (footnote 8).

mandra a Santa Margherita. La mamma quella sera non istava bene,
e si affannava pel lettuccio, cogli occhi spalancati, e non voleva star
più quieta come prima, e voleva questo, e voleva quell'altro, e voleva alzarsi, e voleva che la voltassero dall'altra parte. Carmenio un
po' era corso di qua e di là, a darle retta, e cercare di fare qualche
cosa. Poi si era piantato dinanzi al letto, sbigottito, colle mani nei
capelli.

Il casolare era dall'altra parte del torrente, in fondo alla valle, fra
due grossi pietroni che gli si arrampicavano sul tetto. Di faccia, la
costa, ritta in piedi, cominciava a scomparire nel buio che saliva dal
vallone, brulla e nera di sassi, fra i quali si perdeva la striscia biancastra del viottolo. Al calar del sole erano venuti i vicini della mandra dei fichidindia, a vedere se occorreva nulla per l'inferma, che
non si moveva più nel suo lettuccio, colla faccia in aria e la fuliggine
al naso.

– Cattivo segno! – aveva detto curatolo Decu. – Se non avessi lassù
le pecore, con questo tempo che si prepara, non ti lascierei solo stanotte. Chiamami, se mai!

Carmenio rispondeva di sì, col capo appoggiato allo stipite; ma vedendolo allontanare passo passo, che si perdeva nella notte, aveva un
gran voglia di corrergli dietro, di mettersi a gridare, di strapparsi i
capelli – non sapeva che cosa.

– Se mai – gli gridò curatolo Decu da lontano – corri fino alla mandra dei fichidindia, lassù, che c'è gente.

La mandra si vedeva tuttora sulla roccia, verso il cielo, per quel po'
di crepuscolo che si raccoglieva in cima ai monti, e straforava le macchie dei fichidindia. Lontan lontano, alla Lamia e verso la pianura, si
udiva l'uggiolare dei cani auuuh! . . . auuuh! . . . auuuh! . . . che arrivava appena sin là, e metteva freddo nelle ossa. Le pecore allora si
spingevano a scorazzare in frotta pel chiuso, prese da un terrore
pazzo, quasi sentissero il lupo nelle vicinanze, e a quello squillare
brusco di campanacci sembrava che le tenebre si accendessero di tanti
occhi infuocati, tutto in giro. Poi le pecore si arrestavano immobili,
strette fra di loro, col muso a terra, e il cane finiva d'abbaiare in un ug-
giolato lungo e lamentevole, seduto sulla coda.

– Se sapevo! – pensava Carmenio – era meglio dire a curatolo Decu
di non lasciarmi solo.

Di fuori, nelle tenebre, di tanto in tanto si udivano i campanacci
della mandra che trasalivano. Dallo spiraglio si vedeva il quadro del-
l'uscio nero come la bocca di un forno; null'altro. E la costa
dirimpetto, e la valle profonda, e la pianura della Lamia, tutto si
sprofondava in quel nero senza fondo, che pareva si vedesse soltanto

with his flock to Santa Margherita. That evening, his mother wasn't feeling well; she was breathing heavily on her cot, her eyes wide open, and she didn't want to stay quiet the way she generally did. She wanted this, that, and the other thing, she wanted to get up, and she wanted to be turned over to face the other way. Carmenio had run all around for a while, paying close heed to her wishes and trying to do something. Then he had stood stockstill in front of the bed, alarmed, his hands in his hair.

Their cottage was on the far side of the stream, deep in the valley, between two big crags that protruded over the roof. Opposite, the very steep hillside was beginning to disappear into the darkness that ascended from the ravine, a barren slope dark with rocks, among which the whitish streak of the path faded away. At sunset the neighbors from the "prickly-pear flock" had come to see whether the sick woman needed anything. She was no longer stirring on her cot; her face was looking upward and there was smut on her nose.

"A bad sign!" sheep farmer Decu had said. "If I didn't have my sheep up there, with this storm that's brewing, I wouldn't leave you alone here tonight. Call me if you need me!"

Carmenio said he would, his head leaning on the door jamb; but, when he saw him getting farther away, step by step, and vanishing into the night, he felt a strong urge to run after him, to start shouting, to pull out his hair—he didn't know what.

"In case of trouble," sheep farmer Decu shouted to him from the distance, "run to the 'prickly-pear flock' up there, where there are people."

The flock could still be seen on the crag, against the sky, in the little bit of twilight gathering at the mountaintops and piercing the prickly-pear thickets. Far, far away, at Lamia and toward the lowlands, could be heard the howling of the dogs—ah-oo, ah-oo, ah-oo—which barely reached that far, and which chilled one's bones. Then the sheep fitfully ran around their fold all together, gripped by a mad panic, as if they smelled the wolf nearby, and at that sudden ringing of their bells the darkness seemed to be illuminated with countless fiery eyes, flashing in a circle. Then the sheep stopped still, snuggling up against one another, their muzzles to the ground; and the dog ended his barking with a long, lamenting howl, as he sat on his tail.

"If I had known!" Carmenio thought. "It would have been better to tell farmer Decu not to leave me alone."

Outside in the dark, from time to time you could hear the flock bells as the sheep gave a start. Through the narrow chink of the window you could see the rectangle of the doorway, as black as the mouth of an oven; nothing else. The hillside opposite, the deep valley, and the Lamia lowlands were all submerged in that bottomless blackness;

il rumore del torrente, laggiù, a montare verso il casolare, gonfio e minaccioso.

Se sapeva, anche questa! prima che annottasse correva al paese a chiamare il fratello; e certo a quell'ora sarebbe qui con lui, ed anche Lucia e la cognata.

Allora la mamma cominciò a parlare, ma non si capiva quello che dicesse, e brancolava pel letto colle mani scarne.

– Mamma! mamma! cosa volete? – domandava Carmenio – ditelo a me che son qui con voi!

Ma la mamma non rispondeva. Dimenava il capo anzi, come volesse dir no! no! non voleva. Il ragazzo le mise la candela sotto il naso, e scoppiò e piangere dalla paura.

– O mamma! mamma mia! – piagnucolava Carmenio – O che sono solo e non posso darvi aiuto!

Aprì l'uscio per chiamare quelli della mandra dei fichidindia. Ma nessuno l'udiva.

Dappertutto era un chiarore denso; sulla costa, nel vallone, laggiù al piano – come un silenzio fatto di bambagia. Ad un tratto arrivò soffocato il suono di una campana che veniva da lontano, 'nton! 'nton! 'nton! e pareva quagliasse nella neve.

– Oh, Madonna santissima! – singhiozzava Carmenio – Che sarà mai quella campana? O della mandra dei fichidindia, aiuto! O santi cristiani, aiuto! Aiuto, santi cristiani! – si mise a gridare.

Infine lassù, in cima al monte dei fichidindia, si udì una voce lontana, come la campana di Francofonte.

– Ooooh . . . cos'èeee? cos'èeee? . . .

– Aiuto, santi cristiani! aiuto, qui da curatolo Decuuu! . . .

– Ooooh . . . rincorrile le pecoreee! . . . rincorrileeee! . . .

– No! no! non son le pecore . . . non sono!

In quella passò una civetta, e si mise a stridere sul casolare.

– Ecco! – mormorò Carmenio facendosi la croce. – Ora la civetta ha sentito l'odore dei morti! Ora la mamma sta per morire!

A star solo nel casolare colla mamma, la quale non parlava più, gli veniva voglia di piangere. – Mamma, che avete? Mamma, rispondetemi? Mamma avete freddo? – Ella non fiatava, colla faccia scura. Accese il fuoco, fra i due sassi del focolare, e si mise a vedere come ardevano le frasche, che facevano una fiammata, e poi soffiavano come se ci dessero su delle parole.

Quando erano nelle mandre di Resecone, quello di Francofonte, a veglia, aveva narrato certe storie di streghe che montano a cavallo delle scope, e fanno degli scongiuri sulla fiamma del focolare. Carmenio si rammentava tuttora la gente della fattoria, raccolta ad

it seemed that all that could be sensed was the noise of the stream down there, rising toward the cottage, swollen and threatening.

If he had known—that problem, too!—he would have run to the village before nightfall to call his brother, and surely at that hour he'd have been with him, and so would Lucia and his sister-in-law.

Then his mother started to speak, but he couldn't understand what she was saying, as she fumbled in the bed with her emaciated hands. "Mother! Mother! What do you want?" Carmenio asked. "Tell me, I'm right here with you!"

But his mother didn't reply. Rather, she was shaking her head as if to say no, no, she didn't want to. The boy held the candle near her face and burst out weeping from fear.

"Oh, Mother! Mother!" Carmenio whimpered. "I'm all alone and I can't help you!"

He opened the door to call the people from the "prickly-pear flock." But no one heard.

Everywhere there was a dense glow, on the hillside, in the ravine, down on the plain—like a silence made of absorbent cotton. All at once was heard the muffled sound of a faraway church bell—dong, dong, dong—which seemed to be condensing in the snow.

"Oh, Holy Mother of God!" Carmenio sobbed. "What can that bell be for? Oh, people from the 'prickly-pear flock,' help! Oh, good Christian people, help! Oh, good Christian people, help!" he started to shout.

Finally, up there, on top of the prickly-pear mountain, was heard a faraway voice, like the Francofonte church bell.

"Oh . . . what's wrong? . . . what's wrong? . . ."

"Help me, good Christian people! Help! Here at farmer Decu's place! . . ."

"Oh . . . chase after the sheep . . . chase after them! . . ."

"No! No! It's not about the sheep . . . it's not! . . ."

At that moment an owl flew over and started to hoot on the cottage.

"That does it!" murmured Carmenio, crossing himself. "Now the owl has smelled death! Now my mother is dying!"

Alone in the cottage with his mother, who was no longer speaking, he felt like crying. "Mother, what's wrong? Mother, answer me! Are you cold, Mother?" She wasn't breathing; her face was dark. He lit the fire between the two stones on the hearth, and started watching the branches burning; they blazed up and then puffed as if they were uttering words.

When they had been with the flocks at Resecone, at their evening gatherings a man from Francofonte had told them stories about witches riding brooms and casting spells in the flames of the hearth. Carmenio still recalled how the people in the farmhouse had

ascoltare con tanto d'occhi, dinanzi al lumicino appeso al pilastro del gran palmento buio, che a nessuno gli bastava l'animo di andarsene a dormire nel suo cantuccio, quella sera.

Giusto ci aveva l'abitino della Madonna sotto la camicia, e la fettuccia di santa Agrippina legata al polso, che s'era fatta nera dal tempo. Nella stessa tasca ci aveva il suo zufolo di canna, che gli rammentava le sere d'estate – Juh! juh! – quando si lasciano entrare le pecore nelle stoppie gialle como l'oro, dappertutto, e i grilli scoppiettano nell'ora di mezzogiorno, e le lodole calano trillando a rannicchiarsi dietro le zolle col tramonto, e si sveglia l'odore della nepitella e del ramerino. – Juh! juh! Bambino Gesù! – A Natale, quando era andato al paese, suonavano così per la novena, davanti all'altarino illuminato e colle frasche d'arancio, e in ogni casa, davanti all'uscio, i ragazzi giocavano alla *fossetta,* col bel sole di dicembre sulla schiena. Poi s'erano avviati per la messa di mezzanotte, in folla coi vicini, urtandosi e ridendo per le strade buie. Ah! perché adesso ci aveva quella spina in cuore? e la mamma che non diceva più nulla! Ancora per mezzanotte ci voleva un gran pezzo. Fra i sassi delle pareti senza intonaco pareva che ci fossero tanti occhi ad ogni buco, che guardavano dentro, nel focolare, gelati e neri.

Sul suo stramazzo, in un angolo, era buttato un giubbone, lungo disteso, che pareva le maniche si gonfiassero; e il diavolo del San Michele Arcangelo, nella immagine appiccicata a capo del lettuccio, digrignava i denti bianchi, colle mani nei capelli, fra i zig-zag rossi dell'inferno.

L'indomani, pallidi come tanti morti, arrivarono Santo, la *Rossa* coi bambini dietro, e Lucia che in quell'angustia non pensava a nascondere il suo stato. Attorno al lettuccio della morta si strappavano i capelli, e si davano dei pugni in testa, senza pensare ad altro. Poi come Santo si accorse della sorella con tanto di pancia, ch'era una vergogna, si mise a dire in mezzo al piagnisteo:

– Almeno avesse lasciato chiudere gli occhi a quella vecchierella, almeno! . . .

E Lucia dal canto suo:

– L'avessi saputo, l'avessi! Non le facevo mancare il medico e lo speziale, ora che ho 20 onze.

– Ella è in Paradiso e prega Dio per noi peccatori; conchiuse la *Rossa.* Sa che la dote ce l'avete, ed è tranquilla, poveretta. Mastro Brasi ora vi sposerà di certo.

clustered around to listen, their eyes wide open, in front of the little lamp hanging from the pillar of the big, dark winery; no one was brave enough to go and sleep in his own corner, that evening.

Yes, he had his *abitino della Madonna* under his shirt, and his St. Agrippina's ribbon, darkened with age, tied to his wrist. In his pocket he had his reed pipe, which reminded him of those summer evenings—tootle, tootle—when you allow the sheep to enter the golden-yellow stubble fields all around, and the crickets chirp at midday, and the larks descend with a trill to nest behind the sods at sunset, and the aroma of the calamint and rosemary is awakened. "Yooh, yooh, Baby Jesus!" At Christmas, when he had gone to the village, they were playing that for the novena, in front of the little altar that was illuminated and decorated with orange branches; and in every house, in front of the door, the children were playing *fossetta*,[8] with the lovely December sun on their backs. Then his family had set out for midnight Mass, joining the crowd of neighbors, jostling one another and laughing in the dark streets. Ah, why did he now have that thorn in his heart? And his mother was no longer speaking! It was still a long way till midnight. Amid the stones of the unplastered wall, there seemed to be countless eyes at each hole, staring coldly and blackly inside, into the hearth.

On his pallet in one corner was thrown a jacket, fully spread out, so that its sleeves seemed to be swelling. And the devil subdued by the archangel St. Michael, in the holy picture on the wall over the head of the cot, was gnashing his white teeth, his hands in his hair, amid the red zigzags of Hell.

The next day, all of them as pale as death, came Santo, Redhead with her children tagging behind, and Lucia, who, in her distress, had no thought of concealing her condition. Standing around the dead woman's cot, they tore their hair and punched themselves in the head, their minds on nothing else. Then, when Santo had noticed his sister with such a big belly that it was a disgrace, he started to say, amid all that wailing:

"If at least you had waited until this poor old woman passed on, at least! . . ."

For her part, Lucia said:

"If I had only known, only known! I wouldn't have let her do without the doctor and the pharmacist, now that I have 20 *onze*."

"She's in Heaven and she's praying to God for us sinners," Redhead said in conclusion. "She knows you have your dowry, and she's in peace, poor woman. Master Brasi will surely marry you now."

---

8. "Little hole," a game consisting of tossing a small ball and getting it to fall into a slight round depression in the ground.

LIBERTÀ

Sciorinarono dal campanile un fazzoletto a tre colori, suonarono le campane a stormo, e cominciarono a gridare in piazza: «Viva la libertà!»

Come il mare in tempesta. La folla spumeggiava e ondeggiava davanti al casino dei *galantuomini*, davanti al Municipio, sugli scalini della chiesa: un mare di berrette bianche; le scuri e le falci che luccicavano. Poi irruppe in una stradicciuola.

– A te prima, barone! che hai fatto nerbare la gente dai tuoi campieri! – Innanzi a tutti gli altri una strega, coi vecchi capelli irti sul capo, armata soltanto delle unghie. – A te, prete del diavolo! che ci hai succhiato l'anima! – A te, ricco epulone, che non puoi scappare nemmeno, tanto sei grasso del sangue del povero! – A te, sbirro! che hai fatto la giustizia solo per chi non aveva niente! – A te, guardaboschi! che hai venduto la tua carne e la carne del prossimo per due tarì al giorno!

E il sangue che fumava ed ubbriacava. Le falci, le mani, i cenci, i sassi, tutto rosso di sangue! – Ai *galantuomini*! Ai *cappelli*! Ammazza! ammazza! Addosso ai *cappelli*!

Don Antonio sgattaiolava a casa per le scorciatoie. Il primo colpo lo fece cascare colla faccia insanguinata contro il marciapiede. – Perché? perché mi ammazzate? – Anche tu! al diavolo! – Un monello sciancato raccattò il cappello bisunto e ci sputò dentro. – Abbasso i cappelli! Viva la libertà! – Te'! tu pure! – Al reverendo che predicava l'inferno per chi rubava il pane. Egli tornava dal dir messa, coll'ostia consacrata nel pancione. – Non mi ammazzate, ché sono in peccato mortale – La gnà Lucia, il peccato mortale; la gnà Lucia che il padre gli aveva venduta a 14 anni,

LIBERTY

From the belltower they hung out a tricolored cloth;[1] they sounded an alarm with the bells, and began to shout in the square: "Long live liberty!"

It was like a stormy sea. The crowd heaved and frothed like waves in front of the gentry's club, in front of the village hall, and on the church steps: a sea of white peasant caps; the axes and scythes were gleaming. Then the crowd invaded a narrow street.

"You get it first, Baron! You've had poor folk whipped by your field watchmen!" In front of all the rest went an old hag, with her hair standing up on her head, armed only with her fingernails. "Now it's your turn, devil's priest! You drained the very soul out of us!" "Now for you, you rich glutton! You can't even run away, you've become so fat on poor people's blood!" "Now for you, policeman! You carried out the law only against those who had nothing!" "Now for you, gamekeeper! You sold your own flesh and the flesh of your fellow man for two *tarì* a day!"

And the blood gave off fumes and intoxicated them. Their scythes, their hands, their tattered clothing, the stones, everything was red with blood! "Let's get the gentlefolk! Let's get the felt hats! Kill! Kill! After the felt hats!"

Don Antonio was sneaking away home by shortcuts. The first blow made him fall with his bloodied face against the sidewalk. "Why? Why are you killing me?" "You, too! Go to the devil!" A crippled urchin picked up the soiled hat and spat into it. "Down with the felt hats! Long live liberty!" "Take that! You, too!" they called to the reverend, who used to preach that stealers of bread would go to Hell. He was on his way back from saying Mass, the consecrated wafer in his big belly. "Don't kill me, because I'm in a state of mortal sin!" That mortal sin was Mis' Lucia: Mis' Lucia, whose father had sold her when she was fourteen, during the

---

1. Red, white, and green. These were the colors of the Kingdom of Piedmont, under whose auspices Garibaldi was freeing Sicily from the Kingdom of Naples (Two Sicilies). After the unification of Italy, they became the national colors.

l'inverno della fame, e riempiva la Ruota e le strade di monelli affamati. Se quella carne di cane fosse valsa a qualche cosa, ora avrebbero potuto satollarsi, mentre la sbrandellavano sugli usci delle case e sui ciottoli della strada a colpi di scure. Anche il lupo allorché capita affamato in una mandra, non pensa a riempirsi il ventre, e sgozza dalla rabbia. – Il figliuolo della Signora, che era accorso per vedere cosa fosse – lo speziale, nel mentre chiudeva in fretta e in furia – don Paolo, il quale tornava dalla vigna a cavallo del somarello, colle bisacce magre in groppa. Pure teneva in capo un berrettino vecchio che la sua ragazza gli aveva ricamato tempo fa, quando il male non aveva ancora colpito la vigna. Sua moglie lo vide cadere dinanzi al portone, mentre aspettava coi cinque figliuoli la scarsa minestra che era nelle bisacce del marito. – Paolo! Paolo! – Il primo lo colse nella spalla con un colpo di scure. Un altro gli fu addosso colla falce, e lo sventrò mentre si attaccava col braccio sanguinante al martello.

Ma il peggio avvenne appena cadde il figliolo del notaio, un ragazzo di undici anni, biondo come l'oro, non si sa come, travolto nella folla. Suo padre si era rialzato due o tre volte prima di strascinarsi a finire nel mondezzaio, gridandogli: – Neddu! Neddu! – Neddu fuggiva, dal terrore, cogli occhi e la bocca spalancati senza poter gridare. Lo rovesciarono; si rizzò anch'esso su di un ginocchio come suo padre; il torrente gli passò sopra; uno gli aveva messo lo scarpone sulla guancia e glie l'aveva sfracellata; nonostante il ragazzo chiedeva ancora grazia colle mani. – Non voleva morire, no, come aveva visto ammazzare suo padre; – strappava il cuore! – Il taglialegna, dalla pietà, gli menò un gran colpo di scure colle due mani, quasi avesse dovuto abbattere un rovere di cinquant'anni – e tremava come una foglia – Un altro gridò: – Bah! egli sarebbe stato notaio, anche lui!

Non importa! Ora che si avevano le mani rosse di quel sangue, bisognava versare tutto il resto. Tutti! tutti i *cappelli!* – Non era più la fame, le bastonate, le soperchierie che facevano ribollire la collera. Era il sangue innocente. Le donne più feroci ancora, agitando le braccia scarne, strillando d'ira in falsetto, colle carni tenere sotto i brindelli delle vesti. – Tu che venivi a pregare il buon Dio colla veste di seta! – Tu che avevi a schifo d'inginocchiarti accanto alla povera gente! – Te'! Te'! – Nelle case, su per le scale, dentro le alcove, lacerando la seta e la tela fine. Quanti orecchini su delle facce insanguinate! e quanti anelli d'oro nelle mani che cercavano di parare i colpi di scure!

famine winter, and who filled the streets and the convent's receptacle for foundlings with hungry urchins. If that rabble had amounted to anything, now would have been the time to glut themselves, with the well-to-do being cut to bits with axe blows on the doorsteps of houses and the cobblestones of the streets. Hungry wolves, too, when they attack a flock, don't think about filling their bellies, but slaughter out of rage. They killed the great lady's son, who had come running to see what was going on; the pharmacist, while he was shutting up shop in hot haste; Don Paolo, who was riding his little donkey on his way home from his vineyard, with the thin saddlebags on its cruppers—even though he was wearing an old peasant-style cap that his daughter had embroidered for him long ago, before the plant disease had attacked the vines. His wife saw him succumb in front of the big doorway, while she was waiting with her five children for the scanty provisions contained in her husband's saddlebags. "Paolo! Paolo!" The first attacker hit him in the shoulder with an axe. Another man assailed him with his scythe, and disemboweled him while he clung to the knocker with his bleeding arm.

But the worst occurred as soon as the notary's son went down, a boy of eleven with hair as yellow as gold; no one knew how it happened, he was just knocked over in the crowd. His father had arisen two or three times before dragging himself to a garbage dump, while shouting to him: "Neddu! Neddu!" Neddu was running away in terror, his eyes and mouth wide open, though he was unable to cry out. He was overturned; he, too, rose up on one knee, like his father; the torrent passed over him; one man had put his heavy shoe on his cheek, fracturing it; despite that, the boy was still begging for mercy with a gesture of his hands. He didn't want to die, no, the way he had seen his father killed. It tore your heart out! The woodcutter, out of pity, dealt him a mighty two-handed axe blow, as if he needed to fell a fifty-year-old oak, and he was shaking like a leaf. Another man shouted: "Bah! He would have grown up to be another notary!"

It didn't matter! Now that their hands were red with that blood, they had to spill all the rest. All of them! All the felt hats! It was no longer their hunger, the beatings and outrages they had been subjected to, that made their anger boil over. It was the sight of that innocent blood. The women were even more savage, waving their scrawny arms, shrieking in piercing tones in their rage, their soft skin showing beneath their ragged dresses. "You who came to pray to God in your silk dress!" "You who felt disgusted to kneel down alongside poor people!" "Take that! Take that!" In the houses, on the stairs, in the bed recesses, ripping apart the silk and the fine fabrics. All those earrings on blood-stained faces! All those gold rings on hands trying to fend off axe blows!

La baronessa aveva fatto barricare il portone: travi, carri di campagna, botti piene, dietro; e i campieri che sparavano dalle finestre per vender cara la pelle. La folla chinava il capo alle schioppettate, perché non aveva armi da rispondere. Prima c'era la pena di morte chi tenesse armi da fuoco. – Viva la libertà! – E sfondarono il portone. Poi nella corte, sulle gradinate, scavalcando i feriti. Lasciarono stare i campieri. – I campieri dopo! – Prima volevano le carni della baronessa, le carni fatte di pernici e di vin buono. Ella correva di stanza in stanza col lattante al seno, scarmigliata – e le stanze erano molte. Si udiva la folla urlare per quegli andirivieni, avvicinandosi come la piena di un fiume. Il figlio maggiore, di 16 anni, ancora colle carni bianche anch'esso, puntellava l'uscio colle sue mani tremanti, gridando: – Mamà! mamà! – Al primo urto gli rovesciarono l'uscio addosso. Egli si afferrava alle gambe che lo calpestavano. Non gridava più. Sua madre s'era rifugiata nel balcone, tenendo avvinghiato il bambino, chiudendogli la bocca colla mano perché non gridasse, pazza. L'altro figliolo voleva difenderla col suo corpo, stralunato, quasi avesse avute cento mani, afferrando pel taglio tutte quelle scuri. Li separarono in un lampo. Uno abbrancò lei pei capelli, un altro per i fianchi, un altro per le vesti, sollevandola al di sopra della ringhiera. Il carbonaio le strappò dalle braccia il bambino lattante. L'altro fratello non vide niente; non vedeva altro che nero e rosso. Lo calpestavano, gli macinavano le ossa a colpi di tacchi ferrati; egli aveva addentato una mano che lo stringeva alla gola e non la lasciava più. Le scuri non potevano colpire nel mucchio e luccicavano in aria.

E in quel carnevale furibondo del mese di luglio, in mezzo agli urli briachi della folla digiuna, continuava a suonare a stormo la campana di Dio, fino a sera, senza mezzogiorno, senza avemaria, come in paese di turchi. Cominciavano a sbandarsi, stanchi della carneficina, mogi, mogi, ciascuno fuggendo il compagno. Prima di notte tutti gli usci erano chiusi, paurosi, e in ogni casa vegliava il lume. Per le stradicciuole non si udivano altro che i cani, frugando per i canti, con un rosicchiare secco di ossa, nel chiaro di luna che lavava ogni cosa, e mostrava spalancati i portoni e le finestre delle case deserte.

Aggiornava; una domenica senza gente in piazza né messa che suonasse. Il sagrestano s'era rintanato; di preti non se ne trovavano più. I primi che cominciarono a far capannello sul sagrato si guardavano in faccia sospettosi; ciascuno ripensando a quel che doveva avere sulla coscienza il vicino. Poi, quando furono in molti, si diedero a

The baroness had had her big street door barricaded, placing beams, country carts, and filled casks behind it; and her field watchmen were firing from the windows to sell their lives dearly. The crowd lowered their heads when shots rang out, because they had no weapons to respond with. Earlier there had been a death penalty for bearing firearms. "Long live liberty!" And they broke down the door. Then they swarmed into the courtyard and up the staircases, stepping over the wounded. They let the watchmen alone. "The watchmen later!" First they wanted the baroness's flesh, that flesh composed of partridges and good wine. She ran from room to room with her infant at her breast, all tousled—and there were many rooms. The crowd could be heard howling in anger at that scurrying to and fro; they were coming nearer like a river in full spate. Her older son, a boy of sixteen, he, too, still fair-complexioned, was buttressing the door to the room with both trembling hands and shouting: "Mommy! Mommy!" At the first impetus the door fell in on top of him. He tried to clutch the legs that were trampling him. He was no longer shouting. His mother had taken refuge on the balcony, holding her baby boy tightly and closing his mouth with her hand so he wouldn't call out; she was mad with fear. Her other son, beside himself, tried to defend her with his body, as if he had a hundred hands, seizing all those axes by their cutting edges. Mother and son were separated in a flash. One man grabbed her by her hair, another by her sides, and another by her clothes, lifting her over the railing. The charcoal burner tore the nursing baby from her arms. The second brother saw none of this; all he saw was black and red. He was trampled; his bones were ground by hobnailed heels. He had sunk his teeth into a hand that was squeezing his throat and that refused to let go. There was such a throng that the axes were unable to fall, but merely gleamed in the air.

And in that furious July Carnival, amid the intoxicated howls of the hungry crowd, God's bell continued to sound the alarm, until evening: no noonday chime, no Angelus, just as if it were a Turkish land. They started to disperse, weary of the massacre, feeling dejected, each man avoiding his companions. Before night had set in, all the doors were shut, out of fear, and a light was kept burning in every house. In the narrow streets nothing was heard but the dogs searching every corner, with the sharp sound of bones being gnawed, in the moonlight that bathed the whole scene, revealing the wide-open doors and windows of the deserted houses.

Day was breaking: a Sunday without people in the square or bells ringing for Mass. The sacristan had gone into hiding; not a priest was to be found. The first people who started to gather in front of the church looked one another in the face mistrustfully, each one reflecting on what his neighbor must have on his conscience. Then, when a

mormorare. – Senza messa non potevano starci, un giorno di domenica, come i cani! – Il casino dei *galantuomini* era sbarrato, e non si sapeva dove andare a prendere gli ordini dei padroni per la settimana. Dal campanile penzolava sempre il fazzoletto tricolore, floscio, nella caldura gialla di luglio.

E come l'ombra s'impiccioliva lentamente sul sagrato, la folla si ammassava tutta in un canto. Fra due casucce della piazza, in fondo ad una stradicciola che scendeva a precipizio, si vedevano i campi giallastri nella pianura, i boschi cupi sui fianchi dell'Etna. Ora dovevano spartirsi quei boschi e quei campi. Ciascuno fra di sé calcolava colle dita quello che gli sarebbe toccato di sua parte, e guardava in cagnesco il vicino. – Libertà voleva dire che doveva essercene per tutti! – Quel Nino Bestia, e qual Ramurazzo, avrebbero preteso di continuare le prepotenze dei *cappelli*! – Se non s'era più il perito per misurare la terra, e il notaio per metterla sulla carta, ognuno avrebbe fatto a riffa e a raffa! – E se tu ti mangi la tua parte all'osteria, dopo bisogna tornare a spartire da capo? – Ladro tu e ladro io. – Ora che c'era la libertà, chi voleva mangiare per due avrebbe avuto la sua festa come quella dei *galantuomini*! – Il taglialegna brandiva in aria la mano quasi ci avesse ancora la scure.

Il giorno dopo si udì che veniva a far giustizia il generale, quello che faceva tremare la gente. Si vedevano le camice rosse dei suoi soldati salire lentamente per il burrone, verso il paesetto; sarebbe bastato rotolare dall'alto delle pietre per schiacciarli tutti. Ma nessuno si mosse. Le donne strillavano e si strappavano i capelli. Ormai gli uomini, neri e colle barbe lunghe, stavano sul monte, colle mani fra le cosce, a vedere arrivare quei giovanetti stanchi, curvi sotto il fucile arrugginito, e quel generale piccino sopra il suo gran cavallo nero, innanzi a tutti, solo.

Il generale fece portare della paglia nella chiesa, e mise a dormire i suoi ragazzi come un padre. La mattina, prima dell'alba, se non si levavano al suono della tromba, egli entrava nella chiesa a cavallo, sacramentando come un turco. Questo era l'uomo. E subito ordinò che glie ne fucilassero cinque o sei, Pippo, il nano, Pizzanello, i primi che capitarono. Il taglialegna, mentre lo facevano inginocchiare addosso al muro del cimitero, piangeva come un ragazzo, per certe parole che gli aveva dette sua madre, e pel grido che essa aveva cacciato quando glie lo strapparono dalle

fair number had assembled, they began to murmur. "We can't do without Mass on a Sunday, like dogs!" The gentry's clubhouse was barricaded, and they didn't know where to go to receive their masters' orders for the coming week. The tricolored cloth was still dangling from the belltower, limp in the yellow July heat.

And as the shadows slowly shrank in the churchyard, the whole crowd huddled into one corner. In between two small houses on the square, at the end of a steeply descending narrow street, could be seen the yellowish fields in the lowlands and the somber woods on the slopes of Etna. Now those woods and fields had to be redistributed. Everyone was silently calculating with his fingers the share that would fall to him, while looking daggers at his neighbor. Liberty meant that there should be plenty for everybody! That Nino Beast, and that Ramurazzo,[2] would surely try to continue the highhanded ways of the felt hats! With no more surveyor to measure the land, or notary to draw up a deed, everyone would be scrambling for it, catch as catch can. "And if you eat up your share of it at the inn, do we have to start redistributing all over again?" "You're a thief if I'm a thief!" Now that liberty had arrived, anyone who wanted to eat enough for two would get his head handed to him, just like the gentry! The woodcutter waved his hand in the air as if he were still carrying his axe.

The next day, they heard that the general, the one who made folks shiver, was coming to mete out justice. His soldiers' red shirts were seen slowly ascending the gorge in the direction of the village. All it would take to crush them all was to roll some boulders down from above. But no one budged. The women shrieked and tugged at their hair. By this time the men, swarthy and with long beards, were standing on the mountain, their hands dangling between their thighs, watching the arrival of those weary young men, bent under their rusty rifles, and that tiny general on his big black horse, riding alone in front.

The general ordered straw to be brought into the church, and arranged sleeping quarters for his men as if he were their father. In the morning, before dawn, if they didn't get up when the trumpet sounded, he'd ride his horse into the church, swearing like a Turk. That's the kind of man he was. And immediately he issued orders for five or six men to be shot, Pippo, the dwarf, Pizzanello, the first ones who came to hand. While they were making the woodcutter kneel down against the cemetery wall, he wept like a little boy, on account of a few words that his mother had spoken to him, and because of the

---

2. "Nino Beast" is a punning slur on Nino Bixio, the Garibaldian general who was operating in this part of Sicily. "Ramurazzo" refers to some associate of his, or some politician.

braccia. Da lontano, nelle viuzze più remote del paesetto, dietro gli usci, si udivano quelle schioppettate in fila come i mortaletti della festa.

Dopo arrivarono i giudici per davvero, dei galantuomini cogli occhiali, arrampicati sulle mule, disfatti dal viaggio, che si lagnavano ancora dello strapazzo mentre interrogavano gli accusati nel refettorio del convento, seduti di fianco sulla scranna, e dicendo ahi! ogni volta che mutavano lato. Un processo lungo che non finiva più. I colpevoli li condussero in città, a piedi, incatenati a coppia, fra due file di soldati col moschetto pronto. Le loro donne li seguivano correndo per le lunghe strade di campagna, in mezzo ai solchi, in mezzo ai fichidindia, in mezzo alle vigne, in mezzo alle biade color d'oro, trafelate, zoppicando, chiamandoli a nome ogni volta che la strada faceva gomito, e si potevano vedere in faccia i prigionieri. Alla città li chiusero nel gran carcere alto e vasto come un convento, tutto bucherellato da finestre colle inferriate; e se le donne volevano vedere i loro uomini, soltanto il lunedì, in presenza dei guardiani, dietro il cancello di ferro. E i poveretti divenivano sempre più gialli in quell'ombra perenne, senza scorgere mai il sole. Ogni lunedì erano più taciturni, rispondevano appena, si lagnavano meno. Gli altri giorni, se le donne ronzavano per la piazza attorno alla prigione, le sentinelle minacciavano col fucile. Poi non sapere che fare, dove trovare lavoro nella città, né come buscarsi il pane. Il letto nello stallazzo costava due soldi; il pane bianco si mangiava in un boccone e non riempiva lo stomaco; se si accoccolavano a passare una notte sull'uscio di una chiesa, le guardie le arrestavano. A poco a poco rimpatriarono, prima le mogli, poi le mamme. Un bel pezzo di giovinetta si perdette nella città e non se ne seppe più nulla. Tutti gli altri in paese erano tornati a fare quello che facevano prima. I *galantuomini* non potevano lavorare le loro terre colle proprie mani, e la povera gente non poteva vivere senza i *galantuomini*. Fecero la pace. L'orfano dello speziale rubò la moglie a Neli Pirru, e gli parve una bella cosa, per vendicarsi di lui che gli aveva ammazzato il padre. Alla donna che aveva di tanto in tanto certe ubbie, e temeva che suo marito le tagliasse la faccia, all'uscire dal carcere, egli ripeteva: – Sta' tranquilla che non ne esce più. – Ormai nessuno ci pensava; solamente qualche madre, qualche vecchiarello, se gli correvano gli occhi verso la pianura, dove era la città, o la domenica, al vedere gli altri che parlavano tranquillamente dei loro affari coi *galantuomini*,

cry she had uttered when he was torn out of her arms. From the distance, in the remotest alleys of the village, behind the closed doors,
could be heard those repeated shots, like holiday firecrackers.

Later the real judges arrived, people of the gentry with eyeglasses,
riding on she-mules, haggard from their journey. They were still complaining about the hardship of the trip while they were interrogating
the accused in the convent refectory, sitting sideways on their high-
backed chairs and moaning every time they shifted sides. It was a
long, interminable trial. The guilty parties were brought to the big city
on foot, chained in pairs, between two lines of soldiers with their mus-
kets at the ready. Their wives followed them at a run over the long
country roads, amid the furrows, amid the prickly pears, amid the
vineyards, amid the golden grain; out of breath and limping, they'd
call them by name at every bend in the road, when the faces of the
prisoners could be seen. In the city the men were locked up in the big
prison, as high and vast as a monastery, all riddled with barred windows; if the women wanted to see their husbands, they could do so
only on Mondays, with the guards standing by, behind the iron gate.
And the poor men became yellower and yellower in that permanent
shadow, never catching a sight of the sun. Every Monday they were
more taciturn, barely answering their visitors, and complaining less.
On the other days of the week, if the women loitered in the square
around the prison, the sentries threatened them with their rifles. In
addition, they didn't know what to do, where to find work in the city,
or how to earn their bread. A bed in a stable cost two *soldi*; the white
bread was gulped down in a single mouthful, and didn't fill your stomach; if they squatted at the doorway of a church to spend the night
there, the police arrested them. Little by little they went back home,
first the wives, then the mothers. One fine figure of a girl got ruined
in the city, and nothing was ever heard of her again. All the others
back home had returned to their previous occupations. The gentry
couldn't till the land that they owned with their own hands, and the
poor folk couldn't live without the gentry. They made peace. The
pharmacist's orphan stole Neli Pirru's wife, which he considered a fine
thing to do, to take revenge on the man who had killed his father.
When the woman had uneasy thoughts from time to time, fearing that
her husband might slash her face when he got out of jail, he'd repeat:
"Rest easy; he'll never get out." By this time nobody thought about the
prisoners, except some mother or some old man, if his eyes wandered
toward the lowlands, where the city was located, or on Sundays, seeing the others discussing their business calmly with the gentry in front

dinanzi al casino di conversazione, col berretto in mano, e si persuadevano che all'aria ci vanno i cenci.

Il processo durò tre anni, nientemeno! tre anni di prigione e senza vedere il sole. Sicché quegli accusati parevano tanti morti della sepoltura, ogni volta che li conducevano ammanettati al tribunale. Tutti quelli che potevano erano accorsi dal villaggio: testimoni, parenti, curiosi, come a una festa, per vedere i compaesani, dopo tanto tempo, stipati nella capponaia – ché capponi davvero si diventava là dentro! e Neli Pirru doveva vedersi sul mostaccio quello dello speziale, che s'era imparentato a tradimento con lui! Li facevano alzare in piedi ad uno ad uno. – Voi come vi chiamate? – E ciascuno si sentiva dire la sua, nome e cognome e quel che aveva fatto. Gli avvocati armeggiavano fra le chiacchiere, coi larghi maniconi pendenti, e si scalmanavano, facevano la schiuma alla bocca, asciugandosela subito col fazzoletto bianco, tirandoci su una presa di tabacco. I giudici sonnecchiavano, dietro le lenti dei loro occhiali, che agghiacciavano il cuore. Di faccia erano seduti in fila dodici *galantuomini,* stanchi, annoiati, che sbadigliavano, si grattavano la barba, o ciangottavano fra di loro. Certo si dicevano che l'avevano scappata bella a non essere stati dei galantuomini di quel paesetto lassù, quando avevano fatto la libertà. E quei poveretti cercavano di leggere nelle loro facce. Poi se ne andarono a confabulare fra di loro, e gli imputati aspettavano pallidi, e cogli occhi fissi su quell'uscio chiuso. Come rientrarono, il loro capo, quello che parlava colla mano sulla pancia, era quasi pallido al pari degli accusati, e disse: – Sul mio onore e sulla mia coscienza! . . .

Il carbonaio, mentre tornavano a mettergli le manette, balbettava: – Dove mi conducete? – In galera? – O perché? Non mi è toccato neppure un palmo di terra! Se avevano detto che c'era la libertà! . . .

of the clubhouse, holding their caps in their hands; and they were convinced that the weakest go to the wall.[3]

The trial lasted three years, no less!—three years of prison without seeing the sun; so that the defendants looked as if they had been taken out of the grave, each time they were led to the courtroom in handcuffs. Everyone who was able to had arrived from the village: witnesses, relatives, inquisitive people, as if to a merrymaking, to see their fellow villagers, after all that time, crammed into the jail, that coop for fattening capons—and a man really did become a capon in there! And Neli Pirru was forced to see, right in his face, the face of the pharmacist, who had become a kinsman behind his back! The prisoners were made to rise one by one. "What's your name?" And each one heard himself stating his Christian name, his family name, and what he had done. The lawyers were bustling around amid the chatter, their wide sleeves hanging down, and were getting excited, frothing at the mouth and immediately wiping away the froth with a white handkerchief, then taking a pinch of snuff. The judges were half-asleep behind the lenses of their eyeglasses, which sent a chill to the heart. Facing them, sitting in a row, were twelve men of the gentry, weary, bored, yawning, scratching their beards or mumbling to one another. They were surely telling one another they'd had a lucky escape not to have been the gentlefolk residing in that little village up in the hills when liberty had been proclaimed. And the poor prisoners were trying to read their expressions. Then they went out to deliberate in seclusion, while the pallid defendants waited, their eyes glued to that closed door. When they returned, their foreman, the one who spoke with one hand on his belly, was almost as pale as the defendants when he said: "On my honor and on my conscience! . . ."

When they were putting the handcuffs back on the charcoal burner, he stammered: "Where are you taking me? To jail? Why? I didn't get even an inch of land out of it! And they said we had gotten liberty! . . ."

---

3. Literally: "the rags fly off in the air."

A CATALOG OF SELECTED
DOVER BOOKS
IN ALL FIELDS OF INTEREST

A CATALOG OF SELECTED DOVER
BOOKS IN ALL FIELDS OF INTEREST

CONCERNING THE SPIRITUAL IN ART, Wassily Kandinsky. Pioneering work by father of abstract art. Thoughts on color theory, nature of art. Analysis of earlier masters. 12 illustrations. 80pp. of text. 5⅜ x 8½. 23411-8

ANIMALS: 1,419 Copyright-Free Illustrations of Mammals, Birds, Fish, Insects, etc., Jim Harter (ed.). Clear wood engravings present, in extremely lifelike poses, over 1,000 species of animals. One of the most extensive pictorial sourcebooks of its kind. Captions. Index. 284pp. 9 x 12. 23766-4

CELTIC ART: The Methods of Construction, George Bain. Simple geometric techniques for making Celtic interlacements, spirals, Kells-type initials, animals, humans, etc. Over 500 illustrations. 160pp. 9 x 12. (Available in U.S. only.) 22923-8

AN ATLAS OF ANATOMY FOR ARTISTS, Fritz Schider. Most thorough reference work on art anatomy in the world. Hundreds of illustrations, including selections from works by Vesalius, Leonardo, Goya, Ingres, Michelangelo, others. 593 illustrations. 192pp. 7⅛ x 10¼. 20241-0

CELTIC HAND STROKE-BY-STROKE (Irish Half-Uncial from "The Book of Kells"): An Arthur Baker Calligraphy Manual, Arthur Baker. Complete guide to creating each letter of the alphabet in distinctive Celtic manner. Covers hand position, strokes, pens, inks, paper, more. Illustrated. 48pp. 8¼ x 11. 24336-2

EASY ORIGAMI, John Montroll. Charming collection of 32 projects (hat, cup, pelican, piano, swan, many more) specially designed for the novice origami hobbyist. Clearly illustrated easy-to-follow instructions insure that even beginning papercrafters will achieve successful results. 48pp. 8¼ x 11. 27298-2

THE COMPLETE BOOK OF BIRDHOUSE CONSTRUCTION FOR WOODWORKERS, Scott D. Campbell. Detailed instructions, illustrations, tables. Also data on bird habitat and instinct patterns. Bibliography. 3 tables. 63 illustrations in 15 figures. 48pp. 5¼ x 8½. 24407-5

BLOOMINGDALE'S ILLUSTRATED 1886 CATALOG: Fashions, Dry Goods and Housewares, Bloomingdale Brothers. Famed merchants' extremely rare catalog depicting about 1,700 products: clothing, housewares, firearms, dry goods, jewelry, more. Invaluable for dating, identifying vintage items. Also, copyright-free graphics for artists, designers. Co-published with Henry Ford Museum & Greenfield Village. 160pp. 8¼ x 11. 25780-0

HISTORIC COSTUME IN PICTURES, Braun & Schneider. Over 1,450 costumed figures in clearly detailed engravings–from dawn of civilization to end of 19th century. Captions. Many folk costumes. 256pp. 8⅜ x 11¾. 23150-X

STICKLEY CRAFTSMAN FURNITURE CATALOGS, Gustav Stickley and L. & J. G. Stickley. Beautiful, functional furniture in two authentic catalogs from 1910. 594 illustrations, including 277 photos, show settles, rockers, armchairs, reclining chairs, bookcases, desks, tables. 183pp. 6½ x 9¼. 23838-5

AMERICAN LOCOMOTIVES IN HISTORIC PHOTOGRAPHS: 1858 to 1949, Ron Ziel (ed.). A rare collection of 126 meticulously detailed official photographs, called "builder portraits," of American locomotives that majestically chronicle the rise of steam locomotive power in America. Introduction. Detailed captions. xi+ 129pp. 9 x 12. 27393-8

AMERICA'S LIGHTHOUSES: An Illustrated History, Francis Ross Holland, Jr. Delightfully written, profusely illustrated fact-filled survey of over 200 American lighthouses since 1716. History, anecdotes, technological advances, more. 240pp. 8 x 10¾. 25576-X

TOWARDS A NEW ARCHITECTURE, Le Corbusier. Pioneering manifesto by founder of "International School." Technical and aesthetic theories, views of industry, economics, relation of form to function, "mass-production split" and much more. Profusely illustrated. 320pp. 6⅛ x 9¼. (Available in U.S. only.) 25023-7

HOW THE OTHER HALF LIVES, Jacob Riis. Famous journalistic record, exposing poverty and degradation of New York slums around 1900, by major social reformer. 100 striking and influential photographs. 233pp. 10 x 7⅞. 22012-5

FRUIT KEY AND TWIG KEY TO TREES AND SHRUBS, William M. Harlow. One of the handiest and most widely used identification aids. Fruit key covers 120 deciduous and evergreen species; twig key 160 deciduous species. Easily used. Over 300 photographs. 126pp. 5⅜ x 8½. 20511-8

COMMON BIRD SONGS, Dr. Donald J. Borror. Songs of 60 most common U.S. birds: robins, sparrows, cardinals, bluejays, finches, more—arranged in order of increasing complexity. Up to 9 variations of songs of each species.
Cassette and manual 99911-4

ORCHIDS AS HOUSE PLANTS, Rebecca Tyson Northen. Grow cattleyas and many other kinds of orchids—in a window, in a case, or under artificial light. 63 illustrations. 148pp. 5⅜ x 8½. 23261-1

MONSTER MAZES, Dave Phillips. Masterful mazes at four levels of difficulty. Avoid deadly perils and evil creatures to find magical treasures. Solutions for all 32 exciting illustrated puzzles. 48pp. 8¼ x 11. 26005-4

MOZART'S DON GIOVANNI (DOVER OPERA LIBRETTO SERIES), Wolfgang Amadeus Mozart. Introduced and translated by Ellen H. Bleiler. Standard Italian libretto, with complete English translation. Convenient and thoroughly portable—an ideal companion for reading along with a recording or the performance itself. Introduction. List of characters. Plot summary. 121pp. 5¼ x 8½. 24944-1

TECHNICAL MANUAL AND DICTIONARY OF CLASSICAL BALLET, Gail Grant. Defines, explains, comments on steps, movements, poses and concepts. 15-page pictorial section. Basic book for student, viewer. 127pp. 5⅜ x 8½. 21843-0

THE CLARINET AND CLARINET PLAYING, David Pino. Lively, comprehensive work features suggestions about technique, musicianship, and musical interpretation, as well as guidelines for teaching, making your own reeds, and preparing for public performance. Includes an intriguing look at clarinet history. "A godsend," *The Clarinet,* Journal of the International Clarinet Society. Appendixes. 7 illus. 320pp. 5⅜ x 8½.   40270-3

HOLLYWOOD GLAMOR PORTRAITS, John Kobal (ed.). 145 photos from 1926-49. Harlow, Gable, Bogart, Bacall; 94 stars in all. Full background on photographers, technical aspects. 160pp. 8⅜ x 11¼.   23352-9

THE ANNOTATED CASEY AT THE BAT: A Collection of Ballads about the Mighty Casey/Third, Revised Edition, Martin Gardner (ed.). Amusing sequels and parodies of one of America's best-loved poems: Casey's Revenge, Why Casey Whiffed, Casey's Sister at the Bat, others. 256pp. 5⅜ x 8½.   28598-7

THE RAVEN AND OTHER FAVORITE POEMS, Edgar Allan Poe. Over 40 of the author's most memorable poems: "The Bells," "Ulalume," "Israfel," "To Helen," "The Conqueror Worm," "Eldorado," "Annabel Lee," many more. Alphabetic lists of titles and first lines. 64pp. 5{3/16} x 8¼.   26685-0

PERSONAL MEMOIRS OF U. S. GRANT, Ulysses Simpson Grant. Intelligent, deeply moving firsthand account of Civil War campaigns, considered by many the finest military memoirs ever written. Includes letters, historic photographs, maps and more. 528pp. 6⅛ x 9¼.   28587-1

ANCIENT EGYPTIAN MATERIALS AND INDUSTRIES, A. Lucas and J. Harris. Fascinating, comprehensive, thoroughly documented text describes this ancient civilization's vast resources and the processes that incorporated them in daily life, including the use of animal products, building materials, cosmetics, perfumes and incense, fibers, glazed ware, glass and its manufacture, materials used in the mummification process, and much more. 544pp. 6⅛ x 9¼. (Available in U.S. only.)
                                                                                                 40446-3

RUSSIAN STORIES/RUSSKIE RASSKAZY: A Dual-Language Book, edited by Gleb Struve. Twelve tales by such masters as Chekhov, Tolstoy, Dostoevsky, Pushkin, others. Excellent word-for-word English translations on facing pages, plus teaching and study aids, Russian/English vocabulary, biographical/critical introductions, more. 416pp. 5⅜ x 8½.   26244-8

PHILADELPHIA THEN AND NOW: 60 Sites Photographed in the Past and Present, Kenneth Finkel and Susan Oyama. Rare photographs of City Hall, Logan Square, Independence Hall, Betsy Ross House, other landmarks juxtaposed with contemporary views. Captures changing face of historic city. Introduction. Captions. 128pp. 8¼ x 11.   25790-8

AIA ARCHITECTURAL GUIDE TO NASSAU AND SUFFOLK COUNTIES, LONG ISLAND, The American Institute of Architects, Long Island Chapter, and the Society for the Preservation of Long Island Antiquities. Comprehensive, well-researched and generously illustrated volume brings to life over three centuries of Long Island's great architectural heritage. More than 240 photographs with authoritative, extensively detailed captions. 176pp. 8¼ x 11.   26946-9

NORTH AMERICAN INDIAN LIFE: Customs and Traditions of 23 Tribes, Elsie Clews Parsons (ed.). 27 fictionalized essays by noted anthropologists examine religion, customs, government, additional facets of life among the Winnebago, Crow, Zuni, Eskimo, other tribes. 480pp. 6⅛ x 9¼.   27377-6

FRANK LLOYD WRIGHT'S DANA HOUSE, Donald Hoffmann. Pictorial essay of residential masterpiece with over 160 interior and exterior photos, plans, elevations, sketches and studies. 128pp. 9¼ x 10¾.   29120-0

THE MALE AND FEMALE FIGURE IN MOTION: 60 Classic Photographic Sequences, Eadweard Muybridge. 60 true-action photographs of men and women walking, running, climbing, bending, turning, etc., reproduced from rare 19th-century masterpiece. vi + 121pp. 9 x 12.   24745-7

1001 QUESTIONS ANSWERED ABOUT THE SEASHORE, N. J. Berrill and Jacquelyn Berrill. Queries answered about dolphins, sea snails, sponges, starfish, fishes, shore birds, many others. Covers appearance, breeding, growth, feeding, much more. 305pp. 5¼ x 8¼.   23366-9

ATTRACTING BIRDS TO YOUR YARD, William J. Weber. Easy-to-follow guide offers advice on how to attract the greatest diversity of birds: birdhouses, feeders, water and waterers, much more. 96pp. 5³⁄₁₆ x 8¼.   28927-3

MEDICINAL AND OTHER USES OF NORTH AMERICAN PLANTS: A Historical Survey with Special Reference to the Eastern Indian Tribes, Charlotte Erichsen-Brown. Chronological historical citations document 500 years of usage of plants, trees, shrubs native to eastern Canada, northeastern U.S. Also complete identifying information. 343 illustrations. 544pp. 6½ x 9¼.   25951-X

STORYBOOK MAZES, Dave Phillips. 23 stories and mazes on two-page spreads: Wizard of Oz, Treasure Island, Robin Hood, etc. Solutions. 64pp. 8¼ x 11. 23628-5

AMERICAN NEGRO SONGS: 230 Folk Songs and Spirituals, Religious and Secular, John W. Work. This authoritative study traces the African influences of songs sung and played by black Americans at work, in church, and as entertainment. The author discusses the lyric significance of such songs as "Swing Low, Sweet Chariot," "John Henry," and others and offers the words and music for 230 songs. Bibliography. Index of Song Titles. 272pp. 6½ x 9¼.   40271-1

MOVIE-STAR PORTRAITS OF THE FORTIES, John Kobal (ed.). 163 glamor, studio photos of 106 stars of the 1940s: Rita Hayworth, Ava Gardner, Marlon Brando, Clark Gable, many more. 176pp. 8⅜ x 11¼.   23546-7

BENCHLEY LOST AND FOUND, Robert Benchley. Finest humor from early 30s, about pet peeves, child psychologists, post office and others. Mostly unavailable elsewhere. 73 illustrations by Peter Arno and others. 183pp. 5⅜ x 8½.   22410-4

YEKL and THE IMPORTED BRIDEGROOM AND OTHER STORIES OF YIDDISH NEW YORK, Abraham Cahan. Film Hester Street based on *Yekl* (1896). Novel, other stories among first about Jewish immigrants on N.Y.'s East Side. 240pp. 5⅜ x 8½.   22427-9

SELECTED POEMS, Walt Whitman. Generous sampling from *Leaves of Grass*. Twenty-four poems include "I Hear America Singing," "Song of the Open Road," "I Sing the Body Electric," "When Lilacs Last in the Dooryard Bloom'd," "O Captain! My Captain!"—all reprinted from an authoritative edition. Lists of titles and first lines. 128pp. 5³⁄₁₆ x 8¼.   26878-0

THE BEST TALES OF HOFFMANN, E. T. A. Hoffmann. 10 of Hoffmann's most important stories: "Nutcracker and the King of Mice," "The Golden Flowerpot," etc. 458pp. 5⅜ x 8½. 21793-0

FROM FETISH TO GOD IN ANCIENT EGYPT, E. A. Wallis Budge. Rich detailed survey of Egyptian conception of "God" and gods, magic, cult of animals, Osiris, more. Also, superb English translations of hymns and legends. 240 illustrations. 545pp. 5⅜ x 8½. 25803-3

FRENCH STORIES/CONTES FRANÇAIS: A Dual-Language Book, Wallace Fowlie. Ten stories by French masters, Voltaire to Camus: "Micromegas" by Voltaire; "The Atheist's Mass" by Balzac; "Minuet" by de Maupassant; "The Guest" by Camus, six more. Excellent English translations on facing pages. Also French-English vocabulary list, exercises, more. 352pp. 5⅜ x 8½. 26443-2

CHICAGO AT THE TURN OF THE CENTURY IN PHOTOGRAPHS: 122 Historic Views from the Collections of the Chicago Historical Society, Larry A. Viskochil. Rare large-format prints offer detailed views of City Hall, State Street, the Loop, Hull House, Union Station, many other landmarks, circa 1904-1913. Introduction. Captions. Maps. 144pp. 9⅜ x 12¼. 24656-6

OLD BROOKLYN IN EARLY PHOTOGRAPHS, 1865-1929, William Lee Younger. Luna Park, Gravesend race track, construction of Grand Army Plaza, moving of Hotel Brighton, etc. 157 previously unpublished photographs. 165pp. 8⅞ x 11¾. 23587-4

THE MYTHS OF THE NORTH AMERICAN INDIANS, Lewis Spence. Rich anthology of the myths and legends of the Algonquins, Iroquois, Pawnees and Sioux, prefaced by an extensive historical and ethnological commentary. 36 illustrations. 480pp. 5⅜ x 8½. 25967-6

AN ENCYCLOPEDIA OF BATTLES: Accounts of Over 1,560 Battles from 1479 B.C. to the Present, David Eggenberger. Essential details of every major battle in recorded history from the first battle of Megiddo in 1479 B.C. to Grenada in 1984. List of Battle Maps. New Appendix covering the years 1967-1984. Index. 99 illustrations. 544pp. 6½ x 9¼. 24913-1

SAILING ALONE AROUND THE WORLD, Captain Joshua Slocum. First man to sail around the world, alone, in small boat. One of great feats of seamanship told in delightful manner. 67 illustrations. 294pp. 5⅜ x 8½. 20326-3

ANARCHISM AND OTHER ESSAYS, Emma Goldman. Powerful, penetrating, prophetic essays on direct action, role of minorities, prison reform, puritan hypocrisy, violence, etc. 271pp. 5⅜ x 8½. 22484-8

MYTHS OF THE HINDUS AND BUDDHISTS, Ananda K. Coomaraswamy and Sister Nivedita. Great stories of the epics; deeds of Krishna, Shiva, taken from puranas, Vedas, folk tales; etc. 32 illustrations. 400pp. 5⅜ x 8½. 21759-0

THE TRAUMA OF BIRTH, Otto Rank. Rank's controversial thesis that anxiety neurosis is caused by profound psychological trauma which occurs at birth. 256pp. 5⅜ x 8½. 27974-X

A THEOLOGICO-POLITICAL TREATISE, Benedict Spinoza. Also contains unfinished Political Treatise. Great classic on religious liberty, theory of government on common consent. R. Elwes translation. Total of 421pp. 5⅜ x 8½. 20249-6

MY BONDAGE AND MY FREEDOM, Frederick Douglass. Born a slave, Douglass became outspoken force in antislavery movement. The best of Douglass' autobiographies. Graphic description of slave life. 464pp. 5⅜ x 8½.   22457-0

FOLLOWING THE EQUATOR: A Journey Around the World, Mark Twain. Fascinating humorous account of 1897 voyage to Hawaii, Australia, India, New Zealand, etc. Ironic, bemused reports on peoples, customs, climate, flora and fauna, politics, much more. 197 illustrations. 720pp. 5⅜ x 8½.   26113-1

THE PEOPLE CALLED SHAKERS, Edward D. Andrews. Definitive study of Shakers: origins, beliefs, practices, dances, social organization, furniture and crafts, etc. 33 illustrations. 351pp. 5⅜ x 8½.   21081-2

THE MYTHS OF GREECE AND ROME, H. A. Guerber. A classic of mythology, generously illustrated, long prized for its simple, graphic, accurate retelling of the principal myths of Greece and Rome, and for its commentary on their origins and significance. With 64 illustrations by Michelangelo, Raphael, Titian, Rubens, Canova, Bernini and others. 480pp. 5⅜ x 8½.   27584-1

PSYCHOLOGY OF MUSIC, Carl E. Seashore. Classic work discusses music as a medium from psychological viewpoint. Clear treatment of physical acoustics, auditory apparatus, sound perception, development of musical skills, nature of musical feeling, host of other topics. 88 figures. 408pp. 5⅜ x 8½.   21851-1

THE PHILOSOPHY OF HISTORY, Georg W. Hegel. Great classic of Western thought develops concept that history is not chance but rational process, the evolution of freedom. 457pp. 5⅜ x 8½.   20112-0

THE BOOK OF TEA, Kakuzo Okakura. Minor classic of the Orient: entertaining, charming explanation, interpretation of traditional Japanese culture in terms of tea ceremony. 94pp. 5⅜ x 8½.   20070-1

LIFE IN ANCIENT EGYPT, Adolf Erman. Fullest, most thorough, detailed older account with much not in more recent books, domestic life, religion, magic, medicine, commerce, much more. Many illustrations reproduce tomb paintings, carvings, hieroglyphs, etc. 597pp. 5⅜ x 8½.   22632-8

SUNDIALS, Their Theory and Construction, Albert Waugh. Far and away the best, most thorough coverage of ideas, mathematics concerned, types, construction, adjusting anywhere. Simple, nontechnical treatment allows even children to build several of these dials. Over 100 illustrations. 230pp. 5⅜ x 8½.   22947-5

THEORETICAL HYDRODYNAMICS, L. M. Milne-Thomson. Classic exposition of the mathematical theory of fluid motion, applicable to both hydrodynamics and aerodynamics. Over 600 exercises. 768pp. 6⅛ x 9¼.   68970-0

SONGS OF EXPERIENCE: Facsimile Reproduction with 26 Plates in Full Color, William Blake. 26 full-color plates from a rare 1826 edition. Includes "The Tyger," "London," "Holy Thursday," and other poems. Printed text of poems. 48pp. 5¼ x 7.   24636-1

OLD-TIME VIGNETTES IN FULL COLOR, Carol Belanger Grafton (ed.). Over 390 charming, often sentimental illustrations, selected from archives of Victorian graphics—pretty women posing, children playing, food, flowers, kittens and puppies, smiling cherubs, birds and butterflies, much more. All copyright-free. 48pp. 9¼ x 12¼.   27269-9

PERSPECTIVE FOR ARTISTS, Rex Vicat Cole. Depth, perspective of sky and sea, shadows, much more, not usually covered. 391 diagrams, 81 reproductions of drawings and paintings. 279pp. 5⅜ x 8½. 22487-2

DRAWING THE LIVING FIGURE, Joseph Sheppard. Innovative approach to artistic anatomy focuses on specifics of surface anatomy, rather than muscles and bones. Over 170 drawings of live models in front, back and side views, and in widely varying poses. Accompanying diagrams. 177 illustrations. Introduction. Index. 144pp. 8⅜ x11¼. 26723-7

GOTHIC AND OLD ENGLISH ALPHABETS: 100 Complete Fonts, Dan X. Solo. Add power, elegance to posters, signs, other graphics with 100 stunning copyright-free alphabets: Blackstone, Dolbey, Germania, 97 more–including many lower-case, numerals, punctuation marks. 104pp. 8⅛ x 11. 24695-7

HOW TO DO BEADWORK, Mary White. Fundamental book on craft from simple projects to five-bead chains and woven works. 106 illustrations. 142pp. 5⅜ x 8. 20697-1

THE BOOK OF WOOD CARVING, Charles Marshall Sayers. Finest book for beginners discusses fundamentals and offers 34 designs. "Absolutely first rate . . . well thought out and well executed."–E. J. Tangerman. 118pp. 7¾ x 10⅝. 23654-4

ILLUSTRATED CATALOG OF CIVIL WAR MILITARY GOODS: Union Army Weapons, Insignia, Uniform Accessories, and Other Equipment, Schuyler, Hartley, and Graham. Rare, profusely illustrated 1846 catalog includes Union Army uniform and dress regulations, arms and ammunition, coats, insignia, flags, swords, rifles, etc. 226 illustrations. 160pp. 9 x 12. 24939-5

WOMEN'S FASHIONS OF THE EARLY 1900s: An Unabridged Republication of "New York Fashions, 1909," National Cloak & Suit Co. Rare catalog of mail-order fashions documents women's and children's clothing styles shortly after the turn of the century. Captions offer full descriptions, prices. Invaluable resource for fashion, costume historians. Approximately 725 illustrations. 128pp. 8⅜ x 11¼. 27276-1

THE 1912 AND 1915 GUSTAV STICKLEY FURNITURE CATALOGS, Gustav Stickley. With over 200 detailed illustrations and descriptions, these two catalogs are essential reading and reference materials and identification guides for Stickley furniture. Captions cite materials, dimensions and prices. 112pp. 6½ x 9¼. 26676-1

EARLY AMERICAN LOCOMOTIVES, John H. White, Jr. Finest locomotive engravings from early 19th century: historical (1804–74), main-line (after 1870), special, foreign, etc. 147 plates. 142pp. 11⅜ x 8¼. 22772-3

THE TALL SHIPS OF TODAY IN PHOTOGRAPHS, Frank O. Braynard. Lavishly illustrated tribute to nearly 100 majestic contemporary sailing vessels: Amerigo Vespucci, Clearwater, Constitution, Eagle, Mayflower, Sea Cloud, Victory, many more. Authoritative captions provide statistics, background on each ship. 190 black-and-white photographs and illustrations. Introduction. 128pp. 8⅞ x 11¾. 27163-3

LITTLE BOOK OF EARLY AMERICAN CRAFTS AND TRADES, Peter Stockham (ed.). 1807 children's book explains crafts and trades: baker, hatter, cooper, potter, and many others. 23 copperplate illustrations. 140pp. 4⅝ x 6. 23336-7

VICTORIAN FASHIONS AND COSTUMES FROM HARPER'S BAZAR, 1867–1898, Stella Blum (ed.). Day costumes, evening wear, sports clothes, shoes, hats, other accessories in over 1,000 detailed engravings. 320pp. 9⅜ x 12¼. 22990-4

GUSTAV STICKLEY, THE CRAFTSMAN, Mary Ann Smith. Superb study surveys broad scope of Stickley's achievement, especially in architecture. Design philosophy, rise and fall of the Craftsman empire, descriptions and floor plans for many Craftsman houses, more. 86 black-and-white halftones. 31 line illustrations. Introduction 208pp. 6½ x 9¼. 27210-9

THE LONG ISLAND RAIL ROAD IN EARLY PHOTOGRAPHS, Ron Ziel. Over 220 rare photos, informative text document origin (1844) and development of rail service on Long Island. Vintage views of early trains, locomotives, stations, passengers, crews, much more. Captions. 8⅞ x 11¾. 26301-0

VOYAGE OF THE LIBERDADE, Joshua Slocum. Great 19th-century mariner's thrilling, first-hand account of the wreck of his ship off South America, the 35-foot boat he built from the wreckage, and its remarkable voyage home. 128pp. 5⅜ x 8½. 40022-0

TEN BOOKS ON ARCHITECTURE, Vitruvius. The most important book ever written on architecture. Early Roman aesthetics, technology, classical orders, site selection, all other aspects. Morgan translation. 331pp. 5⅜ x 8½. 20645-9

THE HUMAN FIGURE IN MOTION, Eadweard Muybridge. More than 4,500 stopped-action photos, in action series, showing undraped men, women, children jumping, lying down, throwing, sitting, wrestling, carrying, etc. 390pp. 7⅞ x 10⅝. 20204-6 Clothbd.

TREES OF THE EASTERN AND CENTRAL UNITED STATES AND CANADA, William M. Harlow. Best one-volume guide to 140 trees. Full descriptions, woodlore, range, etc. Over 600 illustrations. Handy size. 288pp. 4½ x 6⅜. 20395-6

SONGS OF WESTERN BIRDS, Dr. Donald J. Borror. Complete song and call repertoire of 60 western species, including flycatchers, juncoes, cactus wrens, many more–includes fully illustrated booklet. Cassette and manual 99913-0

GROWING AND USING HERBS AND SPICES, Milo Miloradovich. Versatile handbook provides all the information needed for cultivation and use of all the herbs and spices available in North America. 4 illustrations. Index. Glossary. 236pp. 5⅜ x 8½. 25058-X

BIG BOOK OF MAZES AND LABYRINTHS, Walter Shepherd. 50 mazes and labyrinths in all–classical, solid, ripple, and more–in one great volume. Perfect inexpensive puzzler for clever youngsters. Full solutions. 112pp. 8⅛ x 11. 22951-3

PIANO TUNING, J. Cree Fischer. Clearest, best book for beginner, amateur. Simple repairs, raising dropped notes, tuning by easy method of flattened fifths. No previous skills needed. 4 illustrations. 201pp. 5⅜ x 8½. 23267-0

HINTS TO SINGERS, Lillian Nordica. Selecting the right teacher, developing confidence, overcoming stage fright, and many other important skills receive thoughtful discussion in this indispensible guide, written by a world-famous diva of four decades' experience. 96pp. 5⅜ x 8½. 40094-8

THE COMPLETE NONSENSE OF EDWARD LEAR, Edward Lear. All nonsense limericks, zany alphabets, Owl and Pussycat, songs, nonsense botany, etc., illustrated by Lear. Total of 320pp. 5⅜ x 8½. (Available in U.S. only.) 20167-8

VICTORIAN PARLOUR POETRY: An Annotated Anthology, Michael R. Turner. 117 gems by Longfellow, Tennyson, Browning, many lesser-known poets. "The Village Blacksmith," "Curfew Must Not Ring Tonight," "Only a Baby Small," dozens more, often difficult to find elsewhere. Index of poets, titles, first lines. xxiii + 325pp. 5⅝ x 8¼. 27044-0

DUBLINERS, James Joyce. Fifteen stories offer vivid, tightly focused observations of the lives of Dublin's poorer classes. At least one, "The Dead," is considered a masterpiece. Reprinted complete and unabridged from standard edition. 160pp. 5$\frac{3}{16}$ x 8¼. 26870-5

GREAT WEIRD TALES: 14 Stories by Lovecraft, Blackwood, Machen and Others, S. T. Joshi (ed.). 14 spellbinding tales, including "The Sin Eater," by Fiona McLeod, "The Eye Above the Mantel," by Frank Belknap Long, as well as renowned works by R. H. Barlow, Lord Dunsany, Arthur Machen, W. C. Morrow and eight other masters of the genre. 256pp. 5⅜ x 8½. (Available in U.S. only.) 40436-6

THE BOOK OF THE SACRED MAGIC OF ABRAMELIN THE MAGE, translated by S. MacGregor Mathers. Medieval manuscript of ceremonial magic. Basic document in Aleister Crowley, Golden Dawn groups. 268pp. 5⅜ x 8½. 23211-5

NEW RUSSIAN-ENGLISH AND ENGLISH-RUSSIAN DICTIONARY, M. A. O'Brien. This is a remarkably handy Russian dictionary, containing a surprising amount of information, including over 70,000 entries. 366pp. 4½ x 6⅛. 20208-9

HISTORIC HOMES OF THE AMERICAN PRESIDENTS, Second, Revised Edition, Irvin Haas. A traveler's guide to American Presidential homes, most open to the public, depicting and describing homes occupied by every American President from George Washington to George Bush. With visiting hours, admission charges, travel routes. 175 photographs. Index. 160pp. 8¼ x 11. 26751-2

NEW YORK IN THE FORTIES, Andreas Feininger. 162 brilliant photographs by the well-known photographer, formerly with *Life* magazine. Commuters, shoppers, Times Square at night, much else from city at its peak. Captions by John von Hartz. 181pp. 9¼ x 10¾. 23585-8

INDIAN SIGN LANGUAGE, William Tomkins. Over 525 signs developed by Sioux and other tribes. Written instructions and diagrams. Also 290 pictographs. 111pp. 6⅛ x 9¼. 22029-X

ANATOMY: A Complete Guide for Artists, Joseph Sheppard. A master of figure drawing shows artists how to render human anatomy convincingly. Over 460 illustrations. 224pp. 8⅜ x 11¼. 27279-6

MEDIEVAL CALLIGRAPHY: Its History and Technique, Marc Drogin. Spirited history, comprehensive instruction manual covers 13 styles (ca. 4th century through 15th). Excellent photographs; directions for duplicating medieval techniques with modern tools. 224pp. 8⅜ x 11¼. 26142-5

DRIED FLOWERS: How to Prepare Them, Sarah Whitlock and Martha Rankin. Complete instructions on how to use silica gel, meal and borax, perlite aggregate, sand and borax, glycerine and water to create attractive permanent flower arrangements. 12 illustrations. 32pp. 5⅜ x 8½. 21802-3

EASY-TO-MAKE BIRD FEEDERS FOR WOODWORKERS, Scott D. Campbell. Detailed, simple-to-use guide for designing, constructing, caring for and using feeders. Text, illustrations for 12 classic and contemporary designs. 96pp. 5⅜ x 8½. 25847-5

SCOTTISH WONDER TALES FROM MYTH AND LEGEND, Donald A. Mackenzie. 16 lively tales tell of giants rumbling down mountainsides, of a magic wand that turns stone pillars into warriors, of gods and goddesses, evil hags, powerful forces and more. 240pp. 5⅜ x 8½. 29677-6

THE HISTORY OF UNDERCLOTHES, C. Willett Cunnington and Phyllis Cunnington. Fascinating, well-documented survey covering six centuries of English undergarments, enhanced with over 100 illustrations: 12th-century laced-up bodice, footed long drawers (1795), 19th-century bustles, 19th-century corsets for men, Victorian "bust improvers," much more. 272pp. 5⅝ x 8¼. 27124-2

ARTS AND CRAFTS FURNITURE: The Complete Brooks Catalog of 1912, Brooks Manufacturing Co. Photos and detailed descriptions of more than 150 now very collectible furniture designs from the Arts and Crafts movement depict davenports, settees, buffets, desks, tables, chairs, bedsteads, dressers and more, all built of solid, quarter-sawed oak. Invaluable for students and enthusiasts of antiques, Americana and the decorative arts. 80pp. 6½ x 9¼. 27471-3

WILBUR AND ORVILLE: A Biography of the Wright Brothers, Fred Howard. Definitive, crisply written study tells the full story of the brothers' lives and work. A vividly written biography, unparalleled in scope and color, that also captures the spirit of an extraordinary era. 560pp. 6⅛ x 9¼. 40297-5

THE ARTS OF THE SAILOR: Knotting, Splicing and Ropework, Hervey Garrett Smith. Indispensable shipboard reference covers tools, basic knots and useful hitches; handsewing and canvas work, more. Over 100 illustrations. Delightful reading for sea lovers. 256pp. 5⅜ x 8½. 26440-8

FRANK LLOYD WRIGHT'S FALLINGWATER: The House and Its History, Second, Revised Edition, Donald Hoffmann. A total revision–both in text and illustrations–of the standard document on Fallingwater, the boldest, most personal architectural statement of Wright's mature years, updated with valuable new material from the recently opened Frank Lloyd Wright Archives. "Fascinating"–*The New York Times.* 116 illustrations. 128pp. 9¼ x 10¾. 27430-6

PHOTOGRAPHIC SKETCHBOOK OF THE CIVIL WAR, Alexander Gardner. 100 photos taken on field during the Civil War. Famous shots of Manassas Harper's Ferry, Lincoln, Richmond, slave pens, etc. 244pp. 10⅝ x 8¼.   22731-6

FIVE ACRES AND INDEPENDENCE, Maurice G. Kains. Great back-to-the-land classic explains basics of self-sufficient farming. The one book to get. 95 illustrations. 397pp. 5⅜ x 8½.   20974-1

SONGS OF EASTERN BIRDS, Dr. Donald J. Borror. Songs and calls of 60 species most common to eastern U.S.: warblers, woodpeckers, flycatchers, thrushes, larks, many more in high-quality recording.   Cassette and manual 99912-2

A MODERN HERBAL, Margaret Grieve. Much the fullest, most exact, most useful compilation of herbal material. Gigantic alphabetical encyclopedia, from aconite to zedoary, gives botanical information, medical properties, folklore, economic uses, much else. Indispensable to serious reader. 161 illustrations. 888pp. 6½ x 9¼. 2-vol. set. (Available in U.S. only.)   Vol. I: 22798-7
Vol. II: 22799-5

HIDDEN TREASURE MAZE BOOK, Dave Phillips. Solve 34 challenging mazes accompanied by heroic tales of adventure. Evil dragons, people-eating plants, blood-thirsty giants, many more dangerous adversaries lurk at every twist and turn. 34 mazes, stories, solutions. 48pp. 8¼ x 11.   24566-7

LETTERS OF W. A. MOZART, Wolfgang A. Mozart. Remarkable letters show bawdy wit, humor, imagination, musical insights, contemporary musical world; includes some letters from Leopold Mozart. 276pp. 5⅜ x 8½.   22859-2

BASIC PRINCIPLES OF CLASSICAL BALLET, Agrippina Vaganova. Great Russian theoretician, teacher explains methods for teaching classical ballet. 118 illustrations. 175pp. 5⅜ x 8½.   22036-2

THE JUMPING FROG, Mark Twain. Revenge edition. The original story of The Celebrated Jumping Frog of Calaveras County, a hapless French translation, and Twain's hilarious "retranslation" from the French. 12 illustrations. 66pp. 5⅜ x 8½.
22686-7

BEST REMEMBERED POEMS, Martin Gardner (ed.). The 126 poems in this superb collection of 19th- and 20th-century British and American verse range from Shelley's "To a Skylark" to the impassioned "Renascence" of Edna St. Vincent Millay and to Edward Lear's whimsical "The Owl and the Pussycat." 224pp. 5⅜ x 8½.
27165-X

COMPLETE SONNETS, William Shakespeare. Over 150 exquisite poems deal with love, friendship, the tyranny of time, beauty's evanescence, death and other themes in language of remarkable power, precision and beauty. Glossary of archaic terms. 80pp. 5³⁄₁₆ x 8¼.   26686-9

THE BATTLES THAT CHANGED HISTORY, Fletcher Pratt. Eminent historian profiles 16 crucial conflicts, ancient to modern, that changed the course of civilization. 352pp. 5⅜ x 8½.   41129-X

THE WIT AND HUMOR OF OSCAR WILDE, Alvin Redman (ed.). More than 1,000 ripostes, paradoxes, wisecracks: Work is the curse of the drinking classes; I can resist everything except temptation; etc. 258pp. 5⅜ x 8½. 20602-5

SHAKESPEARE LEXICON AND QUOTATION DICTIONARY, Alexander Schmidt. Full definitions, locations, shades of meaning in every word in plays and poems. More than 50,000 exact quotations. 1,485pp. 6½ x 9¼. 2-vol. set.
Vol. 1: 22726-X
Vol. 2: 22727-8

SELECTED POEMS, Emily Dickinson. Over 100 best-known, best-loved poems by one of America's foremost poets, reprinted from authoritative early editions. No comparable edition at this price. Index of first lines. 64pp. 5³⁄₁₆ x 8¼. 26466-1

THE INSIDIOUS DR. FU-MANCHU, Sax Rohmer. The first of the popular mystery series introduces a pair of English detectives to their archnemesis, the diabolical Dr. Fu-Manchu. Flavorful atmosphere, fast-paced action, and colorful characters enliven this classic of the genre. 208pp. 5³⁄₁₆ x 8¼. 29898-1

THE MALLEUS MALEFICARUM OF KRAMER AND SPRENGER, translated by Montague Summers. Full text of most important witchhunter's "bible," used by both Catholics and Protestants. 278pp. 6⅝ x 10. 22802-9

SPANISH STORIES/CUENTOS ESPAÑOLES: A Dual-Language Book, Angel Flores (ed.). Unique format offers 13 great stories in Spanish by Cervantes, Borges, others. Faithful English translations on facing pages. 352pp. 5⅜ x 8½. 25399-6

GARDEN CITY, LONG ISLAND, IN EARLY PHOTOGRAPHS, 1869–1919, Mildred H. Smith. Handsome treasury of 118 vintage pictures, accompanied by carefully researched captions, document the Garden City Hotel fire (1899), the Vanderbilt Cup Race (1908), the first airmail flight departing from the Nassau Boulevard Aerodrome (1911), and much more. 96pp. 8⅞ x 11¾. 40669-5

OLD QUEENS, N.Y., IN EARLY PHOTOGRAPHS, Vincent F. Seyfried and William Asadorian. Over 160 rare photographs of Maspeth, Jamaica, Jackson Heights, and other areas. Vintage views of DeWitt Clinton mansion, 1939 World's Fair and more. Captions. 192pp. 8⅞ x 11. 26358-4

CAPTURED BY THE INDIANS: 15 Firsthand Accounts, 1750-1870, Frederick Drimmer. Astounding true historical accounts of grisly torture, bloody conflicts, relentless pursuits, miraculous escapes and more, by people who lived to tell the tale. 384pp. 5⅜ x 8½. 24901-8

THE WORLD'S GREAT SPEECHES (Fourth Enlarged Edition), Lewis Copeland, Lawrence W. Lamm, and Stephen J. McKenna. Nearly 300 speeches provide public speakers with a wealth of updated quotes and inspiration–from Pericles' funeral oration and William Jennings Bryan's "Cross of Gold Speech" to Malcolm X's powerful words on the Black Revolution and Earl of Spenser's tribute to his sister, Diana, Princess of Wales. 944pp. 5⅜ x 8⅜. 40903-1

THE BOOK OF THE SWORD, Sir Richard F. Burton. Great Victorian scholar/adventurer's eloquent, erudite history of the "queen of weapons"–from prehistory to early Roman Empire. Evolution and development of early swords, variations (sabre, broadsword, cutlass, scimitar, etc.), much more. 336pp. 6⅛ x 9¼. 25434-8

AUTOBIOGRAPHY: The Story of My Experiments with Truth, Mohandas K. Gandhi. Boyhood, legal studies, purification, the growth of the Satyagraha (nonviolent protest) movement. Critical, inspiring work of the man responsible for the freedom of India. 480pp. 5⅜ x 8½. (Available in U.S. only.) 24593-4

CELTIC MYTHS AND LEGENDS, T. W. Rolleston. Masterful retelling of Irish and Welsh stories and tales. Cuchulain, King Arthur, Deirdre, the Grail, many more. First paperback edition. 58 full-page illustrations. 512pp. 5⅜ x 8½. 26507-2

THE PRINCIPLES OF PSYCHOLOGY, William James. Famous long course complete, unabridged. Stream of thought, time perception, memory, experimental methods; great work decades ahead of its time. 94 figures. 1,391pp. 5⅜ x 8½. 2-vol. set.
Vol. I: 20381-6   Vol. II: 20382-4

THE WORLD AS WILL AND REPRESENTATION, Arthur Schopenhauer. Definitive English translation of Schopenhauer's life work, correcting more than 1,000 errors, omissions in earlier translations. Translated by E. F. J. Payne. Total of 1,269pp. 5⅜ x 8½. 2-vol. set.   Vol. 1: 21761-2   Vol. 2: 21762-0

MAGIC AND MYSTERY IN TIBET, Madame Alexandra David-Neel. Experiences among lamas, magicians, sages, sorcerers, Bonpa wizards. A true psychic discovery. 32 illustrations. 321pp. 5⅜ x 8½. (Available in U.S. only.) 22682-4

THE EGYPTIAN BOOK OF THE DEAD, E. A. Wallis Budge. Complete reproduction of Ani's papyrus, finest ever found. Full hieroglyphic text, interlinear transliteration, word-for-word translation, smooth translation. 533pp. 6½ x 9¼. 21866-X

MATHEMATICS FOR THE NONMATHEMATICIAN, Morris Kline. Detailed, college-level treatment of mathematics in cultural and historical context, with numerous exercises. Recommended Reading Lists. Tables. Numerous figures. 641pp. 5⅜ x 8½. 24823-2

PROBABILISTIC METHODS IN THE THEORY OF STRUCTURES, Isaac Elishakoff. Well-written introduction covers the elements of the theory of probability from two or more random variables, the reliability of such multivariable structures, the theory of random function, Monte Carlo methods of treating problems incapable of exact solution, and more. Examples. 502pp. 5⅜ x 8½. 40691-1

THE RIME OF THE ANCIENT MARINER, Gustave Doré, S. T. Coleridge. Doré's finest work; 34 plates capture moods, subtleties of poem. Flawless full-size reproductions printed on facing pages with authoritative text of poem. "Beautiful. Simply beautiful."–*Publisher's Weekly.* 77pp. 9¼ x 12. 22305-1

NORTH AMERICAN INDIAN DESIGNS FOR ARTISTS AND CRAFTSPEOPLE, Eva Wilson. Over 360 authentic copyright-free designs adapted from Navajo blankets, Hopi pottery, Sioux buffalo hides, more. Geometrics, symbolic figures, plant and animal motifs, etc. 128pp. 8⅜ x 11. (Not for sale in the United Kingdom.) 25341-4

SCULPTURE: Principles and Practice, Louis Slobodkin. Step-by-step approach to clay, plaster, metals, stone; classical and modern. 253 drawings, photos. 255pp. 8⅛ x 11. 22960-2

THE INFLUENCE OF SEA POWER UPON HISTORY, 1660–1783, A. T. Mahan. Influential classic of naval history and tactics still used as text in war colleges. First paperback edition. 4 maps. 24 battle plans. 640pp. 5⅜ x 8½. 25509-3

THE STORY OF THE TITANIC AS TOLD BY ITS SURVIVORS, Jack Winocour (ed.). What it was really like. Panic, despair, shocking inefficiency, and a little heroism. More thrilling than any fictional account. 26 illustrations. 320pp. 5⅜ x 8½. 20610-6

FAIRY AND FOLK TALES OF THE IRISH PEASANTRY, William Butler Yeats (ed.). Treasury of 64 tales from the twilight world of Celtic myth and legend: "The Soul Cages," "The Kildare Pooka," "King O'Toole and his Goose," many more. Introduction and Notes by W. B. Yeats. 352pp. 5⅜ x 8½. 26941-8

BUDDHIST MAHAYANA TEXTS, E. B. Cowell and others (eds.). Superb, accurate translations of basic documents in Mahayana Buddhism, highly important in history of religions. The Buddha-karita of Asvaghosha, Larger Sukhavativyuha, more. 448pp. 5⅜ x 8½. 25552-2

ONE TWO THREE . . . INFINITY: Facts and Speculations of Science, George Gamow. Great physicist's fascinating, readable overview of contemporary science: number theory, relativity, fourth dimension, entropy, genes, atomic structure, much more. 128 illustrations. Index. 352pp. 5⅜ x 8½. 25664-2

EXPERIMENTATION AND MEASUREMENT, W. J. Youden. Introductory manual explains laws of measurement in simple terms and offers tips for achieving accuracy and minimizing errors. Mathematics of measurement, use of instruments, experimenting with machines. 1994 edition. Foreword. Preface. Introduction. Epilogue. Selected Readings. Glossary. Index. Tables and figures. 128pp. 5⅜ x 8½. 40451-X

DALÍ ON MODERN ART: The Cuckolds of Antiquated Modern Art, Salvador Dalí. Influential painter skewers modern art and its practitioners. Outrageous evaluations of Picasso, Cézanne, Turner, more. 15 renderings of paintings discussed. 44 calligraphic decorations by Dalí. 96pp. 5⅜ x 8½. (Available in U.S. only.) 29220-7

ANTIQUE PLAYING CARDS: A Pictorial History, Henry René D'Allemagne. Over 900 elaborate, decorative images from rare playing cards (14th–20th centuries): Bacchus, death, dancing dogs, hunting scenes, royal coats of arms, players cheating, much more. 96pp. 9¼ x 12¼. 29265-7

MAKING FURNITURE MASTERPIECES: 30 Projects with Measured Drawings, Franklin H. Gottshall. Step-by-step instructions, illustrations for constructing handsome, useful pieces, among them a Sheraton desk, Chippendale chair, Spanish desk, Queen Anne table and a William and Mary dressing mirror. 224pp. 8⅛ x 11¼. 29338-6

THE FOSSIL BOOK: A Record of Prehistoric Life, Patricia V. Rich et al. Profusely illustrated definitive guide covers everything from single-celled organisms and dinosaurs to birds and mammals and the interplay between climate and man. Over 1,500 illustrations. 760pp. 7½ x 10⅛. 29371-8

Paperbound unless otherwise indicated. Available at your book dealer, online at **www.doverpublications.com**, or by writing to Dept. GI, Dover Publications, Inc., 31 East 2nd Street, Mineola, NY 11501. For current price information or for free catalogues (please indicate field of interest), write to Dover Publications or log on to **www.doverpublications.com** and see every Dover book in print. Dover publishes more than 500 books each year on science, elementary and advanced mathematics, biology, music, art, literary history, social sciences, and other areas.